A Diamond for Christmas

SUSAN MEIER
SCARLET WILSON
PATRICIA THAYER

MILLS &
BOON

Published in Great Britain 2015
by Mills & Boon, an imprint of Harlequin (UK) Limited,
Eton House, 18-24 Paradise Road, Richmond, Surrey, TW9 1SR

A DIAMOND FOR CHRISTMAS © 2015 Harlequin Books S. A.

Kisses on Her Christmas List, Her Christmas Eve Diamond and *Single Dad's Holiday Wedding* were first published in Great Britain by Harlequin (UK) Limited.

Kisses on Her Christmas List © 2011 by Linda Susan Meier
Her Christmas Eve Diamond © 2012 Scarlet Wilson
Single Dad's Holiday Wedding © 2012 Patricia Wright

ISBN: 978-0-263-25243-9

05-1215

Harlequin (UK) Limited's policy is to use papers that are natural, renewable and recyclable products and made from wood grown in sustainable forests. The logging and manufacturing processes conform to the legal environmental regulations of the country of origin.

Printed and bound in Spain
by CPI, Barcelona

KISSES ON HER
CHRISTMAS LIST

BY
SUSAN MEIER

Susan Meier spent most of her twenties thinking she was a job-hopper—until she began to write and realized everything that had come before was only research! One of eleven children, with twenty-four nieces and nephews and three kids of her own, Susan has had plenty of real-life experience watching romance blossom in unexpected ways. She lives in western Pennsylvania with her wonderful husband, Mike, three children and two over-fed, well-cuddled cats, Sophie and Fluffy. You can visit Susan's website at www.susanmeier.com.

For my friend Denise.

CHAPTER ONE

SHANNON RALEIGH turned to get a look at herself in the full-length mirror in the bathroom of her executive office suite and gaped in horror. The tall black boots and short red velvet dress she wore exposed most of her legs and the white fur-trimmed *U* at the bodice revealed a sizable strip of cleavage.

"I can't go into a roomful of kids dressed like this!"

Even from behind the closed door, she could hear her assistant Wendy sigh heavily. "Why don't you let me be the judge of that?"

"Because I know you'll say I look fine, when I don't. I can't usher kids to Santa's lap in a skirt so short I can't bend over."

"So don't bend over." Another sigh. "Look, Shannon, it doesn't matter that you're eight inches taller than Carlie. There's nobody else who's even remotely thin enough to fit into that suit. Carlie's car is stuck in a snowdrift. If you don't play Santa's helper there'll be no one to—"

The ring of the phone stopped Wendy midsentence. The next thing Shannon heard was Wendy's happy voice saying, "Raleigh's Department Store. Shannon Raleigh's assistant, Wendy, speaking."

In the lull while Wendy obviously listened to the caller, Shannon cast another critical eye over her reflection. The little red dress was kind of cute. The color complemented her long black hair and made her blue eyes seem bluer. If she were wearing it anywhere else, she'd actually think she looked pretty.

A long-forgotten ache filled her. It was the first time in a year she *felt* pretty, sexy. But sexy wasn't exactly the way a grown woman should dress in a room filled with babies, toddlers and elementary school kids.

The ache was quickly replaced by fear— which was the real reason she didn't want to play Santa's helper. How could she spend four hours in a room full of adorable children? She wanted a baby so badly it hurt, but she couldn't have kids. And seeing all those sweet faces, hearing their cute little lists, would crush her.

"Um, Shannon?"

"I'm not coming out."

"Fine. That was Tammy in the shoe department. No one's come into the store for the past hour and she could tell the storm was getting worse, so she checked the forecast on the internet. They have no clue how much snow we're going to get, but they aren't shy about suggesting we might get another foot."

"Another foot!"

Shannon raced out of her bathroom and pulled back the curtain behind her huge mahogany desk. Thick fluffy snowflakes cascaded from the sky, coating the tinsel and silver bells on the streetlamps of Main Street, Green Hill, Pennsylvania. It blanketed the Christmas lights that outlined shop doorways, and sat on the roof of the park's gazebo like a tall white hat.

"Holy cow!"

Her gaze on the little red Santa's helper outfit, Wendy also said, "Holy cow."

"Don't make fun. We have a serious problem here." Or maybe a way out. She turned from the window. "I think it's time to admit that the storm is keeping shoppers away."

"And most of the staff is scared silly about driving home. The longer we stay, the worse the roads get."

"Okay, announce that the store is closing in fifteen and tell the employees they can go home.

I'll call the radio stations so they can add us to their list of closings. Then I'll lock up."

As the announcement went out over the loud-speaker, Shannon called all the local radio stations and advised them to let listeners know Raleigh's would be closed for the night.

Just as she hung up the phone from the final call, Wendy peeked in. "Okay. Fifteen minutes are up. Store's empty."

"Great. Thanks. Be careful going home."

"My boyfriend's coming to pick me up in his truck. I'll be fine."

Shannon smiled. "See you tomorrow."

"If we can make it."

"We better hope we can make it. The weekend before Christmas is our busiest time."

Wendy shrugged. "If shoppers don't get here tomorrow, they'll just come on Sunday or Monday or Tuesday or whatever. Nobody's going to go without gifts this Christmas. I'd say your profits are safe."

Shannon laughed. Wendy waved and headed off. With a few clicks on her keyboard, she activated the building locks and the alarm system. Reaching for her coat, she peered down at her little Santa's helper outfit. She should change, but knowing the roads were getting worse with every passing minute, she simply yanked her long white wool coat from the closet and ran out.

At the end of the hall, she pushed on the swinging door that led from executive row to housewares. Striding to the elevator, she passed shelves and tables bulging with merchandise, all under loops of tinsel and oversized ornaments hanging from the low ceiling. On the first floor, she hurried past the candy department, to the back door and the employee parking lot. Putting her SUV into four-wheel drive, she edged onto the street and slowly wound along the twisty road that took her out into the country, to her home five miles outside the small city.

As she stepped out into the eighteen inches of snow in her driveway, a sense of disconnect shivered through her. Though it had been a year, it felt like only yesterday that she had been married and living in sunny, happy Charleston, South Carolina, where people didn't often see snow, let alone need winter coats and boots. Then she'd been diagnosed with stage-four endometriosis and forced to have a hysterectomy, her husband had unceremoniously divorced her and she'd returned home to the comforting arms of her parents.

But just when she'd gotten adjusted to being back in town and working at the store, her parents had retired and moved to Florida. Worse, they now wanted her to sell the store to fund their retirement.

Once again, she was alone—and soon she'd be unemployed.

She trudged up the back steps to the kitchen door, scolding herself for being so negative. She knew what was wrong. The near miss with playing Santa's helper had rattled her. Four hours of ushering kids to Santa's throne and listening to their sweet voices as they gave their Christmas lists to the jolly old elf would have been her undoing—a bittersweet reminder to her that she'd never bring a child into this world.

Inside the cold yellow kitchen, she'd just barely unwound the scarf from her neck when the doorbell rang. Confused, she walked up the hall, dodging the boxes of Christmas decorations she'd brought from the attic the night before. She flipped on the porch light and yanked open the door.

A snow-covered state policeman took off his hat. "Evening, ma'am. I'm Trooper Potter."

She blinked. What the devil would the police want with her? "Good evening."

Then Trooper Potter shifted a bit to his left and she saw Rory Wallace. All six foot one, no more than one hundred and eighty-five gorgeous pounds of him. His black hair and topcoat were sprinkled with snow. His dark eyes were wary, apologetic.

"Rory?"

"Good evening, Shannon."

The policeman angled his thumb behind him. "I see you know Mr. Wallace."

"Yes. I do." How could she forget a dark-haired, dark-eyed sex god? While he had dated her roommate, Natalie, their first year at university, Shannon had had a secret crush on him. With his high cheekbones, well-defined chin, broad shoulders and flat abs, he had the kind of looks that made women swoon and Shannon wasn't blind.

"Mr. Wallace was stranded on the interstate. The hotels filled up quickly with travelers and now his only options are a cot in the high school gym or finding someone to take him in. He tells me that he's in Pennsylvania because he has business with you on Monday and—"

"I came a few days early to get a look at the store on my own," Rory interrupted, stepping forward. "But I ran into the storm. I was hoping you wouldn't mind me staying the night. Normally, I wouldn't ask such a big favor, but as you can see I'm desperate."

Mind? She almost laughed. She would bet

that fifty percent of the women he met fantasized about being stuck in a storm with him.

She opened the door a little wider. Not only would having him stay the night get her out of the doldrums about her life, but this also had all the makings of a perfect fantasy. Cold night. Gorgeous guy. And wine. She had tons of wine.

"Daddy, I'm cold."

Her fantasy came to an abrupt halt as she glanced down and saw a little girl standing beside Rory. She wore a pink ski jacket and carried a matching pink backpack. Little strands of yellow hair peeked from beneath her hood.

Her heart pinched with fear. Her breathing stuttered out. Did Fate think it was funny to let her dodge playing Santa's helper only to drop an adorable child on her doorstep?

"You can see why I don't want to stay in a shelter."

Fear and yearning collided as she glanced down at the sweet little girl with big blue eyes and fine yellow hair. As much as she knew spending time with this child would intensify her longing for her own children, she couldn't leave Rory and his daughter out in the cold or ship them to a crowded gym with hundreds of other noisy travelers and a tiny cot.

She also couldn't be a Scrooge. Her problem wasn't their problem. She would be a good hostess.

She stepped back so they could enter. "Yes. Yes, of course."

Carrying a duffel bag and briefcase as he squeezed into the foyer, Rory brushed against her, setting off a firestorm of sensations inside her. She ignored them. Not just because a man with a child was most likely married, but because she probably wouldn't have made a pass at him even if he'd been alone. In the year since her divorce, she hadn't been able to relate to men as anything other than employees. After her husband's anger over her inability to have kids and the way he'd dropped her like a hot potato—no consideration for their five-year marriage, no consideration for her devastation—the fear of another man rejecting her paralyzed her.

Plus, come Monday, they'd be doing business. His family owned a holding company for various types of stores and Raleigh's would probably fit their collection. That's why she'd thought of Natalie's old boyfriend when her parents had decided they wanted to sell the store. It could be a quick, painless sale. She didn't want to jeopardize that.

But, wow. It had been fun to fantasize about being stranded with him, fun for the ten seconds before reality intruded, reminding her she wasn't normal.

As Rory dropped his duffel bag, she said, "It's a terrible storm."

"Worst in ten years," the trooper agreed, staying behind on the porch. "If you're all settled, I need to get back on the road."

"We're fine," Shannon said, as she began to close the door. As an afterthought, she added, "Thank you."

"Yes, thank you," Rory Wallace called out, too.

Already on his way down her front steps, the trooper waved goodbye and trudged through the thick snow on the sidewalk to his car.

Awkward silence reigned as Rory Wallace took in the foyer of Shannon Raleigh's home. As if it wasn't bad enough that he'd been forced to humble himself and ask for shelter from a business associate, it appeared she was moving. Boxes blocked half the corridor that led from the foyer to the kitchen behind it. They littered the living room to the right and the dining room to the left.

Which made him feel even guiltier. "Thank you. I really appreciate this."

She smiled graciously. "You're welcome." Then she shivered, even though she wore a long white coat and the house wasn't that cold, just chilled, as if the heat had been on low all day while she was at work. "Give me a minute to turn on the furnace." She walked to a thermostat on the wall and adjusted it. "You might want to keep your coats on until it heats up in here."

He unbuttoned his topcoat. "Actually, after spending ten hours in a car, your house is warm to us." He stooped to help his daughter with her jacket. Realizing he'd never introduced her, he peeked up at Shannon. "This is my daughter, Finley."

Crouching beside them, Shannon said, "It's nice to meet you, Finley."

Finley mumbled, "Nice to meet you, too," then she looked at him as if wanting to make sure he'd noticed that she'd been polite.

Sliding her arms out of her little pink jacket, he gave her a subtle nod of approval. Lately, Finley had been something of a six-year-old diva. Disciplining her worked, but not always. And some days he was at his wits' end with her. So he was lucky she'd been polite to Shannon Raleigh. He didn't know how he'd deal with her if she insulted the woman who'd rescued them.

"This is the perfect night to be stranded with me," Shannon said, taking Finley's jacket to the closet behind her. "My parents will be home from Florida next Saturday and I promised I'd have the house decorated for Christmas. All these boxes are decorations they left behind when they moved to Florida. You can help me."

While Rory breathed a sigh of relief that he hadn't interrupted her moving, Finley's nose wrinkled and her eyes narrowed with distaste. Before he realized what she was about to do, she spat, "I hate Christmas."

Shannon reared back as if someone had slapped her. Her pretty blue eyes widened in disbelief. "Hate Christmas? How can you hate Christmas?"

"How can you believe that a fat guy in a red suit brings you presents?"

Anger pulsed through Rory's veins and he shot Finley a warning look. He wouldn't yell at her in front of Shannon, but he did need to provide a few rules for behavior when imposing on someone they barely knew. He faced Shannon. "Why don't you tell me where we're sleeping and I'll take Finley to our room and help her get settled in."

Shannon winced. "Actually, there's only one bedroom."

"Oh."

"It's no big deal. We'll give the bed to Finley, and you and I will use sleeping bags. You can put yours on the floor beside the bed and I'll sleep on the sofa."

Mortal embarrassment overwhelmed him. He hadn't realized how much he'd be putting her out when he gave her name to the state policeman. "This is such an imposition. You can't give us your room. Finley and I don't mind sleeping in the living room."

Finley stomped her foot. "I don't want to sleep on the floor."

He flashed Finley another warning look. "You won't. You can have the sofa."

"I want a bed!"

Rory's head pounded. He understood that this time of year wasn't easy for Finley. Her mom had left on Christmas day two years before. So every year, she got moody, and every year he indulged her by taking her on vacation from Christmas Eve to New Year's. For a guy who'd also lost his marriage on Christmas day, a vacation from the holiday was good for him, too. But the foot-stomping and the pouting and the demands that everything go her way, those had just started. And he absolutely refused to get on board with them. He had to spend the next week looking at Raleigh's Department Store for his family's holding company. He couldn't have her acting like a brat all week.

He turned to Shannon. "Would you mind showing us to the bedroom so I can get Finley settled?"

"Not at all."

She led them into a small first-floor bedroom that was as neat and clean as the rest of the house...minus boxes. A feminine white ruffled spread sat on a simple double bed. Red pillows on the bed matched the red shag carpet beneath it and the drapes on the double windows.

He dropped his duffel bag to the floor. "Wow."

She faced him with a smile. Her shiny black hair was a wonderland of long, springy curls. In the years since university, her face had shifted just slightly and she'd become a softer, prettier version of the young girl he remembered.

"Wow?"

"I'm just a little surprised by your room."

Her smile grew. "Really? Why?"

"The red." He felt the same color rising on his cheeks. The room was girlie, yet incredibly sexy. But he certainly didn't feel comfortable saying that to the woman giving him and his daughter shelter, especially not after Finley's minitantrum. Still, he never would have guessed this sexy combination of color and style from the sweet Shannon he knew all those years ago at school.

"There's a private bathroom for the bedroom—" she gestured toward a door to the right "—over there."

"Thank you."

"Just come out when you're ready." She smiled. "I'll start supper. I hope you like toasted cheese sandwiches and soup. I'm not much of a cook."

"On a cold day like this, soup is terrific."

She closed the door behind her and Rory crouched down in front of Finley. Smoothing his hand down her shiny yellow hair, he said, "You're killing me."

She blinked innocently "What?"

"Ms. Raleigh is doing us a favor by letting us stay. We should be polite to her."

"I was polite."

"Saying you want the bed while you stomp your foot is not polite."

Her bottom lip puffed out. "Sorry."

And *this* was why he had trouble disciplining her. The second he pointed out something she'd done wrong, she turned on that little-girl charm. Batted her long black lashes over her pretty blue eyes.

Scrubbing his hand over his mouth, he rose.

"I'll tell you what. You stay in here for a few minutes, while I spend some time getting acquainted with our hostess." And apologizing and doing damage control. "While I'm gone, you can get your pajamas and toothbrush out of your backpack and think about how you'd want a little girl to behave if she were a guest in our house."

Apparently liking her assignment, she nodded eagerly.

"And don't spend all your time thinking about how you'd spoil your little guest, because you wouldn't. If you had to give up your bed for a stranger, you'd want her to be nice to you."

Finley nodded again and said, "Okay. I get it."

Rory was absolutely positive she didn't, but he had to make amends to Shannon. He left Finley in the bedroom and walked up the hall to the kitchen.

The house was small, but comfortable. The furniture was new and expensive, an indication that Raleigh's Department Store did, indeed, make lots of money. So maybe the trip to Pennsylvania might not have been the mistake he'd thought while sitting in his car for ten hours, not moving, on the interstate?

He found Shannon in the kitchen. Still wearing her coat, she drew bread from a drawer and cheese from the refrigerator.

"Thanks again for taking us in."

"No problem." She set the bread and cheese on the center island of the sunny yellow kitchen with light oak cabinets and pale brown granite countertops. She reached for the top button of her coat. "Furnace has kicked in," she said with a laugh, popping the first button and the second, but when she reached for the third, she paused. "I think I'll just take this out to the hall closet."

She walked past him, to the swinging door. Wanting something to do, he followed her. Just as he said, "Is there anything I can do to help with supper?" her coat fell off her shoulders, revealing a bright red dress.

But when she turned in surprise, he saw the dress wasn't really a dress but some little red velvet thing that dipped low at the bodice, revealing an enticing band of cleavage. Tall black boots showcased her great legs.

She was dressed like Mrs. Santa—if Mrs. Santa were a young, incredibly endowed woman who liked short skirts.

His dormant hormones woke as if from a long winter's nap, and he took a step back. These little bursts of attraction he was having toward her were all wrong. He had an unruly daughter who took priority over everything in his life, including his hormones, and he was a guest in Shannon's house. Plus, tomorrow morning, when the storm was over, they'd go into her department store as adversaries of a sort. She'd be trying to sell her family business to him and he'd be looking for reasons not to buy. He couldn't be attracted to her.

He swallowed back the whole filing cabinet of flirtatious remarks that wanted to come out. "That's an interesting choice of work clothes."

She laughed nervously. "I was going to fill in for our Santa's helper in the toy department."

Ah. Not Mrs. Santa but Santa's helper.

"Well, the dress is very…" He paused. He knew the dress was probably supposed to be Christmassy and cute. And on a shorter woman it probably was. But she was tall, sleek, yet somehow still womanly. He didn't dare tell her that. "Festive."

She brought the coat to her neck, using it to shield herself. "That's the look we're after. Festive and happy. And it actually works for the girl who fits into this costume. I was lucky Mother Nature saved me and I didn't have to fill in for her tonight."

Recognizing her acute nervousness, Rory pulled his gaze away from her long, slim legs.

He cleared his throat. "I...um...just followed you to see if I could help you with anything."

She motioned toward his black suit and white shirt. "Are you sure you want to butter bread or stir tomato soup in a suit?"

He took off his jacket, loosened his tie and began rolling up his sleeves.

And Shannon's mouth watered. Damn it. She'd already figured out she couldn't be fantasizing about him. Sure, his shoulders were broad, his arms muscled. And she'd always been a sucker for a man in a white shirt with rolled-up sleeves looking like he was ready to get down to business. But as far as she could tell, he was married. That shut down the possibility of any relationship right then and there. Plus, she wanted him to buy her parents' store. She couldn't be drooling on him.

She hung up her coat, then scurried past him, into the kitchen and directly to the laundry room. Leaning on the closed door, she drew in a deep breath. God, he was gorgeous. But he was also married.

Married. Married. Married.

She forced the litany through her head, hoping it would sink in, as she grabbed a pair of sweats and a T-shirt from the dryer and changed into them.

When she returned to the kitchen he stood at the center island, buttering bread. "While we have a few seconds of privacy, I also wanted to apologize for Finley. I brought her because she's on Christmas break from school and I hate to leave her with her nanny for an entire week. But I know she can be a handful."

Walking over to join him, she said, "She's just a little girl."

"True, but she's also recently entered a new phase of some sort where she stomps her foot when she doesn't get her own way."

Standing so close to him, she could smell his aftershave. Her breathing stuttered in and out of her lungs. So she laughed, trying to cover it. "A new phase, huh?"

"She was perfectly fine in preschool and kindergarten, but first grade is turning her into a diva."

"Diva?"

"Yeah." Smiling, he caught her gaze, and every nerve ending in her body lit up like the lights on the Christmas tree in Central Park. Spinning away from him, she repeated the litany in her head again.

Married. Married. Married!

"You know, I can easily handle this myself.

You can use the den for privacy if you need to call your wife."

He snorted a laugh. "Not hardly."

She set the frying pan for the sandwiches on the stove and faced him again. "I'm sure she's worried."

"And I'm sure she and her new husband aren't even thinking about me and Finley right now."

"Oh." Nerves rolled through her. He was divorced? Not married?

Their gazes caught. Attraction spun through her like snowflakes dancing in the light of a streetlamp. She reminded herself that they were about to do business, but it didn't work to snuff out the snap and crackle of electricity sizzling between them.

She pivoted away from him. Pretending she needed all her concentration to open two cans of soup, she managed to avoid conversation. But that didn't stop the chatter in her brain. As difficult as it might be to have a little girl around, she was abundantly glad Finley was with him. She might have had that quick fantasy of being stranded with him, but now that sanity had returned, she knew the sale of the store had to take precedence over a night of…she swallowed…passion? Good God, she hadn't even *thought* the word in a year, let alone *experienced* it. She'd probably dissolve into a puddle if he made a pass at her.

Finley came out of the bedroom just as Rory set the sandwiches on the table and Shannon had finished ladling soup into the bright green bowls sitting on the pretty yellow place mats. She crawled onto a chair and spread her paper napkin on her lap.

Longing hit Shannon like an unexpected burst of winter wind. She remembered dreams of buying pretty dresses for her own little girl, her dreams of taking her to the park, gymnastics, dance lessons and soccer—

She stopped her thoughts, cut off the sadness and grief that wanted to engulf her. Surely, she could have a little girl in her house without breaking into a million shattered pieces? She hadn't given up on the idea of becoming a mother altogether. She knew that once she adjusted to not having her own child, she could adopt. So maybe this was a good time to begin adjusting?

Finley sighed. "I don't like red soup."

Sounding very parental, Rory said, "That's okay. Just eat your sandwich."

Finley sighed heavily again, as if it were pure torture not to get her own way. Rory ignored her. Shannon studied her curiously, realizing

that with Diva Finley she really would get a
solid understanding of what it took to be a parent. She was like a little blond-haired litmus test
for whether or not Shannon had what it took to
adopt a child and be a mom.

Rory turned to her and said, "This is certainly
a lovely old house."

She faced Rory so quickly that their gazes
collided. He had the darkest eyes she'd ever
seen. And they were bottomless. Mesmeriz-
ing...

She gave herself a mental shake. It was pointless to be attracted. He wouldn't make a pass at
her with his daughter around, and she wouldn't
make a pass at him because they were about
to do business. She had to stop noticing these
things.

She cleared her throat. "The parts I've re-
stored are great. But the whole heating system
needs to be replaced."

"Well, you've done a wonderful job on the
renovations you have done."

"Really?" She peeked up at him.

And everything Rory wanted to say fell out of
his head. Her big blue eyes reminded him of the
sky in summer. The black curls that curved around
her face had his hand itching to touch them.

Finley sighed heavily. "I don't want this soup."

Rory faced her. "We already agreed that you didn't have to eat it."

"I don't like that it's here."

"Here?"

"In front of me!"

Before Rory had a chance to react, Shannon rose with a smile. "Let me take it to the sink."

She reached across the table, lifted the bowl and calmly walked it to the sink. Then she returned to the table and sat as if nothing had happened.

Technically nothing *had* happened. She'd diffused the potentially problematic soup episode just by reacting calmly.

Of course, he knew that was what *he* should have done, but after ten grueling hours on the road, he was every bit as tired and cranky as Finley. And this confusing attraction he felt for Shannon wasn't helping things.

"I don't want this sandwich."

Here we go again. "Finley—"

"I'm tired."

Before Rory could remind her he was, too, Shannon rose. "I have just the cure for being tired. A bubble bath."

Finley instantly brightened. "Really?"

"I have all kinds of bubbles in my bathroom.

It's right beside the bedroom you're using. Why don't we go get a bath ready for you?"

Finley all but bounced off her chair. "All right!"

They disappeared down the hall to the bedroom, and Rory ran his hand down his face.

He didn't know what would drive him crazy first, his daughter or his hormones.

CHAPTER TWO

SHANNON WALKED OUT of the kitchen with a happy Finley skipping behind her to the bathroom. Her self-pity long forgotten and her new mission in place, she was glad to help tired, frazzled Rory with his daughter. It would give her a chance for some one-on-one time with Finley, a chance to prove to herself that she was strong enough to be around kids. Strong enough to adopt one of her own, if she wanted to.

Unfortunately, the second they were out of Rory's earshot, Finley the Diva returned. "You can go. I'll fill the tub myself."

Having watched her friends in Charleston handle their children, if nothing else, Shannon knew the grown-up in charge had to stay in charge. "I'm sure you could, but I want to do it."

Finley crossed her arms on her chest and huffed out a sigh.

For Rory's sake, Shannon didn't laugh. "I like this scent," she said, picking up her favorite bubble bath. "But you can choose whichever one you want."

Finley chose another scent. Shannon shrugged. It didn't matter to her which scent Finley used. She turned on the tap, poured in the liquid and faced Finley with a smile. "I'm going to leave the room while this fills up so you can undress. Call me when you're ready to step in the tub."

"I don't need help."

And with that comment, Shannon decided she had experimented enough for one night. She didn't have the right to discipline this little girl and she definitely needed a firm hand. So she left this battle for Rory. "Okay. That's great."

She walked out of the bathroom and directly into the kitchen. "Tub is almost full and Finley's stripping. You might want to go in and supervise."

Rory rose. "She can bathe herself but I like to be in the next room just in case." He glanced at the dishes and winced. "Sorry about that."

She waved a hand in dismissal. "I can load a few dishes into the dishwasher. You go on ahead."

Alone in the kitchen for forty minutes, she

wasn't sure if Finley had decided to have an Olympic swim in her tub or if Rory was reading her a story...or if they'd found the TV and decided to stay on their own in the bedroom.

Whatever had happened, Shannon was fine with it. She knew they were both tired, weary. And once the dishes were stacked in the dishwasher and the kitchen cleaned, she had decorating to do. But just as she dragged the box of garland over to the sofa, Rory walked into the living room.

"Well, she's down for the night."

"I suspected she was tired."

"Exhausted."

"She'll be happy in the morning."

With a weary sigh, Rory fell to the couch. "How'd you get so smart about kids?"

His praise surprised her. Though she'd spent years watching her friends' kids, longing for her own, she'd also all but ignored them this past difficult year. "I had some friends in South Carolina who had children. I used to babysit."

He laughed. "You *volunteered* to hang around kids?"

"It's always easier to handle children who aren't yours." She brushed her hands together to rid them of attic dust and stepped away from the box of decorations. Eager to change the subject, she said, "You sound like you could use a glass of wine."

"Or a beer, if you have one."

"I do." She left the living room, got two beers from the refrigerator and gave one to Rory.

He relaxed on the couch, closed his eyes. "Thanks."

"You're welcome." She glanced at the decorations, thinking she really should get started, but also knowing Rory was embarrassed about imposing and at his wits' end. Deciding to be a Good Samaritan and give him someone to talk to, she gingerly sat on the sofa beside him. "Must have been some drive."

"There was a point when I considered turning around because I could see things were getting worse, but the weather reports kept saying the storm would blow out soon." He peered over at her. "It never did."

"This will teach you to listen to weathermen."

He laughed. Relaxed a little more. "So you ended up taking over your family's business?"

"By default. I was perfectly happy to work with the buyers and in advertising for Raleigh's. But my dad wanted to retire and I'm an only child." She paused then smiled at him. "I see you also ended up in your dad's job."

Rory tilted his head, studying her. Her smile

was pretty, genuine. Not flirtatious and certainly not enough to get his hormones going, but an odd tingle took up residence in his stomach. "Yeah. I did. Who would have thought ten years ago that we'd be running the two businesses we always talked about while I waited for Natalie for our dates?"

"Well, you were a shoo-in for your job. You're the oldest son of a family that owns a business. I thought I was going to be a lawyer. Turns out law school is really, really dull."

He laughed again, then realized he couldn't remember the last time he'd laughed twice, back-to-back, in the same night. Warmth curled through him. Not like arousal from flirting. Not like happiness, but something else. Something richer. Not only was Shannon Raleigh a knockout and good with kids, but she was also easy to talk to—

Good grief. This strange feeling he was having was attraction. Real attraction. The next step beyond the hormone-driven reaction he had when he saw her in the little red dress.

Damn it. He was here to look at her family's store to see if it was an appropriate investment for his family. He couldn't be attracted to her. Not just that, but he was already a loser at love. He'd given in to the fun of flirting once. He'd let himself become vulnerable. Hell, he'd let himself tumble head over heels for someone, and he knew how that had turned out—with her leaving him on Christmas day two years ago, and all but deserting their daughter.

When he'd finally found her and asked about visitation, she'd told him she didn't want to see Finley. Ever. Hoping that she'd change her mind in the two years that had passed, he'd run out of excuses to give Finley for missed birthdays and holidays. Pretty soon he was going to have to tell a six-year-old girl that her mother didn't want her.

That broke his heart. Shattered it into a million painful pieces. Made him want to shake his ex-wife silly.

Which was why he'd never marry again. At this point in his life he wasn't even sure he'd date again.

He rose from the sofa. "You know what? I'm tired, too. I'm going to have to figure out how to get my car from the interstate in the morning and I'm guessing for that I'm going to need a good night's sleep." He gave her a warm smile. "Thanks again for letting us stay."

With that he turned and all but raced toward the door, but he didn't get three steps before Shannon stopped him. "Rory?"

He turned.

She pointed at the sleeping bag rolled up at by the door. "You might want to take that."

He sucked in a breath. The whole point of coming into the room had been to get his sleeping bag. Two minutes in her company and he'd forgotten that. "Yeah. Thanks."

He scooped the sleeping bag from the floor. He hadn't been this foolish around a woman in years.

He was glad he was leaving in the morning.

Shannon was awakened by the feeling of soft breath puffing in her face. She batted at it only to have her hand meet something solid.

Finley yelled, "Ouch!"

Shannon bolted up on the couch as several things popped into her head at once. First, she was sleeping in her living room. Second, she had company. Third, Finley was not the nicest child in the world. But, the all-important fourth, she would be alone with a child until Rory woke up.

"I'm hungry." Finley's tiny face scrunched. Her nose became a wrinkled button. Her mouth pulled down in an upside-down *U*.

Shannon pressed her lips together to keep from laughing. Which heartened her. Because

Finley was forceful and demanding, not a cute little cuddle bug, it was easier for Shannon to deal with being around her.

She rolled out of her sleeping bag. Her friends had complained about being awakened by their children at ungodly hours. But a glance at the wall clock told her it was after eight. She couldn't fault Finley for waking her. It might be Saturday, but she still had to be at the store by ten to open it.

Fortunately, she had enough time to make something to eat. "Well, I enjoy cooking breakfast so it looks like we're both lucky this morning."

That confused Finley so much that her frown wobbled.

Laughing, Shannon ruffled her hair. "Which do you prefer pancakes or waffles?"

"Do you have blueberries?"

"Of course."

"Then I'd like pancakes."

Shannon headed for the kitchen. "You and I are going to get along very well."

As she pulled the ingredients for pancakes from the cupboards, Finley took a seat at the table. Before she started to make the batter, Shannon picked up the remote for her stereo and turned it on. A rousing rendition of "Here Comes Santa Claus" poured into the room.

"Would you like a glass of milk?"

"Yes, please."

Shannon dipped into her refrigerator as Finley slid off her seat. Watching Finley walk to the counter, she grabbed the gallon of milk and pulled it out of the fridge. But before she could reach the counter, Finley had picked up the remote and turned off the music.

She blinked. "I was listening to that."

"It was stupid."

"It was a Christmas song."

"And Christmas is stupid."

Shannon gaped at her. Not just because she had the audacity to turn off the music without asking, but that was the second time she'd mentioned she didn't like Christmas.

The temptation was strong to ask why, as she poured Finley a glass of milk, but she wasn't quite sure how to approach it. Did she say, *Hey, kid, everybody likes Christmas. You get gifts. You get cookies. What's the deal?*

As curious as she was, that seemed a lot like interfering and she was just getting accustomed to being around a child. She wasn't ready for deep, personal interaction yet. Plus, saying she hated Christmas could just be a part of one of

Finley the Diva's tantrums. Or a way to manipulate people.

So, she turned to the counter and began preparing pancakes. A happy hum started in her
throat and worked its way out, surprising her.
Breakfast was one of the few meals she was
well versed in. She could make a pancake or a
waffle with the best of them. But it was a happy
surprise to be able to be in the same room with
Finley without worrying that she'd fall apart or
dwell on her inability to have kids herself.

"So where do you go to school?"

"Winchester Academy."

"Is that a private school?"

Finley nodded.

"Do you like school?"

"Sometimes. Artie Regan brings frogs and
scares me. And Jenny Logan beats me to the
swing."

A motherly warmth flowed through her.
When she wasn't demanding her own way, Finley was normal. And here she was handling her.
Talking to her. No flutters of panic. No feeling
sorry for herself.

The kitchen door opened and Rory walked
into the room yawning. "Sorry about that."

"About what?" Shannon faced him with a

smile, but the smile disappeared as her mouth went dry.

His dark hair was sticking out in all directions. His eyes didn't seem to want to open. A day-old growth of beard sexily shadowed his chin and cheeks. He wore a white undershirt and navy blue sweats that loosely clung to his lean hips.

"About sleeping in. Normally, I'm up—" He paused. "Are you making pancakes?"

"Blueberry."

"Wow. We should get stranded on an interstate more often."

She laughed. *Laughed.* She had a sexy man and a cute little girl in her kitchen and she wasn't stuttering or shattering, she was laughing.

But a little warning tweaked her brain. Not only was she enjoying this way too much, but it also would be over soon. They'd eat breakfast, pack up the few things they'd brought with them and head out.

She had about twenty minutes over breakfast before she'd be alone again.

Rory ambled to the counter, where the coffeemaker sputtered the last drops of fresh coffee into the pot. "Can I get you a cup?"

"That'd be great, thanks. Mugs are in the cupboard by the sink."

But as he reached into the cupboard to get the mugs, his arm stopped. "Holy cats!"

Shannon paused her spoon in the pancake batter. "What?"

"There's got to be two feet of snow out there."

"That was the eventual predication after we already had eighteen inches."

"Yeah, well, it doesn't look like the snowplow went through."

She dropped the spoon, hustled to the window beside him. "Wow."

He turned and caught her gaze. "Even with that big SUV I saw in the driveway, I'll bet you can't get us out to a main road."

Her heart lodged in her throat. Could they actually be forced to stay another day? Could she handle another day?

The answer came swiftly, without hesitation. She couldn't just handle another day; she *wanted* another day.

"With all that snow, I'm not sure the main roads are even clear."

"I'll check the internet."

"If the roads are still closed, you know you're welcome to stay, right?"

"I think we may have to take you up on that."

Though her heart leaped with anticipation, she pasted a disappointed-for-them look on her face. "I'm sorry."

"I'm the one who's sorry."

"Don't be." She brightened her expression. "I don't mind."

Rory nudged his head toward Finley, who sat quietly at the kitchen table.

Lowering her voice, Shannon said, "She'll be fine."

"You want to be the one to tell her?"

"What do you say we get a pancake into her first?"

He tapped her nose. "Excellent idea."

The friendly tap shouldn't have made Shannon's heart race, but it did. She pivoted away from him and returned to her pancake batter. They were staying another day as guests. Friends. Nothing more. But being friends meant no stress. No pressure. They could have a good time.

A good time, instead of a lonely, boring weekend.

Who would have thought the day before, when she'd stood trembling with fear over playing Santa's helper, that today she'd welcome having a little girl spend the day with her?

She ladled batter onto the already warm grill

and within minutes the sweet scent of pancakes filled the air.

As she piled pancakes on three plates, Rory found the maple syrup and took the pot of coffee to the table.

Finley eagerly grabbed her plate from Shannon. Without as much as a blink from her dad, she said, "Thank you."

Shannon's heart tweaked again. She glanced from happy Finley to relieved Rory. They had no idea how much their presence meant to her. Worse, they probably didn't realize she was actually glad the snowplow hadn't yet gone through. Their misery changed her incredibly lonely, probably bordering-toward-pathetic weekend into time with other people. Company for dinner the night before. Someone to make pancakes for. People who would eat lunch and maybe dinner with her.

And maybe even someone to bake sugar cookies with? A little girl who'd paint them with her child's hand, giving them strokes and color and even mistakes only a child could make. Turning them into real Christmas cookies.

Rory pointed at his pancake. "These are great."

Finley nodded in agreement. "These are great."

"Thanks."

Rory laughed and caught her gaze. "Thought you said you couldn't cook?"

Her heart stuttered a bit. Not because he was paying attention to her, but because his dark eyes were filled with warmth and happiness. Casual happiness. The kind of happiness real friends shared. "I can't, except for breakfast. But breakfast foods are usually easy."

Turning his attention back to his plate, he said, "Well, these are delicious."

Warmth filled her. Contentment. She gave herself a moment to soak it all in before she reached for her fork and tasted her own pancake.

Picking up his coffee cup, Rory said, "I can't believe how much snow fell."

"It is Pennsylvania."

"How do you deal with it?"

"Well, on days like this, those of us who can stay in."

"You play games maybe?"

Ah, she got what he was doing. He was paving the way to tell Finley they couldn't leave. Probably hoping to show her she'd have a good day if they stayed.

"We do. We play lots of games. But we also bake cookies."

Finley didn't even glance up. Happily involved in her blueberry pancake, she ignored them.

Rory said, "I love cookies."

"These are special cookies. They're sugar cookies that I cut into shapes and then paint."

"Paint?"

"With icing. I put colored icing on houses, churches, bells—"

Finley glanced up sharply. "You mean Christmas bells."

Shannon winced. "Well, yes. I'm baking cookies for my family when we celebrate Christmas next week. But it's still fun—"

"I hate Christmas!"

This was the third time Finley had said she hated Christmas. It wasn't merely part of a tantrum or even a way to manipulate people. This little girl really didn't like Christmas.

"Okay. So instead of baking cookies, how about if we play cards?"

"I thought we were leaving."

Rory set his hand on top of Finley's. "I'd like to leave. But I have to check to see if the roads are open. There's a good possibility that we're stranded here for another few hours, maybe even another day."

Finley sighed heavily, like a billion-dollar heiress who'd just received bad news, and who would, at any second, explode. Shannon found herself holding her breath, waiting for Finley's reply. Which was ridiculous. The kid was six. The weather wasn't anybody's fault. She was stuck and that was that.

Setting her fork on her plate, Shannon rose and said, "While I go to my room to check on the roads and call my staff, you drink your milk and finish your breakfast. Then we'll put the dishes in the dishwasher and we'll play Go Fish."

Finley's eyes narrowed and her mouth formed the upside-down *U* again. But Shannon ignored her. From her peripheral vision she watched Finley glare at her dad.

Without looking at her, Rory said, "I haven't played Go Fish in years. I'm not sure I remember the rules."

"It's an easy game, Daddy."

"Good. Then I should catch on quickly."

Shannon took her plate to the sink. "Or maybe she'll beat you."

That brought a light to Finley's eyes. When Shannon returned from checking the road conditions on the internet, calling her staff to say she wasn't opening the store and calling the radio stations to alert the community that the store would be closed again, she returned to the kitchen. Finley eagerly helped clear the table, stacked dishes in the dishwasher and rifled through a kitchen drawer for a deck of cards.

"I had to close the store."

Rory held up his cell phone. "I figured. I checked the road conditions. Nothing's really open. Customers can't get there anyway."

As Finley approached the table with the cards, Shannon said, "So we'll have some fun."

Pulling a chair away from the round kitchen table, Rory said, "Yes, we will. Right, Finley?"

Finley sighed and shrugged, but also pulled out a chair and sat.

Shannon noticed that Rory more or less let Finley win the first game, so she went along, too. But when Rory handily won the second game, Shannon didn't think it was out of line to play the third game without deference to Finley. But when she won, Finley exploded.

"You cheated!"

Shannon laughed. "No. Cheating takes all the sport out of a game. There's no fun in winning if you haven't really won."

"I don't care!" She swung her arm across the table, sending cards flying. But before her hand could slow down, she also thwacked her milk. The glass went airborne and landed on the floor. Sticky white milk poured everywhere.

Mortally embarrassed by Finley's outburst, Rory bounced from the table. "Finley!"

Finley bounced off her chair and raced to the kitchen door. "I hate you!"

The swinging door slammed closed when she flew through it.

Shannon rose and grabbed the paper towels. "Sorry. I should have let her win again."

Rory rubbed his hand across the back of his neck. "No. We were playing a game. She knows she can't win every time." He rubbed his neck again. He'd only ever told his parents about the trouble in his marriage and he certainly hadn't intended to tell Shannon because, technically, they didn't really know each other. But deep down Finley was a sweet little girl who deserved defending.

He fell to his seat again. "Finley's behavior isn't the fault of a confused six-year-old, but a mom who abandoned her."

Using a paper towel to sop up the milk, Shannon said, "What?"

"Her mom," Rory said, not quite sure how to broach this subject because he hadn't spoken with anyone about his ex. So he had no practice, no frame of reference for what to say.

He lifted his eyes until he could catch Shannon's gaze. "Finley's mom left us two years ago on Christmas day."

Shannon took the wet paper towels to the trash. Confusion laced her voice when she said, "Your ex left you on Christmas day?"

"Yeah, that's why Finley's sensitive about Christmas. But what's worse is that her mom doesn't want to see her at all. She doesn't like kids. Didn't want kids."

Shannon returned to the table and fell to her chair, trying to force all that to sink in but not quite able to comprehend. She'd spent her entire adult life attempting to get pregnant, longing for a child, and Finley's mom had left her without a backward glance?

"My ex never did anything she didn't want to do." He rose from the chair, pushed it out of his way and stooped to pick up the scattered cards.

"That's amazing."

He shrugged, but his pinched expression told her he wasn't so cavalier about it. "She'd said at the outset of our marriage that she didn't want kids." Finished gathering the cards, he rose. "Her getting pregnant was a surprise, but I thought we were ready. Turns out she wasn't."

Shannon sat in stunned silence. Rory's wife had *abandoned* her daughter? Disbelief thundered through her, along with a sense of injustice. While she'd do anything, give anything, to be able to have a child, Finley's mom had simply abandoned one?

How could a woman be so cruel?

CHAPTER THREE

RORY NEATLY STACKED the cards on the table. "I need to check on her."

"Okay. I'll start lunch."

As she had the night before, Shannon made soup and sandwiches. This time, she chose chicken soup—a soup with not even a red vegetable in it—and prepared a plate of cold cuts and some bread.

Finley walked into the kitchen in front of her dad, who had both hands on her little shoulders. Looking at the floor, she mumbled, "I'm sorry."

Shannon's heart ached for her, but she didn't think it was appropriate to say, "Hey, it's not your fault. Your mom's a horrible woman who shouldn't have left you." So, instead, she said, "That's okay. I didn't make red soup today."

Finley peeked at her. "You didn't?"

"No. I made chicken noodle."

"I like chicken noodle."

"So do I."

Rory got bowls from the cupboard and he and Finley set them on the place mats Shannon had already put out. Finley found soup spoons. Shannon set the cold cuts on the table. Everybody did everything without saying a word.

Shannon felt oddly responsible. Should she have tried to lose at the card game? Should she have reacted differently to the cheating accusation? She honestly didn't know. But she did know Finley deserved a bit of happiness and if she could, she intended to provide it.

She sucked in a breath. "You know...I still have a few sleds from when my dad and I used to slide down Parker's Hill when I was a little girl."

Finley's face instantly brightened. "Really?"

"There's a bit of a hill behind this house. I never tried it out for sledding because I just moved here last year, but I'm guessing there might be a place we could sled-ride."

This time Rory said, "Really?"

"Sure. It would be fun. Even if we can't go sledding, getting outside for some fresh air would do us all good."

Rory inclined his head. "Maybe." He faced his daughter. "What do you think?"

"I'd like to sled-ride."

"And we will if we can," Shannon quickly assured her. "As I said, I've never checked out that hill."

"I don't have snow pants."

"You can wear two pair of jeans," Rory suggested.

"And we'll put them in the dryer as soon as we come inside, so they'll be good for tomorrow morning."

The mood clearing the lunch dishes improved significantly from the mood when setting out those same dishes. Finley hurriedly dressed in the multiple jeans and double sweaters. Shannon found a pair of mittens to put over Finley's tiny multicolored striped gloves.

When Finley was ready, Shannon quickly dressed in a pair of jeans and two sweaters. She put her dad's old parka over herself and used insulated gloves for her hands.

They stepped outside onto the back porch and the glare off the snow almost blinded them.

"Wow. It's beautiful."

Shannon glanced around proudly at the snow-covered fir trees that surrounded her little home. "Yes. It is. I loved living in South Carolina—close to the beach," she added, slanting a look at Rory. "But this is home. As annoying as snow is, it is also beautiful."

They trudged from the house to the shed behind the garage and found an old sled and two red saucer sleds. Shannon and Finley took the saucers and Rory hoisted the bigger runner sled off its hook and followed them out, into the bright sunshine again.

Again they trudged through the snow, walking the twenty or thirty feet from the outbuilding to the dip behind the house.

"There are trees."

Shannon glanced at Rory. "I know. That's why I couldn't say for sure we could sled. Without a wide path between the trees, there'd be too much chance we'd hit one and somebody could be hurt."

He walked fifty feet to the left. "Too many trees this way." Then fifty feet to the right. "I found something!" he called, motioning for Shannon and Finley to come over. "There's a perfect space right here."

The "hill" was more of a slope. It eased down nicely for about thirty feet. A wide ledge would stop them before they reached what looked to be a bigger hill. Still, given that Finley was only six, Shannon didn't think they should try to go beyond the ledge.

She tossed her saucer to the snow. "I'm ready."

Finley followed suit. "I'm ready, too."

They plopped onto their saucers, scooted a bit to get them going then careened down the hill. Finley's squealing giggles filled the quiet air. Hearing her, Shannon laughed. They flew down the slope and, as predicted, their saucers ran out of steam on the ledge.

Finley bounced up. "Let's go again!" She grabbed her saucer and started up the hill.

"Walk along the side!" Shannon called. "We don't want to make our slope bumpy from footprints."

To Shannon's complete amazement, Finley said, "Okay!" and moved to the side of the hill.

When they reached the top, Rory said, "Okay, everybody out of my way. I'm taking this puppy for a ride."

He threw the runner sled onto the snow and landed on top of it, sending it racing down the hill. He hit the ledge, but his sled didn't stop. The ledge didn't even slow the sleek runners. Smooth and thin, they whizzed across the ledge as if it were nothing. In seconds Rory and his sled headed down the bigger hill and disappeared.

Finley screamed.

Thinking she was terrified, Shannon spun to face her, but the little girl's face glowed with laughter. Shannon's lips twitched. Then she burst out laughing, too.

"Do you think we'll ever see him again?"

Finley's giggles multiplied. "How far down does the hill go?"

"I don't know. I've never been back that far."

The world around them grew silent. Now that the fun of seeing him disappear was over, Shannon's tummy tugged with concern. As fast as he was going, he could have hit a tree. He could be at the bottom of the hill, unconscious.

"We better go check on him."

"Can we ride our sleds down to the ledge?"

Shannon laughed and patted Finley's head. Kids really had no comprehension of danger. But before she could reply, Rory called, "I'm okay!"

His voice echoed in the silence around them. But knowing he was fine, Shannon tossed her saucer to the ground. "Race you to the ledge."

Finley positioned her sled and jumped on. They squealed with laughter as they sped down the hill. On the ledge, both popped off their sleds, ran to the edge and peered over. At least fifty feet below, Rory dragged his sled up the hill.

He waved.

Finley waved. "Hi, Daddy!" Then she glanced

around when her voice echoed around her. "That is so cool."

"It's a cool place." She turned Finley toward the top of the hill again. "I'll bet we can sled down twice before your dad gets to the ledge."

Finley grabbed her sled. "Okay!"

They raced down another two times before Rory finally joined them on the ledge. "That was some ride."

Shannon peered over the edge. A reasonably wide strip wound between the rows of trees, but the hill itself was steep and long. "I'll bet it was."

He offered the runner sled to her. "Wanna try?"

She laughed. "Not a chance."

"Hey, sledding was your idea. I thought you were a pro."

"I haven't really gone sledding in years—"

Before she could finish her sentence Rory tossed the sled to the ground and punched into her like a linebacker. She fell on the sled. He fell on top of her and they took off down the hill. For several seconds she had no breath. When she finally caught a gulp of air, she screamed. Really screamed. But soon her screams of fear became screams of delight. The thrill of the speed whooshed through her. The wind whipping across her face felt glorious.

They hit the bottom with a thump.

Obviously paying attention to the grove of trees ahead of them, Rory banked left, toppling the sled to a stop. She rolled on the ground. He rolled beside her.

She turned her head to face him; he turned to face her and they burst out laughing.

Finley's little voice echoed down the hill. "Me next, Daddy!"

He bounced up and held his hand out to Shannon, helping her up.

"That was amazing."

He picked up the sled. "I know. It was like being a kid again. Fun. Free." Holding the sled with one hand, he looped his other arm across her shoulders. "Now we have to trudge about fifty feet up a hill."

She laughed, but her insides tickled. Even working at the store, she'd been nothing but lonely in the past year. Not because she didn't have friends. She did. Lots of them. Not because she missed her husband. Any man who'd desert a woman the day she had a hysterectomy was an ass. But because she'd missed belonging. With Rory and Finley she felt as if she belonged.

She sucked in a breath, erasing that thought.

These two would be with her for one more day—well, one evening and one night. Maybe breakfast in the morning. She couldn't get attached to them.

Still, when they reached the top and found Finley bouncing with delight, happiness filled her again. Finley was a sweet little girl who deserved some fun. Maybe even a break from the reality of her life—that her mom didn't want her.

Rory scooped her off the ground and fell with her onto the sled. The weight of their bodies set the sled in motion and it slid down the little slope. Shannon fell to her own sled and careened behind them so she could jump off when she reached the ledge and watch them as they whipped down the bigger hill.

Finley's squeals of pleasure echoed through the forest. Shannon's chest puffed out with pride. She'd thought of the idea that had turned a potentially dismal afternoon into an afternoon of joy.

She watched Finley and Rory plod back up the hill. When they reached the ledge, she stooped down and hugged Finley. "That was fun, wasn't it?"

Her eyes rounded with joy. "It was great!" She turned to her dad. "Let's go again."

"Hey, I just slogged up that hill three times. I need a break." He headed up the slope again. "But you can ride your saucer down the little hill as much as you want."

Surprisingly, Finley said, "Okay," and followed him up the slope. At the top, she set her butt on the saucer and sent herself lobbing down the hill.

Rory dropped to the snow. "I am seriously tired."

Shannon plopped beside him. "After three little rides?"

He tweaked a curl that had escaped from her knit cap. "Three *little* rides? You try walking up that hill three times in a row with no break."

Finley's final whoop of laughter as she slid to a stop on the ledge reached them. Shannon's heart swelled again, filled with warmth and joy. This was what it would feel like to have a real family. A loving husband. An adorable child.

Watching Finley trudge up the slope with her saucer, Rory said, "This is why I love having a kid. The fun. When Finley's not in a mood, she can be incredibly fun." He peeked at Shannon. "And spontaneous. The things she says sometimes crack me up."

She glanced down the hill at Finley, saw the

joy on her face, the snow on her tummy, and she laughed. "Yeah. She's cute."

Shannon's laughter filled Rory with peace. The whole afternoon had been fun, even though he'd told her about his ex-wife. Or maybe because he'd told her about his ex-wife. She seemed to feel enough sympathy for Finley that she'd gone out of her way to make his little girl happy.

"You really love Finley, don't you?"

Her question surprised him so much that he glanced over at her again. The sun sparkled off the snow that clung to her. Her full lips bowed up in a smile of pure pleasure as she watched his child—his pride and joy—pick herself up and head up the hill.

"I adore her. I love being a dad."

Her smile trembled a bit. "I bet you do."

He snorted a laugh. "You've seen the bad side of parenting in the past twenty-four hours. Most of the time Finley makes me laugh, fills in my world." He shrugged. "Actually, she makes my world make sense, gives all the work I do a purpose."

"You're a great dad."

"Yeah, too bad I won't have any more kids."

Her face registered such a weird expression that he felt he needed to explain. "When a spouse leaves the way mine did, no explanation, no trying to work things out, just a plain old 'I don't love you anymore and I certainly don't want to be a mom…'" He shrugged again, forced his gaze away from her, over to the blue, blue sky. "Well, you're left with a little bit more than a bad taste in your mouth for marriage."

"Marriage doesn't have anything to do with having kids."

He laughed. "You're right. Not in this day and age, with adoption and surrogate mothers." He caught her gaze again. "But it's difficult enough to handle Finley—one child—without a mom. I couldn't imagine adding another. So it's just me and Finley for the rest of our lives."

"Even though you love kids, you wouldn't try any of the other options?"

"Nope. But if I had a wife I would. Of course, if I had a wife I could have kids the old-fashioned way." He waggled his eyebrows, but the truth of that settled over him and he stopped being silly. "If I could commit again, I'd love to have more kids. *My* kids. A little boy who'd look like me. Another little girl who might look like her mom."

When he caught her gaze again, her eyes were soft and sad. He could have been confused by her reaction, except he knew his voice had gotten every bit as soft and sad. He'd revealed some personal tidbits that she probably wasn't expecting. Hell, even he hadn't realized he felt all those things about kids until the conversation had turned that way.

Of course, she'd sort of turned it that way.

Now that he thought about it, she owed him some equally personal tidbits. "So what about you? No husband? No kids? Married to your store?"

She brushed her hand along the top of the snow. "This time last year I was married."

"Oh?" Something oddly territorial rattled through him, surprising him. Sure, he was attracted to her...but jealous? Of a guy from her past? That was just stupid.

She batted a hand. "I got dumped pretty much the same way you did." Avoiding his gaze, she ran her mittened hand along the surface of the snow again. "One day he loved me. The next day he didn't."

"I'm sorry."

"It's certainly not your fault." She caught his gaze, laughed lightly. "And I'm over him."

"Oh, yeah?"

She shrugged. "Only a fool pines for someone who doesn't want her."

"I'll drink to that."

She craned her neck so she could see Finley again, then she faced him. "She's going to sleep like a rock tonight."

Rory said, "Yeah," but his mind was a million miles away. The easy way she'd dismissed her marriage had caused his jealousy to morph into relief that she wasn't just free, she was happy to be free. That somehow mixed and mingled with his suddenly active hormones and he wanted to kiss her so badly he could taste it.

But that was wrong. Not only had he been hurt enough to never want to risk a relationship again, but she'd also been hurt. After less than twenty-four hours in her company he knew she was a sweet, sincere woman, who might take any romantic gesture as much more than he would intend it.

Still, that didn't stop him from wanting to kiss her. With the snow in her hair, on her jacket, covering her jeans. If he slid his hands under her knit hat, to the thicket of springy black curls, and pulled her face to his, he could kiss her softly, easily just because they were having fun.

But would she realize it was a kiss of pure happiness over the fun afternoon? Or would she make more of it?

He pulled back. They were having too much fun—Finley was having too much fun—for him to spoil it over a craving for something he shouldn't take.

He rose, put his hand down to help Shannon stand. "She'll be back any second."

"Do you think she'll want to go down again?"

"Undoubtedly."

"Hope you're rested."

He grinned. "Hope *you're* rested because I'm taking the saucer and you get the runner sled."

With that he grabbed the saucer and joined Finley at the top of the slope. Shannon pretended great interest in the sled he'd left for her, but she didn't even really see it. Her heart pounded in her chest and her insides had all but turned to mush. For a few seconds there, when their conversation had paused, she could have sworn he was going to slide his hand behind her neck and pull her forward so he could kiss her.

Kiss her!

What a crazy thing to think! Ridiculous wishful thinking on her part, that's what it was. They might be having fun with his daughter, but that was no reason for a man to kiss a woman. She was simply too much of a romantic.

But figuring all this out now was actually a good thing. Rory had come right out and said that if he married again, he would want kids.

His own kids. A son of his own. Another adorable daughter.

And didn't that sound painfully familiar? The last man she would have expected to leave her over not being able to have kids was her seemingly wonderful ex-husband. He'd loved her. She'd never had any doubt. Yet, once she couldn't give him a son—a real son, his flesh-and-blood son—he'd bolted. She wasn't sure she could handle that kind of rejection again. So she was glad they'd had this little talk early on. There'd be no more wishful thinking. No more hoping he'd kiss her.

But right here and right now, she was a lonely woman, and she had both Rory and his daughter in her yard, enjoying her company. She'd be crazy to be upset. Crazier still to withdraw just because there couldn't be anything romantic between her and Rory. The smart thing to do would be to simply relax and enjoy their company.

She picked up the sled. Studied it. Could she ride this down the slope and get it stopped on the ledge? Or would she go racing down the hill?

She smiled. Either way she'd probably make Finley laugh. So why not?

* * *

When they returned to the house, Shannon realized she hadn't taken anything out of the freezer for dinner. Her only choice was to thaw some hamburgers in the microwave and make use of the frozen French fries her mom always bought in bulk then had to give away because she and her dad couldn't eat them all.

As soon as they stepped into the kitchen, she walked to the refrigerator, removed the meat from the freezer section and tossed it on the counter. Unzipping her dad's big parka, she said, "That was fun."

Rory helped Finley out of sweater number one. "Really fun."

Finley grinned. "Lots of fun." She sat on the floor as her father tugged off her little pink boots, then helped her slide out of the first of her two pair of jeans. "But I'm hungry."

"Me, too! I thought I'd make burgers and fries."

Finley bounced up. "All right."

Rory ruffled her hair. "Go wash your hands while Shannon and I get started on the food."

She nodded and all but skipped out of the room.

Shannon unwrapped the hamburger, set it in a bowl and put it in the microwave on low.

As it hummed behind her, Rory said, "What can I do?"

"I guess we could plug in the fryer to heat the oil for the fries."

She rummaged through a cupboard beside the sink and found the fryer. After pouring in fresh oil, she plugged it in.

Rory laughed. "That still leaves me with nothing to do."

"You could go check on Finley."

"I probably should. She had such a busy afternoon that I may find her asleep on the bed."

While he was gone, Shannon hung her parka in the hall closet and took the breakfast dishes out of the dishwasher.

When he and Finley returned to the kitchen a few minutes later, Finley was carrying a little laptop. Rory joined Shannon at the counter where she was forming the hamburgers. "She can play a game or two while we cook." He pointed at the hamburgers. "How many of these should we make?"

"How many do you want?"

"I'll eat two. Finley will eat one."

"And I'll eat one." She glanced down at the plate. "We already have four. So it looks like we're done."

He nudged her aside. "I'll take it from here.

Usually I grill hamburgers, but I can use a frying pan, too."

Shannon retrieved plates and utensils and stacked them on the table. She grabbed a handful of paper napkins and set them beside the plates.

Finley glanced up. "Can I help?"

Surprised, but not about to turn down help, Shannon said, "You can arrange the plates and silver while I start the French fries."

Finley nodded. Shannon walked back to the refrigerator, removed the frozen fries and put them into the fryer.

Dinner conversation was very different from the quiet lunch. Finley chattered about how much fun she'd had sledding and how silly her dad looked on a sled. Rory reminded her that she didn't think him silly the times he rode down the big hill with her and she giggled.

Shannon basked in the ordinariness of it. A happy little girl and her father who clearly adored her. They bantered back and forth as Rory cut her burger in half and poured ketchup for her fries.

Shannon took a bite of her own hamburger. Rory was a nice guy, with a big heart, trying to raise a daughter abandoned by her mother. She supposed that was why he'd pulled away rather

than kiss her that afternoon. He was too busy
to be looking for a romance. But as quickly as
she thought that she reminded herself of her decision not to even ponder a romance with him
anyway. She'd seen the expression on his face
when he talked about having more kids. A son.
No matter what he said or how busy he was,
someday he'd want to remarry. He'd want that
family. Those kids.

And she couldn't have any.

The aching pain filled her as it always did
when confronted by her barrenness. The loss.
The unfairness.

For the first time in months she wanted to
flirt. Wanted to be pretty to somebody—and
she had to pull back.

For both of their sakes.

CHAPTER FOUR

"WELL, SHE'S ASLEEP." Rory plopped down on the sofa beside Shannon, who was pulling strands of tinsel through her fingers to untangle them. Supper had gone well. But after the dishes had been cleared, Finley had begun to nod off, so Rory had taken her for a bath. "She went out like a light the second her head hit the pillow." Rolling his head across the sofa back, he smiled at her. "You're great with her."

Shannon laughed. "Not really. In case you didn't notice my strategy, I simply kept her busy until she dropped from exhaustion."

He laughed.

"I'm serious. She's obviously a smart little girl. She bores easily. The trick to preventing tantrums might be simply keeping her busy."

"I can't always do that. I have a company to run. So it's her nanny, Mrs. Perkins, who gets the brunt of her moods. Though she spends a lot of time entertaining Finley, there are days when Finley only wants me. If she breaks down and calls me and I come home, we feel like we're rewarding Finley for bad behavior."

"You are." She turned her attention to her tangled tinsel again. She didn't like to pry, but he needed help and now that she'd spent a little time with Finley, she realized she'd learned a great deal watching her friends and their children in South Carolina. "There are lots of things you can do to discipline her. The first is to get her accustomed to hearing the word *no*. But you have to be smart about it. If she's tired or hungry, she won't take well to it. If you don't watch her mood, and discipline her when she's not open, it'll make things worse."

He tweaked her hair. "How'd you get so smart?"

She shrugged. "I pay attention?"

He laughed. "Right." He paused, obviously waiting for her to say more, and when she didn't he said, "I'm serious. I've asked you this before, but you always blew me off. And I'm curious. Did you read a book or something? Because if you did, I'd like to get that book."

"No book." She ran some more tinsel through her fingers, once again debating how much to tell him. After a few seconds, she said, "When

I lived in South Carolina with my ex, all of our friends had children. We'd be invited to picnics and outings and I'd see how they handled their kids. My husband really wanted children and I wanted to be a good mom. So I'd watch." She laughed slightly at how stupid she probably sounded. "Technically, I spent my entire marriage watching other people raise kids."

The room grew silent. Every pop and snap of the logs in the fireplace echoed in the quiet room.

Rory finally broke the silence. "So what happened?"

She peeked at him. "Happened?"

"To your marriage."

Once again, she thought before answering. There was no way she'd tell him the truth. It was humiliating to be deserted by the man you loved on the day you needed him the most. Humiliating that a man who'd truly loved her couldn't stay. Humiliating that she'd been abandoned for a physical defect.

Plus, Rory was in Green Hill to buy her store. They might be spending some personal time together because of the storm, but at the end of the weekend they would be business associates.

Still, they were stranded together and he'd

told her some personal things. So she couldn't totally ignore the question.

She ran the last of the first strand of tinsel through her fingers and began spooling it around her hand so it would be ready to hang the next day when Rory and Finley left.

"I suspect my ex was a little like your ex."

He laughed. "Really?"

"He had very definite ideas of how he wanted his life." She continued spooling so she didn't have to look at him. "He wanted things to be a certain way. When we hit a point where I couldn't make those things happen, he dumped me."

He sat forward, dropped his clasped hands between his knees, then straightened again and caught her gaze. "I'm sorry your ex was a jerk."

"I'm sorry your marriage didn't work out."

Once again silence reigned and unspoken thoughts rippled through her brain. He was a nice guy and, at her core, Finley was a sweet little girl. She'd give anything to have had a good husband and a beautiful child. Anything.

Rory leaned toward her and her heart expanded in her chest. They were only a foot apart. A shift forward by him, a shift forward by her and their lips could touch.

But uncertainty leaped in the dark depths of

his deep brown eyes. Though he didn't say a word, she knew the litany undoubtedly rattling through his head right now. They were both wounded. He had a child. And as soon as they got out of his storm, they'd be doing business. They shouldn't get involved.

He pulled back, away from her, confirming her suspicions, and disappointment shuddered through her.

He rose. "I guess I'd better head off to bed myself. I'll see you in the morning."

She smiled. "Sure. See you in the morning."

But something splintered inside her heart. Since Bryce, she'd lived with a feeling of inadequacy. Not being good enough. Never feeling womanly enough. Though Rory had good reasons not to kiss her, those feelings of inadequacy reverberated through her. Whispering like demons, reminding her that for lots of men she wasn't whole, wasn't good enough... couldn't ever be good enough.

The next morning the world was still a winter wonderland. Rory ambled into the kitchen to find Shannon sitting at the table, drinking a cup of coffee.

She smiled at him over the rim. "No Finley?"

"She's still sleeping."

"Good, then I can tell you I watched the local news this morning."

He winced. "Bad?"

She laughed. "Depends on your point of view. Raleigh's employees get another unexpected vacation day. We got another six inches of snow last night and the roads haven't been cleared from the first storm."

Rory didn't care. Finley was well-behaved, happy, for the first time in the two years they'd struggled without her mom. Another day of not looking at the store didn't bother him. Unfortunately, he wasn't the only person in this equation.

"I'm sorry that you're losing revenue."

"Funny thing about running the only department store in a twenty-mile radius. You might think we'd lose a lot of business by being closed for the entire weekend before Christmas, but the truth is we'll just be busier Monday through Friday." She smiled. "We'll be fine."

Rory got a cup of coffee and headed to the table. Sitting across from her, he noticed she wasn't wearing a lick of makeup. Her hair had been combed but not styled and the riot of curls made her look young, carefree. Kissable.

His heart cartwheeled in his chest as longing sprinted through him. But he'd already been through this in his head the night before, so he ignored the yearning in favor of the more important issue. In spite of the fact that he'd almost kissed her the night before, she wasn't upset, angry or even standoffish. She still liked having him and Finley at her home.

He picked up his coffee, drank a long swallow, then said, "How about if I make omelets this morning?"

"Oh, I love omelets!" Her face brightened in a way that shot an arrow of arousal through him. He didn't know what it was about this woman that attracted him so, but he did know that these feelings were inappropriate. She'd done so much for them in the past two days that he owed her. He shouldn't be ogling her or fantasizing about kissing her.

"I have some ham, some cheese. I'll bet there's even a green pepper or two in the refrigerator."

"Western omelets it is, then."

Yawning, Finley pushed open the swinging door. "Morning."

Rory scooped her off the floor. "Morning to you, too." He kissed her cheek. "I'm making omelets."

Her eyes widened with delight. "Good!" She scooted down. "I'll set the table."

Shannon caught his gaze, her eyebrows rising in question. He shrugged. But he knew why Finley was so helpful, so accommodating. He'd like to take credit, but he couldn't. Shannon was the one who'd so easily guided her into helping with meals and setting the table, keeping her busy so she wouldn't get bored and misbehave.

And the way he thanked her was with inappropriate thoughts of kissing her?

Not good, Rory. Seriously, not good.

Shannon chopped the green peppers and ham, while he gathered eggs, beat them in a bowl. They worked together companionably, happily, as Finley set out plates and silver. But when breakfast was over, Finley slid off her seat. "Are we going now?"

Rory looked at Shannon. Then realized what he'd done. He hadn't just turned to her for help with Finley. He trusted her. He wanted her advice.

That was not good. Not because she couldn't help, but because his reaction had been automatic. Instinctive.

"Are we ever going to get out of here?"

Shannon rose from the table, taking Finley's plate with her. "Aren't you having fun?"

Her lip thrust out. "Yeah. Sort of."

"The roads are still pretty bad," Rory said. He

walked over to her and lifted her into his arms. "Unless the snowplow comes through sometime today, we're still stuck here."

Her lower lip jutted out even farther. "Okay."

Shannon understood her cabin fever, but multiplied by about fifty. Not only was she stuck in her house, but she was also stuck with a man she was really coming to like who wouldn't want her if he knew the truth about her. Even if he was interested and asked her out, she'd never accept a date. Lying awake the night before, she'd realized that if they dated, at some point she'd have to tell him she couldn't have kids. The last man she'd told hadn't taken it so well. Just like Bryce, Rory wanted kids. Was it worth a few weeks or months of *her* happiness to put *him* in a position of having to dump her when she told him?

It wasn't. Which was why the subject of a date or romance or even liking each other would never come up, if she could help it. And why needing to keep Finley busy was such a lucky, lucky thing.

She walked over to the six-year-old. "I have an idea. I have a neighbor who lives over there." She pointed over Finley's shoulder, out the window. "She's a little bit older and her husband died last year. So when we get stranded like this, she's all by herself. Imagine being all by yourself for three days, no company, nobody to talk to."

Finley gasped and pressed her hands over her mouth. "I'll bet she's scared."

"Maybe not scared. But lonely. So, since the weather's not so bad that we can't go out, I was thinking we could bake a cake and take it to her." She glanced at Rory, silently asking for his approval as she detailed her plan. "We'd have to walk, but we could think of it as fun, like we did yesterday when we were sledding."

Rory frowned. "How far away does she live?"

"Not far," she assured him. "Just far enough that we'd get a good walk in the fresh air." She faced Finley. "So, do you want to try to bake a cake?"

"What kind?"

"I have a box mix for a chocolate cake and one for a yellow. We could make peanut-butter icing for the chocolate. Or chocolate icing for the yellow."

Finley slid out of her father's arms and to the floor. "I like peanut butter."

"So do I." She nudged Finley to the door. "Go back to the bedroom and change out of your pj's and we'll get to work."

Finley nodded and raced out of the room. Rory followed her. "I'll help her."

By the time they returned, Shannon had the box cake mix on the center island, along with a mixing bowl, mixer, eggs, butter and water.

"Give me two minutes to put on jeans and a sweatshirt and we'll get this into the oven."

She scooted out of the kitchen and into her bedroom. The bed was neatly made. The bathroom was also neat as a pin. But the Wallace family scent lingered around her. Finley's little-girl smells mixed with Rory's aftershave and created a scent that smelled like home. Family. She didn't even try to resist inhaling deeply. She might not ever become a permanent part of their lives, but she liked these two. This weekend was her chance to be with them. She might not kiss him, but she wouldn't deprive herself of the chance to enjoy them.

Once in jeans and a University of Pittsburgh sweatshirt, she ambled out to the kitchen. Finley climbed onto a stool beside the center island. "What can I do?"

"I don't know? What can you do?" She laughed.

But not getting the joke, Finley frowned.

Rather than explain, Shannon said, "Can you break eggs into a bowl?"

She glanced back at Rory. He shrugged. "There's a first time for everything."

Shannon set the bowl in front of Finley. Pulling an egg from the carton, she said, "You take an egg, like this—" Demonstrating by putting the egg against the bowl's edge, she continued, "And crack it against the edge of the bowl like this." The egg broke in half, its contents spilling into the bowl.

"My turn." Finley grabbed an egg and hit it on the rim. Miraculously, the white and yoke tumbled into the bowl. She tossed the shell beside Shannon's and clapped her hands together with glee. "I did it!"

"Yes, you did." Shannon handed her the open box of cake mix. "Take out the plastic container. We'll open it and dump that into the bowl, too."

With Shannon giving Finley the opportunity to be involved in every step of the process of cake baking, it took a long time to get the cake into the oven. They played two games of Go Fish while it baked. After lunch, they made simple peanut-butter icing, spread it across the two layers and slid the cake into a carrier.

Once again, they dressed Finley in two pair of jeans and two sweaters. When they stepped outside, the snow glowed like a million tiny diamonds. Rory carried Finley across the field that separated the two houses. They stomped the snow off their boots as they walked across Mary O'Grady's back porch to the kitchen door.

Mary answered on the first knock. Short and round, with shaped gray hair, Mary wore a festive Christmas sweater and jeans. "Shannon!" She glanced at Finley and Rory. "And who is this?"

"Mary O'Grady, this is Rory Wallace and his daughter, Finley."

As Shannon made the introduction, Rory hoped Finley wouldn't say something awful about the sweet-looking woman's sweater.

"Rory was on his way to Green Hill to take a look at the store when they were stranded on the highway and had the state police bring them to my house." She offered the cake. "Since we're all getting a little bored, we brought a cake to share."

"Well, aren't you sweet," Mary said, opening her door to invite them in. She pinched Finley's cheek. "And aren't you adorable!" She smiled at Rory. "It's nice to meet you."

"It's nice to meet you, too," he said, sliding Finley through the door. The kitchen hadn't been remodeled the way Shannon's had. Old-fashioned oak cupboards dominated the room.

A rectangular table, with four ladder-back chairs, sat in the center.

Mary fussed over Finley. "Let me help you with your jacket."

Finley glanced at her dad. Rory nodded his head slightly, indicating she should just go with it.

Unzipping Finley's coat, Mary faced Shannon. "Sweetie, why don't you put on a pot of coffee so we can enjoy that cake properly?"

Shannon laughed. "You're a woman after my own heart, Mary."

After removing her coat, she walked to the counter with the ease of someone who'd been there before. Rory watched her root through the cupboards to find the filters and coffee. She got water and measured grounds.

Mary helped Finley onto a chair. "And what can I get you to drink, sweetie?"

Rory held his breath. She hadn't mentioned the sweater, but she'd gotten a little nervous over having a stranger help her with her jacket. They weren't out of the woods yet.

Finley smiled. "Milk."

Rory breathed again, as Shannon retrieved some plates and coffee mugs from the cupboard and joined them at the table. "That'll only take a minute."

Rory faced Mary. "You have a lovely home."

She batted a hand in dismissal. "I had such plans for this, then my Joe died. And I just sort of lost interest."

"But we're hoping to have a contractor out here next summer, aren't we, Mary?"

Mary's face saddened a little more. "I thought you were leaving if you sold the store."

"Probably." She glanced at Rory, then back at Mary. "But we already looked at the books with the cupboard samples. All you need to do is finalize your choices and you can easily have the entire kitchen remodeled before fall. If you want, you can call me every night with an update or tell me your problems and I'll help you figure out how to solve them."

Mary sat beside Shannon and patted her hand. "You're very good to me."

Rory suppressed a smile. It seemed he and Finley weren't the only strays that Shannon cared for. A few times it had popped into his head that her kindness to him and Finley might be an act of sorts to keep herself in his good graces when he looked at her store on Monday. He'd dismissed that thought, but now he could totally put it out of his mind. Shannon Raleigh was a genuinely nice woman.

His heart twisted a bit. She *was* a nice woman.

And Finley liked her. If he were in the market for a romance, she'd be at the top of the candidates list.

But he wasn't looking for a romance.

The coffeemaker groaned its final release and Mary jumped from the table. "Cut the cake, sweetie, and I'll get the coffee."

In a few minutes, everyone had a slice of cake and a cup of coffee or glass of milk. They talked some more about Mary's plans to remodel her house, then Mary asked Finley about school and Finley launched into an unusually happy, unusually lengthy discussion of her classes, her classmates and recess.

Mary seemed to soak it all up, but Shannon really listened, really participated in the conversation with Finley.

When the cake was gone and the conversation exhausted, Shannon rose from the table and gathered their plates, which she slid into the dishwasher. "We really have to get going. Not only do we have to make something for dinner, but it will also be dark soon."

Mary rose, too. "That's the bad thing about winter. It gets dark too early. And with all these clouds, you can't count on the light of the moon to get you home."

Finley laughed. "That's funny."

Mary tickled her tummy. "I'm a funny lady." She pulled Finley's jacket from the back of her chair and helped her slide into it. "You can come back anytime you like."

Finley nodded.

"Just always remember to bring cake."

At that, Finley giggled.

After sliding into her parka, Shannon picked up her cake carrier and headed for the door. "I'll call you tomorrow."

"Oh, you don't have to. I'm fine."

"I know, but Mom and Dad are arriving one day this week for the holiday. So you'll be invited to Christmas Eve dinner. I'll need to give you the time."

"Sounds great."

Shannon gave her a hug, opened the door and stepped out onto the cold porch.

Carrying Finley, Rory followed her. "She's great."

Leading them down the stairs, Shannon said, "She is. But she was even funnier when her husband was alive." She peeked back at Rory. "He had a heart attack two years ago. She's really only now getting back into the swing of things."

"That's hard."

"Yeah." She caught his gaze again. "But lots of life is hard."

He knew she was referring to her divorce, which she'd barely explained. Still he could tell that life—marriage—hadn't treated her any more fairly than it had treated him. It was no wonder they got along so well. Both had been burned. Both knew nothing was certain.

They finished the walk chitchatting about nothing, making conversation to alleviate the boredom. But when they got into the house and Shannon pulled off her knit cap, throwing snow around her kitchen when she freed her hair, a knot formed in Rory's stomach.

He liked her. He wanted to kiss her so much that he'd almost acted on the impulse twice.

He didn't want to get married again. He wasn't even sure he wanted to get in a serious relationship again.

But he *liked* her.

And he wanted to kiss her.

And if he didn't soon get out of this house he was going to act on that impulse.

CHAPTER FIVE

THE SNOW ITSELF might have stopped by Sunday morning, but on Monday morning the air was still cold, the wind wicked.

They set out to get Rory's car from the interstate at seven o'clock, but discovered it had been towed—with all the other stranded cars—to a used car dealership in the next town over, so the roads could be plowed.

By the time they returned to Green Hill, the store was already open for business. When they entered the crowded first-floor sales department, color, scent and sound bombarded them. Throngs of noisy people crowded the sales tables. Red, green and blue Christmas ornaments hung from the ceiling, along with strings of multicolored lights and tinsel. The scent of chocolate from the candy department wafted through the air. "Jingle Bells" spilled from the overhead speakers.

Shannon cast a quick glance at Finley, who was being carried by her dad. Her eyes had grown huge. Her mouth was a little *O*, as if she were totally surprised or totally horrified. When she threw arms around Rory and buried her face against his neck, Shannon guessed she was horrified.

Rory held her tightly. "Finley, honey, we've been over this already. I told you the store would be decorated for the holiday. I told you there would be Christmas songs."

Finley only snuggled in closer.

After the lovely weekend that had caused her to begin to bond with a man and child she couldn't have, Shannon had promised herself she would keep her distance. No more private conversations with Rory. No more helping to discipline Finley.

But a frightened child had to be an exception to her rule. She grabbed Rory's hand and led him in the direction of the elevators.

"Come on," she said, ignoring the *thump, thump, thump* of her heart from the feeling of Rory's hand tucked inside of hers. "Before you know it we'll be in my office where, I swear, there isn't as much as a poinsettia."

Pushing through the crowd, Shannon got them to the elevator and immediately dropped

Rory's hand. She pressed the button for the third floor. The door closed, blocking out most of the sights and scents of Christmas, but "Jingle Bells" still piped into the little box.

Finley huddled against Rory. She wasn't upset or panicky. Just huddled. Once they got into the undecorated administrative offices she would be fine.

Shannon faced Rory. "Even though we lost the weekend, we can get down to work right away. There are four administrative departments. Buyers, human resources, accounting and advertising. If you take one day with each department, that will give you a full day on Friday to walk the store and some time for questions and explanations."

"Sounds good."

The elevator reached the second floor. "Jingle Bells" became "Rudolph the Red Nosed Reindeer." Finley looked to be getting antsy, so Shannon kept talking. "I only have four departments because I combined a lot of things for efficiency."

"That makes sense—if you've combined the right departments."

"MIS with accounting. Public relations with advertising."

He shrugged. "Should work."

The elevator pinged. Shannon sucked in a breath. Though they were entering the housewares department, it was as decorated with shiny red, green and blue ornaments as every other floor in the store. And the Christmas music? Well, that was piped everywhere, except into the administrative offices. So "Rudolph" still echoed around them.

She hurriedly ushered Rory around the tables of sheets and towels, past the shelves of small appliances, past the rows of dishes, glasses and stemware.

When they finally reached the swinging door into the administrative offices, she pushed it open with a sigh of relief. The second it swung closed behind them, "Rudolph" became a soft hum. As they hurried down the hall, even the hum echoed away.

At the end of the long, thin corridor, she opened the door that led to her office suite. Wendy was already seated at her desk.

"Good morning, Ms. Raleigh."

Shannon shrugged out of her coat. "No need to be formal for Mr. Wallace's sake. We spent the weekend together."

Wendy's eyes widened. "The whole weekend?"

Rory slid Finley to the floor and helped her

out of her little pink jacket. "Couldn't get to my car until today."

"It was a mess," Wendy agreed, scrambling to take Finley's coat and Rory's topcoat and hang them on the coat tree. "So what are you planning for today?"

"Since we're late, I'm only introducing Rory to the staff this morning. Then he can pick a department to spend time with this afternoon."

Wendy said, "Sounds good to me," but her gaze fell on Finley.

Rory put his hands on his daughter's shoulders. "She'll just come with us."

Since she'd promised herself she would distance herself from Rory and Finley, Shannon didn't argue that Finley would be bored. Instead, she set her briefcase on her desk then led the Wallaces into the hall again.

"Accounting is in the suite closest to the door. Buyers are in the next suite. Advertising and PR are in the third suite and the human resources department is on the fifth floor. They need extra space for testing and continuing education so they have half the floor. The cafeteria has the other." She met Rory's gaze. "So where to first?"

With a quick glance down at Finley, he said,

"Let's just stay behind the door for as long as we can."

Understanding that he didn't want to take Finley out into the decorations and music until he had to, Shannon said, "How about buyers then?"

"Sounds great."

She led Rory and Finley to the first door and opened it onto a narrow office with a row of desks that led to an executive office in the back. Papers were everywhere. Invoices, catalogues, samples.

Shannon faced him. "I'm sure you're not surprised that we're finalizing our spring merchandise."

He laughed. "Not in the least."

She stopped at the first desk. "Lisa, Robbie, Jennifer, Bill..." All four employees glanced up at her. "This is Rory Wallace. He's our first prospective buyer."

Everyone perked up. Superenthusiastic hellos greeted Rory. He stifled a laugh. Everybody was clearly trying to give a good first impression.

He met Missy McConnell, the head buyer, then Shannon herded him and Finley out of that office and into accounting. Five desks had been crammed into the narrow space and everyone sat staring at a computer screen.

Having already established a drill, Shannon simply introduced people as she walked by their desks. Though this group looked a little more wary than the enthusiastic buyers, Rory nodded and smiled.

In department three, advertising and PR, copy layout littered a big table in the center of a much wider main room. Employees sat at drafting table desks. The department head, John Wilder, was just a tad too happy for Rory's tastes. Finley wasn't thrilled with him, either.

"So are you going to sit on Santa's lap?"

Finley's little mouth tuned down into her perfect *U* frown. "No."

"Ah. Too old for that now, huh?"

"No, I don't believe he exists."

John laughed, but Finley tugged on Rory's hand. "I don't like it here."

Rory covered for her with a little laugh. "We've been meeting people since we arrived. She's probably ready for a break."

Shannon moved them toward the door. "That's a great idea." In the hall, she stooped in front of Finley. "How about if we go up to the cafeteria and have a soda?"

Her little mouth pulled down even farther. "I want to go home."

Shannon shot a glance up at Rory, and he

crouched beside Finley. Putting his hands on her shoulders, he said, "I told you this would be boring and you said you didn't care as long as we went to the beach afterward."

Her bottom lip puffed out. "I know."

"So you've got to keep up your end of the bargain."

Her lip quivered. "I don't have anything to do while you talk."

"Things will slow down this afternoon and we'll stay in one department. We'll find you a chair and you can sit and play on your computer."

"It's noisy when you talk."

"It is," Shannon agreed suddenly. "And lots of those offices don't have room for an extra chair."

Rory glanced up at her, mortified that she was agreeing with Finley, ruining his defense.

"So why don't we set you up in my office? Wendy will be right outside the door, if you need anything. And I have a TV in case your computer games get boring."

"If you have Wi-Fi, I can watch TV on my computer."

Shannon laughed. "My screen's bigger."

Finley laughed, too.

Rory peeked over at Shannon again. Her

abilities with Finley were amazing. She'd said she'd babysat some of her friends' kids, but she seemed so much smarter than a part-time, fill-in caregiver.

Unless he was just lacking?

Ah, hell. Who was he kidding? Ever since Finley entered this new diva phase, he'd been behind the eight ball, playing catch up rather than proactively parenting. Shannon, an objective person, knew exactly what to do because she saw things more clearly than he did.

They walked Finley back to the office at the end of the hall. Wendy looked up as they entered. "That was fast."

Shannon said, "We took a quick introduction tour and Finley got bored. So, we've decided to let her watch TV in my office while we go up to human resources."

Wendy rose. "That's a great idea. I also think we have some cola in your refrigerator...maybe even some candy."

"No candy before lunch," Rory said.

Shannon smiled. "I should think not. We've got a great cafeteria upstairs." She caught Finley's gaze. "They make the best French fries. Give us an hour to talk with the people in human resources and I'll race you upstairs. Winner gets a milk shake."

Finley gasped with excitement. Wendy laughed and took her hand. "You two go on. Finley and I will channel surf until we find some cartoons."

When they were in the hall, Rory ran his hand along the back of his neck. "Thanks."

Shannon began walking up the hall. "For what?"

He hurried to catch up with her. "For being so good with Finley."

"Finley is a very easy child to love."

That made him laugh, but Shannon didn't join him. "You're serious."

For that she stopped. "Yes. Why are you surprised?"

He pointed at his chest. "I love her because she's mine. But this diva phase has even me backing off sometimes."

"That's because you take everything too personally."

"She is my daughter."

"Right."

"You know, we've got five whole days of entertaining her."

"I know."

"And Finley's not going to settle into your office for an entire week and just play baby angel."

That time she did laugh.

"So what do you say we form an alliance?"

She peeked at him. "An alliance?"

"A partnership. My side of the bargain is that I need help. Your side is to provide that help. It's win-win."

She laughed again.

And something soft and warm floated through Rory. He hadn't exactly forgotten what it felt like to be in the company of a woman, but he had forgotten some things. Like how everything around them always smelled pretty. Or how their laughs were usually musical.

"I love it when you laugh."

Shannon took a step back, and though she'd pulled away before, avoided him before, this morning it gave him an odd feeling in the pit of his stomach. She had a real problem with him complimenting her.

After nearly three days together he should be at least allowed to compliment something neutral like her laugh.

"Why does that make you mad?"

She started walking again. "It doesn't make me mad."

"It makes you something because you stopped laughing. Pulled away." He paused, watching her race away from him. "Now you're all but running away."

"We have work to do."

"And we also spent the weekend together. We can't spend the week behaving like strangers."

"Not strangers, just people working out a business deal."

Catching up to her, he said, "Ah, so this is your business face."

She motioned a circle in front of the bright red jacket of her suit. "This is the whole business demeanor." Then she sighed. "Look, I'm seriously trying to sell you my store. It would help if you'd forget that I love to sled-ride. And that I can't cook. And I haven't even started decorating for Christmas yet."

He studied her pretty blue eyes, which were shiny with what he could only guess was fear that something personal might cause him to walk away from their negotiations. His voice was soft, careful, when he said, "Why would that help? People who like each other usually make better deals."

She looked away. "Friendships can also backfire."

Ah. "Did you have a friendship backfire?"

"No, I'm just saying—"

"And I'm just saying relax. We like each other—" For once he didn't try to deny it. All weekend long he'd been coming to know her, getting to like her. Being trapped in her little house with a strong desire to kiss her hadn't been good. But in a store filled with people and with a business deal to discuss she had nothing to fear.

Or was that he had nothing to fear?

No matter. They were both safe.

"We got to be friends over the weekend. I've even asked for help with Finley. Surely, I should be allowed to say you have a pretty laugh."

She stiffened. Then, as if realizing she was making too much out of nothing, she drew in a breath. "Yes. Of course, I'm sorry."

"No need to be sorry. Just relax."

She smiled. "Okay."

"Okay."

They spent an hour in human resources and returned to her office to pick up Finley for lunch. In the huge, bustling cafeteria they drank milk shakes and ate French fries. But Finley tossed her head back and covered her ears when "Here Comes Santa Claus" replaced the more sedate Christmas song that had been playing.

"You know what puzzles me?" Shannon said, tugging one of Finley's hands away from her ears. "How can you watch cartoons?"

Finley's eyes narrowed.

Shannon picked up a French fry. "I mean,

they're not any more real than Santa. Yet you like cartoons. Wendy told me you did."

Finley's mouth scrunched up.

Shannon dipped her fry in ketchup. "So why don't you start thinking of Santa the same way you do a cartoon character?"

Finley glanced at Rory and he laughed. "It sounds perfectly logical to me."

Finley raised her gaze to the ceiling as if she could see the music.

"Listen to the words and pretend Santa is a cartoon character."

Finley's face contorted with little-girl concentration, then she smiled. "It's funny."

"Of course, it is. That's why people like to listen. It makes them laugh."

As if to prove that, Finley giggled.

Rory laughed, too. But when he realized he was laughing and Finley was laughing because Shannon had turned Finley's hatred of Christmas songs into acceptance, his laughter stopped.

This woman was really special.

Really special.

She wasn't just pretty or sexy or even really smart. She was attuned to life. People. It was as if she saw things other people missed and knew how to use that information to make everybody feel wanted, needed...happy.

He said nothing as they returned to her office and deposited Finley with Wendy. But when they entered the office for the buyers that afternoon, he noticed something that he probably could have noticed that morning if he'd been clued in to look for it. These people loved her.

"So what are you going to do, Shannon, if the store sells?"

That question came from Julie Hughes, a woman in her twenties who gazed at Shannon with stars in her eyes, as if she were the epitome of everything Julie wanted to be when she got a little older.

"I'm not sure." Shannon smiled, casually leaned her hip on the corner of Julie's desk, clearly comfortable with her staff. "This is only Mr. Wallace's first day here. He may look around and decide he doesn't want to buy us."

"He'd be crazy," Fred Cummings said, leaning back in his chair. "We make a ton of money." He pointed at Shannon. "Due in no small part to changes this woman made after her dad let go of the reins."

Shannon laughed. "I did a few things. They've only been up and running a few months."

Fred said, "Right."

But Rory got the message. Fred wouldn't push anymore because he wouldn't insult the last company president, Shannon's dad, in front of Shannon. But it was clear things hadn't always gone so smoothly at Raleigh's Department Store.

Heading back to the administrative officer, he said, "This is some place."

Though she'd downplayed her efforts in front of her staff, in the hall, away from anyone who could see, her face blossomed with pride. "Thank you."

"But I do have one really big question."

"Fire away. There's no question too sacred."

"Why are you selling Raleigh's? It's clear you love this store. You're also very good at what you do. Why would you want to give it up?"

"My parents need the money from the sale to fund their retirement."

"Right. I get that. But you love it." He paused, then asked the question that had been bothering him for the past few hours. "Why don't you buy it?"

She stopped. Faced him. "I tried. I couldn't get financing."

"Oh. Did you try finding a partner?"

"Are you offering?"

He winced. "My family doesn't partner. We either buy outright or nothing at all."

"I didn't think so."

But Rory wasn't so easily put off. "You said I'm the first person you approached. Surely there are others, investors who might consider a partnership—"

She laughed slightly. "Rory. Are you trying to talk me out of selling to you?"

"No. It's just that it's obvious to me that you're going to miss the store." He paused. When she didn't reply, he said, "There's more to this story. I need to hear it."

For a few seconds it looked like she wouldn't reply. Finally she said, "I've actually only been working at the store a year. My husband had unceremoniously dumped me and I was devastated. So I came home. I expected to sleep away the next few months, but my dad wouldn't let me." She smiled, as if remembering. "Anyway, he got me working in the store, and when he retired a few months ago, he made me company president. Nobody expected that I'd blossom the way I did. I like the work enough that I could have stayed here the rest of my life." She shrugged. "But my parents need the money, so I have to move on. But, on the bright side, at least now I know what I want to do with my life."

"Run another store?"

"Maybe. Or maybe just head up the buyers."

She smiled. "Or the advertising department, public relations…"

He laughed. "You won't be happy unless you can have your finger in every pot."

But even as he laughed, an uncomfortable lump formed in his stomach. "I feel like I'm taking away your dream."

She shook her head. "Running my parents' store is not my dream. It's just a really great job."

"So what is your dream?"

She started walking again, but he'd seen the sadness that shadowed her face.

If he wasn't taking away her dream by buying the store, something was up with her. He considered that maybe she couldn't handle another change in her life only one year after her divorce. But she was a strong, competent woman. He believed her when she said she was over her ex and the accompanying sadness from her divorce.

So what was it?

Why did he know, deep in his gut, that something serious haunted her and somehow, some way, he contributed to it?

He caught her arm and stopped her.

When he didn't say anything, she said, "Question?"

He stared into her pretty blue eyes. All the physical reactions he'd held at bay all weekend came flooding back. Only now they were combined with emotions. He cared about her. He cared about her a lot. He didn't want to take away her dreams. He *liked* her.

The urge to kiss her itched through him again and he was growing tired of fighting it. Tired of fighting the first good thing that had happened to him in two long years.

When his head lowed toward hers, he didn't try to stop himself. For the first time since his divorce, he wasn't just physically attracted to a woman. He liked her.

Their lips met tentatively, just a quick brush. But response shivered through him. Attraction. Arousal. Wonderful forgotten sensations that he'd avoided, ignored or smothered over the past two years.

He deepened the kiss, pressing his mouth against hers and though he felt her hesitate, she pressed back.

She liked him.

Just when he would have deepen the kiss, made it a real kiss, she pulled away.

Smoothing her hand along her cascade of dark curls, she turned and started up the hall again. "We should get back to Finley."

CHAPTER SIX

AT SIX O'CLOCK that night Rory and Finley stepped into a very comfortable hotel room. A double bed sat in the middle of the room, and, as he'd requested when he made his reservation, a cot for Finley sat beside the bed. As he tossed their suitcases into the closet and slid his briefcase onto the desk, the feelings from the kiss he'd shared with Shannon that afternoon still vibrated through him. Unfortunately, all those wonderful sensations were mitigated by the awkwardness afterward. Worse, he couldn't stop thinking about Shannon herself. Her future. What would she do without the store?

He might not be taking away her "dream" but he was taking away her job. And maybe her home. With only one department store in her small city, there was no other store in town for her to manage. She'd definitely have to move away.

They'd been so busy all afternoon that she'd

easily avoided talking abut her life and that kiss. But he had to talk to her again. He couldn't sit here in a hotel all night and wonder. Plus, he'd finally figured out she probably didn't want to talk about her decisions in the hallway of an office where she could be overheard.

Finley shrugged out of her jacket, but he pushed it up her arms again.

"Hey!"

He stooped down in front of her. "I have a favor to ask."

She blinked.

"You know how Shannon took us in this weekend?"

She nodded.

"Well, she did us a favor."

She tilted her head in question. "Uh-huh."

"So now we have to return the favor."

"We do?"

"Yes." He pulled in a breath. It wasn't a fabulous plan, but it was the only plan he could come up with, so he was running with it. "Shannon was supposed to decorate her house for Christmas over the weekend."

Finley's eyes grew round and large. She wasn't a dummy. She knew what was coming.

He sucked it up and just told her straight out. "But because we were in her home, she didn't decorate. She entertained us. So since we owe her for taking us in, I was thinking we should go to her house and help her do the work she would have done had we not needed her help."

He'd couched his request in such a way Finley would see how much they were in Shannon's debt. Still, she frowned. "I don't want to."

"I don't doubt that. But didn't she give you a way to think about Christmas today that made it seem easy for you?"

"Yeah."

"So, she's done us more than one favor and now we're going to repay her. That's the way life works."

Her lower lip jutted out.

He rose anyway. "Suck it up, kid. We owe her. We're doing this. And no hissy fits or diva behavior. You might not like Christmas but Shannon does and I won't spoil this for her. So we're going."

She sighed heavily but didn't argue.

He found a phone book and ordered Chinese food before shepherding Finley back to the car. They stopped for the takeout food, and were on Shannon's front porch within the hour.

She answered their knock quickly, as if she'd been standing right by the door. When she saw them, a smile of pleasure blossomed on her pretty face, making Rory realize he'd made the right choice. "Hey."

He held up the Chinese food. "I brought a peace offering."

She motioned for them to step inside. "Peace offering?"

He handed her the bags of food, and wrestled out of his topcoat. "We wasted your entire weekend. So we decided to help you decorate."

Her gaze flew to Finley. "Really?"

"Yes." He glanced down at his daughter. "Right?"

Finley sighed. "Right."

Shannon led them into the kitchen. "Well, thank you very much. I can use the help." Depositing the food on the center island, she added, "Would you rather eat first and decorate second, or eat as we decorate?"

"How about eat as we decorate?" He slid his gaze to Finley, hoping Shannon would get the message that if Finley was busy eating then she wouldn't actually have to decorate. An easy way to avoid trouble.

She nodded slightly, indicating she'd caught his drift. "I have some paper plates we can use." She walked to the cupboard to get them. "We'll make it like a picnic."

They set everything up on the coffee table between the floral sofa and twin sage-green club chairs. When it came to dealing with Finley, Shannon was fine. But when the room grew quiet and Finley was busy eating rice and sweet-and-sour chicken, shivers of fear sprinkled her skin.

He'd kissed her. Spontaneously. Wonderfully. And everything inside of her had responded. It wasn't a kiss of lust or surprise, as it would have been had he kissed her over the weekend. This kiss had been...emotional.

They liked each other. Two and a half days of forced company coupled with a day of walking through her store, finding out about each other, had taken their physical attraction and turned it into an emotional attachment.

It was wonderful...and scary...and wrong.

She knew the end of this rainbow. If they got involved—dated—at some point she'd have to tell him she couldn't have kids.

And everything between them would change. Even the way he saw her—

Especially the way he saw her.

She pulled in a breath. Told herself to settle down. If he bought the store, she would leave. If he didn't, he would leave. He'd go back to his life and company in Virginia, and she would stay here. Distance alone would keep them from dating. And if they didn't date, she wouldn't have to tell him.

So why not enjoy the evening?

Or use it as a chance to bring Finley along? No child should hate a holiday filled with wonder and magic. Her mom should be ashamed for ruining one of the best times of the year for her daughter. But in the past three days, Finley gone from being horrified about anything even related to the holiday, to actually laughing at the Christmas songs piped into the cafeteria. Maybe it was time to nudge her a little more?

Catching a piece of chicken in her chopsticks, she said, "You know, I like Christmas music when I decorate. You laughed about the Christmas songs today at lunch. So I'm just going to pop in a CD right now."

Finley glanced at Rory. He shrugged. "Just think of them like cartoons. The way Shannon told you this afternoon."

Finley sighed. Shannon found the Christmas music but kept the volume low. A soft mellow song drifted into the room. Finley turned her attention to her dinner. Wanting to get as much done as she could while Finley was cooprerative, Shannon grabbed the spools of tinsel she'd created the night before.

"I'm going to hang these from the ceiling."

Rory glanced over at her. "Is that code for I need a tall person to help me?"

She laughed. "Yes."

He took the tinsel from her hand. She pointed at a corner. "What my dad used to do at our old house was string the tinsel from one corner to the center, and from the center to the opposite corner, making two loops. Then we'd do that again from the other corners."

He frowned. "Why don't you just direct me?"

"Okay. Walk to the corner, attach the tinsel with a tack, then loop it to the center of the ceiling."

He did as she said. When they met in the center, she tacked the tinsel in place. "Now walk to the opposite corner and tack the tinsel up there."

When the line of tinsel was in place, he smiled. "Not bad. Sort of festive."

"Glad you like it." She handed him another strand of tinsel. "Because now we've got to do the other two corners."

He happily took the strand of tinsel and repeated the looping process.

When he was done, she offered him the ball of mistletoe her dad always put in the center. "Just hang this where the strands meet."

He looked at the mistletoe, looked at her.

Then it hit her. The mistletoe was pretty, but it

was plastic. They'd hung the silly thing in their living room for years and, basically, no one paid any attention to the fact that it was mistletoe or the traditions that surrounded it.

Obviously, Rory wasn't so casual about it.

Embarrassment should have shot through her. Instead, when their gazes met, the warmth of connection flooded her. She really liked this guy.

But she'd already figured out that they weren't right for each other. Plus, once he made a decision about her store, they'd never see each other again. They had no time to form a deep emotional attachment. There'd be no time for a real commitment. They'd spend so little time together there wouldn't even be a brush with one. Was it so wrong to want another kiss?

It might not be wrong, per se, but it did lead them down a slippery slope. A slope she might not recover from if she actually fell for him in this little span of time they had together. If they fell, and he asked her to stay or asked her to come to Virginia with him, or ask for any kind of commitment at all, she'd have to tell him.

And she couldn't do that. Not again.

She caught his gaze. "We don't have to bow to the whims of superstition or tradition."

He bounced the ball of mistletoe on his palm. "But what if we want to?"

Frissions of delight raced through her bloodstream. She couldn't stop the pleasure that blossomed in her chest. But that only made her realize how easily she could fall and how careful she'd have to be spending the next few days with him at the store.

Still, she didn't want to make a big deal out of this. She tapped his arm playfully. "Just hang the darn thing."

They hung more tinsel in her dining room and threaded it around her doorways. With the shiny silver tinsel in place, she handed Rory a box of bright blue Christmas-tree balls. "Hang these on the tinsel…about three feet apart."

"Okay." He glanced at Finley, who had finished her dinner and was sitting, watching them. He offered the box to her. "Want to hand these to me?"

She shrugged. "I suppose." She scrambled up from her seat beside the coffee table and took the box.

Shannon gathered their dishes and carried them to the kitchen. When she returned to the living room, Rory and Finley had a little assembly line going. Finley would hand him a blue ball. He'd hang it on the tinsel. By the time he turned for another ornament, Finley already had one in her hand for him.

"What do you think I should do with the drapes?"

Rory glanced over. "Do?"

"Should I loop some tinsel across the top?" She pulled some plastic fir garland from the big box on the floor. "Or maybe some of this fake fir stuff."

Finley said, "It's too green," surprising both Shannon and Rory.

"Too green?"

"Yeah. The curtains are green."

Understanding what Finley was saying, Shannon said, "Right. Maybe we should loop some tinsel around the garland so it stands out a bit."

"Or just put up lights."

"Lights!" Shannon said, liking that idea. "My parents left me all kinds of lights." She rummaged through the box of ornaments again. She presented two sets. "What do you think? Little twinkle lights or these bigger lights that don't blink?"

"I think you'll see the bigger ones better."

Rory laughed at Finley's answer. "When did you become an expert?"

Finley's nose wrinkled. "What's an expert?"

"Someone who knows what she's doing," Shannon replied. "You're a natural."

Finley shrugged. But Shannon dug out the bigger lights. With her hands full, she kicked a stepstool over to the front window.

But before she could climb up to reach the top rod, Rory was behind her. "Need help looping those?"

She turned so quickly that she nearly bumped into him. Warmth exploded through her. So did ridiculous need. She didn't remember ever being so spontaneously attracted to a man. But she was to him. And she'd already decided it was wrong. Or pointless. Or both.

She stepped back, putting some necessary space between them. "Just loop them across the top."

Finley ran to the step stool. "I'll help."

Rory laughed. "You're certainly enthusiastic suddenly."

She shrugged. "This is kinda fun."

Shannon ruffled her hair. "I told you."

As Rory and Finley strung the brightly colored lights across the top of the drapes, Shannon rummaged for more decorations from the boxes her parents had left behind when they moved to Florida. She pulled out figurines of two kids skiing and figurines of people sledding and set them out on the end tables. She found a gold table runner and set it on the coffee table with red and green candles.

Seeing Rory and Finley were still stringing the lights, she decided this would be a good time for her to make some cocoa and headed for the kitchen. But she'd barely gotten the milk in the pan before Rory walked in.

"After the way you shot me down over the mistletoe, I'm guessing I should apologize for kissing you this afternoon."

His comment surprised her so much that she turned from the stove. The repentant look on his face squeezed her heart. Because she'd been as much of a party to that kiss as he'd been, she'd be a real hypocrite if she let him take the blame. "No apology necessary."

"Really? Because you're kind of standoffish."

She drew in a breath. What could she say? *There's no chance of a relationship between us, so I'm being careful?* She'd look like an idiot. Especially since in this day and age a kiss didn't necessary equate to a relationship. Hell, for some people sex didn't necessarily equate to a relationship.

"I'm tired."

"Yeah, me, too." He took a few more steps into the room, walking to the center island, where she'd set three mugs on a tray. "What's this?"

"Mugs for cocoa."

He glanced up. Smiled. "I love cocoa. I haven't had it since I was about eight."

"Then it's time you did."

He laughed. "That's exactly why I didn't want to apologize for kissing you. I wanted to kiss you."

Pleasure exploded inside her again. Why did he have to be so sweet? "Because I make cocoa?"

"Because you make me laugh. You're a nice person. A good person. I'd be an idiot if I didn't see how you're turning Finley around. She's actually humming a Christmas song in there."

She walked over to the stove, stirred the cocoa mix into the warm milk. "I'm not really doing much of anything. I think Finley's finally ready to be turned. I just have more Christmas things at my disposal than you do."

He shook his head. "No. I think she's ready because you nudge her along."

She walked to the island, brusquely picked up the tray of mugs to take to the counter by the stove. But he caught her hand. "Why won't you let me compliment you?"

"Because I'm not doing anything. It's the season. The time she's spending at the store." She shrugged, wishing he'd let go of her hand so she could scamper away. Wishing he'd hold on to it because it felt so good to have a man touch her again. And not just any man. Someone she liked.

"Well, we're at the store because of you...so we're back to you being responsible."

Humor crinkled the corners of his eyes, pulled his full lips upward. Her heart stuttered a bit, filled with hope. How easy it would be to simply laugh and accept what was happening. Part of her longed to do just that. To relax. To enjoy. No matter what he decided about the store, they'd separate. She didn't have to fear getting involved in something so deep it would force her to tell her big secret.

But the other part knew that she couldn't spend another four days with this man without falling head-over-heels in love. She was so needy, so desperate, that every scrap of attention he threw her drew her in like a kitten to a bowl of fresh milk. She had to keep her distance.

Still, she argued with her wiser self. Couldn't she enjoy this, breathe it in, savor it...so she'd have pleasant memories for the long cold nights ahead?

She didn't know. If in her desperation she fell

in love, those wonderful memories she was creating could actually haunt her.

So she simply shrugged. "I see myself more as having fun with Finley than being responsible for her turnaround."

"And we are a team."

She smiled slightly. She'd forgotten they'd formed a team that morning. "You're right."

"Seriously, you're great with kids. You're going to make a wonderful mother."

Tears sprang to her eyes. His comment wasn't out of line. It wasn't even unusual. But she hadn't been prepared for it.

She yanked the tray of empty mugs from the center island, effectively pulling her wrist out from underneath his hand and scurried to the stove to grab a ladle to scoop hot cocoa into the mugs.

"Want to get the marshmallows?" she asked, her voice cracking just a bit.

He pulled away from the center island. "Sure. Where are they?"

She pointed. "Second shelf, second cupboard."

He opened the cabinet door and pulled out the marshmallows.

"Grab a bowl from that cupboard over there," she said, pointing at a cabinet across the room.

"And put about a cupful in the bowl. That way you and Finley can take as many marshmallows as you want."

He filled the bowl with marshmallows, set it on the tray in the center of the three cups of steaming cocoa. But he didn't move his hand so she could lift the tray.

So she stepped away again. "You know what?" She walked to the refrigerator and opened the door of the small freezer section on top. "I have some Christmas cookies from a batch I made last weekend." She retrieved a plastic bag of fruit horn cookies. "Since Finley's handling the Christmas music, maybe it's time to indoctrinate her into cookies."

He laughed. "They don't look like Christmas cookies."

But when she brought a plateful of the cookies to the microwave to thaw them, he was in her way again.

She edged past him, first to get a plate to lay them out on, then to open the microwave door. When she set the timer and turned away, once again he was right in front of her.

"My little girl had lost Christmas and you're helping her find it again."

"*We're* helping her find it again," she pointed out, reminding him of the team they'd formed.

"It's more you." As he said the words, his hands fell to her shoulders and his head descended. She realized his intention about two seconds before his lips met hers, but by then it was too late to pull away.

Sensation exploded inside her. Sweet, wonderful need. Her arms ached to wrap around his shoulders. Her body longed to step into his, feel the total length of him pressed up against her. But fear shadowed every thought, every feeling. What would he say if she told him she couldn't have kids? How would he react? Would he be so loving then? Or angry as Bryce had been?

She swallowed. She didn't want to test him.

Still, there was no need. They'd really only just met. In a few days, they'd part. Couldn't she keep the situation so light that there'd be no worry about falling in love?

Maybe.

Hope bubbled up inside her. They also had a built-in chaperone in Finley. He wouldn't go too far in front of his daughter. Since he was so persistent and she couldn't seem to evade him, maybe she should just enjoy this?

It felt incredibly wrong to be wishing a relationship wouldn't last. Even more wrong to bask in the joy of the knowledge that time and distance would ultimately part them. Right at that moment, with his lips brushing hers and sweet sensation teasing her, she didn't care. For once in her life she wanted to think of herself.

That resurrected her wiser self. Even in her head the voice she heard was hard, scolding. *Your life is not as simple, your problems not as easily solved, as other women's. You cannot be flip.*

Just when she knew he would have deepened the kiss, she pulled away. Sadness bumped into anger and created an emotion so strong, so foreign she couldn't even name it.

But she did know she was mad at her wiser self.

You are such a sap. Such a scaredy-cat sap. Surely you can kiss a man, be attracted to a man, enjoy a man without thinking forever?

The answer came back quick, sharp. *No. You can't.*

She made the mistake of catching his gaze as she stepped back. The confusion in his dark orbs made her swallow hard. But she comforted herself with the knowledge that it was better for both of them if she didn't explain.

She picked up the tray. "Let's get this cocoa to Finley before it's cold."

CHAPTER SEVEN

TUESDAY MORNING Shannon walked through the employee entrance of Raleigh's Department Store a nervous wreck. After the kiss debacle, Rory had gone quiet. He'd enjoyed his cocoa and allowed Finley to drink hers, but he hadn't stayed after. He'd just gone.

Absolutely positive she'd blown her opportunity to spend time with Finley—and that she didn't need to have any more internal debates about how to handle their attraction because she'd pretty much killed any feelings he might have been having for her—she was more than annoyed with her subconscious. Especially when she'd fallen asleep and had a wonderful dream about them. The three of them. Not just her and Rory married, but her and Rory raising Finley.

She walked through the dark, silent first floor of Raleigh's. The light coming in from the big front windows reflected off the shiny oversize Christmas ornaments hanging from the ceiling and lit her way to the elevator. Inside, she pressed the button for the third floor and drew in a long, cleansing breath.

Watching herself interact with a child, even in a dream, had intensified her yearning for her own little boy or girl. She'd awakened with a tight chest and a longing so sweet in her tummy that she knew beyond a shadow of a doubt that she needed to adopt a child. Or maybe two children. Or maybe a whole gaggle of kids. In her gut, she knew she was made to be a mom. Since Mother Nature had stolen her normal child-getting avenue away from her, she would simply go an alternative route.

That solid, irrevocable decision was the good effect of the dream. If she wanted to be a mom, she could be.

But…

Now that she was so sure she would become a mom, shouldn't she want to spend as much time as she could with children? Especially one-on-one time like the kind she got with Finley? And shouldn't she also want to spend time with parents, the way she had in South Carolina? Learning the ins and outs of the things they did automatically. Rory might have stumbled a bit dealing with Finley the Diva, but he did so many things automatically, instinctively. Like get her coat. Slide her little arms into sweaters. Make sure she had ketchup.

She'd been watching other people with kids her entire adult life, preparing to become a mom. Now that she had up-close-and-personal time with a daddy and daughter, wasn't she stupid to throw it away?

She licked her lower lip and remembered every second of both kisses Rory had given her. She remembered the flash of heat that accompanied the sweet, romantic caresses. She remembered the yearning to step into his embrace, the longing to wrap her arms around him, and knew it would be risky to her heart to spend any more time with him.

But just as quickly, she reminded herself that she wasn't weak. In the past year, she'd lost a part of herself, then lost her husband because she wasn't whole anymore. She'd come home. Taken over her family's store. Gotten over her pain.

Surely, she could direct a relationship between herself and Rory away from romantic to a place where they could be friends.

Of course she could. She was strong. Her problems had made her strong. Now that she had sorted all this out in her head and had a solid course of action, she was even stronger. More determined. With her mind set, she could spend a lifetime in his company and not waver.

She walked into her dark, quiet office. Turned on the light. She could do this. She *would* do this.

Twenty minutes later, Rory and Finley strolled in. Finley raced over to her desk and gave her a hug. "I had fun last night."

Closing her eyes, she squeezed the little girl affectionately. Without Finley she might have taken years to make her decision to adopt. For as much as Rory thought he owed her with Finley, she knew she owed Finley more.

"I had fun last night, too."

Shannon rose and helped Finley out of her jacket. "Did you bring your laptop?"

Finley nodded.

"I have a surprise." She lifted a new video game off her desk. "I bought you a game."

Finley's face lit up. "What is it?"

She glanced at the CD. "I'm not sure. Something with frogs and dragons. Wendy said her grandkids love it."

Finley eagerly took the game Shannon handed her.

Shannon laughed and faced Rory. "So what do you want to do today?"

Obviously avoiding her gaze, he shrugged out of his topcoat. "Chat with the people in advertising and public relations."

She pressed her intercom button. "Wendy, we're ready for you to help Finley install her new game. Mr. Wallace and I will be with advertising."

Wendy said, "Great," and within seconds was in the doorway to Shannon's office.

Shannon walked around the desk and headed for the door. "She's all yours." She pointed at Rory. "You come with me."

Rory swung Finley up and gave her a smacking kiss goodbye. "We'll be back in time for lunch."

Finley said, "Okay," then slithered down.

As Rory and Shannon walked out, Finley eagerly raced to Shannon's chair, where Wendy sat booting up her laptop.

In the hall, Rory glanced over at Shannon. The night before, she'd acted very oddly with him, refusing to let him compliment her, getting nervously quiet after he'd kissed her. He didn't need to be hit on the head with a rock. She didn't want him kissing her.

So that morning in the shower, he'd given himself a stern lecture. Kissing her had been wrong. Her reaction to the mistletoe should have clued him in, but he was so damned sure his charm and good looks would smooth things over that he'd made a mistake. A big blunder. But this morning he would fix that by apologizing.

Except, she didn't seem to need an apology. She seemed strong and in control. No moodiness. No nerves.

He could have been insulted by the second, annoyed that she was denying the attraction he knew hummed between them, but he wasn't that much of an idiot. He might be feeling the stirrings of being interested in a relationship, but it was clear she wasn't. His divorce was two years in the past. Hers was one. He was incredibly physically attracted to her. She might not be incredibly attracted to him. He liked her. She... Well, he might not be as charming as he'd always thought.

Plus, they were together because of a business deal. Once the deal was done, she might feel differently. She could be standoffish right now because she wanted to get a fair price for her store. And if she did like him, if she was only pulling back because of their business deal, wouldn't he be an idiot to push her?

Of course, he would.

When she reached the door marked Advertising, he hustled in front of her and grabbed the knob. It certainly wouldn't hurt to start being a gentleman, and show her his charming, likable side, while they were doing business so that once their business was concluded he might be able to ask her out.

Even the thought sent a ripple of excitement through him. He couldn't believe he'd spent two long years on his own. But he had. And that was probably for the best. But now, he was ready.

She smiled at him as he walked through the door and his heart swelled with ridiculous hope. She obviously wasn't holding a grudge against him for kissing her. He had three or four days left for him to mend his reputation, show her he was a nice guy, and then, when the deal was done, he could pounce.

Good God, he liked having a plan!

John Wilder, obviously having been alerted by Wendy, stood in the center of the big room. "What would you like to see first?"

"Actually, I'd like to talk first." He glanced around the room. "With everyone."

John's brows rose. "Individually?"

He laughed. "We have all day. And I'd like to get a good feel for what this division does to justify its existence."

John straightened with affront. "You can't have a department store without ads in the local paper."

Rory laughed. "Relax." He glanced at a red-haired woman who was the only one in the department still working. "I'd like to start with her."

She glanced up, pointed at her chest. "Me?"

"Yes. You are…"

"I'm Rose."

"And you do what?"

"Layout mostly."

"Great. Where can we talk?"

John gestured toward a small conference room and Rory motioned for Rose to join him there.

Unusually comfortable with Shannon, Rory didn't think twice about the fact that she was always with him when he made his visits, until she stepped into the conference room with him and Rose. It was only day two of his tour, but he suddenly realized that he'd never once been alone with anyone from her staff. Worse, he hadn't once questioned the fact that Shannon stuck to him like glue. Normally, he'd ask for time on his own. Time to see the store. Time to get the real scoop from employees. Yet, with Shannon, he'd never even thought of it.

By eleven o'clock they'd interviewed everyone and were back in John's office. At the end of that time he'd also concluded that he'd never questioned Shannon's continuing presence because he liked her and he liked spending time with her. But even friends checked up on each other's facts and figures in a business deal. He'd been so preoccupied with the personal side of their relationship that he'd fallen down on the job. He might not insist she back off from his department visits just yet, but before this week was out, he'd get some private time with everyone. He'd also spend the evening on the internet, checking things out even more. Then, in the morning, before he came to the store, he'd talk with some of her vendors.

"So are you ready to break for lunch?"

Jarred out of his reverie, Rory said, "Yeah. Sure."

John rose from his seat. Papers of various and sundry kinds and sizes littered his desk. "Why don't I come with you? We can continue our discussions over a hot roast beef sandwich?"

Rory was about to decline with an apology, but Shannon beat him to it. "That would be great, but Rory has his daughter with him. She's been stuck in my office all morning. I don't think we should bore her with business."

John easily backed off. "I'll see you after lunch then."

Shannon said, "Great."

But Rory kept himself a step or two behind her as they walked out of the advertising offices, concerned that she'd answered for him. Normally, he wouldn't care, except the night before she'd been so quiet. And today she was all but bursting with confidence.

Of course, she was trying to sell him her company. And from what he'd seen of her dealings with staff, she was a take-charge person.

His libido instantly wondered how that would play out in bed and in his head he cursed himself. It was that kind of thinking that had gotten them to this place. He'd already promised himself that he wouldn't make another move, wouldn't say another inappropriate word until they had this deal done. And he wouldn't.

When they entered Shannon's office, Finley was deep in play. Striding over to the desk, he said, "Hey, aren't you ready for French fries?"

She didn't take her eyes off her computer screen. "Just one more minute."

He glanced over at Shannon and the look of love on her face for his little girl nearly did him in. How could he not fall for the woman who loved his daughter? Especially when her own mom hadn't?

He sucked in a breath, told himself to think about this later and said, "Come on, Finley. I have lots of work to do this afternoon. We need to go now."

She sighed heavily, but got off the chair and scampered over to Shannon, who took her hand and led her out of the office.

A strange sensation invaded his chest. Four days ago, he thought he'd never see his normal daughter again. But a little bit of time with Shannon had changed everything.

And he wondered if that wasn't a big part of why he liked her so much, why he was so ready suddenly to jump into another relationship.

Was he really seeing Shannon romantically or was he only falling for her because he wanted help with his daughter?

They walked through the cafeteria line, choosing their lunches, and when Finley picked whipped-cream-covered cherry gelatin and pie as her main course, Rory simply took those dishes off her plate and told her to choose again.

But Shannon smiled and said, "I'll bet your dad would let you keep the gelatin as your dessert if you picked a better main course."

Frowning, Finley studied the available food.

Finally, she took a salad and an order of fries. But Rory stared at Shannon. He remembered that they'd formed an alliance. He'd been the one to suggest it. But his question about his motives in wanting a relationship with Shannon came back full force. He suddenly felt as if he were using her. And, even worse, that he might be thinking of Shannon romantically just because he wanted a mother for his child.

Nerves skittered down his spine. What if he was? Oh, lord. What if he was?

Then he was scum.

They found a table in the back and once Rory opened Finley's little packet of ranch dressing and poured it on her salad, she started to eat. Her mouth full of lettuce, she said, "I really like the game, Shannon."

Shannon and Rory both said, "Don't talk with your mouth full."

Shannon quickly looked down at her own salad, but those odd feelings floated through Rory again. It was wonderful to have a partner. Wonderful to have backup. With Shannon around, it wasn't just him against Finley. He had an ally.

Finley chewed and swallowed then said, "I also forgot to say thanks."

The guilty sensations bombarding him intensified. That morning he should have prompted Finley to thank Shannon and he'd forgotten. He was proud as hell that Finley had remembered, but it served as yet another reminder that he wasn't as good with Finley as he needed to be. And he was getting comfortable with Shannon picking up the slack.

Shannon said, "You're welcome. It was my pleasure. I appreciate you being so patient while I show your dad my store."

Kicking her feet under the table, Finley grinned.

Rory's heart about burst in his chest. Not from love or even pride. From some hideous emotion he couldn't name. He didn't have to ponder or think this through. Finley liked Shannon. She liked having a woman around. Having a woman around settled her. Was it any wonder he was interested in Shannon? Any wonder he wasn't demanding to see her store on his own? He wanted to stay in her company and in her good graces. He didn't want any friction between them so she'd continue to help him with Finley.

He was double scum.

Once they returned Finley to Shannon's office and Wendy's care, they started up the hall to the advertising department again, but Rory stopped her by placing his hand on her forearm.

"Wait."

She turned, smiled. "What?"

"I want some time alone with the people in advertising."

She didn't hesitate, her smile didn't slip. "Sure. No problem. I understand that you'd want to see what they'd say when the boss isn't around."

"And I think I'd like to be by myself tomorrow when I spend the day with accounting."

Again, her smile didn't slip. No hesitation when she said, "Sure." Her smile actually grew. "I'll be happy to spend this afternoon and tomorrow with Finley."

His heart lurched. She really did love Finley.

"And I also thought it would be a good idea for the two of you to come to my house for a little more decorating tonight."

She might not have hesitated, but he did. He wasn't at all sure that was a good idea. Except, he was confused about his feelings for Shannon and maybe a little private time would clear everything up for him?

"Are you sure we're not an imposition?"

She laughed her wonderful musical laugh and his heart about kicked its way out of his chest.

How could he ever worry that he only wanted to spend time with Shannon because she was a good mom to Finley? He *liked* her. God, if he liked her any more he wouldn't be able to hold off telling her until after he made a decision about the store.

"I love having you around."

He caught her gaze and found himself trapped in her pretty blue eyes. "Thanks."

"You're welcome. And don't bring food. I'll cook."

He chuckled, glad she'd said something that could bring him back to reality. "Thought you couldn't cook?"

"I wasn't thinking anything fancy. Just macaroni and cheese and hot dogs. Things Finley might be missing since you're on the road."

His heart expanded again. She was so good to Finley that it was easy for him to see how he could be confused. But he wasn't confused anymore. She was beautiful. Smart. Fun. He liked her.

Ha! Take that, Fate. He *liked* her.

He frowned. Great. He liked her. But he couldn't tell her or make a move until after their deal was done. And he was about to spend private time in her company. This night might not be the piece of cake that he thought.

* * *

That night when they arrived at Shannon's house, she opened the door and welcomed them inside, proud of the scent of macaroni and cheese and hot dogs that greeted them.

Impatient while her dad helped her out of her jacket, Finley cried, "Hot dogs!"

"Yep. And macaroni."

"All right!"

She turned to take Finley's jacket and saw Rory shrugging out of his coat and she did a double take. He wasn't wearing his usual dress shirt and dress pants. Instead, he wore jeans and a T-shirt. She'd seen him in jeans, of course, but that was over the weekend when everything was awkward. Tonight he looked so relaxed, so casual in her home, that her pulse fluttered.

She sucked in a breath. Reminded herself she could do this. For the opportunity to spend time with Finley, she could be with Rory without giving in to her attraction.

"Right this way."

She led them into the kitchen and walked directly to the stove. Pulling a tray of hot dogs from the broiler, she said, "Everything's ready. Take a seat."

At the table, Rory put a hot dog on a bun for Finley, who eagerly bit into it. "This is good!"

Shannon took a quick swipe over her mouth

with her napkin to keep from scolding Finley for talking with her mouth full. Rory had been giving her odd looks all day. It had taken a while but she'd finally figured out that she might be overstepping her boundaries by constantly mothering Finley. Whether he'd asked for help or not, she was just a bit too helpful. So it was best to back off a bit.

She served yellow cake for dessert then accepted Rory and Finley's help clearing the table. When the kitchen was cleaned, she turned from the sink and said, "Okay, everybody, let's get our coats on."

Rory's eyebrows rose. "Coats?"

"We're going to put up the outside lights."

Finley clapped. Rory frowned. "It's dark."

"I know. But my dad has a big spotlight that we can use." She laughed. "It'll light up the whole yard."

"Setting up seems like it will take more time than the actual decorating."

"I know. But my parents will be home soon. And I was going to do this last Saturday—" She paused. She didn't want them to help because of a guilt trip. "Never mind. I didn't mean that like it sounded. I only meant that I was running out of time."

But it was too late. Rory said, "Of course, you're right. We'll set up the big light and decorate."

After shrugging into his coat and assisting Finley with hers, Rory followed Shannon out to the shed behind her house. Though they'd been there on Saturday to get the sleds, he took a closer look this time around, as Shannon dug through a mountain of junk stored in her shed.

"What is all this?"

She peeked up. "My parents had no use for a lot of their things when they moved to Florida." She pointed at a snowblower. "Especially winter things." She went back to working her way through boxes and containers. "So they left it all with me."

He looked around in awe. "I'm not sure if I envy you or feel sorry."

"Feel sorry. Because if I have to move to a warmer climate when I sell Raleigh's, I'm going to have to have a huge yard sale. If I stay in snow country, I've gotta move all this stuff to whatever city I end up in."

He laughed.

"Ah-ha! Here it is." She struggled to get the big light out of a box and he raced over to help her. Their gloved hands brushed and though

Rory felt an instant connection, Shannon didn't even react.

Which was fine. They were wearing gloves. Besides, did he really expect her to have heart-racing, pulse-pounding reactions every time they touched?

Hoisting the light out of the box, he frowned. *He* was having heart-racing, pulse-pounding reactions around her. It only seemed fair that she would have them, too.

After they set the light on the floor, she scrambled away. "I have an extension cord."

He glanced over his shoulder and saw that she held a huge, orange heavy-duty extension cord.

She grabbed the neatly bound electrical cord of the spotlight and connected it to the extension cord. "I'll unwind as you walk out to the yard. When the cord stops, that's where the light sits. Anything that isn't lit by the light doesn't get decorated."

He chuckled. "Sounds like a plan."

He walked out into the snowy front yard. When he ran out of extension cord, he unwound the light's cord and went another ten feet.

"That's it!" he called and Shannon and Finley came out of the shed. Shannon held a huge roll of multicolored lights. Finley skipped behind her.

"I'd like to put these around the porch roof."

He glanced over at it. "We'll need a ladder."

She motioned with her head to the shed behind her. "It's on the wall. I'll turn on the spotlight."

He easily found the ladder and when he carried it out of the shed, he quickly noticed two things. First, the spotlight could illuminate a small village. Second, she and Finley sat on the porch steps, laughing, waiting for him.

He stopped walking. He loved that she was so affectionate with Finley, but right now, dressed in simple jeans and her dad's big parka, with the flood light making her hair a shiny sable and her big blue eyes sparkling, he liked *her*. He liked everything about her. He even liked that she'd sort of conned him into helping her with the big job of outdoor decorating.

And he was getting a little tired of pretending. A little tired of holding back. He'd waited two long years to find somebody else. He didn't want to wait another ten minutes to enjoy her. He wanted her now.

He headed to the porch again. Since they'd already proven that they could be professional at work even though they had a totally different connection outside the office, he was going for it. He might not seduce her or even kiss her, but tonight by his behavior he would show her that he liked her. And if he was lucky he might even force her to admit she saw him as more than a potential purchaser for her store.

And after that, let the chips fall where they may.

He thumped the ladder against the porch roof. "Okay," he said, huffing just a bit because the ladder was heavy. "I think we need an assembly line. Put the lights on the porch."

Shannon turned and set the big roll of lights on the floor behind her.

"Finley, you stand by the roll and carefully unwind them as Shannon feeds them to me."

He grabbed the ladder, jostled it to be sure it was steady, and said, "I'll be up here."

He paused, faced Shannon. "Once I get up there, is there something to hang the lights on?"

"The previous owner left her hooks. They're about six feet apart."

He started up the ladder. "Perfect."

He looped the string of lights on the first hook on the right side of the porch and strung them on hooks until he couldn't reach the next one. Then he climbed down to reposition the ladder.

At the bottom of the ladder, he smiled at Shannon. She quickly looked away.

Deciding he'd simply caught her off guard, he moved the ladder over to the center of the porch, climbed up and hung the rest of the lights. When he came down, Shannon skittered away from the ladder.

Okay. He hadn't imagined that, but she could be eager to get done, not in the mood for tom-foolery.

He brushed his gloved hands together, knocking the roof dust and snow from them. "What now?"

"Now, I have a Santa's sleigh to set up in the front yard."

He peered at her. "Really?"

"Hey, my dad loves Christmas. It would be a disappointment for him if we didn't set up the sleigh."

"Okay."

They walked into the shed and Shannon went directly to a lump covered by a tarp. Flinging it off, she revealed a life-size Santa's sleigh, complete with a plastic life-size Santa.

Finley crept over. "Wow."

Rory laughed, amazed that things Finley used to hate now amused her simply because Shan-

non got her to relate to Santa the same way she
did cartoon characters.

She turned to him with wide eyes. "It's so
big."

"Yeah, it is," Shannon agreed. "But my dad
loves it."

Rory walked over. He knocked on the sleigh
and confirmed his suspicions. "It's plastic."

"Yeah. That's how I know we can lift it."
Shannon faced him, so he smiled at her.

She quickly turned away. "Anyway, it's light.
Won't be hard to carry out. We just have to an-
chor it."

Disappointment rose, but he smashed it down.
They were working. She was single-minded in
her determination to get the house and yard decorated for her dad. She wasn't rebuffing him as
much as she was simply focused.

Once they got into the house, he'd be better
able to gauge her mood.

They worked like a well-oiled machine. Rory
took one side of the sleigh. Shannon took the
other. Because Rory was walking backward,
Finley directed their steps. When they had the
sleigh set up, they brought the reindeer out and
lined them up them in front of the sleigh. Shannon arranged small red and green floodlights

around the big plastic sleigh and turned off the huge spotlight.

Multicolored lights twinkled around the porch. Santa's sleigh sat in a flood of red and green light. Finley jumped up and down, clapping her hands. Shannon looked extremely pleased that the decorating was done. And he was feeling downright jolly himself. Now that the work was done, they could play. So he reached down, grabbed two handfuls of snow, patted them into a ball and threw it at her.

She turned just in time to see it and ducked. "Hey!"

"Hey, yourself." He reached down again, grabbed more snow and tossed it before she could react. This snowball thumped into her thigh.

Finley screeched with joy and bolted behind Santa's sled for cover.

Shannon brushed idly at the snow on her jeans, glanced over at him and casually said, "You want a war?"

He motioned with his hands for her to bring it. "You think you can beat me?"

Rather than answer, Shannon bent, scooped snow and hurled a snowball at him. He dived behind an available bush. But that only gave

Shannon time to scoop up two more handfuls of snow and heave them at him.

She was good. Fast. Having been raised in snow country, she seemed to have a system down pat. And Virginia boy that he was, he didn't quite have the technique she did.

The battle lasted no more than five minutes and ended when he saw Finley shiver.

Walking out from behind the bush, he raised his hands in surrender. "Finley's cold."

Shannon thwacked one final snowball into his chest. "You lose."

"Hey, I'm from the south. Considering that we get about two snows a year, I think I held my own."

She laughed.

And his heart did a small dance. He'd been correct. She'd missed all his smiles and cues because she was focused on decorating. But things would be different now that they were done.

When he reached the porch steps, he caught Finley's hand and slid his other arm across Shannon's shoulders. She immediately slid out from underneath it.

Running up the steps, she said, "I'll make cocoa!"

Finley scrambled after her.

But Rory stayed at the bottom of the steps.

What the heck was going on here? He wasn't so bad at reading signals that he was misinterpreting Shannon's. She felt something for him. He knew she had.

He frowned. *Had*. Maybe *had* was the operative word? Maybe they'd *had* fun over the weekend, but she didn't feel anything more, anything deeper?

CHAPTER EIGHT

WALKING INTO Raleigh's Department Store the next morning, Rory had the unshakable feeling that whatever he and Shannon had been feeling for each other over the weekend, it had slipped away.

Disappointment lived in his gut. But with his gloved hand wrapped around Finley's much smaller hand as they walked through the brightly decorated store, he reminded himself that he had a child who was his first priority and a potential store purchase that was his second. Sure, Shannon was the first woman in two years to catch his eye, but she clearly wasn't interested.

He had to be a man and accept that.

He walked into Shannon's office with Finley in tow and she jumped off her seat. "Finley! I've got a great day planned for us."

He should have been happy that she was so

eager to amuse his daughter while he worked, except he had the weird feeling that their roles had flipped. She now liked Finley more than she liked him.

Which was cute and nice, but he felt like last year's handbag. A must-have when it was in style, totally forgotten now that it was old news.

Finley skipped over. "What are we going to do?"

"Well, first I have to get some work done. But that should only take me a couple of hours. After that I thought we'd go outside and stroll through the park. So you can see a bit of the city." She glanced at Rory. "If that's okay."

If her eyes shone a bit, it was over the prospect of having fun with Finley. Not because she was happy to see him, or tremblingly aware of their chemistry.

"Sure. It's fine." His heart beat hollowly in his chest. There was no more doubt in his mind. If she'd ever felt anything for him, she'd rejected it. He took off his topcoat, hung it on her coat tree, walked over to Finley and stooped down in front of her. "You be good for Shannon."

She nodded. "I will."

Shannon rounded her desk. "I'm sure she will, too."

Rory peeked up at her. Her pretty black hair

spilled around her, a tumble of springy curls. Her blue eyes sparkled with happiness. She was, without a doubt, one of the most beautiful women he'd ever seen. And she was sweet. Nice. Smart. Fun.

An ache squeezed his heart. He'd lost her even before he'd had a chance to fully decide if he wanted her.

Realizing that was probably for the best, he gave Finley another reminder to behave then headed for the accounting department. An examination of the books confirmed what he'd suspected from looking at the annual statements she'd sent him. Raleigh's Department Store made a lot of money even when her dad ran it. But profits had leaped when she'd taken the reins.

At noon, he ambled back to Shannon's office suite. Wendy wasn't at her desk, so he walked back to Shannon's office, only to discover Shannon wasn't there, either. With a sigh, he strolled to the window and gazed out. The city below bustled with activity. Silver bells and tinsel on the streetlamps blew in the breeze. The gazebo in the center of the little park looked like it was wearing a white snow hat. The city was small, comfortable. It would be a good place to raise a child. And, if he bought this store, he'd need to spend so much time here for the first three or four years of ownership that it might be a good idea to move here.

"She's happier than I've ever seen her, you know?"

Wendy's unexpected comment caused his heart to jump. He spun from the window. "Excuse me?"

"Shannon. The past few days she's been happier than I've ever seen her. She came back from South Carolina broken. Genuinely broken." Wendy paused for a second, then shook her head. "Whatever her husband did to her, it was devastating. She doesn't talk about it, but she didn't have to. It was easy to see he broke her."

Indignation roared through him. He'd like to find the bastard and give him a good shaking.

"Then you came along. Spent that snowy weekend with her and she came in that Monday different." She smiled. "Happy. Whatever you're doing, keep doing it."

He snorted. "She might have started off enjoying my company, but she's been a bit standoffish lately."

Leaning against the doorjamb, Wendy shrugged. "I told you. Her ex really hurt her. I don't blame her for being cautious." She glanced at the floor then caught his gaze. "I just… Well, she'd be crazy not to like you and I can see from the way you look at her that you're interested and…" She sucked in a breath. "Just don't give up, all right?"

Giving up was the last thing he wanted to do. Especially since he now knew she was cautious. Not standoffish. Not disinterested. But cautious. For heaven's sake. All this time that he'd been jumping to conclusions, he'd missed the obvious one. A bad divorce had made her cautious. He nearly snorted with derision. He of all people should have recognized the signs.

Finley suddenly appeared in the doorway. She pushed past Wendy and ran over to him. He scooped her off the floor. "Hey."

"Hey! They have a candy store. And a toy store."

Rory met Shannon's gaze over Finley's head. "You took her to see the competition?"

She laughed. "They're fun, interesting shops."

"I'll bet."

Unbuttoning her long white coat, Shannon said, "They really are. And because they're unique and interesting they bring shoppers to town. Those same shoppers buy their one unique, interesting Christmas gift for the year at one of the specialty shops, then they come to us for the normal things like Christmas pajamas, tea sets and trucks."

He slid Finley to the floor. "Makes sense." His entire body tingled with something he couldn't define or describe.

It wasn't fear, though there was a bit of fear laced in there. He should be as cautious as Shannon. His heart had been stomped on, too.

It wasn't excitement, though he couldn't deny that every time he saw her his stomach flipped or his heart squeezed or his chest tightened.

It wasn't anticipation, though how could he not feel a bit eager at the fact that Shannon didn't dislike him? She was simply being cautious. Wendy had more or less given him a green light and now that he had it he didn't know what to do with it.

How did a man woo a woman who'd been hurt?

Finley tugged on his hand. "Shannon said that if it was okay with you we could go shopping with her tonight."

"Shopping?" He laughed lightly, so uncertain about what to do or say. He knew exactly what Shannon was feeling. The hurt of rejection. The sting of not being wanted, not being good enough anymore for the person who took a vow to love you. He knew how shaky she felt.

He'd felt it, too. But attraction to her had quickly gotten him beyond it. Unfortunately, that hadn't left him a road map for how to help her. "Why would a person who owns a department store need to go shopping?"

"For a Christmas tree," Finley answered.

The words came out through a giggle and something that felt very much like a fist punched into his heart. Finley, the child he firmly believed would never experience the joy of Christmas had her joy back. Shannon was responsible for that. Her generosity of spirit was part of the reason he'd fallen for her so hard and so fast.

So maybe he should show her he could be generous, too? "Wendy, would you mind taking Finley into your office for a minute?"

Wendy reached down and took Finley's hand. "Sure. No problem." Very astutely, Wendy closed the door as they walked out.

Cautious himself now, Rory caught Shannon's gaze. "I'd love to go tree shopping, too...if you really want us."

She caught his gaze, smiled sheepishly, hopefully. "There's a huge difference between going tree shopping as a single adult and going tree shopping with a little girl who is seeing the holiday for the first time."

Boy, didn't he know that? Technically, this

would be *his* first time of seeing the joy on Finley's face when she walked through a forest of evergreens and chose the perfect one to sit in their big front window, so the whole town could see the lights.

He felt his own Christmas spirit stir, remembered the first time he walked into the woods with his dad to get the family's tree, remembered decorating it, remembered seeing it shining with lights on Christmas morning. His heart tugged a bit.

He swallowed. She wasn't just changing Finley. She was changing him. "All right, then. We're happy to go with you."

Shannon insisted they take her big SUV to the Christmas tree farm on the top of the hill outside of town. Without streetlights, the world was incredibly dark. A new storm had moved in. Though it was nothing like the storm that had stranded Rory and Finley at her home the weekend before, it blew shiny white flakes in front of the SUV's headlights.

She pointed at the big illuminated sign that said Wendell's Christmas Trees. "Take the next right."

Rory smoothly maneuvered the SUV onto the slim country road. After a minute, the lights of the farm came into view. A minute after that she directed him to turn down the lane. Snow coated the firs that formed a tunnel to a bright red barn that was surrounded by four white plank outbuildings. Floodlights lit the area. Cars were parked wherever appeared convenient. Some in front of buildings. Some at the side of the lane. Tree shoppers walked the thin lines between the rows of tall, majestic firs.

They stopped in front of the first outbuilding. Rory helped Finley out of the car seat they'd installed in the back of Shannon's SUV for her. She glanced around in awe. "Wow."

Rory stooped down in front of her. "I'm going to let you walk until you get tired. But as soon as you get tired, you need to tell us. It's too cold to be out here too long."

Even as he said that a gust of wind blew away the tiny white flakes of snow that glittered in his hair and fell to the shoulders of his black leather jacket. Shannon watched, mesmerized. He was so gorgeous, yet so normal.

He rose and took Finley's hand. "So how do we do this?"

Shannon took Finley's other hand. "We get a tag from the cashier over there." She pointed at a young girl who stood in front of a table holding a cash register. "Then we walk down the rows until we see a tree that we like and we tag it. One of us goes out to get one of the helpers to cut down our tree while the other two stay with the tree." She looked around at the large crowd of tree shoppers. It might not have been such a wise idea to wait until this close to Christmas to choose her tree. Of course, with last weekend's storm she hadn't had much choice. "Since they're busy, this might take a while."

Finley grinned. "I don't care."

Rory laughed. "Yeah, *you* wouldn't. If you get cold or tired, somebody's going to carry you."

She giggled.

Shannon laughed, too. Not just because of Finley but because Rory was such a good dad. So easygoing with Finley and so accepting of her limitations.

After getting a tag from the cashier, they headed into the first row and Shannon drew in a deep breath of the pine-scented air.

Rory reverently said, "This is amazing."

Shannon glanced around, trying to remember what the tree farm had felt like to her the first time she'd seen it. Tall pines towered around them. Snow pirouetted in the floodlights illuminating the area. The scent of pine and snow enveloped them.

She smiled. "Yeah. It is amazing."

He glanced over. The smile he gave her was careful, tentative. A wave of guilt washed through her. She'd been so standoffish with him the past two days that he probably thought she hated him.

"Did you come here often as a child?"

"Every year with my dad." She laughed, remembering some of the more memorable years. "He always had a vision of the tree he wanted. Some holidays it was a short, fat tree. Others it was a tree so tall it barely fit into our living room."

He smiled. "Sounds fun."

"It was." She swallowed. After her behavior the past two days, he would be within his rights to be grouchy with her. Actually, he could have refused to take this trip with her. Instead, here he was, with his daughter, ready to help pick out a tree and carry it into her house for her.

With a quick breath for courage, she said, "What about you? Did you have any Christmas traditions as a kid?"

"Not really traditions as much as things we'd pull out of a hat every year to make it special or fun."

"Like what?"

He peeked over at her. "Well, for one, we'd make as big of a deal out of Christmas Eve as we did Christmas. My mom would bake a ham and make a potato salad and set out cookies, cakes, pies and then invite everyone from the neighborhood." He chuckled. "Those were some fun nights. We never knew what to expect. Sometimes the neighbors would have family visiting and they'd bring them along. Some nights, we'd end up around the piano singing carols. One night, we all put on our coats and went caroling to the people on the street who couldn't make it to our house for some reason."

"Sounds fun."

"It was fun."

He said the words as if he were resurrecting long-forgotten memories and it hit her that he'd been left that Christmas two years ago as much as Finley had been. She wondered how much of his own Christmas joy had been buried in the pain of the past two years.

"Tell me more."

"After the big shindig on Christmas Eve, you'd think Christmas day would be small potatoes, but my mom always found a way to make it special." He laughed. "I remember the year she tried to make apple-and-cinnamon pancakes."

"Sounds yummy."

"Only if you like charcoal. She got it into her

head for some reason or another that they'd taste better if she didn't use the grill but fried them in a frying pan the way her mom used to when she was little."

"Uh-oh."

"She couldn't adjust the temperature and most of them burned. At one point the pan itself started burning." He shook his head and laughed. "I've always been glad my dad was quick with a fire extinguisher."

Finley began swinging their arms back and forth. Rory took another deep breath of the pine-scented air. A small shudder worked through Shannon's heart. It was the perfect outing. Just like a mom and dad with their daughter, they walked the long thin rows, looking for the tree that would make their living room complete. And every time they'd start walking after pausing to examine a tree, Finley would swing their hands.

"What about this one?"

Rory had stopped at a towering blue spruce. Shannon studied it critically. "You don't think it's too tall?"

"Better too tall than too short. If it's too tall, we can always shave a few inches from the bottom."

She looked at it again. The needles were soft

but bushy. Healthy. The branches were thick. There were no "holes," as her father would say. No places where you could see the wall behind the tree because there was no branch filling in the space.

"I like it."

"Then let's tag it," Rory said, reaching out to grab a branch and attach the tag. His arm brushed against her and Shannon jumped back. When their gazes met, she immediately regretted it.

He was so good to her, so kind and she was nothing but jumpy.

She swallowed. "I'm sorry."

He pulled away. "You're just nervous."

That sounded like as good of an excuse as any. Especially since it was true. He did make her nervous. He made her shaky and antsy and all kinds of things because she liked him. Still, she didn't need to tell him why she was nervous.

"It's cold. It's close to Christmas. I have lots of work to do." She shrugged. "So, yes, I'm nervous."

He cast a quick glance down at Finley, who was preoccupied with fitting her little pink boot into the footprint of someone who had walked down the row before them. "You're not nervous because you like me?" He smiled endearingly. "Not even a little bit?"

His question was so unexpected that she pulled her bottom lip between her teeth, stalling, trying to figure out what to say. She didn't want to insult or encourage him.

Finally, confused and out of her element, she said, "I'm not sure."

He laughed. "You like me."

Her breath stuttered into her lungs at his confidence. She was on the verge of denying it, like a third grader confronted by the cute guy in class and too afraid to admit her crush, but he didn't give her time.

He turned and faced Finley. "Want to stay with Shannon or walk back with me so that we can get one of the tree cutters back here to help us out?"

She didn't even hesitate. "I'll stay with Shannon."

He gave Shannon a wink before he turned and headed down the row. Finley said, "I like your tree."

Shannon glanced down with a smile. "I do, too."

"My dad picked out a good one. He's smart."

"Yes, he is smart," Shannon agreed, but her throat was closing and her knees were growing weak. He hadn't confronted her about liking him to give her a chance to argue. He'd made a statement of fact, then walked away, as if giving her time to accept it.

Accept it?

She *knew* she liked him. She fought her feelings for him every day. He hadn't needed to tell her. He hadn't needed to get it out in the open for them to deal with.

She sucked in a breath. Stupid to panic. In another day or two, he'd be done looking at her store. Then he'd leave. And the rest of their dealings would be done through lawyers. Even if they had to meet to sign an agreement, it would be at a lawyer's office.

They wouldn't spend enough time together for her "liking him" to mean anything. Even if he liked her back.

Which he did—

Oh, dear God. That's why he'd said that! He was preparing her to hear him tell her that he liked her.

With a glance down the row, she saw Rory returning with the tree cutter. She moved Finley out of the way as they approached.

As if he hadn't just dropped the bombshell that threatened to destroy the entire evening,

Rory said, "You can go down and pay if you want."

She nodded, and, holding Finley's hand, she raced down to the cashier. She paid for the tree and directed Finley to the SUV, where Rory and the farm employee were tying her blue spruce to her vehicle's roof.

As they got inside the vehicle and headed home, Shannon and Rory were quiet. But Finley chatted up a storm.

"So how do we get the tree in the house?"

Rory said, "We'll park as close as we can to the porch, then I'll hoist it on my shoulder and hope for the best."

Finley giggled. Shannon almost laughed, too. She could picture him wobbling a bit with an entire tree on his shoulder.

"And then what do we do with it?"

He looked over at Shannon. "I'm guessing Shannon has a tree stand."

"What's a tree stand?"

Shannon took this one. "That's the thing that holds up the tree. Since it doesn't have roots anymore, it needs help standing."

Finley nodded sagely. "Oh." Then she grinned. "Do we get hot cocoa after that?"

"As much as you want."

Rory peeked over at Shannon. "But not so much that she's too wired to go to sleep tonight."

An unexpected longing shot an arrow straight to her heart. She wanted them to stay the night. She wanted to put the tree up in the living room, make hot cocoa and decorate the tree with them. Not just Finley, but Rory, too. She'd liked his stories of happy Christmas Eves and Christmases. She liked that his mom couldn't cook any better than she could. She liked that he didn't mind telling stories of his past. She liked that he didn't mind leaving her with his child, doing the heavy lifting of the tree... Who was she kidding? She also liked that he was good-looking, funny, smart—and that he liked her.

She turned to look out the window. *He liked her.* Her heart swelled with happiness, even as her stomach plummeted. He could like her until the cows came home, but that didn't change the fact that they wouldn't ever be together.

Pulling into her driveway, Rory said, "I think the easiest way to get the tree off the SUV is for me to stand on one side, while you stand on the other. You untie your side of the ropes first. I'll do mine second. Then I'll ease the tree off on my side."

"Sounds like a plan."

Finley leaned forward. "Yeah. Sounds like a plant."

Rory laughed. "She said plan. It sounds like a plan."

"But a tree is a plant!"

Shannon slanted him a look. "She's got you there."

They got out of the SUV laughing. Rory stood on the driver's side, while Shannon stayed on the passenger's side.

"Okay," he called. "You untie the ropes on your end."

As quickly as she could, Shannon undid the ropes currently holding the tree to her side of the SUV.

"Okay!"

"Okay!" Rory called back. "Now, I'll untie mine."

The branches of the blue spruce shimmied a bit as he dealt with the ropes. Then suddenly it shivered a little harder, then began to downright shake. Before Shannon knew what was happening, it rolled toward her, and then tumbled off the roof.

Finley screamed and raced up the porch. Shannon squealed and jumped out of the way, but the tree brushed her as it plopped into the snow.

Rory came running over. In a move that appeared as instinctive as breathing, he grabbed her and pulled her to him. "Oh, my God! Are you all right?"

Even through his jacket she could feel his heart thundering in his chest. Feel his labored, frightened breathing.

"It just brushed me." She tried to say the words easily, but they came out slow and shaky. It had been so long since a man had cared about her so much that he hugged her without thinking, so long since she'd been pressed up against a man's chest, cocooned in a safe embrace. Loved.

She squeezed her eyes shut. There it was. The thing that scared her about him. He was tumbling head over heels in love with her, as quickly as she was falling for him. She'd spent days denying it. Then another two days avoiding it, thinking it would go away. But it wasn't going away.

They were falling in love.

CHAPTER NINE

RORY PULLED THE TREE UP and hoisted it over his shoulder the way he'd told Finley he would.

Shannon watched him. Her heart in her throat with fear that he might hurt himself, then awe at the sheer power and strength of him. He might work in an office all day, but he was still a man's man. Still strong. Masculine. Handsome.

Oh, Lord, she had it bad.

And the worst part was, he knew.

Thanking God for the built-in chaperone of Finley, she scrambled up the stairs behind him. She could hear Finley's little voice saying, "Okay, turn left, Daddy." She squealed. "Duck down! Duck down! You're going to hit the doorway!"

Shannon quickened her pace.

Rory dropped the tree to the living-room floor with a gentle thump. He grinned at her. "You women. Afraid of a little bit of dirty work."

Shannon glanced down at the pine needles around her feet. "A little bit of dirty work? I'll be vacuuming for days to get these needles up."

Rory laughed. "Where's your tree stand?"

"It's by the window."

He made short order of getting the tree in the stand. After removing her boots and coat, Finley stood on the club chair nearby giving orders. "It's leaning to the left."

He moved it.

"Now it's leaning to the right."

They were so cute, and it was so wonderful to have them in her house, that her heart filled with love. Real love. She knew beyond a shadow of a doubt that she had fallen in love with them. Especially Rory. Finley would grow up and move on. But she could see herself growing old with Rory.

And that was wrong. Really wrong. So she ducked out of the living room for a minute or two of private time in the kitchen.

Busying herself with making cocoa for Finley, she chided herself. "So you're falling in love. Big deal. He's gorgeous. He's good with his daughter. And—" She sucked in a breath. "He likes you, too. Is it any wonder you're being drawn in?"

The kitchen door swung open. Rory walked in. "Are you talking to yourself?"

Her blood froze in her veins. This was a consequence of living alone for the past few months. She did talk to herself. Out loud.

Hoping he hadn't heard what she'd said, only the mumbling of her talking, she brushed it off. "Old habit." Turning from the stove to face him, she said, "Not a big deal."

Then she looked into his eyes, saw the attraction she'd been denying and avoiding, and her pulse skittered. What she wouldn't give to be able to accept this. To run with it. Step into his arms and look into his eyes and just blatantly flirt with him.

As if reading her mind, he walked over, caught her elbows and brought her to him. "Thanks for tonight. Finley had a great time and I did, too."

His entire body brushed up against hers, touching, hinting, teasing her with thoughts of how it would feel to be held by him romantically. Her heart tumbled in her chest. Her brain said, *Say you're welcome and step away,* but her feet stood rooted to the spot. She'd longed to be wanted for an entire year, yearned for it. And here he was a whisper away.

"Do you think we should have a little conversation about what I told you at the tree farm?"

Her tongue stayed glued to the roof of her mouth. Little starbursts of possibility exploded inside her. But her brain rebuked her. *Step away. Pretend you don't understand what he's getting at.*

He nudged her a little closer. Her breasts swept against his chest. Their thighs brushed. The starbursts of possibilities became starbursts of real attraction, arousal. He was here. Hers for the taking. All she had to do was say a word. Or two. Or maybe even just smile.

"I know you're attracted to me." He laughed. "I haven't been out of the game so long that I don't recognize the signs." He nudged her closer still. "And I like you."

His head began to descend and she knew he was going to kiss her. She couldn't have told if it had taken ten seconds or ten minutes for their lips to meet. Caught in his gaze, mesmerized by his soft words, she stood frozen, yearning egging her on while fear stopped her.

But when his lips met hers, pure pleasure punched through her objections. Her brain went blank and she simply let herself enjoy the forbidden fruit he offered. His lips nibbled across the sensitive flesh of her mouth. Shivers of de-

light raced down her spine. He deepened the
kiss, parting her lips and sliding his tongue inside her waiting mouth. Yearning ricocheted
through her. Not just for physical satisfaction,
but for everything connected to it. Love. Commitment. Family.

But she couldn't give him a family. And pretending she could, stringing him along, was
wrong.

She reluctantly, painfully stepped away. The
jackhammer beat of her pulse reduced to a low
thud. The tingles of desire flooding her system
mocked her.

Rory's voice softly drifted to her, breaking in
on her personal agony. "Why are you fighting
this?"

She leaned against the counter. Tears swam
in her eyes. The arousal coursing through her
blood competed with the anger and frustration
battering her brain.

"If you're worried about the distance, about
the fact that you may have to leave town if I buy
Raleigh's, you could always continue working
for me."

She squeezed her eyes shut as pain shot
through her. He liked her enough that he was
already making compromises.

"I'd have to stay in Virginia, but it's only

a four-hour drive. One week you could drive down to me, the next I could drive up to you." He chuckled. "I'd give you every Friday off. It's one of the advantages of dating the boss."

The tears stinging her eyes became a flood. He liked her enough that he was *planning a future*. A real future. One with kids and a dog and a white picket fence and a husband and wife who really would love each other until death parted them.

When she didn't answer, he walked up behind her. Slid his hands around her waist. "Shannon?"

The tears spilled over. Her heart splintered into a million pieces. Her lips trembled.

"Why are you upset, when I've already worked it all out for us?" He chuckled softly. "I can understand that you'd be afraid of starting something because of your ex. But I'm not like your ex. Not only would I never hurt anyone, but I like you. A lot. More than I ever thought I could like—"

She cut him off when she turned in his arms. Blinking back tears she let herself study his face, his fathomless black eyes, his wonderful, perfect mouth, the mouth that kissed so well.

She wanted to remember this. She wanted to remember what it looked like when a man really wanted her. With the pain shredding her heart, shattering her soul, at the knowledge that she was going to have to tell him she couldn't have kids, she knew beyond a shadow of doubt that she would never, ever get close to a man again. So she'd memorize Rory. Never forget him. Never forget what it felt like to be wanted. If only for a little while.

He tried to pull her close but she shrugged out of his hold. She couldn't handle it if he dropped his arms from around her when she told him the truth. Because she had to tell him the truth. Not only did he like her enough that she had to be fair, but she also liked him enough that she could accept nothing less from herself than total honestly.

She stepped away. Cleared the lump filling her throat. Quietly, with the burden of pain it always brought, she said, "I can't have kids."

His face contorted with confusion. "What?"

She drew a harsh breath, caught his gaze. When reality had to be faced, it was best to face it head-on. Bravely. Now that she had her bearings she could do just that.

"My ex left me the day I had a hysterectomy. I had the kind of endometriosis that compromises vital organs. I had no choice."

His features softened with sympathy for her. "I'm so sorry."

"And you love kids." Swallowing back a waterfall of tears that wanted to erupt, she turned away. "I see how you are with Finley, but we've also discussed this. The day we went sledding you told me how much fun it was to have Finley and that if—" Her voice faltered. "If you ever found someone to love again you would want more kids."

He stepped up behind her. "Those were words—"

"That was *truth*," she shot back harshly. She didn't want him saying things tonight that he'd regret in the morning. She turned, faced him. She refused to let her misery compromise her pride. "You love kids. You wouldn't even have to say the words. Anybody who saw you with Finley would know. But you told me. You told me plainly that if you ever fell in love again, it would be to remarry...to have kids." She paused long enough to draw in some much needed air. "If we acknowledge that honestly, and stop what's happening between us now, there'll be no hard feelings. No one will get hurt because we barely know each other."

He brushed at the tear sitting on the rim of her eyelash. "Shannon..." Her name was a soft question that she didn't know how to answer.

So she shrugged away from him, swallowed and said, "Don't. Really. I'm fine with this."

He didn't pull her to him again, but she still stood close enough that he brushed at the second tear. "Then why are you crying?"

For a million reasons. She wanted to say it. Hell, she wanted to shout it. Life had stolen her ability to have kids and with it slimmed down her pool of potential life partners. Her husband had dumped her. She hadn't really been held by a man in an entire year. She'd gone through the worst situation life had ever handed her and she'd gone through it alone.

She was crying because she was tired. Alone. Afraid to hope. And when she looked at him, she hoped.

Rory drew a sharp breath, her pain was a living, breathing thing in the room, tormenting them both. He wanted to tell her he wasn't going anywhere. That he didn't care about having kids. That he liked her enough to explore what was happening between them, then Finley ran into the room.

"Where is everybody?"

Shannon spun away from the door so Finley couldn't see her crying and Rory's heart broke for her again. He longed to take her into his arms, to let her cry, but he respected her privacy.

If he did something like that, Finley would see and ask questions. But they could—*would*—talk about this in the morning.

He walked over and swept Finley up off the floor. "Hey, kiddo. Tree's up. It's time for us to go home."

"But I didn't get cocoa."

"We'll stop somewhere along the way."

"Okay."

But carrying his daughter to the front hall, strange feelings enveloped him. He remembered the day she was born, remembered walking the floor with her after her two-o'clock feedings. The memories tripped something in his psyche...a love so profound and so deep that it could have only come from the inner sanctum of his soul. Shannon would never know this. But, if he stayed with her, pursued what was happening between them, he would never know it again.

He'd never have a son. His flesh and blood. A little miniature of himself, but with complementing gifts from his mother's gene pool. He'd never teach *his* little boy how to play baseball. Never proudly introduce him around on the first tee of the country club golf course.

Selfish, he knew, but when he thought of life

without those things, something tore a hole in his lungs. He felt like he couldn't breathe.

It was a lot to be confronted with out of the blue. This time last week, he didn't believe he'd ever consider dating again, let alone having more kids. Now, he felt like he was in the raging pit of hell because he finally liked someone but she couldn't have kids. And he had to make a choice. A huge choice. A life-altering choice.

He found Finley's jacket on the chair in the living room where she'd tossed it while he'd settled the tree into the stand. He found her mittens on the foyer floor. By the time he had her dressed for outside and had shrugged into his leather jacket, Shannon walked out of the kitchen.

Quiet, but composed, she stooped in front of Finley. "Button up. It gets colder at night."

Finley nodded.

Shannon hugged her. And Rory's chest ached. Now he knew why she'd been so happy to spend time with Finley. Now he knew why she hadn't even hesitated when they'd needed a place to stay.

She loved kids.

And she couldn't have any.

CHAPTER TEN

THAT NIGHT RORY lay awake while Finley snored softly in the cot beside his bed. Staring at the dark ceiling, he struggled with the myriad thoughts that battled in his brain. Was she right? Would he reject her, the way her ex-husband had, because she couldn't have kids?

He didn't know. He honestly didn't know. But he did know that if he followed her lead, pulled back from a relationship, as she had, he'd never be put in the position where he'd have to make a choice. Which might be why she'd been so standoffish. She liked him enough that she didn't want to put him in the position where he had to choose. Then, as she'd pointed out, neither one of them would be hurt.

He fell asleep around four and woke at seven, tired but agreeing that the thing to do would be to follow her lead. Pull back. Hold back. Don't give her hope only to snatch it away again later if he just plain wasn't ready to handle a relationship. Or, God help him, if he couldn't come to terms with never having any more of his own children.

As he and Finley walked into Shannon's office, she rose from her desk. Wearing a red dress, with bright gold earrings shaped like Christmas ornaments, she looked festive. But her smile was cautious, wary.

"So, Miss Finley, are you staying with me this morning while your dad spends some time in human resources?"

She bounced up and down. "Yes! Are we going to do something fun?"

"Well, first I have to get my morning paperwork done." She clicked on her big-screen TV. "You can watch cartoons while I do that. Then I thought we'd just take a walk in the park, get some fresh air." She stooped down in front of Finley. "There should be carolers there this morning."

"Carolers?"

"People who sing Christmas songs."

Not enthusiastic, but at least not pouting or throwing a tantrum, Finley shrugged. "Sounds okay."

Shannon rose. "Okay? It's going to be fun."

She smiled tentatively at Rory. "So you'll be back around noon?"

He swallowed. She might be cool and collected, but he knew her heart had been broken. Irrevocably. Life couldn't do anything crueler to a woman who wanted children than to deprive her of the privilege of conceiving them.

He tried to smile, but knew the effort was lacking. "Yeah. I'll be back around noon."

When he turned to go, she caught his forearm. He faced her again.

"Don't worry about me."

"I'm not..."

"You are. But I'm fine. Really. In the past year I've adjusted, and in the past week I've made some decisions about what I want to do with the rest of my life. You just do your part. Decide if you want to buy Raleigh's. And I'll take care of everything else."

He left her office with a strange feeling of finality swamping him. *She'd* made the choice. It didn't sit right, still part of him sighed with relief. He'd just come from a bad, bad, bad marriage. Until he'd met Shannon he'd all but decided never to get close to a woman again. It scared him silly to think he even wanted to try. And the first time he tried it was with a woman who couldn't be hurt, someone who needed promises up front. Promises he was too shaky to make.

So maybe Shannon was right? Maybe it was best that there be nothing between them?

He headed for human resources, but halfway to the door to housewares, Wendy called to him. "Wait! Wait!"

He stopped. Thinking she had a message from Shannon or Finley, he said, "What's up?"

"Nothing…" She sighed heavily. "It's just that Shannon came in sad this morning and I…" She winced. "I just wanted to know if something happened last night."

His breath caught, but he refused to give in to the emotion. She'd made the choice and he respected that—if only because his own failed marriage had left him so cautious that he couldn't promise that he'd give her the love she needed. Not after only a few days together.

"Nothing happened last night." Nothing that he'd tell one of Shannon's employees. But as quickly as he thought that, it dawned on him that if Wendy, her trusted secretary, didn't know why Shannon was so heartbroken then Shannon might not have told anyone.

Except him.

He felt burdened and honored both at the same time.

"I've been divorced. I know how difficult the first Christmas alone can be. Give her some space. She'll be fine."

With that he pushed open the swinging door. He spent the morning listening to the human resources director explain Raleigh's hiring policies, its wage structure, its bonus and pension plans. Glad for the distraction, he listened intently, but the second he left the big office and headed downstairs to Shannon's office, the weight of her troubles sat on his shoulders again.

When he arrived at her office, Finley raced into his arms. "We went to the park! Saw the people sing. They were funny."

"Funny?"

Shannon laughed. "One of the singers dressed up as a reindeer when they sang 'Rudolph the Red-Nosed Reindeer.' It was hysterical."

He smiled. He couldn't help it. Finley was really coming around about Christmas. If she kept this up, in a few more days she might actually like the holiday. But, more importantly, Shannon looked better. More peaceful. He knew that was due in part to Finley's company, but he genuinely believed that since they hadn't really "fallen in love" she'd very quickly gotten beyond their near-miss romance.

"So…" He caught her gaze. "Are we ready for lunch?"

She looked away. "You go on without me."

Finley whined, "Awww!!"

Shannon peeked up, smiled at her. "Sorry, but because we played all morning I have a little work I'd like to catch up on."

A combination of fear and guilt clenched in his stomach. She didn't want to be around him anymore. Or maybe she wasn't having as much fun around Finley as she seemed? Maybe having a child around was pure torture? "If Finley's a bother, I can have her sit in a room with me."

Her eyes softened. "Finley's never a bother."

And he nearly cursed. Of all the mistakes he'd made around Shannon that was probably the stupidest. It had been clear from the beginning that she loved being around Finley. He was the one with the problem. He had absolutely no clue how to relate to Shannon anymore. Probably because he knew something about her that wasn't true for most women, and he was barely accustomed to dealing with "most" women. Of course, he was clumsy and awkward around her.

But at lunch he decided that he wasn't going to abandon her. He might stop his romantic advances. He definitely wouldn't kiss her again. Those things only seemed to make her unhappy, but he wouldn't, by God, take Finley away from her in the last two days of their trip.

That evening, after they'd eaten supper in a little Italian restaurant, he loaded Finley back into the car.

"Where're we goin'?"

"Shannon's."

"All right!"

"I have no idea what she's going to be doing tonight, but whatever it is, we're going to help her."

Blissfully clueless, Finley shrugged. "Okay."

"I mean it, Finley. This might be a little hard for you to understand, but Christmas means a lot to Shannon and I don't want any tantrums if she says or does something you don't like."

"Okay."

He bit back a sigh. He couldn't be sure that Finley really got it. But he did know he couldn't let Shannon alone that night.

She answered the door wearing a bright Christmas-print apron over jeans and a red sweater. Her dark hair swirled around her sexily, but the drop of flour on the tip of her nose made her look just plain cute.

"Hey!"

She stepped away to allow them to enter.

Rory guided Finley inside. "We weren't sure

what you would be doing tonight but we suspected you might need some help." He caught her gaze, smiled tentatively. "So we're here."

She headed for the kitchen, motioning for them to follow her. "I'm baking cookies."

Finley gasped. "What kind?"

Shannon turned and caught her gaze. "Christmas cookies."

Finley frowned but Shannon laughed. "Don't you think it's about time you learned how to bake them?"

"I'm six."

Shannon headed for the kitchen again. "I know. But next year you'll be seven and the year after that eight and before you know it you'll be twelve or so and you'll want to be the one who bakes the cookies. So, just trust me."

Finley wrinkled her nose and glanced up at her father. Recognizing she might be more opposed to the work than the idea that the cookies were for a holiday she didn't really like, he said, "Well, you don't think I'm going to bake our cookies, do you?"

In the kitchen, the dough had already been prepared. Shannon had it rolled into a thin circle. Cookie cutters sat scattered along the side of the cookie dough bowl.

He ambled to the center island as Finley

hoisted herself onto one of the tall stools in front of it.

"You see these?" Shannon displayed a bunch of the cookie cutters to Finley. "We push these into the dough." She demonstrated with a Christmas-tree-shaped cutter. "Then pull it out and like magic we have a cookie that's going to look like a tree."

Finley grabbed for the tree cutter. "Let me."

Rory tugged her hand back. "What do we say?"

She huffed out a sigh. "Please, can I do one?"

Shannon laughed. "You may do as many as you like." She laughed again. "As long as there's dough."

And Rory's heart started beating again. He hadn't realized how worried he was, how guilty he felt, until Shannon laughed and some of the burden began to lift.

Finley and Shannon cut twelve shapes and Shannon removed the cookie dough from around them. They lifted the shapes from the countertop onto a baking sheet and Shannon rolled another circle of dough.

They worked like that for about twenty minutes. When Rory also joined in the fun, it took even less time to cut out all the cookies in a circle of dough. As they cut shapes and filled cookie sheets, Shannon slid the trays into the oven. Using a timer, she kept close track of their baking times and in exactly twelve minutes she removed each pan of cookies.

When they finished the last tray, Shannon walked over to the cookies cooling on the round kitchen table and said, "These are ready to be painted."

Finley frowned. "With a brush?"

"With a lot of little brushes." She brought a plate of cooled cookies over to the counter then headed for the refrigerator, where she had icing cooling. She filled four soup bowls with icing.

"Now we put some food coloring in the bowls and make different colors of icing."

Grabbing two bottles of the coloring, Rory helped her create red, blue, green, yellow and pink icing.

She carefully caught his gaze. "You're good at this."

He laughed, relieved that she finally seemed comfortable with him in the room. "It's not we're like mixing rocket fuel."

She laughed a little, too. Finley snatched a cookie and one of the thin paintbrushes lying beside the icing bowls.

Now that the cookies had baked, they'd fluffed out a bit and didn't exactly look like their intended design. So Rory said, "That's a bell."

Finley sighed as if put upon. "I know."

Hoping to cover for the insult, he said, "So what color are you going to paint it?"

"The song they sang in the park today said bells are silver. But there is no silver icing."

"Silver bells are silver," Shannon agreed. "But cookie bells can be any color you want."

"Then I'll make mine pink."

"A pink bell sounds lovely."

Though Rory had pitched in and helped cut the cookies and even create the colored icing, he had no interest in painting cookies. He glanced around. "Would you mind if I made a pot of coffee?"

Shannon peeked over at him again. This time more confidently. "Or you could make cocoa."

Rory's shoulders relaxed a bit more. If they kept this up, by the time he was ready to take Finley home, he and Shannon might actually be comfortable in each other's company again.

He found the milk and cocoa. While Shannon and Finley happily painted cookies, he made their cocoa and served it to them. They barely paused. Seeing that it would take hours if he didn't help, Rory lifted a brush and began to paint, too.

They worked until nine. When they were through, and the cookies drying on the kitchen table, Rory told Finley to get her coat while he helped Shannon clean the dishes and brushes. In spite of the goodwill that had seemed to grow between them as they made cookies, once Finley left the room Shannon again became quiet.

Rory still didn't quite know what to say. With every minute of silence that passed, a little more distance crept between them. He knew part of that was his fault. He'd only decided he was ready to date. The decisions thrown at him the night before were usually the kinds of things people discovered after months of dating. When they were comfortable and confident in their feelings.

But he understood why Shannon had told him. They were growing close and she didn't want to.

With the dishwasher humming, she dried her hands on the dishtowel and then tossed it on the counter. "I wonder if she's struggling with her boots."

He laughed. "She always struggles with those damn things. But she loves them. So we deal with it."

Heading out of the kitchen, Shannon tried to laugh, but the sound that came out of her throat was a cross between a hum and a sigh. The whole evening had been strained. Rory tried to pretend things weren't different between them, but they were. This time yesterday, he would have flirted with her. He also would have found something to do in her living room rather than watch her and Finley make cookies. He'd clearly been bored. Yet, he stayed in the room. As if he didn't trust her not to break down.

Expecting to see Finley on the foyer floor struggling with her boots, she paused when she saw the empty space. "Wonder where she is?"

Rory's steps quickened as he ran to the closet. But as he passed the living room entryway, he stopped. "Look."

She peered into the living room and there, on the sofa, sleeping like an angel was Finley. Warmth enveloped her like a soft sigh of contentment. "She's so cute."

"Yeah," Rory agreed, slowly walking toward her. Gazing down at his daughter he said, "You've done so much for her, helping her to get into the spirit of Christmas."

She swallowed. "It was my pleasure."

"I wonder what other things she might like?"

"Might like?"

"About Christmas." He glanced over. "We've decorated, made cookies. You've even gotten her to like carols. But that's just the tip of the holiday iceberg. There are lots of things she's never experienced. Now that she's open, I'd like to introduce her to everything…make her like everything so that this time next year she'll be excited for Christmas, not sad."

Shannon bit her lower lip. She knew exactly what it was like not to look forward to the holiday. She knew what it felt like to wish every day could be normal because the special days only pointed out that you had no one to share them with. "Maybe we could get her to sit on Santa's lap."

Rory laughed as if he didn't think she'd been serious. He caught her gaze again. "That's like asking a guy who's just learned to hike if he wants to try Everest."

"I suppose." But a weird, defensive feeling assaulted her. Up to this point Rory had taken every suggestion she'd given him. Now that he knew she couldn't have kids, it was as if he didn't trust her. That might have even been why he'd stayed in the kitchen with them during cookie making.

Sadness shimmied through her. She turned and headed for the closet. "I'll get her coat and boots."

"Thanks."

When she returned to the living room, Rory sat on the edge of the sofa cushion beside Finley. Shannon handed him Finley's boots. She didn't even stir as he slid them on. But he had to lift her to get her into her coat and hat. Still, though she stirred, she really didn't waken. She put her head on Rory's shoulder when he lifted her into his arms and carried her to the foyer.

Shannon raced to open the door for them. With Finley sound asleep, it was the first time they'd said a private goodbye at the door.

"Thanks for coming over tonight. Even with the extra time to teach Finley, your help cut my cookie-making time in half." She tried to give him a confident happy smile, but it wobbled. It had meant the world to her to have Finley to teach. To have people to share her cookie-making joy with. Just to have people around who cared about her. Deep down, she knew that was why he'd come, why he'd brought Finley. He now knew she was sad. So he'd tried to cheer her.

But that's all it was. The kindness of one human being to another. Not a gesture of love as it might have been the day before—when he didn't know she couldn't have kids.

The injustice of it punched through her, made her want to rail at the universe. But she didn't.

She was the one who had made the choice to tell him, and for good reason. She couldn't be angry that she had.

Rory smiled awkwardly. "We were glad to help." He cleared his throat. "You know, today, when I asked if Finley was a bother—" He cleared his throat again. "I was just worried that she kept you from getting your work done. She likes being with you. I like letting her spend time with you."

Relief rolled through her, stole her breath, thickened her throat. She whispered, "Thanks."

"So tomorrow, while I'm walking around on the sales floor, talking with staff, watching how things are done, you could keep her all day if you like."

"Yes. That would be great."

"Okay."

"Okay."

Silence ensued again. If she hadn't yet told him, she knew he'd probably try to kiss her good-night right now. Her heart stumbled in her chest. She'd hurt both of them, because she was afraid of a bigger hurt to follow.

But it had been the right thing to do.

It had to be.

Because if it wasn't, she was missing out for nothing.

She twisted the doorknob, opened the door. "I'll see you in the morning then."

"Yes."

"Drive carefully."

He nodded, gave her one last look, then walked out to the porch.

She waited until Finley was securely buckled in and Rory had jumped behind the steering wheel, before she turned off the porch light, closed the door and leaned against it. She had another entire day of Finley's company and, if she was lucky, a little time Christmas Eve morning before they returned to Virginia. She should be overjoyed.

Instead sadness softened her soul. She liked Rory. Really liked him. Probably loved him. And she'd chased him away.

CHAPTER ELEVEN

THE NEXT MORNING Rory kissed Finley good-bye before he walked out of Shannon's office to investigate the store. Dressed in jeans and a leather jacket, so the cashiers and shoppers wouldn't guess who he was, he looked so cute that Shannon felt a lightning bolt of longing. But she contented herself with the fact that she had Finley all day again.

"So any thoughts on what you'd like to do today?"

From her seat on the sofa near the big-screen TV, Finley peeked over at her. "Don't you have papers?"

She laughed. "Yes. But I came in early to review them. I'm all yours this morning. So what do you want to do? Go to the candy store again? Maybe the toy store?" she suggested, hoping Finley would say yes so she could buy her a gift. Something special. Something she knew Finley would want. And maybe keep to remember her by.

Finley sucked in a breath. "I'd sorta like to go shopping."

"Great! Where? The toy store?"

She shook her head, sending her fine blond hair swinging. "I wanna buy a present for Daddy."

"Oh." Wow. She'd never thought of that. A little kid like Finley, especially a child with only one parent, probably didn't get a lot of chances to shop for Christmas gifts. But considering Finley's life, a more important question popped into her head. "Have you ever bought your dad a Christmas gift?"

She shook her head again. "No."

Though her heart twisted with a combination of love and sadness for sweet little Finley, she deliberately made her voice light and teasing so Finley's first experience of Christmas shopping would be fun. "Well, then this is your lucky day because we have an excellent men's department here at Raleigh's."

Finley rewarded her with a giggle.

"Let's go!" She caught her hand and led her to the elevator. Inside the little box with "We Wish You a Merry Christmas" spilling from the speakers, she pressed the button for the second floor. Menswear.

As they stepped out, Finley glanced around in awe at the tables of shirts, racks of ties and mannequins dressed in suits. Customers milled about everywhere, examining underwear and pajamas displayed in long tables, studying ties.

"Ohhhh."

Shannon also looked around, trying to see the store as Finley saw it. Because Finley was only a little over three feet tall, she suspected everything looked huge.

"So what do you think? Shirt? Tie? Rodeo belt buckle?"

Finley giggled.

"We also have day planners, pen-and-pencil sets for a daddy's desk and all kinds of computer gadgets in electronics, if you don't see something you like here."

"You sound funny."

"I'm being a salesman."

Finley giggled again, but out of the corner of her eye, Shannon saw Rory talking to one of the salesclerks. Grasping Finley's shoulders, she raced them behind one of the columns holding a mirror.

Finley said, "What?"

"Your dad is here."

"Oh."

"And if we want to keep your gift for him a surprise, we'll have to be careful where we walk."

Finley nodded her understanding.

They slipped to the far side of the sales floor. Customers, Christmas ornaments, racks of suit jackets, rows of jeans and walls of ties all provided good cover so that Rory wouldn't see them.

As Finley inspected a table full of dress shirts, Shannon sneaked a peek at Rory. With his hands stuffed into the front pockets of his jeans and his shoulders filling out his leather jacket, he could have been any other extremely gorgeous shopper. He chatted happily with a salesclerk, who eagerly showed him suit jackets and ties, probably expecting a nice commission.

She hated to see him disappoint the clerk, but she couldn't stop herself from watching as he took off his jacket and tried on the suit coat suggested by the clerk. His muscles bunched and flexed as he reached around and took the jacket, then shrugged into it.

"I like this one."

Shannon glanced down at Finley. "Huh?"

Finley waved a shirt at her. Folded neatly so that it fit into a rectangular plastic bag, the shirt was a shade of shocking pink so bold that Shannon had to hold back a gasp.

"That one?"

She nodded.

"Um…have you looked at any of the others?"

She nodded. "I like this one."

"It's very nice, but…um…usually men don't like to wear pink shirts."

"Why not?"

"I don't know.…" And she also wasn't sure why she was arguing with a six-year-old. Rory had enough money that he didn't need a new shirt, and the pink one, the one chosen by his daughter with all the enthusiasm in her little pink-loving heart, would be a nice memento. He could keep it forever. Save it to show her when she got her first gift from her own child. Tears sprang to her eyes. It would actually be fun to see that. To remember this day. Share it with Rory. Make him laugh.

She swallowed hard. "You know what? I like that shirt, too."

She glanced up to see which cash register could take their money, and she saw Rory going to the checkout beside the row of suits. The clerk was taking information from him—probably contact information for when the trousers had been hemmed and/or alterations made—and he was pulling out a credit card.

Her heart swelled with love for him. He *wasn't* going to disappoint the clerk who'd spent so much time with him. He was actually buying something. She pressed her hand to her chest. He was such a great guy.

"You know…I don't really hate Christmas anymore."

Stunned back to the real world by Finley's remark, Shannon peeked down at her. "I was beginning to wonder about that."

Finley grinned. "I like presents."

Shannon laughed. "I do, too. I like to give them as much as get them."

Finley nodded eagerly.

"We'll sneak to that register over there—" she pointed at the register in the far corner where Rory wouldn't see them "—and pay for this, then I'm going to buy you ice cream."

"It's morning!"

"I know. But I think you've earned it."

"What's 'earned'?"

"It means that you did something nice, so I'm going to do something nice for you."

Finley grinned.

Shannon paid for the shirt and the clerk handed the bag containing the bright pink shirt to her. She nudged her head so that the clerk would give it to Finley.

With a smile, the clerk shifted the bag over to Finley. "Thank you, ma'am, for shopping at Raleigh's. Come again."

Finley giggled.

Shannon caught her hand. "Want me to carry your bag?"

Finley clutched it tightly, her little hand wrapped around the folded-down end. "I've got it."

She was quiet as they walked out of menswear and to the elevator. When they stepped inside, amazingly, it was empty.

Shannon almost hit the button for the third floor then remembered she'd promised Finley ice cream and pressed the button for the cafeteria floor.

Finley wiggled a little bit. After the doors closed, her tiny voice tiptoed into the elevator. "Some days I miss my mom."

Shannon glanced down, her heart in her throat because she didn't know what to say. It wasn't her place to talk about Finley's mom, but she certainly couldn't ignore her. "I'm sure you do."

"I don't remember her."

Stooping down in front of her, Shannon said,

"You were very small, so you probably don't remember. But you should really talk to your dad about this. I'd love to talk with you about it, but you and your dad were both part of your mom leaving." She swallowed. "And you're family. This is the kind of stuff you talk about with your family."

Her blue eyes solemn and sad, Finley nodded. "Okay."

The urge to hug Finley roared through her. Not just because she was sad, but because they were connected. They might not be family, but somewhere along the way they'd bonded. She wished with all her heart she could have talked with Finley about this. Could have eased her pain a bit. But it really was Rory's place.

Still, though she couldn't speak, she could hug, so she wrapped her arms around Finley's tiny shoulders and squeezed.

Finley snuggled against her. "I wish you were my mom."

She closed her eyes. Only with great effort did she stop herself from saying, "I do, too." Instead, she tightened her hold, pressing her lips together to stop their trembling.

The elevator bell dinged. The doors opened. Shannon rose, took Finley's hand and headed to the cafeteria. They could both use some ice cream now.

She managed to avoid having lunch with Finley and Rory. Partially because she hoped Finley would use the private time to ask her dad about her missing mom. She knew a cafeteria wasn't the best place to have the conversation, but recognized that Rory would be smart enough to stall a bit while they were in public. That would give him time to think through what he wanted to say that night when they were alone in the hotel room.

She spent the afternoon with Finley, taking her downstairs to the gift-wrap department to have Rory's new pink shirt properly wrapped in paper covered in elves and candy canes. When Rory arrived at her office around five to take Finley home, she rose from her office chair.

"So, you're ready to go?"

"Yes." He ambled into her office. "The store is fantastic, by the way. Your clerks are very cheerful."

"Hey, some of them work on commission. And the Christmas season puts a lot of money in their pockets."

He laughed. "Ready to go, Finley?"

She scooted off the sofa. "I need my coat."

Shannon walked to the coatrack. "I'll get it."

She slid Finley's arms into the jacket, her heart aching at seeing them leave. Plus, she wanted to talk to Rory about Finley asking about her mom. The need to invite them to her house that evening trembled through her. More time with Finley was a good thing. More time with Rory was tempting fate.

With Finley's coat zipped, Shannon turned her toward her dad. "See you tomorrow."

Rory scooped her up. "Yep. We'll see you tomorrow."

It was wiser to simply let them go. She could leave Finley with Wendy the following morning, track Rory down on the sales floor, and ask for a few private minutes to talk about Finley's question about her mom. That was a much better plan than asking them to her house again that night. Especially since she was decorating the tree. And that would just feel too much like a family thing.

But, oh, she wanted it.

As their feet hit the threshold of her office door, she blurted, "I'm decorating the tree tonight, if you're interested?"

Rory turned, an odd expression on his face. But Finley clapped with glee. "Yes! I want to see the tree when it's all pretty!"

He cast her a puzzled frown. "It's not decorated yet. She wants us to decorate the tree to-night."

Finley grinned. "I know."

He shrugged. "Okay." He faced Shannon. "It looks like we're happy to help. But this time it's my turn to bring food." He caught her gaze. "Anything in particular you like?"

A million sensations twinkled through her. She nearly said, *I want you to stay. I want you to love me.* But she only smiled. "I like chicken."

"You mean fried chicken?"

She nodded.

"Fried chicken it is."

She was ready for them when they arrived a little after six. Paper plates and plastic forks were already on the kitchen table, so they wouldn't have much clean up and could get right to decorating the tree.

She opened the door with a big smile, but from the shell-shocked look on Rory's face, Shannon suspected that Finley had asked him about her mom.

She hustled them inside. "I set up the kitchen table. We can eat first, decorate second."

Not thinking about her own longings, and more concerned about how Rory had handled "the" question, she shooed Finley ahead and stopped Rory short of the door.

"She asked you, didn't she?"

He rubbed his hand down his face. "About her mom?"

She nodded.

"Yeah."

"What did you say?"

"The truth. Or at least as much of it as I could say without hurting her." He sucked in a breath. "She's six. I don't want to tell her that her mom doesn't love her—doesn't even want to see her."

"Of course not."

"She was oddly accepting of the fact that Bonnie left. Almost as if she was just curious about where she was."

Shannon let out the breath she didn't even realize she was holding. "So that's good."

"Yeah. But I have a feeling bigger questions will be coming."

"Maybe."

He chuckled. "Probably."

Finley pushed open the swinging door. "I'm hungry!"

When she spun around and the door swung closed behind her, Shannon started for the kitchen, but Rory stopped her.

"Thanks."

Her eyebrows rose. "For what?"

"For being so good to her. For listening to me when I need somebody to talk about this stuff with."

"Haven't you talked about these things with your friends?"

He cast her a look. "Do you tell your friends about your divorce?"

She felt her face redden. "Not really."

"That's why it's so nice to have someone to talk to. Someone who will listen without judging."

Understanding, she inclined her head. Even though telling him about her inability to have kids had been painful, it had been nice finally to have someone to talk to.

Someone who understood.

A little bit of her burden lessened. He did understand. She might have effectively ended the romantic aspect of their relationship, but maybe she didn't need a romance as much as she needed somebody who truly understood her pain. Somebody who truly understood that sometimes life could be incredibly unfair.

She smiled at him. "I think we better get into the kitchen."

He laughed, slung his arm across her shoulder. "Yep."

The casualness of the gesture seeped into her soul. He liked her. She liked him. They were friends. Real friends, who knew the worst about each other's lives and didn't feel sorry, didn't feel put off, simply accepted and understood. She didn't have to hide things from him. He didn't have to tiptoe around her. More important, she didn't have to worry about him finding out. *He knew.* It was amazing. Suddenly freeing.

They walked into the kitchen to discover that Finley had already opened the bucket of chicken, chosen a leg and was wrestling with the container of coleslaw.

Rory said, "I'll get that."

Shannon opened the mashed potatoes and gravy. "And I'll get this." She offered the potatoes to Finley. "Would you like some of these?"

"Yes, please."

They ate dinner having a surprisingly relaxed conversation, considering that Finley had asked the big question that afternoon.

As soon as she was done eating, Finley slid off her chair and tossed her paper plate and plastic fork into the trash. She skipped to the door. "I'm going to get started."

Rory bounced off his seat. "Not without us!" He headed for the door, then doubled back and

tossed his plate and plastic fork into the trash.
"If you have any valuable ornaments, I'd eat
quickly and get into the living room before she
tries to hang them."

With that he raced away and Shannon chuckled, shaking her head. What she wouldn't give
to have them as her real family.

But she couldn't. And she did have another
night with them. So she rose, tossed her plate
and utensils, closed the bucket, put the remaining chicken into the refrigerator and joined them
in her living room.

To her relief, she found Rory stringing lights
on the tree, as Finley unspooled them.

"That's going to be pretty."

Finley beamed. "Yep."

Heading to the box containing the ornaments
her parents had left behind, she said, "I'll un-
wrap these and we can get started."

They worked in silence for the next five minutes while Rory finished the lights and Shannon
carefully removed the white tissue paper from
the ornaments.

When the lights had been hung on the
branches and the star sat at the top of the tree,
she said, "Plug them in. We'll decorate around
them."

Rory plugged in the lights and the tree twinkled and sparkled, causing Finley to gasp.

Shannon said, "It's pretty, isn't it?"

She nodded. "Very pretty."

Hanging the ornaments wasn't as simple as stringing the lights. Finley wanted to know the story behind every ornament and if an ornament didn't have a story, Shannon had to make one up.

It was ten o'clock before they got all the ornaments hung. When it was time to leave, after Finley had had sufficient time to ohhh and ahhh, Rory carried the cocoa tray to Shannon's kitchen, leaving Finley with the instruction to put on her boots and coat.

Shannon held the kitchen door open for Rory. As they walked into the kitchen "White Christmas" was playing on the stereo.

"Oops. Forgot to turn that off."

She reached for it as Rory set the tray on the center island, but before she could click it off, he caught her hand. "I love this song."

"I'll bet! With only two or three snowfalls a year, a white Christmas is probably pretty high on your wish list. But here in snow country there's never really a happy storm."

He laughed, then surprised her by swinging her into his arms to dance. Holding her close, he said, "It's a pretty song. A happy song. A song about someone wishing for something he might just get." He laughed again. "Don't spoil it for me."

She said, "I won't," but inside her chest her heart pounded like a jackhammer. She told herself that they were only friends. Reminded herself that having a friend, a real friend who knew her secrets and understood her, was a blessedly wonderful feeling. But the sensations rippling through her were every bit as wonderful. She wanted him to like her as more than a friend.

But she'd snuffed out that possibility, headed it off herself. Her choice.

The song ended and they pulled away. Gazing into each other's eyes, they stepped back. Their initial chemistry kicked up again, but she swung away. Carrying the tray to the sink, she laughed shakily. "Somebody who likes snow... sheesh."

"Hey. It's hard to hate something that frequently gets you a day off."

She laughed, then heard the sound of the door as he left the kitchen. Knowing he was gone, she braced herself against the countertop and squeezed her eyes shut, letting herself savor the sensation of being held by him. Danced with. Only when she had memorized every feeling swimming through her, tucked it away to pull out on snowy winter nights without him, did she turn from the sink and go out to the foyer.

Already in her little coat and pink boots, Finley snuggled into her dad's neck, preparing for sleep. Shannon stood on tiptoes and kissed her cheek. "Good night, sweetie."

"G'night."

"I'll see you in the morning?" She made the statement as a question because he'd never really told her a time or day he was leaving. Given that they were spending another night in Green Hill, she suspected he'd stop in the store in the morning.

She peeked at him expectantly.

"Yes. We'll be there in the morning. I want to see Christmas Eve sales. But we do have a four-hour drive, so we'll be leaving around noon."

"Okay."

He smiled. "Okay."

They stared at each other for a few seconds. She swore she saw longing in his eyes. The same longing that tightened her tummy and put an ache in her chest. Then he broke away and headed for the door.

When they were gone she sat in front of the tree for twenty minutes. Just looking at it. Wishing she could keep it up forever.

CHAPTER TWELVE

AFTER BUCKLING Finley into her car seat, Rory slid behind the wheel of his car, his heart thumping in his chest. Not with excitement, but with recrimination. He knew she was sad. He knew he was responsible for at least a little bit of that sadness.

But everything between them had happened so fast. Worse, he wasn't even a hundred-percent sure he was capable of trusting someone enough to love them. He wasn't steady enough on his feet to believe he should try a relationship with a normal woman. Someone as special as Shannon was too delicate to be his romantic guinea pig.

The next morning at the store, he wasn't surprised when Shannon again offered to take Finley around the store for a few hours. Needing to see to a few details, Rory shrugged. "I'll be walking around the store, too. You don't have to do this."

She smiled. "I want to."

Then she gave him some kind of head signal that he didn't quite understand. So he laughed. Which amazed him. Even as upset as he knew she was, she still had the ability to make him laugh. And to think of others.

She angled her head toward Finley and nudged twice.

He still didn't have a clue.

So he just went with the program. "Okay. You take Finley and I'll be a secret shopper again."

Finley jumped up and down. "Okay!"

They walked together to the elevator, but when he got off on the second floor, they continued to the main floor. He walked through the menswear department and poked around in the electronics and small appliances, but couldn't seem to focus. Technically, he'd seen enough the day before. He could report back to his dad that Raleigh's had a huge, faithful group of shoppers. At Christmas time, they seemed to sell goods faster than they could restock shelves.

The store had some drawbacks. It only broke even most months of the year and two months of the year it actually lost money. But Christmas made up for that. In spades.

So why did he need to walk around anymore? He didn't.

He took the stairs to the first floor and glanced around, looking for Shannon and Finley. But the store was packed with customers. He barely squeezed through the aisles on his quest to find Shannon and his daughter, but finally he saw them standing by the candy counter.

He edged his way up. "Hey."

"Hey!" Shannon turned, smiled at him. "I thought you were shopping?"

"I think I shopped enough already."

She winced. "Is that good or bad news for me?"

"I shouldn't really tell you anything because I have to report back to my dad, and he and my brothers and I have to make an official decision…but…I can't see any reason we'd shy away from a deal."

Her eyes sparkled. "Really?"

Seeing her so happy put the air back in his lungs, the life back in his heart. After everything that had happened between them, this was at least one good thing he could do for her.

"So Finley and I can go home now."

Her head snapped around. "What?"

"I'm done. We can go home."

"But I…" She paused, nudging her head toward Finley. "I didn't get to buy someone a gift."

"You did," he said. "Remember? You bought a g-a-m-e."

"I can spell, Daddy."

Rory laughed, but Shannon's face appeared to be frozen. "I just…you know…I thought we'd have the whole morning."

He glanced at his watch, then out the wall of windows fronting the store, at the heavy snowflakes falling. "I thought that, too, but look at the weather."

Shannon turned to look, then swallowed. "I thought you liked snow."

"In its proper place and time."

"Oh."

Her eyes filled with tears and Rory suddenly got it. She wanted this time with Finley. He glanced at the snow again. If anything, it seemed to be coming down harder.

He caught her gaze. "I'm sorry. Really. But if it's any consolation I can bring Finley back when my dad and I come to present our offer."

She swallowed, stepped away. "No. That's okay. I'm fine."

She wasn't fine. She was crying. *He'd made*

her cry. Guilt and sorrow rippled through him. "I'm sorry."

Finley stomped her foot. "Daddy! We were supposed to stay."

And Finley the Diva was back. As if it wasn't bad enough that he had to leave Shannon. Now he had to deal with Ms. Diva.

"Finley, it's snowing—"

"I want to see Santa!"

Shannon looked down. "What?"

"I want to see Santa. I want to sit on Santa's lap." She stomped her foot. "Right now!"

Rory had had his fill of giving in to her tantrums, but this one he understood. From the confused look on Shannon's face, he didn't think she had promised to take Finley to see Santa, but he did suspect that Finley had intended to ask her to. She'd been taking steps all along toward acclimating to Christmas and now she was finally here.

Tantrum or not, he wouldn't deny her this. "Okay."

Shannon glanced at him. "Okay?"

He shrugged. "She's been deprived too long. I think I should do this." He paused, caught her gaze again. "Want to come?"

She smiled. The sheen of tears in her eyes told the whole story even before she said, "Sure."

He directed Finley away from the candy counter. "Let's go then."

They headed for the elevator and the toy department in the mezzanine that overlooked the first floor like a big balcony. Santa's throne was in an area roped off and called Santa's Toy Shop. Shannon led the way as Finley skipped behind her.

Rory didn't know whether to laugh or cry. In spite of the long line, Rory kept his patience as they waited. Finley was not so good. She stepped from foot to foot.

"Don't be nervous."

She glanced at Shannon. "I'm not nervous. I need to get there!"

Finally, their turn came. Finley raced over to Santa as if he were her long-lost best friend.

Rory snorted a laugh. "Look at her. This time last year—this time last week!—she didn't even believe in him. Just a few days ago, she thought of him as a cartoon character. Now look at her!"

Shannon blinked back tears. "I think she's cute."

His heart stuttered a bit. Shannon always behaved like a mom to Finley and when he saw her tears his own perspective changed. He swallowed the basketball-size lump in his throat. "Yeah, she is cute."

"Ho, ho, ho!" Santa said. "And what would you like for Christmas, little girl?"

"Can you really give me what I want?" she demanded.

Rory hung his head in shame. "Oh, no. This could get ugly."

Shannon put her hand on his bicep. "Just be patient. Give her a chance."

He glanced down at her, once again grateful for her support, his heart hurting in his chest. He liked her so much. But it had all happened so fast and the choices he'd have to make were too big, but the most important thing was he didn't want to risk hurting her.

Santa boomed a laugh. Glancing at Rory and Shannon he winked. "Well, I can't make promises, but I do try my best."

"Okay, then I want you to make Shannon happy again."

Santa frowned. "What?"

Finley pointed at Shannon. "That's Shannon. She's my friend. I wish she was my mother. But this morning she got sad. Really sad." Her nose wrinkled. "I even think I saw her cry." She faced Santa. "I don't want her to be sad. Make her happy again."

Santa—aka Rick Bloom, manager of the toy department—cast an awkward look in Shannon's direction. He clearly didn't know what to say.

Shannon's eyes filled with tears. Though it was strange having a child announce her sadness in front of a roomful of kids and parents waiting to see Santa, her heart looked past that and saw the small child who cared about her enough to ask Santa to make her happy again.

Rory slowly walked over to Santa. He stooped in front of Finley. "Santa actually only handles requests for gifts."

Finley's face puckered. "Why? If he can fly around the world in one night, he can do all kinds of things."

"Yeah, but—" Obviously confused, Rory glanced back at her.

Holding back her tears, Shannon went over. She also stooped in front of Finley. "Honey, all of Santa's miracles pretty much involve toys."

"Well, that's a bummer."

Shannon couldn't help it. She laughed. Rory laughed, too. Santa chuckled. The parents waiting in line with their kids laughed and shuffled their feet.

But in spite of her laughter, Shannon's heart squeezed with love. She would miss this little girl terribly. When the tears sprang to her eyes again, she rose and whispered, "Tell Santa what toys you want for Christmas. Okay?"

Finley nodded. She glanced back at Rick and rattled off a list of toys. Rory stepped over beside her. "I'll have to remember to get all those things."

She nodded, but turned away. Real tears burned in her throat now. He liked her. He understood her. He needed her. And his daughter liked her.

Rory's hand fell to her shoulders. "Hey. Are you okay?"

She sniffed. "Finley's just so sweet."

He laughed. "Only because of you."

Because her back was to him, she squeezed her eyes shut.

"Are you not going to look at me?"

She shook her head. If she turned around he'd see her tears and she was just plain tired of being pathetic.

A few seconds went by without him saying anything. Finally, he turned her around, saw her tears.

He looked at the ceiling then sighed. "I'm so sorry this didn't work out."

She swiped at her tears, aware that at least thirty parents, thirty *customers,* were watching her. Not to mention employees. People who didn't know her secrets. People she didn't *want* to know her secrets.

"It's fine. You want the store. That's why you came. To see the store." She swallowed again. "It's fine."

"Don't you think I wish it could have been different between us? I like you. But I'm more damaged than you are. I won't take the risk that I'll hurt you more."

She sniffed. Nodded. "I get it."

"I don't think you do—"

"Ho, ho, ho!"

Recognizing the voice as her father's, Shannon snapped her head up and spun around. "Daddy?"

Dressed as Santa himself, carrying a sack of gifts, Dave Raleigh strode toward Santa's throne, gesturing broadly. "I'd like to thank my helper here for taking my place for a while this morning, but I'm here now." He dropped the sack just as her mom strode over.

Dressed in a festive red pantsuit, with her hair perfectly coiffed, Stacy Raleigh said, "Silly old coot. I tried to talk him out of this but you know how he loves Christmas."

Just then Finley scampered over. Her mom smiled. "And who is this?"

"Mom—" she gestured to Rory "—this is Rory Wallace."

Her mom extended her hand to shake his. "Ah, the gentleman who came to see the store."

"Yes." She motioned to Finley. "And this is his daughter, Finley."

Stacy stooped down. "Well, aren't you adorable?"

Finley said, "Yes, ma'am."

And Shannon laughed. But she also saw her way out of this painful and embarrassing situation. She caught Rory's arm and turned him in the direction of the stairway off the Santa-throne platform. "Thank you for a wonderful visit. We'll look forward to hearing from you after the holidays."

She stooped and kissed Finley's cheek. Unable to stop herself she wrapped Finley in a big hug and whispered, "I love you," in her ear.

Finley squeezed back and whispered, "I love you, too."

Then she rose and relinquished Finley into her dad's custody. She watched them walk down the stairs, then raced to the half wall of the mezzanine and watched as they squeezed through the first-floor sales floor, watched as they walked through the door and out into the falling snow.

Her mom caught her forearm. "Shannon?"

The tears welling in her eyes spilled over. "I want to go home."

CHAPTER THIRTEEN

SHANNON'S MOTHER deposited her in the living room, left and returned with a cup of tea. "Drink this."

Her tears now dried up, she took the tiny china cup and saucer from her mother's hands. "Did you remember sugar?"

Her mom smiled. "Yes."

She took a sip, closed her eyes and sighed.

"Are you going to tell me what's wrong?"

Her automatic response was to say, "I'm fine." But remembering the wonderful sense of release she had being around Rory after having confessed the truth, she wouldn't let herself lie, not even to protect her mom.

She cleared her throat. "I…um…told Rory that I couldn't have kids."

Her mom's eyes narrowed. "Why?"

"Because he was starting to like me and I felt he needed to know the truth."

Her mom's face fell in horror. "You scared him off?"

Oh, Lord. She's never thought of it that way. "I didn't want him to get involved in something that wouldn't work for him."

Stacy drew Shannon into her arms and hugged her. "You always were incredibly fair."

She squeezed her eyes shut, grateful that her mom understood and even more grateful that the feeling that she'd done the wrong thing had disappeared. "He's a good man who wants more kids."

"And you can always adopt—"

She pulled out of her mom's embrace, caught her gaze. "I am going to adopt."

"On your own?"

"Yes."

She hugged her again. "And you always were brave, too." She squeezed her tighter. "I'm glad."

Shannon returned her mother's hug, closed her eyes and contented herself with the fact that being around Finley had given her enough confidence that she could go on with the rest of her life. So what if it was without Rory? So what if she didn't have someone she felt connected to? Someone who made her feel special? Someone who loved her unconditionally?

Her heart broke a bit. Though Rory and Finley had helped her to make the decision to adopt, she couldn't begin looking immediately. She didn't want to associate getting a child to losing Rory and Finley. She wanted her child to come into her life when she was totally over the loss.

And she didn't think she would be for a while.

Two hours later, Rory was battling traffic on I-95, wondering why so many people needed to be out on Christmas Eve. It was two o'clock in the afternoon when people should be at home with their families.

"So, then, I kinda peeked at Santa's ear and I think I saw something holding his beard on."

Rory absently said, "You might have."

"Because it was fake?"

He glanced at her. Now that she was "into" Christmas a whole new set of problems had arisen. Her beliefs were so precarious and so fragile that he didn't want to spoil the magic. But she was a smart kid, a six-year-old, somebody who probably would have been realizing by now that Santa wasn't real.

He had no idea what to say and reached for his cell phone to call Shannon. She would know.

His hand stopped. His chest tightened. He couldn't call her. He'd hurt her. Walking out of Ralcigh's he'd convinced himself that leaving was sad, but justified, because he wasn't sure he loved her and didn't want to hurt her. But that was a rationalization. He had already hurt her. In a few short days, they'd fallen into some romantic place where it didn't matter if they wanted to like each other. It didn't matter if they spent every waking minute together or thirty seconds a day—they still wanted more. They'd clicked, connected.

But he was afraid.

Who was he kidding? He was terrified.

"So was his beard fake?"

He glanced at Finley, all bright eyes and childlike smiles. "Well, you saw the real Santa come in and take over. So the guy whose lap you sat on was like his helper." A thought came to him and he ran with it. "There's a Santa in every shopping mall around the world for the six weeks before Christmas. The real one can't be in all those places. So he trains lots of helpers."

"Oh." She frowned, considering that.

A few miles went by with Rory maneuvering in and out of the traffic. He spent the time alternating between wondering if he'd told Finley the right thing and forcing his mind away from the sure knowledge that Shannon would have known exactly what to say. Then a worse thing happened. Suddenly, he began wishing he could call her tonight and tell her about this conversation.

"So if there are lots of Santas, that explains how he gets everywhere on Christmas Eve to deliver presents."

"Exactly."

"So that means not everybody gets a real Santa. Most of us get a fake!"

Panicked, Rory glanced at her. "No. No. He's a special magic guy who can go around the world all in one night. Because he's special." He floundered, grasping for words. "Magic. It all has to do with magic."

"But you told me magic is just some guy who knows how to do things really fast or by getting you to look away from what he's really doing."

Caught in the web of an explanation he'd given Finley after they'd seen a young man doing magic tricks on the beach a few months before, he wanted to bounce his head off the steering wheel. This is what he got for having a super-intelligent child. "That is true with most magic. But this is Christmas magic."

"What's the difference?"

He peered over at Finley again. Shannon would have handled this so easily. She would have told Finley the truth. And maybe that was what he needed to do. Tell her the truth. Not the big truth that Santa wasn't real. But the other truth. The truth most parents hated admitting.

"I don't know."

"Why not?"

"Because I'm a guy who buys stores and fixes them up so that they make lots of money. I'm not the guy in charge of Santa. So I'm not in on those secrets."

She nodded sagely, leaned back in her car seat. "I miss Shannon."

He struggled with the urge to close his eyes. Not in frustration this time, but because he missed Shannon, too. He swallowed. "So do I."

"She was pretty."

Gorgeous. He couldn't count the times he'd longed to run his fingers through her thick, springy black curls. He couldn't count the times he'd noticed that her eyes changed shades of blue depending upon what she wore. He couldn't count the time he'd itched to touch her, yearned to kiss her, thought about making love to her.

"She was smart, too."

He'd definitely have to agree with that. Not only was there a noticeable difference in Raleigh's income from when her dad ran the store and when she'd taken over, but she also ran that store like a tight ship. And she always knew what to say to him, how to handle Finley.

She'd thought of sled riding and baking a cake on days when he probably would have been stumped for entertainment for himself, let alone himself and a six-year-old.

A pain surrounded his heart like the glow of a firefly. He could still see her laughing as she slid down the hill on her saucer sled, hear her screams of terror that turned into squeals of delight when he forced her down the big hill on the runner sled.

His throat thickened. He could also remember the sorrow in her voice when she told him she couldn't have kids. She believed herself unlovable—

It hurt to even think that, because she was the easiest person to love he'd ever met.

He drove another mile or two before the truth of that really hit him. Not that she was easy to love, but that he knew that. How could he know she was easy to love, if he didn't love her?

Shannon's dad arrived home around five. The store stayed open until nine for late shoppers, but Santa's throne was deserted at five with a note that told children that he was on his way to the North Pole to begin delivering gifts.

In the kitchen, where Shannon and her mom were making Christmas Eve supper, he shrugged out of his coat. He'd already removed his fake beard and white wig, but his salt-and-pepper hair had been flattened against his head. He still wore the Santa suit but the top two buttons of the jacket were undone. "So what did Wallace have to say? Is he going to buy the store?"

Shannon watched her mom shoot her dad one of those warning looks only a wife can give a husband and she laughed. "It's okay, Mom. We can talk about it."

Her dad headed for the table. "Talk about what?"

"About Rory Wallace breaking our daughter's heart."

His eyes widened, his forehead creased. "What?"

Shannon batted a hand. She didn't mind talking to her mom, but her dad had a tendency to make mountains out of mole hills. "I'm fine. We just sort of began to get close while he was here and I might have taken a few things he said to heart that he didn't mean."

"Scoundrel!"

"No, Dad. It was me. We were attracted, but he sort of laid everything out on the table early on in the week. He had a wife who left him, who doesn't want anything to do with their daughter."

He fell to one of the chairs at the table. "Oh."

"Then he mentioned a time or two that he loved being a dad and wanted more kids."

He glanced up sharply, held her gaze. "You're not out of that game. You can always adopt."

Though she and her father had never come right out and talked about this, she wasn't surprised that he'd thought it through, that he'd already come to this conclusion. She smiled shakily. "I know."

"So what's the deal? Why can't we talk about him?"

"Because in spite of the fact that I knew we weren't a good match I sort of let myself fall." She sucked in a breath. "But I'm okay now. And I can tell you that he's definitely interested in the store. He has to talk to his family first."

"Maybe I don't want to sell it to him."

For the first time in hours, she laughed. "Don't cut off your nose to spite your face. The Wallaces own a big company, with lots of capital. I'm sure they'll make you a very fair offer."

"Everything in life isn't about money."

She laughed again, glowing with the fact that her dad loved her enough not to take a deal.

Even though that was idiotic and she planned to talk him out of it, she said, "That's the first time you've ever said that."

"Well, it's true." He scooted his chair closer to the table. "Are we going to eat tonight or what?"

His mom brought him a drink. "It's only a little after five. I invited Mary to dinner at seven. Have a drink, go get a shower, and before you know it Mary will be here."

A sudden knock at the door had her mom turning around. "Maybe she's early?"

"Maybe," Shannon said, heading out of the kitchen. "But, seriously, Dad, supper's not ready until seven. So you might as well get a shower."

With that she pushed through the swinging door and walked up the hall. She opened the door with a jolly "Merry Christmas," only to have Finley propel herself at her knees.

"Merry Christmas, Shannon!"

Shocked, she looked up at Rory. Their gazes caught. "Merry Christmas, Shannon."

Her heart tumbled in her chest. It was wonderful to see them. Fabulous that they were still in Pennsylvania this late. That probably meant they wanted to share Christmas with her.

But it was also bad because she'd finally, finally stopped crying and finally, finally reminded herself that she could adopt on her own.

Create the family she wanted. Seeing them again only brought back her sad sensations of loss.

"Can we come in?"

Shaking herself out of her stunned state, she said, "Yes. Yes, of course."

Her mom pushed open the kitchen door and came into the hall. Obviously expecting to see Mary, she frowned. "Oh, Mr. Wallace? What can we do for you?"

"Actually, I'd like to talk to Shannon."

Her mother's perfectly shaped brows arched in question.

Shannon said, "My dad is here. If you want to talk about the store…"

He caught her gaze again. "I want to talk to you. Privately."

Finley huffed out a sigh, walked to Shannon's mom. "That means he wants us to go." She caught Stacy's hand. "We can make cocoa."

Stacy laughed. "I'll give you five minutes. After that, I won't be responsible for what the kitchen looks like."

When the kitchen door swung closed behind them, Shannon stood staring it at. After a few seconds, Rory put his hands on her shoulders, turned her around.

"First, I'm sorry."

She shrunk back. "That's okay. I get it. You had to go." She smiled sheepishly. "I'm surprised you're here now. Isn't your family going to miss you?"

"My parents are in Arizona with my sister and her family for the holiday."

"Oh. So this will be good for Finley then—"

He tightened his hold on her shoulders. "Stop. I'm trying to tell you something here." He sucked in a breath. "I think I love you. I know it's crazy. We've known each other only a few days. But hear me out. We've both been hurt. So we're both smart about love. We don't give away our hearts frivolously, so for me to have lost mine, I know this has to be right. Now you can argue, but I—"

Catching his cheeks in her hands, Shannon rose to her tiptoes and pressed her mouth to his. She let the joy of following an impulse flow through her as she deepened the kiss, expressed every ounce of crazy feeling inside of her through one hot press of her mouth to his.

Then she pulled away, stared into his eyes and said the words she'd been aching to say for days. "I love you, too."

He grinned. "Really? In a few days? You don't think we're crazy?"

"Oh, we're definitely crazy, but that's okay."

She patted her chest with her right hand. "I know here that it's right."

"So you won't think it out of line for me to ask you to marry me?"

"I think it will go easier on us at the adoption agency if we're married."

He sucked in a breath. "So you won't mind adopting kids? Because I really do want to raise more kids."

"We can adopt seven if you want."

He laughed, caught her around the waist and hauled her to him. This time he kissed her. He let his tongue swirl around hers, nudged her so close that their hearts beat against each other. Savored the moment he knew, truly knew, that he loved her.

And that this time love would last.

Then he heard the swinging door open and he broke the kiss. Seeing Finley slinking into the foyer, he smiled down at Shannon and nudged his head in the direction of his daughter, alerting her to Finley's presence.

"So now that all that's settled, Finley would like to know how Santa gets all around the world in one night."

Her eyes widened in horror. "Seriously, you want me to field this?"

"I already tried and failed."

Smiling, Finley blinked at her expectantly.

She glanced up at him and he raised his eyebrows, letting her know he, too, was eager to hear what she said.

She stooped in front of Finley. "Santa's sleigh is powered by love."

Finley squinted. "Love?"

"It's the love of all the parents in the world that gets his sleigh to get to every house in one night."

Finley pondered that, but Rory's heart expanded. Leave it to Shannon to know exactly what to say. Was it any wonder he loved her?

Shannon glanced up at Rory and said, "Without love nothing really works." She looked back at Finley. "But with love, everything works." She hugged her tightly, then rose and wrapped her arms around Rory. "You do realize we have to sleep on the floor."

"Huh?"

"My parents get the bedroom. We get the sleeping bags—"

Finley let out a whoop of joy. "And I get the sofa!" She headed for the living room. "Let's turn on the fireplace. Oh, and the tree lights. We can have the tree lights on all night!"

Rory cast a confused look toward the living room. "Do you think she'll fall asleep long enough for me to grab the gifts I bought Thursday afternoon from the back of my trunk?"

Shannon laughed. "She better."

"Or?"

She nestled against him. "Or we won't get any snuggle time, either."

Rory said, "Ah." Then he bent his head and kissed her.

EPILOGUE

THE FOLLOWING Christmas Eve, Rory stood near the half wall of the mezzanine watching Finley play Santa's helper. Over the course of the year that had passed, she'd finally caught on to the whole Santa thing. Due in no small part to the new friends she'd made in Green Hill when he and Shannon had bought Mary O'Grady's house. She'd thought the place too big and decided she liked Shannon's house better, so they'd swapped. She took the little house that was remodeled. They got the old house and were in the process of redoing it to accommodate at least four kids.

Finley had discovered a little girl her age about a mile up the road and they'd had enough play dates that they behaved more like sisters than friends. Right now Finley and Gwen wore little green-and-red elf suits with red-and-green-striped tights. Each held a clipboard and pen.

They were the naughty and nice elves, writing down names. Finley kept track of the nice. Gwen was in charge of naughty. Funny thing was, Santa never put a kid on the naughty list. Only the nice.

Shaking his head, Rory laughed and glanced down at the first-floor sales floor. Hundreds of customers swarmed around tables and racks. The line at the candy department was six deep. Congratulating himself on the money they'd be making, he glanced at the door and straightened suddenly.

Shannon's parents had arrived. Early.

As if they had radar, they headed for the mezzanine steps. Within seconds, they were beside him.

"Hey, Rory!" Stacy hugged him.

"Rory." A bit more standoffish, Shannon's dad reluctantly offered his hand to shake his.

"I'm glad you're here early. You can see Finley in action."

Stacy glanced over. "Oh, she's adorable!"

Even Shannon's dad's expression softened a bit. "She's quite a kid."

"Due in no small part to your daughter," Rory said, desperately trying to make points with this guy, who still wasn't over the fact that Rory had left Christmas Eve the year before. Never mind that he'd come back and proposed marriage to his daughter even though they'd only known each other a week. Nope. Dave still held a grudge. "She's a wonderful mother. I couldn't raise Finley without her."

Stacy looked around. "Speaking of Shannon, where is she?"

He didn't know. She'd been missing in action all morning and he wasn't sure it was wise to tell her parents that. He hadn't lost her. She was a grown woman, allowed to go Christmas shopping on her own if she chose, but somehow he didn't think her dad would like that answer.

Still, he sucked in a breath, ready to say, "I'm not sure where she is," when he saw Shannon get off the elevator and stride toward him.

The happy expression on her face hit him right in the heart. He couldn't believe he'd almost walked away from her the year before.

She strode over, directly into his open arms. "Can I talk to you?"

He turned her to see that her parents were already there.

"Mom? Dad? You're early."

Her dad scowled. "Why, is that bad?"

"It's not bad, Dad. It's just that I have something to tell Rory."

Her dad harrumphed. "You can tell him in front of us…unless there's something wrong."

"Nothing wrong," Rory assured him, then prayed there wasn't.

Shannon cleared her throat. "Okay, then—" She slid her arm around Rory again. "I've spent the morning with the adoption agency." She turned in Rory's arms. "Melissa Graham had her baby. She chose us as the parents."

Rory's heart stopped. As he grabbed Shannon and hugged her, he noticed Shannon's parents' faces fall in disbelief. "We get a baby?"

Her eyes glowed. "A boy."

His breath stuttered out. "A boy."

She hugged him again. "A baby. Our baby boy."

The speakers above them began to play the hallelujah chorus. Shannon laughed. Rory bit back tears, not wanting Shannon's dad to see him cry.

Pulling out of his embrace, Shannon said, "Who gets to tell Finley that she's about to be a big sister?"

Rory turned her toward Santa's throne. He put his arm around Stacy's shoulders and tugged on Shannon's dad's arm. "Let's tell her together."

* * * * *

HER CHRISTMAS EVE
DIAMOND

BY
SCARLET WILSON

Scarlet Wilson wrote her first story aged eight and has never stopped. Her family have fond memories of "Shirley and the Magic Purse", with its army of mice all with names beginning with the letter "M". An avid reader, Scarlet started with every Enid Blyton book, moved on to the Chalet School series, and many years later found Mills & Boon.

She trained and worked as a nurse and health visitor, and currently works in public health. For her, finding Medical Romances was a match made in heaven. She is delighted to find herself among the authors she has read for many years.

Scarlet lives on the West Coast of Scotland, with her fiancé and their two sons.

This book is dedicated to the children
I've watched grow up over the years
from excitable toddlers into responsible adults.

Carissa Hyndman, Jordan Dickson, Dillon Glencross
and Carly Glencross. Life is what you make it—
reach for the stars!

And to my new editor Carly Byrne.
Thanks for all your support and encouragement.
Writing can be tricky business and you make it all
so much easier—I think we make a good team!

PROLOGUE

30 September

CASSIDY raised her hand and knocked on the dilapidated door. Behind her Lucy giggled nervously. 'Are you sure this is the right address?'

Cassidy turned to stare at her. 'You arranged this. How should I know?' She glanced at the crumpled piece of paper in her hand. 'This is definitely number seventeen.' She leaned backwards, looking at the 1960s curtains hanging in the secondary glazed double windows that rattled every time a bus went past. 'Maybe nobody's home?' she said hopefully.

This had to be the worst idea she'd ever had. No. Correction. It hadn't been her idea. In a moment of weakness she'd just agreed to come along with her colleagues to see what all the fuss was about.

'Where did you find this one, Lucy?'

Lucy had spent the past year whisking her friends off to as many different fortune-tellers as possible. By all accounts, some were good, some were bad and some were just downright scary. Cassidy had always managed to wriggle out of it—until now.

'This is the one my cousin Fran came to. She said she was fab.'

Cassidy raised her eyebrows. 'Cousin Fran who went on the reality TV show and then spent the next week hiding in the cupboard?'

Lucy nodded. 'Oh, great,' sighed Cass.

'I wonder if she'll tell me how many children I'll have,' murmured Lynn dreamily. She stuck her pointed elbow into Cassidy's ribs. 'She told Lizzie King she'd have twins and she's due any day now.'

'I just want to know if Frank is ever going to propose,' sighed Tamsin. 'If she doesn't see it in the future then I'm dumping him. Five years is long enough.'

Cassidy screwed up her nose and shook her head. 'You can't dump Frank because of something a fortune-teller says.'

But Tamsin had that expression on her face—the one that said, *Don't mess with me.* 'Watch me.'

There was a shuffle behind the door then a creak and the door swung open. 'Hello, ladies, come on in.'

Cassidy blinked. The smell of cats hit her in the face like a steamroller.

She allowed the stampede behind her to thunder inside then took a deep breath of clean outside air, before pulling the door closed behind her. A mangy-looking cat wound its way around her legs. 'Shoo!' she hissed.

'Come on, Cassidy!'

She plastered a smile on her face and joined her colleagues in smelly-cat-woman's front room. The peeling noise beneath the soles of her feet told her that the carpet was sticky. She dreaded to think what with.

Her three friends were crowded onto the brown sofa. Another cat was crawling across the back of the sofa behind their heads. Cassidy's eyes started to stream and she resisted the temptation to start rubbing them. Once she started, she couldn't stop. Cat allergies did that to you.

'So who wants to go first?'

Cassidy glanced at her watch. How had she got roped into this?

'You go first, Cass,' said Lucy, who turned to smelly-cat woman. 'You'll have to do a good job, Belinda. Our Cassidy's a non-believer.'

The small, rotund woman eyed Cassidy up and down. Her brow was as wrinkled as her clothes. 'This way, dear,' she muttered, wandering down the hallway to another room.

Cassidy swallowed nervously. Maybe it would be easier to get this over and done with. Then at least she could wait outside in the car for the others.

The room was full of clutter. And cats.

As Belinda settled herself at one side of the table and shuffled some cards, Cassidy eyed the squashed easy chair on the other side. A huge marmalade cat was sitting in pride of place, blinking at her, daring her to move him.

Her gorgeous turquoise-blue velvet pea coat would attract cat hairs like teenage girls to a Bieber concert. She should just kiss it goodbye now.

'Move, Lightning!' Belinda kicked the chair and the cat gave her a hard stare before stretching on his legs and jumping from the seat, settling at her feet.

Cassidy couldn't hide the smile from her face. It had to be the most inappropriately named cat—ever.

Belinda fixed her eyes on her. How could such a soft, round woman have such a steely glare? Her eyes weren't even blinking. She was staring so hard Cass thought she would bore a hole through her skull.

She looked around her. Books everywhere. Piles of magazines. Shelves and shelves of ornaments, all looking as though they could do with a good dust. Another allergy to set off. One, two, no, three…no, there was another one hiding in the corner. Four cats in the room. All looking at her as if she shouldn't be there. Maybe they knew something that she didn't.

'So, what do we do?' she asked quickly.

Belinda's face had appeared kindly, homely when she'd answered the door. But in here, when it was just the two of them, she looked like a cold and shrewd businesswoman. Cassidy wondered if she could read the thoughts currently in her head. That would account for the light-sabre stare.

Belinda shuffled the cards again. 'We can do whatever you prefer.' She spread the cards face down on the table. 'I can read your cards.' She reached over and grabbed hold of Cassidy's hand. 'I can read your palm. Or…' she glanced around the room '…I can channel some spirits and see what they've got to say.'

The thought sent a chill down Cassidy's spine. She wasn't sure she believed any of this. But she certainly didn't want to take the risk of channelling any unwanted spirits.

The TV special she'd watched the other day had claimed that all of this was based on reading people. Seeing the tiny, almost imperceptible reactions they had to certain words, certain gestures. Cassidy had come here tonight determined not to move a muscle, not even to blink. But her cat allergy seemed to have got the better of her, and her eyes were a red, blinking, streaming mess. So much for not moving.

She didn't like the look of the cards either. Knowing her luck, she'd turn over the death card—or the equivalent of the Joker.

'Let's just do the palm, please.' It seemed the simplest option. How much could anyone get from some lines on a palm?

Belinda leaned across the table, taking Cassidy's slim hand and wrist and encapsulating them in her pudgy fingers. There was something quite soothing about it. She wasn't examining Cassidy's palm—just holding her hand. Stroking her fingers across the back of her hand for a few silent minutes, then turning her hand over and touching the inside of her palm.

A large smile grew across her face.

The suspense was killing her. Cassidy didn't like long silences. 'What is it?'

Belinda released her hand. 'You're quite the little misery guts, aren't you?'

'What?' Cassidy was stunned. The last she'd heard, these people were only supposed to tell you good things. And certainly not assassinate your character.

Belinda nodded. 'On the surface you're quite the joker with your friends at work. On the other hand, you always see the glass half-empty. Very self-deprecating. All signs of insecurity.' She took a deep breath. 'But very particular at work. Your attention to detail makes you hard to work with. Some of your colleagues just don't know how to take you. And as for men...'

'What?' Right now, men were the last thing on her mind. And the word 'insecurity' had hit a nerve she didn't want to acknowledge. It was bad enough having parents who jet-setted around the world, without having a fiancé who'd upped and left. The last thing she wanted was some random stranger pointing it out to her.

'You're a clever girl, but sometimes you can't see what's right at the end of your nose.' She shook her head. 'You've got some very fixed ideas, and you're not very good at the art of compromise. Just as well Christmas is coming up.'

Cassidy was mad now. 'What's that got to do with anything? Christmas is still three months away.'

Belinda folded her arms across her chest, a smug expression on her face. 'You're going to be a Christmas bride.'

'What?'

The woman had clearly lost her cat-brained mind.

'How on earth can I be a Christmas bride? It's October tomorrow, and I don't have a boyfriend. And there's nobody I'm even remotely interested in.'

Belinda tapped the side of her nose, giving her shoulders an annoying little shrug. 'I only see the future. I don't tell you how you're going to get there.' She leaned over and touched the inside of Cassidy's palm. 'I can see you as a Christmas bride, along with a very handsome groom—not from around these parts either. Lucky you.'

Cassidy shook her head firmly. It had taken her months to get over her broken engagement to her Spanish fiancé—and it had not been an experience she wanted to repeat. 'You're absolutely wrong. There's no way I'm going to be a Christmas bride. And particularly not with a groom from elsewhere. I've had it with foreign men. The next man I hook up with will be a true fellow Scot, through and through.'

Belinda gave her *the look*. The look that said, *You've no idea what you're talking about.*

'That's us, then.'

Cassidy was aghast. Twenty quid for that? 'That's it?'

Belinda nodded and waved her hand. 'Send the next one in.'

Cassidy hesitated for a second, steeling herself to argue with the woman. But then the fat orange cat brushed against her legs and leapt up onto the chair beside her, determined to shed its thousands of orange cat hairs over her velvet coat. She jumped up. At least she was over and done with. She could wait outside in the car. It was almost worth the twenty quid for that alone.

She walked along the corridor, mumbling to herself, attempting to brush a big wad of clumped cat hair from her coat.

'Are you done already? What did she tell you?'

Cassidy rolled her eyes. 'It's not even worth repeating.' She jerked her head down the corridor. 'Go on, Tamsin. Go and find out when you're getting your proposal.'

Tamsin still had that determined look on her face. She stood up and straightened her pristine black mac—no orange cat hairs for her. 'You mean *if* I'm getting my proposal.' She swept down the corridor and banged the door closed behind her.

Lucy raised her eyebrows. 'Heaven help Belinda if she doesn't tell Tam what she wants to hear.' She turned back to Cassidy. 'Come on, then, spill. What did she say?'

Cassidy blew out a long, slow breath through pursed lips. She was annoyed at being called a 'misery guts.'

And she was beyond irritated at being called insecure. 'I'm apparently going to be a Christmas bride.'

'What?' Lucy's and Lynn's voices were in perfect tandem with their matching shocked expressions.

'Just as well Tamsin didn't hear that,' Lucy muttered.

'Oh, it gets worse. Apparently my groom is from foreign climes.' She rolled her eyes again. 'As if.'

But Lucy's and Lynn's expressions had changed, smiles creeping across their faces as their eyes met.

'Told you.'

'No way.'

Cassidy watched in bewilderment as they high-fived each other in the dingy sitting room.

'What's with you two? You know the whole thing's ridiculous. As if *I'm* going to date another foreign doctor.'

Lynn folded her arms across her chest. 'Stranger things have happened.' She had a weird look on her face. As if she knew something that Cassidy didn't.

Lucy adopted the same pose, shoulder to shoulder with Lynn. Almost as if they were ganging up on her.

Her gaze narrowed. 'I'm willing to place a bet that Belinda could be right.'

Cassidy couldn't believe what was happening. The crazy-cat-woman's disease was obviously contagious. A little seed planted in her brain. She could use this to her advantage. 'What's it worth?'

Lucy frowned. 'What do you mean?'

Cassidy smiled. 'I'll take that bet. But what's it worth?'

'Night shift Christmas Eve. Oh.' The words were out before Lucy had had time to think about them. She had her hand across her mouth. It was the most hated shift on the planet. Every year they had to draw straws to see who would take it.

'You're on.' Cassidy held out her hand towards Lucy, who nodded and shook it firmly. She had no chance of losing this bet. No chance at all.

CHAPTER ONE

1 October

CASSIDY pulled the navy-blue tunic over her head. These new-style NHS uniforms were supposed to be made from a revolutionary lightweight fabric, designed for comfort and ease of fit. The reality was they were freezing and not designed for Scottish winters in a draughty old hospital. She pulled a cardigan from her locker and headed for the stairs. Maybe running up three flights would take the chill out of her bones.

Two minutes later she arrived in the medical ward. She took a deep breath. There it was. The hospital smell. Some people hated it and shuddered walking through the very doors of the hospital. But Cassidy loved it—it was like a big security blanket, and she'd missed it. It was just before seven and the lights were still dimmed. Ruby, the night nurse, gave her a smile. 'Nice to see you back, Cassidy. How was the secondment?'

Cassidy nodded, wrapping her cardigan further around her torso. Her temperature was still barely above freezing. 'It was fine, but three months was long enough. The new community warfarin clinic is set up—all the teething problems ironed out. To be honest, though, I'm glad to be back. I missed this place.'

And she had. But at the time the three-month secondment had been perfect for her. It had given her the chance to sort out all the hassles with her gran, work regular hours and get her settled into the new nursing home—the second in a year. Her eyes swept over the whiteboard on the wall, displaying all the patient names, room numbers and named nurses. 'No beds?' She raised her eyebrows.

'Actually, we've got one. But A and E just phoned to say they're sending us an elderly lady with a chest infection, so I've put her name up on the board already. She should be up in the next ten minutes.'

Cassidy gave a nod as the rest of the day-shift staff appeared, gathering around the nurses' station for the handover report. She waited patiently, listening to the rundown of the thirty patients currently in her general medical ward, before assigning the patients to the nurses on duty and accepting the keys for the medicine and drugs cabinets.

She heard the ominous trundle of a trolley behind her. 'I'll admit this patient,' she told her staff. 'It'll get me back into the swing of things.'

She looked up as Bill, one of the porters, arrived, pulling the trolley with the elderly woman lying on top. A doctor was walking alongside them, carrying some notes and chatting to the elderly lady as they wheeled her into one of the side rooms. He gave her a smile— one that could have launched a thousand toothpaste campaigns. 'This is Mrs Elizabeth Kelly. She's eighty-four and has a history of chronic obstructive pulmonary disease. She's had a chest infection for the last seven days that hasn't responded to oral antibiotics. Her oxygen saturation is down at eighty-two and she's tachycardic. The doctor on call wanted her admitted for IV antibiotics.'

For a moment the strong Australian accent threw her—she hadn't been expecting it. Though goodness knows why not. Her hospital in the middle of Glasgow attracted staff from all over the world. His crumpled blue scrubs and even more crumpled white coat looked as though he'd slept in them—and judging by his blond hair, sticking up in every direction but the right one, he probably had.

She didn't recognise him, which meant he must be one of the new doctors who had started while she was away on secondment. And he was too handsome by far. And that cheeky twinkle in his eye was already annoying her.

After three months away, some things appeared to have changed around the hospital. It was usually one of the A and E nurses who accompanied the patient up to the ward.

Cassidy pumped up the bed and removed the headboard, pulling the patslide from the wall and sliding the patient over into the bed. The doctor helped her put the headboard back on and adjusted the backrest, rearranging the pillows so Mrs Kelly could sit upright. Cassidy attached the monitoring equipment and changed the oxygen supply over to the wall. The doctor was still standing looking at her.

For a second she almost thought he was peering at her breasts, but as she followed his gaze downwards she realised her name and designation was stitched on the front of her new tunics.

She held out her hand towards him. 'Cassidy Rae. Sister of the medical receiving unit. Though from the way you're staring at my breasts, I take it you've gathered that.'

His warm hand caught her cold one, his eyes twinkling. 'Pleased to meet you, Dragon Lady. I hope your heart isn't as cold as your hands.'

She pulled her hand away from his. 'What did you call me?'

'Dragon Lady.' He looked unashamed by the remark. 'Your reputation precedes you. I've been looking forward to meeting you, although from what I hear it's usually you who does the name-calling.'

She folded her arms across her chest, trying to stop the edges of her mouth turning upwards. 'I've no idea what you're talking about.' She picked up the patient clothing bag and bent down, starting to unpack Mrs Kelly's belongings into the cabinet next to her bed.

'I heard you called the last lot Needy, Greedy and Seedy.'

She jumped. She could feel his warm breath on her neck. He'd bent forward and whispered in her ear.

'Who told you that?' she asked incredulously. She glanced at her watch. Ten past seven on her first morning back, and already some smart-alec doc was trying to get the better of her.

'Oh, give me a minute.' The mystery doctor ducked out of the room.

It was true. She had nicknamed the last three registrars—all for obvious reasons. One had spent every waking minute eating, the other hadn't seen a patient without someone holding his hand, and as for the last one, he'd spent his year sleazing over all the female staff. And while the nursing staff knew the nicknames she'd given them, she'd no idea who'd told one of the new docs. She'd need to investigate that later.

She stood up and adjusted Mrs Kelly's venturi mask, taking a note of her thin frame and pale, papery skin. Another frail, elderly patient, just like her gran. She altered the alarms on the monitor—at their present setting they would sound every few minutes. With a history of COPD, Mrs Kelly had lower than normal oxygen levels.

'How are you feeling?' She picked up the tympanic thermometer and placed it in Mrs Kelly's ear, pressing the button to read her temperature then recording her observations in the chart. Mrs Kelly shook her pale head.

She sat down at the side of the bed. 'I need to take some details from you, Mrs Kelly. But how about I get you something to eat and drink first? I imagine you were stuck down in A and E for hours. Would you like some tea? Some toast?'

'Your wish is my command.' The steaming cup of tea and plate of buttered toast thudded down on the bedside table. 'See, Mrs Kelly? I make good on my promises.' He shook his head at Cassidy. 'There was *nothing* to eat down in A and E and I promised I'd get her some tea once we got up here.'

'Thank you, son,' Mrs Kelly said, shifting her mask and lifting the cup to her lips, 'My throat is so dry.'

He nodded slowly. Oxygen therapy frequently made patients' mouths dry and it was important to keep them hydrated.

Cassidy stared at him. Things had changed. She couldn't remember the last time she'd seen a doctor make a patient a cup of tea. It was almost unheard of.

She smiled at him. 'Makes me almost wish we could keep you,' she said quietly. 'You've obviously been well trained.'

His blue eyes glinted. 'And what makes you think you can't keep me?'

'I imagine A and E will have a whole load of patients waiting for you. Why did you come up here anyway? Was it to steal our chocolates?' She nodded towards the nursing station. The medical receiving unit was never short of chocolates, and it wasn't unknown for the doctors from other departments to sneak past and steal some.

He shook his head, the smile still stuck on his face. He held out his hand towards her. 'I forgot to introduce myself earlier. I'm one of yours—though I dread to think what nickname you'll give me. Brad Donovan, medical registrar.'

Cassidy felt herself jerk backwards in surprise. He looked too young to be a medical registrar. Maybe it was the scruffy hair? Or the Australian tan? Or maybe it was that earring glinting in his ear, along with the super-white teeth? He didn't look like any registrar she'd ever met before.

Something twisted inside her gut. No, that wasn't quite true. Bobby. For a tiny second he reminded her of Bobby. But Bobby's hair had been dark, not blond, and he'd worn it in a similar scruffy style and had the same glistening white teeth. She pushed all thoughts away. She hadn't thought about him in months. Where had that come from?

She focused her mind. This was a work colleague—albeit a cheeky one. She shook his hand firmly. 'Well,

Dr Donovan, if you're one of mine then maybe I should tell you the rules in my ward.'

His eyebrows rose, an amused expression on his face. 'You really are the Dragon Lady, aren't you?'

She ignored him. 'When you finally manage to put some clothes on, no silly ties. In fact, no ties at all and no long sleeves. They're an infection-control hazard.' She ran her eyes up and down his crumpled scrubs, 'Though from the look of you, that doesn't seem to be a problem. Always use the gel outside the patients' rooms before you touch them. And pay attention to what my nurses tell you—they spend most of their day with the patients and will generally know the patients ten times better than you will.'

His blue eyes fixed on hers. Quite unnerving for this time in the morning. His gaze was straight and didn't falter. The guy was completely unfazed by her. He seemed confident, self-assured. She would have to wait and see if his clinical competence matched his demeanour.

'I have been working here for the last two months without your rulebook. I'm sure your staff will give me a good report.' She resisted the temptation to reply. Of course her staff would give him a good report. He was like a poster boy for Surfers' Central. She could put money on it that he'd spent the last two months charming her staff with his lazy accent, straight white teeth and twinkling eyes. He handed her Mrs Kelly's case notes and prescription chart.

'I've written Mrs Kelly up for some IV antibiotics, some oral steroids and some bronchodilators. She had her arterial blood gases done in A and E and I'll check them again in a few hours. I'd like her on four-hourly obs in the meantime.' He glanced at the oxygen supply, currently running at four litres. 'Make sure she stays on the twenty-eight per cent venturi mask. One of the students in A and E didn't understand the complications of COPD and put her on ten litres of straight oxygen.'

Cassidy's mouth fell open. 'Please tell me you're joking.'

He shook his head. The effects could have been devastating. 'Her intentions were good. Mrs Kelly's lips were blue from lack of oxygen when she was admitted. The student just did what seemed natural. Luckily one of the other staff spotted her mistake quickly.'

Cassidy looked over at the frail, elderly lady on the bed, her oxygen mask currently dangling around her neck as she munched the toast from the plate in front of her. The blue tinge had obviously disappeared from her lips, but even eating the toast was adding to her breathlessness. She turned back to face Brad. 'Any relatives?'

He shook his head. 'Her husband died a few years ago and her daughter emigrated to my neck of the woods ten years before that.' He pointed to a phone number in the records. 'Do you want me to phone her, or do you want to do that?'

Cassidy felt a little pang. This poor woman must be lonely. She'd lost her husband, and her daughter lived thousands of miles away. Who did she speak to every day? One of the last elderly patients admitted to her ward had disclosed that often he went for days without a single person to speak to. Loneliness could be a terrible burden.

The doctor passed in front of her vision again, trying to catch her attention, and she pushed the uncomfortable thoughts from her head. This one was definitely too good to be true. Bringing up a patient, making tea and toast, and offering to phone relatives?

Her internal radar started to ping. She turned to Mrs Kelly. 'I'll let you finish your tea and come back in a few minutes.

'What are you up to?' She headed out the door towards the nursing station.

He fell into step beside her. 'What do you mean?'

She paused in the corridor, looking him up and down. 'You're too good to be true. Which means alarm bells are ringing in my head. What's with the nice-boy act?'

She pulled up the laptop from the nurses' station and started to input some of Mrs Kelly's details.

'Who says it's an act?'

Her eyes swept down the corridor. The case-note trolley had been pulled to the end of the corridor. Two other doctors in white coats were standing, talking over some notes. She looked at her watch—not even eight o'clock. 'And who are they?'

Brad smiled. 'That's the other registrars. Luca is from Italy, and Franco is from Hungary. They must have wanted to get a head start on the ward round.' He gave her a brazen wink. 'I guess they heard the Dragon Lady was on duty today.'

She shook her head in bewilderment. 'I go on secondment for three months, come back and I've got the poster boy for Surfers' Paradise making tea and toast for patients and two other registrars in the ward before eight a.m. Am I still dreaming? Have I woken up yet?'

'Why?' As quick as a flash he'd moved around beside her. 'Am I the kind of guy you dream about?'

'Get lost, flyboy.' She pushed Mrs Kelly's case notes back into his hands. 'You've got a patient's daughter in

Australia to go and phone. Make yourself useful while I go and find out what kind of support system she has at home.'

He paused for a second, his eyes narrowing. 'She's not even heated up the bed yet and you're planning on throwing her back out?'

Cassidy frowned. 'It's the basic principle of the receiving unit. Our first duty is to find out what systems are in place for our patients. Believe it or not, most of them don't like staying here. And if we plan ahead it means there's less chance of a delayed discharge. Sometimes it can take a few days to set up support systems to get someone home again.' She raised her hand to the whiteboard with patient names. 'In theory, we're planning for their discharge as soon as they enter A and E.'

The look on his face softened. 'In that case, I'll let you off.' He nodded towards his fellow doctors. 'Maybe they got the same alarm call that I did. Beware the Dragon!' He headed towards the doctors' office to make his call.

Dragon Lady was much more interesting than he'd been led to believe. He'd expected a sixty-year-old, grey-haired schoolmarm. Instead he'd got a young woman with a slim, curvy figure, chestnut curls and deep brown eyes. And she was feisty. He liked that.

Cassidy Rae could be fun. There it was, that strange, almost unfamiliar feeling. That first glimmer of interest in a woman. That tiny little thought that something could spark between them given half a chance. It had been so long since he'd felt it that he almost didn't know what to do about it.

He'd been here a few months, and while his colleagues were friendly, they weren't his 'friends'. And he didn't want to hang around with the female junior doctors currently batting their eyelids at him. Experience had taught him it was more trouble than it was worth.

Distraction. The word echoed around his head again as he leaned against the cold concrete wall.

Exactly what he needed. Something to keep his mind from other things—like another Christmas Day currently looming on the horizon with a huge black stormcloud hovering over it. He'd even tried to juggle the schedules so he could be working on Christmas Day. But no such luck. His Italian colleague had beat him to it, and right now he couldn't bear the thought of an empty Christmas Day in strange surroundings with no real friends or family.

Another Christmas spent wondering where his little girl was, if she was enjoying her joint birthday and Christmas Day celebrations. Wondering if she even remembered he existed.

He had no idea what she'd been told about him. The fact he'd spent the last eighteen months trying to track down his daughter at great time and expense killed him—especially in the run-up to her birthday. Everyone else around him was always full of festive spirit and fun, and no matter how hard he tried not to be the local misery guts, something inside him just felt dead.

Christmas was about families and children. And the one thing he wanted to do was sit his little girl on his knee and get her the biggest birthday and Christmas present in the world. If only he knew where she was…

There was that fist again, hovering around his stomach, tightly clenched. Every time he thought of his daughter, Melody, the visions of her mother, Alison, a junior doctor he'd worked with, appeared in his head. Alison, the woman who only liked things her way or no way at all. No negotiation. No compromise.

More importantly, no communication.

The woman who'd left a bitter taste in his mouth for the last eighteen months. Blighting every other relationship he'd tried to have. The woman who'd wrangled over every custody arrangement, telling him he was impinging on her life. Then one day that had been it. Nothing. He'd gone to pick up two-year-old Melody as planned and had turned up at an empty house. No forwarding address. Nothing.

The colleagues at the hospital where Alison had worked said she'd thought about going to America—apparently she'd fallen head over heels in love with some American doctor. But no one knew where. And he'd spent the last few years getting his solicitor to chase false leads halfway around the world. It had taken over his whole world. Every second of every day had revolved around finding his daughter. Until he'd finally cracked and some good friends had sat him down firmly and spoken to him.

It had only been in the last few months, since moving to Scotland, that he'd finally started to feel like himself again. His laid-back manner had returned, and he'd finally started to relax and be comfortable in his own skin again.

While he would still do everything in his power to find his daughter, he had to realise his limitations. He had to accept the fact he hadn't done anything wrong and he still deserved to live a life.

And while the gaggle of nurses and female junior

doctors didn't appeal to him, Cassidy Rae did. She was a different kettle of fish altogether. A fierce, sassy woman who could help him make some sparks fly. A smile crept over his face. Now there was just the small matter of the duty room to break to her. How would she react to that?

Cassidy went back to Mrs Kelly and finished her admission paperwork, rechecked her obs and helped her wash and change into a clean nightdress. By the time she'd finished, Mrs Kelly was clearly out of breath again. Even the slightest exertion seemed to fatigue her.

Cassidy hung the IV antibiotics from the drip stand and connected up the IV. 'These will take half an hour to go through. The doctor has changed the type of antibiotic that you're on so hopefully they'll be more effective than the ones you were taking at home.'

Mrs Kelly nodded. 'Thanks, love. He's a nice one, isn't he?' There was a little pause. 'And he's single. Told me so himself.'

'Who?' Cassidy had started to tidy up around about her, putting away the toilet bag and basin.

'That handsome young doctor. Reminds of that guy on TV. You know, the one from the soap opera.'

Cassidy shook her head. 'I don't watch soap operas. And anyway...' she bundled up the used towels and sheets to put in the laundry trolley '...I'm looking for a handsome Scotsman. Not someone from the other side of the world.'

She walked over to the window. The old hospital building was several storeys high, on the edge of the city. The grey clouds were hanging low this morning and some drizzly rain was falling outside, but she could still see some greenery in the distance.

'Why on earth would anyone want to leave all this behind?' she joked.

Mrs Kelly raised her eyebrows. 'Why indeed?'

Cassidy spent the rest of the morning finding her feet again in the ward. The hospital computer system had been updated, causing her to lose half her patients at the touch of a button. And the automated pharmacy delivery seemed to be on the blink again. Some poor patients' medicines would be lost in a pod stuck in a tube somewhere.

Lucy appeared from the ward next door, clutching a cup of tea, and tapped her on the shoulder. 'How does it feel to be back?'

Cassidy gave her friend a smile. 'It's good.' She picked up the off-duty book. 'I just need to get my head around the rosters again.' Her eyes fell on the sticky notes inside the book and she rolled her eyes. 'Oh, great. Seven members of staff want the same weekend off.'

Lucy laughed. 'That's nothing. One of our girls got married last weekend and I had to rope in two staff from the next ward to cover the night shift. Got time for a tea break?'

She shook her head and pointed down the corridor. 'The consultant's just about to arrive for the ward round.'

Lucy crossed her arms across her chest as she followed Cassidy's gaze to the three registrars at the bottom of the corridor. 'So what do you make of our new docs?'

Cassidy never even lifted her head. 'Funky, Chunky and Hunky?'

Lucy spluttered tea all down the front of her uniform. She looked at her watch. 'Less than two hours and you've got nicknames for them already?'

Cassidy lifted her eyebrows. 'It wasn't hard. Although Luca is drop-dead gorgeous, he's more interested in his own reflection than any of the patients. And Franco has finished off two rolls with sausages and half a box of chocolates in the last half hour.'

'So none of them have caught your eye, then?'

Cassidy turned her head at the tone in her friend's voice. She looked at her suspiciously. 'Why? What are you up to?'

Lucy's gaze was still fixed down the corridor. 'Nothing. I just wondered what you thought of them.' She started to shake her behind as she wiggled past, singing along about single ladies.

Cassidy looked back down the corridor. Her eyes were drawn in one direction. Brad's appearance hadn't improved. He was still wearing his crumpled scrubs and coat. His hair was still untamed and she could see a shadow around his jaw.

But he had spent nearly half an hour talking to Mrs Kelly's daughter and then another half hour talking Mrs Kelly through her treatment for the next few days. Then trying to persuade her that once she was fit and well, she might want to take up her daughter's offer of a visit to Australia.

Most doctors she worked with weren't that interested in their patients' holistic care. Their radar seemed to switch off as soon as they'd made a clinical diagnosis.

There was the sound of raucous laughter at the end of the corridor, and Cassidy looked up to see Brad almost bent double, talking to one of the male physios.

She shook her head and scoured the ward, looking for one of the student nurses. 'Karen?'

The student scuttled over. 'Yes, Sister?'

'Do you know how to assess a patient for the risk of pressure ulcers?'

The student nodded quickly as Cassidy handed her a plastic card with the Waterlow scale on it. 'I want you to do Mrs Kelly's assessment then come back and we'll go over it together.'

Karen nodded and hurried off down the corridor. Cassidy watched for a second. With her paper-thin skin, poor nutrition and lack of circulating oxygen, Mrs Kelly was at real risk of developing pressure sores on her body. For Cassidy, the teaching element was one of the reasons she did this job. She wanted all the students who came through her ward to understand the importance of considering all aspects of their patients' care.

There was a thud beside her. Brad was in the chair next to her, his head leaning on one hand, staring at her again with those blue eyes. He couldn't wipe the smile from his face. 'So, which one am I?'

Cassidy blew a wayward chestnut curl out of her face. 'What are you talking about now?'

He moved closer. 'Hunky, Chunky or Funky? Which one am I?' He put his hands together and pleaded in front of her. 'Please tell me I'm Hunky.'

'How on earth did you…?' Her eyes looked down the corridor to where Pete, the physio, was in conversation with one of the other doctors. He must have overheard her. 'Oh, forget it.'

She wrinkled her nose at him, leaning forward wickedly so nobody could hear. 'No way are you Hunky. That's reserved for the Italian god named Luca.' Her eyes fell on Luca, standing talking to one of her nurses. She whispered in Brad's ear, 'Have you noticed how he keeps checking out his own reflection in those highly polished Italian shoes of his?'

Brad's shoulders started to shake.

She prodded him on the shoulder. 'No. With that excuse of a haircut and that strange earring, you're definitely Funky.' She pointed at his ear. 'What is that anyway?'

Her head came forward, her nose just a few inches off his ear as she studied the twisted bit of gold in his ear. 'Is it a squashed kangaroo? Or a surfboard?'

'Neither.' He grinned at her, turning his head so their noses nearly touched. 'Believe it or not, it used to be a boomerang. My mum bought it for me when I was a teenager and I won a competition.' He touched it with his finger. 'It's a little bent out of shape now.'

Her face was serious and he could smell her perfume—or her shampoo. She smelled of strawberries. A summer smell, even though it was the middle of winter in Glasgow. He was almost tempted to reach out and touch her chestnut curls, resting just above her collarbone. But she was staring at him with those big chocolate-brown eyes. And he didn't want to move.

If this was the Dragon Lady of the medical receiving unit, he wondered if he could be her St George and try to tame her. No. That was the English patron saint and he was in Scotland. He'd learned quickly not to muddle things up around here. The Scots he'd met were wildly patriotic.

Her face broke into a smile again. Interesting. She hadn't pulled back, even though they were just inches from each other. She didn't seem intimidated by his closeness. In any other circumstances he could have leaned forward and given her a kiss. A perfect example of the sort of distraction he needed.

'Come to think of it, though...' She glanced up and down his crumpled clothes. How could she ever have thought he reminded her of Bobby? Bobby wouldn't have been seen dead in crumpled clothes. He'd always been immaculate—Brad was an entirely different kettle of fish. 'If you keep coming into my ward dressed like that, I'll have to change your name from Funky to Skunky.'

Brad automatically sat backwards in his chair, lowering his chin and sniffing. 'Why, do I smell? I was on call last night and I haven't been in the shower yet.' He started to pull at his scrub top.

She loved it. The expression of worry on his face. The way she could so easily wind him up. And the fact he had a good demeanour with the patients and staff. This guy might even be a little fun to have around. Even if he was from the other side of the world.

She shook her head. 'Stop panicking, Brad. You don't smell.' She rested her head on her hands for a second, fixing him with her eyes. Mornings on the medical receiving unit were always chaotic. Patients to be moved to other wards, new admissions and usually a huge battery of tests to be arranged. Sometimes it was nice just to take a few seconds of calm, before chaos erupted all around you.

He reached over and touched her hand, resting on top of the off-duty book. The invisible electric jolt that shot up her arm was instantaneous.

'I could help you with those. The last place I worked in Australia had a computer system for duty rosters.

You just put in the names, your shift patterns and the requests. It worked like a charm.'

Her eyes hadn't left where his hand was still touching hers. It was definitely lingering there. She'd just met this guy.

'You're going to be a pest, aren't you?' Her voice was low. For some reason she couldn't stop staring at him. It didn't help that he was easy on the eye. And that scraggy hair was kind of growing on her.

He leaned forward again. 'Is that going to be a problem?' His eyes were saying a thousand different words from his mouth. Something was in the air between them. She could practically feel the air around her crackle. This was ridiculous. She felt like a swooning teenager.

'My gran had a name for people like you.'

He moved even closer. 'And what was that?' He tilted his head to one side. 'Handsome? Clever? Smart?'

She shook her head and stood up, straightening her tunic. 'Oh, no. It was much more fitting. My gran would have called you a "wee scunner".'

His brow wrinkled. 'What on earth does that mean?'

'Just like I told you. A nuisance. A pest. But it's a much more accurate description.' She headed towards the duty room, with the off-duty book in her hand. She had to get away from him. Her brain had taken leave of her senses. She should have taken Lucy up on that offer of tea.

Brad caught her elbow. 'Actually, Cassidy, about your duty room...'

He stopped as she pushed the door open and automatically stepped inside, her foot catching on something.

'Wh-h-a-a-t?'

CHAPTER TWO

CASSIDY stared up at the white ceiling of her duty room, the wind knocked clean out of her. Something was sticking into her ribcage and she squirmed, causing an array of perilously perched cardboard boxes to topple over her head. She squealed again, batting her hands in front of her face.

A strong pair of arms grabbed her wrists and yanked her upwards, standing her on the only visible bit of carpet in the room—right at the doorway.

Brad was squirming. 'Sorry about that, Cassidy. I was trying to warn you but...'

He stopped in mid-sentence. She looked mad. She looked *really* mad. Her chestnut curls were in complete disarray, falling over her face and hiding her angry eyes. 'What is all this rubbish?' she snapped.

Brad cleared his throat. 'Well, actually, it's not "rubbish", as you put it. It's mine.' He bent over and started pushing some files back into an overturned box. They were the last thing he wanted anyone to see.

Her face was growing redder by the second. She looked down at her empty hand—obviously wondering where the off-duty book she'd been holding had got to. She bent forward to look among the upturned boxes then straightened up, shaking her head in disgust.

She planted her hands on her hips. 'You'd better have a good explanation for this. No wonder you were giving me the treatment.'

'What treatment?'

She waved her hand in dismissal. 'You know. The smiles. The whispers. The big blue eyes.' She looked at him mockingly. 'You must take me for a right sap.'

All of a sudden Brad understood the Dragon Lady label. When she was mad, she was *mad*. Heaven help the doctor who messed up on her watch.

He leaned against the doorjamb. 'I wasn't giving you the *treatment*, as you put it, Cassidy. I was trying to connect with the sister of the ward I work in. We're going to have to work closely together, and I'd like it if we were friends.'

Her face softened ever so slightly. She looked at the towering piles of boxes obliterating her duty room. 'And all this?'

He shot her a smile. 'Yes, well, there's a story about all that.'

She ran her fingers through her hair, obviously attempting to re-tame it. He almost wished he could do it for her. 'Please don't tell me you've moved in.'

He laughed. 'No. It's not that desperate. I got caught short last night and was flung out of my flat, so I had to bring all my stuff here rather than leave it all sitting in the street.'

She narrowed her eyes. 'What do you mean, you got caught short? That sounds suspiciously like you were having a party at five in the morning and the landlord threw you out.'

Brad nodded slowly. 'Let's just say I broke one of the rules of my tenancy.'

'Which one?'

'Now, that would be telling.' He pulled a set of keys from his pocket with a brown tag attached. 'But help is at hand. I've got a new flat I can move into tonight—if I can find it.'

'What do you mean—if you can find it?' Cassidy bent over and read the squiggly writing on the tag.

Brad shrugged his shoulders. 'Dowangate Lane. I'm not entirely sure where it is. One of the porters put me onto it at short notice. I needed somewhere that was furnished and was available at short notice. He says its only five minutes away from here, but I don't recognise the street name.'

Cassidy gave him a suspicious look. 'I don't suppose anyone told you that I live near there.'

'Really? No, I'd no idea. Can you give me some directions?'

Cassidy sighed. 'Sure. Go out the front of the hospital, take a left, walk a few hundred yards down the road, take a right, go halfway down the street and go down the nearby close. Dowangate Lane runs diagonally off it. But the street name fell off years ago.'

Cassidy had a far-away look in her eyes and was gesturing with her arms. Her voice got quicker and quicker as she spoke, her Scottish accent getting thicker by the second.

'I have no idea what you just said.'

Cassidy stared at him—hard. 'It would probably be easier if I just showed you.'

'Really? Would you?'

'If it means you'll get all this rubbish out of my duty room, it will be worth it.'

'Gee, thanks.'

'Do you want my help or not?'

He bent forward and caught her gesturing arms. 'I would love your help, Cassidy Rae. How does six o'clock sound?' There it was again—that strawberry scent from her hair. That could become addictive.

She stopped talking. He could feel the little goose-bumps on her bare arms. Was she cold? Or was it something else?

Whatever it was, he was feeling it, too. Not some wild, throw-her-against-the-wall attraction, although he wouldn't mind doing that. It was weird. Some kind of connection.

Maybe he wasn't the only person looking for a Christmastime distraction.

She was staring at him with those big brown eyes again. Only a few seconds must have passed but it felt like minutes.

He could almost hear her thought processes. As if she was wondering what was happening between them, too.

'Six o'clock will be fine,' she said finally, as she lowered her eyes and brushed past him.

Brad hung his white coat up behind the door and pulled his shirt over his head. He paused midway. What was he going to do with it?

Cass stuck her head around the door. 'Are you ready yet?' Her eyes caught the tanned, taut abdomen and the words stuck in her throat. She felt the colour rush into her cheeks. 'Oops, sorry.' She pulled back from the door.

All of a sudden she felt like a teenager again. And trust him to have a set of to-die-for abs. Typical. There was no way she was ever taking her clothes off in front of Mr Ripped Body.

Where had that come from? Why on earth would she ever take her clothes off in front of him? That was it. She was clearly losing her marbles.

Almost automatically, she sucked in her stomach and looked downwards. Her pink jumper hid a multitude of sins, so why on earth was she bothering?

Brad's hand rested on the edge of the door as he stuck his head back round. 'Don't be so silly, Cassidy. You're a nurse. It's not like you haven't seen it all before. Come back in. I'll be ready in a second.'

She swallowed the huge lump at the back of her throat. His shoulder was still bare. He was obviously used to stripping off in front of women and was completely uninhibited.

So why did that thought rankle her?

She took a deep breath and stepped back into the room, trying to avert her eyes without being obvious. The last thing she wanted was for him to think she was embarrassed. With an attitude like his, she'd never live it down.

He was rummaging in a black holdall. Now she could see the muscles across his back. No love handles for him. He yanked a pale blue T-shirt from the bag and pulled it over his head, turning round and tugging it down over his washboard stomach.

'Ready. Can we go?'

Cassidy had a strange expression on her face. Brad automatically looked down. Did he have a huge ketchup stain on his T-shirt? Not that he could see. Her cheeks were slightly flushed, matching the soft pink jumper she was wearing. A jumper that hugged the shape of her breasts very nicely. Pink was a good colour on her. It brought out the warm tones in her face and hair that had sometimes been lost in the navy-blue tunic she'd been wearing earlier. Her hair was pulled back from her face in a short ponytail, with a few wayward curls escaping. She was obviously serious about helping him move. No fancy coats and stiletto heels for her. Which was just as well as there were around fifty boxes to lug over to his new flat.

'Will you manage to carry some of these boxes down to my car?'

'I'll do better than that.' She opened the door to reveal one of the porters' trolleys for transporting boxes of equipment around the hospital. The huge metal cage could probably take half of his boxes in one run.

'Genius. You might be even more useful than I thought.'

'See, I'm not just a pretty face,' she shot back, to his cheeky remark. 'You do realise this is going to cost you, don't you?' She pulled the cage towards the duty room, letting him stand in the doorway and toss out boxes that she piled up methodically.

'How much?' As he tossed one of the boxes, the cardboard flaps sprang open, spilling his boxers and socks all over the floor.

Cassidy couldn't resist. The colours of every imagination caught her eyes and she lifted up a pair with Elmo from *Sesame Street* emblazoned on the front. 'Yours?' she asked, allowing them to dangle from one finger.

He grabbed them. 'Stop it.' He started ramming them

back into the box, before raising his eyebrows at her. 'I'll decide when you get to see my underwear.'

When. Not if. The thought catapulted through her brain as she tried to keep her mind on the job at hand. The boxes weren't neatly packed or taped shut. And the way he kept throwing them at her was ruining her precision stacking in the metal cage.

'Slow down,' she muttered. 'The more you irritate me, the more my price goes up. You're currently hovering around a large pizza or a sweet-and-sour chicken. Keep going like this and you'll owe me a beer as well.'

The cheeky grin appeared at her shoulder in an instant. 'You think I won't buy you a beer?' He stared at the neatly stacked boxes. 'Uh-oh. I sense a little obsessive behaviour. One of your staff warned me about wrecking the neatly packed boxes of gloves in the treatment room. I can see why.'

'Nothing wrong with being neat and tidy.' Cassidy straightened the last box. 'Okay, I think that's enough for now. We can take the rest downstairs on the second trip.'

Something flashed in front of his eyes. Something wicked. 'You think so?'

He waited while she nodded, then as quick as a flash he shoved her in the cage, clicking the door behind her and pushing the cage down the corridor.

Cassidy let out a squeal. For the second time today she was surrounded by piles of toppling boxes. 'Let me out!' She got to her knees in the cage as he stopped in front of the lifts and pushed the 'down' button.

His shoulders were shaking with laughter as he pulled a key from his pocket for the 'Supplies Only' lift and opened the door. 'What can I say? You bring out the wicked side in me. I couldn't resist wrecking your neat display.'

He pulled the cage into the lift and sprang the lock free, holding out his hands to steady her step. The lift started with a judder, and as she was in midstep—it sent her straight into his arms. 'Ow-w!'

The lift was small. Even smaller with the large storage cage and two people crammed inside. And as Brad had pressed the ground-floor button as he'd pulled the cage inside, they were now trapped at the back of the lift together.

She was pressed against him. He could feel the ample swell of her breasts against his chest, her soft pink jumper tickling his skin. His hands had fallen naturally to her waist, one finger touching a little bit of soft flesh. Had she noticed?

Her curls were under his nose, but there was no way he was moving his hands to scratch the itch. She lifted her head, capturing him with her big brown eyes again.

This was crazy. This was madness.

This was someone he'd just met today. It didn't matter that he felt a pull towards her. It didn't matter that she'd offered to help him. It didn't matter that for some strange reason he liked to be close to her. It didn't matter that his eyes were currently fixed on her plump lips. He knew nothing about her.

Her reputation had preceded her. According to her colleagues she was a great nurse and a huge advocate for her patients, but her attention to detail and rulebook for the ward had become notorious.

More importantly, she knew nothing about him. She had no idea about his history, his family, his little girl out there in the world somewhere. She had no idea how the whole thing had come close to breaking him. And for some reason he didn't want to tell her.

He wanted this to be separate. A flirtation. A distraction. Something playful. With no consequences. Even if it only lasted a few weeks.

At least that would get him past Christmas.

'You can let me go now.' Her voice was quiet, her hands resting on his upper arms sending warm waves through his bare skin.

But for a second they just stood there. Unmoving.

The door pinged open and they turned their heads. His hands fell from her waist. She turned and automatically pushed the cage through the lift doors, and he fell into step next to her.

The tone and mood were broken.

'Are you sure you don't mind helping me with this? You could always just draw me a map.'

She stuck her elbow in his ribs. 'Stop trying to get out of buying me dinner. What number did you say the flat was? If I find out I've got to carry all these boxes up four flights of stairs I *won't* be happy.'

They crossed the car park and reached his car. She blinked. A Mini. For a guy that was over six feet tall.

'This is your car?'

'Do you like it?' He opened the front passenger door, moved the seat forward and started throwing boxes in the back. 'It's bigger than you think.'

'Why on earth didn't you just leave some stuff in the car?'

Brad shrugged. 'Luca borrowed my car last night after he helped me move my stuff. I think he had a date.' And some of his boxes were far too personal to be left unguarded in a car.

Cassidy shook her head and opened the boot, trying to cram as many of the boxes in there as possible. She was left with two of the larger ones still sitting on the ground.

She watched as he put the passenger seat back into place and shrugged her shoulders. 'I can just put these two on my lap. It's only a five-minute drive. It'll be fine.'

Brad pulled a face. 'You might need to put something else on your lap instead.'

She felt her stomach turn over. What now?

'Why do I get the distinct impression that nothing is straightforward with you?'

He grabbed her hand and pulled her towards the porter's lodge at the hospital gate, leaving the two boxes next to his unlocked car. 'Come on.'

'Where on earth are we going?'

'I've got something else to pick up.'

He pushed open the door to the lodge. Usually used for deliveries and collections, occasionally used by the porters who were trying to duck out of sight for five minutes, it was an old-fashioned solid stone building. The front door squeaked loudly. 'Frank? Are you there?'

Frank Wallace appeared. All twenty-five stone of him, carrying a pile of white-and-black fur in his hands. 'There you are, Dr Donovan. He's been as good as gold. Not a bit of bother. Bring him back any time.'

Frank handed over the bundle of black and white, and it took a few seconds for Cassidy to realise the shaggy bundle was a dog with a bright red collar and lead.

Brad bent down and placed the dog on the floor at their feet. It seemed to spring to life, the head coming up sharply and a little tail wagging furiously. Bright black eyes and a pink panting tongue.

'Cassidy, meet Bert. *This* is the reason I lost my tenancy.'

Cassidy watched in amazement. Bert seemed delighted to see him, jumping his paws up onto Brad's shoulders and licking at his hands furiously. His gruff little barks reverberated around the stone cottage.

He was a scruffy little mutt—with no obvious lineage or pedigree. A mongrel, by the look of him.

'Why on earth would you have a dog?' she asked incredulously. 'You live in Australia. You can't possibly have brought him with you.' Dogs she could deal with. It was cats that caused her allergies. She'd often thought about getting a pet for company—a friendly face to come home to. But long shifts weren't conducive to having a pet. She knelt on the floor next to Brad, holding her hand out cautiously while Bert took a few seconds to sniff her, before licking her with the same enthusiasm he'd shown Brad.

'I found him. A few weeks ago, in the street outside my flat. He looked emaciated and was crouched in a doorway. There was no way I could leave him alone.' *And to be honest, I needed him as much as he needed me.* Brad let the scruffy dog lick his hands. Melody would love this little dog.

'So what did you do?'

'I took him to the emergency vet, who checked him over, gave me some instructions, then I took him home.'

'And *this* is why you got flung out your flat?' There was an instant feeling of relief. He hadn't been thrown out for non-payment of rent, wild parties or dubious women. He'd been thrown out because of a dog. She glanced at his face as he continued to talk to Bert. The mutual admiration was obvious.

The rat. He must have known that a dog would have scored him brownie points. No wonder he'd kept it quiet earlier. She would have taken him for a soft touch.

She started to laugh. 'Bert? You called your dog Bert?'

He shrugged his shoulders. 'What's wrong with Bert? It's a perfectly good name.'

'What's wrong with Rocky or Buster or Duke?'

He waved his hand at her. 'Look at him. Does he look like Rocky, Buster or Duke?'

He waited a few seconds, and Bert obligingly tipped his head to one side, as if he enjoyed the admiration.

Brad was decisive. 'No way. He's a Bert. No doubt about it.'

Cassidy couldn't stop the laugh that had built up in her chest. Bert wasn't a big dog and his white hair with black patches had definitely seen better days. But his soft eyes and panting tongue were cute. And Brad was right. He looked like a Bert—it suited him. She bent down and started rubbing his ears.

'See—you like him. Everyone should. He's a good dog. Not been a bit of bother since I found him.'

'So how come you got flung out the flat? And what about the new one? I take it they're happy for you to have a dog?'

Brad pulled a face. 'One of my neighbours reported me for having a dog. And the landlord was swift and ruthless, even though you honestly wouldn't have known he was there. And it was Frank, the porter, who put me onto the new flat. So I'm sorted. They're happy for me to have a dog.'

Cassidy held out her arms to pick up the dog. 'I take it this is what I'm supposed to have on my lap in the car?'

Brad nodded. 'Thank goodness you like dogs. This could have all turned ugly.'

She shook her head, still rubbing Bert's ears. 'I'm sure it will be fine. But let's go. It's getting late and I'm starving.'

They headed back to the car and drove down the road past Glasgow University and into the west end of Glasgow. Lots of the younger hospital staff stayed in the flats around here. It wasn't really designed for kids and families, but for younger folks it was perfect, with the shops, restaurants and nightlife right at their fingertips.

'So what do you like best about staying around here?'

Cassidy glanced around about her as they drove along Byres Road. She pointed to the top of the road. 'If you go up there onto Western Road and cross the road, you get to Glasgow's Botanic Gardens. Peace, perfect peace.'

Brad looked at her in surprise. 'Really? That's a bit unusual for someone your age.'

'Why would you think that? Is it only pensioners and kids that can visit?' She gestured her thumb over her shoulder. 'Or if you go back that way, my other favourite is the Kelvingrove Art Gallery and Museum— as long as the school trips aren't there! There's even a little secret church just around the corner with an ancient cemetery—perfect for quiet book reading in the summer. Gorgeous at Christmastime.'

Brad stared at her. 'You're a dark horse, aren't you? I never figured you for a museum type.'

She shrugged her shoulders. 'It's the peace and quiet

really. The ward can be pretty hectic. Some days when I come out I'm just looking for somewhere to chill. I can be just as happy curled up with a good book or in the dark at the cinema.'

'You go to the cinema alone?'

She nodded. 'All the time. I love sci-fi. My friends all love romcoms. So I do some with my friends and some on my own.' She pointed her arm in front of them. 'Turn left here, then turn right and slow down.'

The car pulled to a halt at the side of the road next to some bollards. Cassidy looked downwards. Bert had fallen asleep in her lap. 'Looks like it's been a big day for the little guy.'

Brad jumped out of and around the car and opened the passenger door. He picked up the sleeping dog. 'Let's go up and have a look at the flat before I start to unpack the boxes.'

'You haven't seen it yet?'

He shook his head. 'How could I? I was on call last night and just had to take whatever I could get. I told you I'd no idea where this place was.'

Cassidy smiled. 'So you did. Silly me. Now, give me the key and we'll see what you've got.'

They climbed up the stairs in the old-style tenement building, onto the first floor, where number five was in front of them. Cassidy looked around. 'Well, this is better than some flats I've seen around here.' She ran her hand along the wall. 'The walls have been painted, the floors are clean, and...' she pointed to the door across the hallway '...your neighbour has some plants outside his flat. This place must be okay.'

She turned the key in the lock and pushed open the

door. Silently praying that she wouldn't be hit with the smell of cats, mould or dead bodies.

Brad flicked the light switch next to the door and stepped inside. He was trying to stop his gut from twisting. Getting a flat that accepted dogs at short notice—and five minutes away from the hospital—seemed almost too good to be true. There had to be a catch somewhere.

The catch was obvious. Cassidy burst into fits of laughter.

'No way! It's like stepping back in time. Have we just transported into the 1960s?' She turned to face him. 'That happened once in an old *Star Trek* episode. I think we're just reliving it.'

Brad was frozen. The wallpaper could set off a whole array of seizures. He couldn't even make out the individual colours, the purples and oranges all seemed to merge into one. As for the shag-pile brown carpet...

Cassidy was having the time of her life. She dashed through one of the open doors and let out a shriek. 'Avacado! It's avocado. You have an avocado bathroom! Does that colour even exist any more?' Seconds later he heard the sounds of running water before she appeared again, tears flowing down her cheeks. 'I love this place. You have to have a 1960s-style party.'

She ducked into another room then swept past him into the kitchen, while Brad tried to keep his breathing under control. Could he really live in this?

He set down the dog basket on the floor and placed the sleeping Bert inside. His quiet, peaceful dog would probably turn into a possessed, rabid monster in this place.

He sagged down onto the purple sofa that clashed

hideously with the brown shag-pile carpet. No wonder this place had been available at a moment's notice.

He could hear banging and clattering from next door—Cassidy had obviously found the kitchen. He cringed. What colour was avocado anyway? He was too scared to look.

Cassidy reappeared, one of her hands dripping wet, both perched at her waist. 'Kitchen's not too bad.' She swept her eyes around the room again, the smile automatically reappearing on her face. She walked over and sat down on the sofa next to Brad, giving his knee a friendly tap. 'Well, it has to be said, this place is spotlessly clean. And the shower's working.' She lifted her nose and sniffed the air. 'And it smells as if the carpets have just been cleaned. See—it's not so bad.'

Not so bad. She had to be joking.

And she was. He could see her shoulders start to shake again. She lifted her hands to cover her face, obviously trying to block out the laughter. His stomach fell even further.

'What is it?'

He could tell she was trying not to meet his gaze. 'Go on. What else have you discovered in this psychedelic temple of doom?' He threw up his hands.

Cassidy stood up and grabbed his hand, pulling him towards her. For a second he was confused. What was she doing? Sure, this had crossed his mind, but what did she have in mind?

She pulled him towards the other room he hadn't looked at yet—the bedroom. Surely not? He felt a rush of blood to the head and rush of something else to the groin. This couldn't be happening.

She pushed open the door to the room, turning and

giving him another smile. But the glint in her eyes was something else entirely. This was no moment of seduction. This was comedy, through and through.

He stepped inside the bedroom.

Pink. Everywhere and everything. Pink.

Rose-covered walls. A shiny, *satin* bedspread. Pink lampshades giving off a strange rose-coloured hue around the room. Pink carpet. Dark teak furniture and dressing table. He almost expected to see an eighty-year-old woman perched under the covers, staring at them.

Cassidy's laughter was building by the second. She couldn't contain herself. She spun round, her hands on his chest. 'Well, what do you think? How's this for a playboy palace?'

His reaction was instantaneous. He grabbed her around the waist and pulled her with him, toppling onto the bed, the satin bedspread sliding them along. He couldn't help it. It was too much for him and for the next few minutes they laughed so hard his belly was aching.

They lay there for a few seconds after the laughter finally subsided. Brad's eyes were fixed on the ceiling, staring at yet another rose-coloured light shade.

He turned his head to face Cassidy's. 'So, tell me truthfully. Do you think this flat will affect my pulling power?'

Cassidy straightened her face, the laughter still apparent in her eyes. She wondered how to answer the question. Something squeezed deep inside her. She didn't want Brad to have pulling power. She didn't want Brad to even consider pulling. What on earth was wrong with her? She'd only met this guy today. Her naughty streak came out. 'Put it this way. This is the first time

I've lain on a bed with a man, panting like this, and still been fully dressed.'

His eyebrows arched and he flipped round onto his side to face her. 'Well, Sister Rae, that almost sounds like a challenge. And I like a challenge.'

Cassidy attempted to change position, the satin bed-spread confounding her and causing her to slide to the floor with a heavy thud.

Brad stuck his head over the edge of the bed. 'Cass, are you okay?'

She held up her hand towards him and shook her head. 'Just feed me.'

Fifty boxes later and another trip back to the hospi-tal, they both sagged on the sofa. Brad pulled a bunch of take-away menus from a plastic bag. 'I'd take you out for dinner but I don't think either of us could face sitting across a table right now.'

Cassidy nodded. She flicked through the menus, picking up her favourite. 'This pizza place is just around the corner and it's great. They don't take long to deliver. Will we go for this?'

'What's your favourite?'

'Thin crust. Hawaiian.'

'Pineapple—on a pizza? Sacrilege. Woman, what's wrong with you?'

She rolled her eyes. 'Don't tell me—you're a meat-feast, thick-crust man?'

He sat back, looking surprised. 'How did you know?'

'Because you're the same as ninety per cent of the other males on the planet. Let's just order two.' She picked up the phone, giving it a second glance. 'Wow, my parents had one of these in the seventies.' She listened for a dial tone. 'Never mind, it works.' She dialled the number and placed the order.

'So, what do you think of your new home? Will you still be talking to Frank in the morning?'

Brad sighed. 'I think I should be grateful, no matter how bad the décor is. I needed a furnished flat close by—it's not like I had any furniture to bring with me—so this will be fine.' He took another look around. 'You're right—it's clean. That's the most important thing.' Then he pointed to Bert in the corner. 'And if he's happy, I'm happy.' The wicked glint appeared in his eyes again. 'I can always buy a new bedspread—one that keeps the ladies on, instead of sliding them off.'

There it was again. That little twisting feeling in her gut whenever he cracked a joke about other women. For the first time in a lifetime she was feeling cave-woman primal urges. She wanted to shout, *Don't you dare!* But that would only reveal her to be a mad, crazy person, instead of the consummate professional she wanted him to think she was.

He rummaged around in a plastic bag at his feet. 'I'm afraid I can't offer you any fancy wine to drink. I've got orange or blackcurrant cordial.' He pulled the bottles from the bag. 'And I've got glasses in one of those boxes over there.'

Cassidy reached over and opened the box, grabbing two glasses and setting them on the table. 'So what's your story? What are you doing in Scotland?' *And why hasn't some woman snapped you up already?*

'You mean, what's a nice guy like me doing in a place like this?' He gestured at the psychedelic walls.

She shrugged. 'I just wondered why you'd left Australia. Do you have family there? A girlfriend?'

She couldn't help it. She really, really wanted to know. She'd wanted to ask if he had a wife or children, but that had seemed a bit too forward. He wasn't wearing a wedding ring, and he hadn't mentioned any significant other. And he'd been flirting with her. Definitely flirting with her. And for the first time in ages she felt like responding.

'I fancied a change. It seemed like a good opportunity to expand my experience. Scottish winters are notorious for medical admissions, particularly around old mining communities.' He paused for a second and then added, 'And, no, there's no wife.' He prayed she hadn't noticed the hesitation. He couldn't say the words 'no children'. He wouldn't lie about his daughter. But he just didn't want to go there right now. Not with someone he barely knew.

Cassidy nodded, sending silent prayers upwards for his last words, but fixed her expression, 'There's around two and half thousand extra deaths every winter. They can't directly link them to the cold. Only a few are from hypothermia, most are from pneumonia, heart disease or stroke. And last year was the worst. They estimated nine pensioners died every hour related to the effects of the cold. Fuel payments are through the roof right now. People just can't afford to heat their homes. Some of the cases we had last year broke my heart.'

Brad was watching her carefully. Her eyes were looking off into the distance—as if she didn't want him to notice the sheen across her eyes when she spoke. He wondered if she knew how she looked. Her soft curls shining in the dim flat light, most of them escaping from the ponytail band at the nape of her neck. It was clear this was a subject close to her heart—she knew her stuff, but as a sister on a medical receiving unit he would have expected her to.

What he hadn't expected was to see the compassion in her eyes. Her reputation was as an excellent clinician, with high standards and a strict rulebook for the staff on her ward. But this was a whole other side to her. A side he happened to like. A side he wanted to know more about.

'So, what's the story with you, then?'

She narrowed her eyes, as if startled he'd turned the question round on her. 'What do you mean?'

'What age are you, Cassidy? Twenty-seven? Twenty-eight?' He pointed to her left hand. 'Where's your other half? Here you are, on a Monday night at...' he looked at his watch '...nearly nine o'clock, helping an orphaned colleague move into his new flat. Don't you have someone to go to home to?'

Cassidy shifted uncomfortably. She didn't like being put on the spot. She didn't like the fact that in a few moments he'd stripped her bare. Nearly thirty, single and no one to go home to. Hardly an ad for Mrs Wonderful.

'I'm twenty-nine, and I was engaged a few years ago, but we split up and I'm happy on my own.' It sounded so simple when she put it like that. Leaving out the part about her not wanting to get out of bed for a month after Bobby had left. Or drinking herself into oblivion the month after that.

His eyebrows rose, his attention obviously grabbed. 'So, who was he?'

'My fiancé? He was a Spanish registrar I worked with.'

'Did you break up with him?'

The million-dollar question. The one that made you

look sad and pathetic if you said no. Had she broken up with him? Or had Bobby just told her he was returning to Spain, with no real thought to how she would feel about it? And no real distress when she'd told him she wouldn't go with him.

Looking back she wondered if he'd always known she wouldn't go. And if being with her in Scotland had just been convenient for him—a distraction even.

She took a deep breath. 'What's with the questions, nosy parker? He wanted to go home to Spain. I wanted to stay in Scotland. End of story. We broke up. He's back working in Madrid now.' She made it sound so simple. She didn't tell him how much she hated coming home to an empty house and having nobody to share her day with. She didn't say how whenever she set her single place at the table she felt a little sad. She didn't tell him how much she hated buying convenience meals for one.

'Bet he's sorry he didn't stay.'

Cassidy's face broke into a rueful smile and she shook her head. 'Oh, I don't think so. He went home, had a whirlwind romance and a few months later married that year's Miss Spain. They've got a little son now.'

She didn't want to reveal how hurt she'd been by her rapid replacement.

He moved a little closer to her. 'Didn't that make you mad? He left and played happy families with someone else?'

Cassidy shook her head determinedly. She'd had a long time to think about all this. 'No. Not really. I could have been but we obviously weren't right for each other. When we got engaged he said he would stay in Scotland, but over time he changed his mind. His heart was in Spain.'

SCARLET WILSON 57

Her eyes fell downwards for a few seconds as she drew in a sharp breath, 'And I'd made it clear I didn't want to move away. I'm a Scottish girl through and through. I don't want to move.'

Brad placed his hand on her shoulder. 'But that seems a bit off. Spain's only a few hours away on a plane. What's the big deal?'

Cassidy looked cross. He made it all sound so simple. 'I like it here. I like it where I live. I don't want to move to...' she lifted her fingers in the air '...*sunnier climes*. I want to stay here...' she pointed her finger to the floor '...in Scotland, the country that I love. And I have priorities here—responsibilities—that I couldn't take care of in another country.' She folded her arms across her chest.

'So I made myself a rule. My next other half will be a big, handsome fellow Scot. Someone who wants to stay where I do. Not someone from the other side of the planet.'

The words hung between them. Almost as if she was drawing a line in the sand. Brad paused for a second, trying to stop himself from saying what he really thought. Should he say straight away that he would never stay in Scotland either? That he wanted his life to be wherever his daughter was—and he was prepared to up sticks and go at a moment's notice?

No. He couldn't. That would instantly kill this flirtation stone dead. And that's all this would ever be—a mild flirtation. Why on earth would what she'd just said bother him? He was merely looking for a distraction—nothing more. Something to take his mind off another Christmas without his daughter.

'Just because someone is from Scotland it doesn't

mean they'll want to stay here. There have been lots of famous Scots explorers—David Livingstone, for example.' He moved forward, leaning in next to her. 'Anyway, that's a pretty big statement, Cassidy. You're ruling out ninety-nine per cent of the population of the world in your search for Mr Right. Hardly seems fair to the rest of us.' He shot her a cheeky grin. 'Some people might even call that a bit of prejudice.'

'Yeah, well, at least if I think about it this way, it saves any problems later on. I don't want to meet someone, hook up with them and fall in love, only to have my heart broken when they tell me their life's on the other side of the planet from me.' *Been there. Done that.* 'Why set myself up for a fall like that?'

'Why indeed?' He'd moved right next to her, his blue eyes fixed on hers. She was right. Cassidy wanted to stay in Scotland. Brad wanted to go wherever in the world his little girl was. A little girl he hadn't even told her about. Anything between them would be an absolute disaster. But somehow he couldn't stop the words forming on his lips.

'But what happens if your heart rules your head?' Because try as he may to think of her as a distraction, the attraction between them was real. And it had been a long time since he'd felt like this.

She could see every tiny line on his face from hours in the Australian sun, every laughter line around the corners of his eyes. His hand was still resting on her arm, and it was making her tingle. Everything about this was wrong.

She'd just spelled out all the reasons why this was so wrong. He was from Australia. The other side of the planet. He was the worst possible option for her. So why, in the space of a day, was he already getting under her skin? Why did she want to lean forward towards his lips? Why did she want to feel the muscles of his chest under the palms of her hands? He was so close right now she could feel his warm breath on her neck. It was sending shivers down her spine.

She didn't want this to be happening. She didn't want to be attracted to a man there was no future with. So why couldn't she stop this? Why couldn't she just pull away?

Ding-dong.

Both jumped backwards, startled by the noise of the bell ringing loudly. Even Bert awoke from his slumber and started barking.

Cassidy was still fixed by his eyes, the shiver continuing down her spine. A feeling of awakening. 'Pizza,' she whispered. 'It must be the pizza.'

'Saved by the bell,' murmured Brad as he stood up to answer the door. At the last second he turned back to her. A tiny little part of him was feeling guilty— guilty about the attraction between them, guilty about not mentioning his daughter, and completely irritated by her disregard for most of the men in the world.

Her mobile sounded, and Cassidy fumbled in her bag. 'Excuse me,' she murmured, glancing at the number on the screen.

She stepped outside as he was paying for the pizzas and pressed the phone to her ear. 'Hi, it's Cassidy Rae. Is something wrong with my grandmother?'

'Hi, Cassidy. It's Staff Nurse Hughes here. Sorry to call, but your gran's really agitated tonight.'

Cassidy sighed. 'What do you need me to do?' This was happening more and more. Her good-natured, placid gran was being taken over by Alzheimer's disease, at times becoming confused and agitated, leading to outbursts of aggression that were totally at odds with her normal nature. The one thing that seemed to calm her down was hearing Cassidy's voice—whether over the phone or in person.

'Can you talk to her for a few minutes? I'll hold the phone next to her.

'Of course I will.' She took a deep breath. 'Hi, Gran, it's Cassidy. How are you feeling?' Her words didn't matter. It was the sound and tone of her voice that was important. So she kept talking, telling her gran about her day and her plans for the week.

And leaving out the thoughts about the new doctor that were currently dancing around in her brain.

Brad sat waiting patiently. What was she doing? Who was she talking to outside in that low, calm voice? And why couldn't she have taken the call in here?

More importantly, what was *he* doing?

Getting involved with someone he worked with hadn't worked out too great for him the last time. He'd had a few casual dates in the last year with work colleagues, but nothing serious. He really didn't want to go down that road again.

So what on earth was wrong with him? His attraction to this woman had totally knocked him sideways. Alison had been nothing like this. A few weeks together had proved they weren't compatible. And the pregnancy had taken them both by surprise. And although his thoughts had constantly been with his daughter, this was the first time that a woman had started to invade his mind.

His brain wasn't working properly, but his libido was firing on multiple cylinders. Which one would win the battle?

CHAPTER THREE

11 October

Cassidy's fingers hammered on the keyboard, responding to yet another bureaucratic email.

'What's up, girl?' As if by magic, Brad was leaning across the desk towards her. 'You've got that ugly frown on your face again. That usually spells trouble for the rest of us.'

Cassidy smiled. For the last ten days, every time she'd turned around he'd been at her elbow. His mood was generally laid-back and carefree, though a couple of times she'd thought he was going to steer a conversation toward something more serious. She turned the computer monitor towards him. 'Look at this. According to "customer care" principles, we've got to answer the ward phone on the third ring.'

'Since when did our patients become "customers"?'

'Oh, don't get me started. I just replied, pointing out that patients are our first priority on the medical unit and I won't be leaving a patient's bedside to answer the phone in three rings.'

'Are you still short-staffed?' Brad looked around the

ward, noting the figures on the ward and trying to work out if everyone was there.

Cassidy pointed to the board. 'There were seven staff sick last week, but they should all be back on duty either today or tomorrow.' Her frown reappeared. 'Why, what are you about to tell me?'

Brad walked around to her side of the desk and wheeled her chair towards him. 'I was going to invite you to breakfast. It's Saturday morning, the ward's pretty quiet, so it seemed like a good time.' He pulled a face. 'Plus, those five empty beds you've got are about to be filled. I've got five patients coming into A and E via the GP on-call service who will all need to be admitted.'

Cassidy stood up. 'So what's this, the calm before the storm?'

'Something like that. Come on.' He stuck his elbow out towards her. 'You'll probably not get time for lunch later.'

Cassidy handed over the keys to one of her staff nurses and headed down to the canteen with Brad.

There was something nice about this. The easy way they'd fallen into a friendship. She'd mentioned her front door was jamming and he'd appeared around at her flat to fix it. Then they'd walked to the Botanic Gardens a few times on days off and taken Bert out in the evenings. Even though they were tiptoeing around the edges of friendship, there was still that simmering 'something' underneath.

'I see you actually managed to put some clothes on today.' She ran her eyes up and down his lean frame, taking in his trousers and casual polo shirt. 'I was beginning to wonder if you actually owned any clothes.'

They'd reached the canteen and Brad picked up a tray. 'It's a deliberate ploy. If I live my life in scrubs then the hospital does my laundry for me. And I haven't got my washing machine yet.'

Cassidy nodded. 'Ah...the truth comes out.' She walked over to the hot food and lifted a plate. 'Why didn't you just say? You could have used my washing machine.'

'You'd do my washing for me?'

Cassidy shuddered. 'No. I said you could *use* my washing machine. I didn't say *I* would do it for you. Anyway, that's one of my rules.'

He watched as she selected a roll, put something inside and picked up a sachet of ketchup.

'What do you mean—one of your rules?'

She lifted a mug and pressed the button for tea. 'I have rules. Rules for the ward, rules for life, rules for men and rules for Christmas.'

He raised his eyebrows. 'Okay, now you've intrigued me. Either that, or you're a total crank—which is a distinct possibility.' He picked up his coffee. 'So, I'm interested. I know about the rules for the ward but tell me about these rules for men.'

She handed over her money to the cashier and sat down at a nearby table. 'They're simple. No overseas men.'

'Yeah, yeah. I've heard that one. And I'm not impressed. What else?'

'No washing. No ironing. No picking up after them. I'm not their mother. Do it a few times and they start to expect it. I get annoyed, then I start picturing them as Jabba the Hut, the fat, lazy monster from *Star Wars*, and yadda, yadda, yadda.' She waved her hand in the air.

'I was right. You *are* a crank.' He prodded her roll. 'And what is that? Everyone around here seems to eat it and I've no idea what it is.'

'It's slice.'

'Slice? A slice of what?'

'No. That's what it's called—slice. It's square sausage. A Scottish delicacy.'

'That's not a sausage. That looks nothing like a sausage.'

'Well, it is. Want to try a bit?' She held up her roll towards him.

He shook his head. 'That doesn't look too healthy. Apart from the pizza the first night I met you, you seem to spend your life eating salads or apples. I've never even seen you eat the sweets on the ward.'

'But this is different. This is Saturday morning. This is the bad-girl breakfast.' She had a twinkle in her eye as she said it.

Brad moved closer, his eggs abandoned. 'Should I keep a note of this for future reference?'

There it was again—that weird little hum that seemed to hang in the air between them. Making the rest of the room fall silent and fade away into the background. Making the seconds that they held each other's gaze seem like for ever.

But he kind of liked that. He kind of liked the fact that she didn't seem to be able to pull her gaze away any more than he could. He kind of liked the fact that once he was in the vicinity of Cassidy, his brain didn't seem to be able to focus on anything else. And from right here he could study the different shades of brown in her eyes—some chocolate, some caramel, some that matched her chestnut hair perfectly.

Whoa! Since when had he, Brad Donovan, ever thought about the different shades of colour in a woman's eyes? Not once. Not ever. Until now. Where had his brain found the words 'chocolate', 'caramel' and 'chestnut'?

'Maybe you should.' The words startled him. There it was again, something in the air. The way at times her voice seemed deeper, huskier, as if she was having the same sort of thoughts that he was.

But what did she think about all this? Was he merely a distraction? After all, she didn't want a man from the other side of the world; she wanted a Scotsman. And he clearly wasn't that. So why was she even flirting with him?

But now her eyes were cast downwards, breaking his train of thought. There was a slight flush in her cheeks. Was she embarrassed? Cassidy didn't seem the bashful type. Maybe she was having the same trouble he was— trying to make sense of the thoughts that seemed to appear as soon as they were together.

He didn't like silence between them. It seemed awkward, unnatural for two people who seemed to fit so well together.

He picked up his fork and started eating his eggs. 'So, tell me about the Christmas rules?'

Cassidy sat back in her chair, a huge smile appearing on her face in an instant. Her eyes went up towards the ceiling. 'Ah, Christmas, best time of year. I love it, absolutely love it.' She counted on her fingers. 'There are lots of rules for Christmas. You need to have a proper advent calendar, not the rubbish chocolate kind. You need the old-fashioned kind with little doors that open to pictures of mistletoe and holly, sleighs, presents and reindeer. Then your Christmas tree needs to go up on the first of December.' She pointed her finger at him. 'Not on the twelfth or Christmas Eve, like some people do. You need to get into the spirit of things.'

'Should I be writing all this down?'

'Don't be sarcastic. Then there's the presents. You don't put them under the tree. That's a disaster. You bring them out on Christmas Eve.'

Brad was starting to laugh now. The enthusiasm in her face was brimming over, but she was deadly serious. 'Cassidy, do you still believe in Santa Claus?'

She sighed. 'Don't tell me you're a Christmas Grinch. There's no room for them in my ward.'

The Christmas Grinch. Actually, for the last few years, it would have been the perfect name for him. It was hard to get into the spirit of Christmas when you didn't know where your little girl was. Whether she was safe. Whether she was well. Whether she was happy. Cassidy did look literally like a child at Christmas. This was obviously her thing.

He tried to push the other thoughts from his mind. He was trying to be positive. This year he wasn't going to fall into the black hole he'd found himself in last year, dragged down by the parts of his life he couldn't control.

'Any other Christmas rules you need to tell me?'

'Well, there's all the fun stuff. Like trying to spot the first Christmas tree someone puts up in their window. I usually like to try and count them as I walk home from work every day. Then trying to guess who has got your name for the secret Santa at work. And the shops—I love the shops at Christmas. The big department store on Buchanan Street has the most gorgeous tree and decorations. They'll be up in a few weeks. You have to go and see them. And there will be ice skating in George Square. We have to go to that!'

'But it's still only October. We haven't had Hallowe'en yet.' Brad took a deep breath. He had an odd feeling in the pit of his stomach.

'We celebrate Christmas in Australia, too, you know. It might be a little different, but it's every bit as good as it sounds here. Where I live in Perth, everyone has Christmas lights on their houses. We have a huge Christmas tree in Forrest Place that gets turned on every November. Okay—maybe the temperature is around forty degrees and we might spend part of the day on the beach. But it's still a fabulous time. I'm gutted I won't be there this year.'

He was pushing his Christmas memories aside, and curiosity was curling at the bottom of his stomach. Little pieces of the puzzle that was Cassidy Rae were clicking into place. 'Have you ever celebrated Christmas anywhere else?'

Cassidy shook her head fiercely. 'I couldn't for a minute imagine being anywhere other than here at Christmas. Sometimes it even snows on Christmas Eve and Christmas Day. Then it's really magical.'

Brad frowned. 'Didn't you even celebrate Christmas in Spain with your fiancé?'

Cassidy looked at him as if he had horns on his head. 'Absolutely not.'

He folded his arms across his chest. 'Surely it doesn't matter where you celebrate Christmas—it's about who you celebrate with. It's the people, Cass, not the place.' He willed his voice not to break as he said the words. She would have no idea how much all this hurt him.

Cassidy was still shaking her head, and Brad had the distinct feeling he'd just tiptoed around the heart of the matter. She didn't want to move. She didn't want to leave. She wouldn't even consider moving anywhere else.

In some circumstances it might seem fine, patriotic even. But it irritated Brad more than he wanted to admit. How could Cass be so closed-minded? Was this really why she wouldn't even consider a relationship with him? Not that he'd asked her. But every day they were growing closer and closer.

Why hadn't he told her about Melody yet? The most important person in his life and he hadn't even mentioned her existence. He'd heard from his lawyer yesterday. Still no news. Still no sign. America was a big place. They were searching every state to see if Alison had registered as a doctor, though by now she could be married and working under a different name. If that was the case, they might never find her. And that thought made him feel physically sick.

His brain was almost trying to be rational now. Trying to figure out why Alison hadn't contacted him.

He was a good father—committed to Melody and her upbringing. He'd wanted a say in everything and that had kind of spooked Alison, who liked to be in control. And if she'd really met someone and fallen in love, he could almost figure out why she'd done things this way.

If she'd told him she wanted to move to the US, there would have been a huge custody battle. But to steal his daughter away and let eighteen months pass with no contact? That, he couldn't understand—no matter what.

He almost wanted to shout at Cassidy, *It's the people, Cass—always the people.* He couldn't care less where he was in this world, as long as he was near his daughter.

His mind flickered back to the four tightly packed boxes stuffed in the bottom of the wardrobe in his bedroom. Eighteen months of his life, with a private investigator in Australia and one in the US. Eighteen months when almost all his salary had gone on paying their fees and jumping out of his skin every time the phone rang.

No one could keep living like that. Not even him. It destroyed your physical and mental health. So he'd tried to take a step back, get some normality back into his life. He was still looking for his daughter and still had a private investigator in the US. But now he didn't require a daily update—an email once a week was enough. And the PI was under strict instructions to phone only in an emergency.

He looked at the woman across the table. He still couldn't get to the bottom of Cassidy Rae. She'd received another one of those phone calls the other day and had ducked out the ward, talking in a low, calm voice.

What on earth was going on?

Cassidy stared across the table. Maybe she'd gone a little overboard with the Christmas stuff. She always seemed to get carried away when the subject came up. It looked as if a shadow had passed across Brad's eyes. Something strange. Something she didn't recognise. Was it disappointment? She drew her breath in, leaving a tight feeling in her chest. She didn't like this.

But she didn't know him that well yet. She didn't feel as if she could share that it was just her and her gran left. And she wanted to hold on to what little family she had left. Of course Christmas was about people—even if they didn't know you were there.

She reached across the table and touched his hand. Every single time she touched him it felt like this. A tingle. Hairs standing on end. Delicious feelings creeping down her spine. The warmth of his hand was spreading through her.

He looked up and gave her a rueful smile, a little sad maybe but still a smile.

'Let's talk about something else. Like Hallowe'en. We usually have a party for the staff on the ward. I had it in my flat last year, but I think yours would be the perfect venue this time.'

Brad's smile widened. He looked relieved by the change of subject. 'I guess a Hallowe'en party wouldn't be out of the question in the House of Horrors.'

'It's not a House of Horrors. Why don't we just tell people we've got a theme for the year? It could be Hallowe'en-slash-fancy-dress, 1960s-style?'

He nodded slowly. 'I suppose we could do that. Are you going to help me with the planning?'

'Of course.' Cassidy stood up and picked up her plate and mug, 'Come on, it's time to go back upstairs. We can talk about it as we go.'

He watched her retreating back and curvy behind. One thing was crystal clear. This woman was going to drive him crazy.

30 October

Brad opened the door as yet another party reveller arrived. Bert had retreated to his basket, now in Brad's pink bedroom, in sheer horror at the number of people in the small flat. It seemed that inviting the 'medical receiving unit' to a party also included anyone who worked there, used to work there or had once thought about working there.

It also included anyone who'd ever passed through or seen the sign for the unit.

'Love the outfit!' one of the junior doctors shouted at Brad. He looked down. Cassidy had persuaded him to go all out, and his outfit certainly reflected that. The room was filled with kipper ties, psychedelic swirls, paisley patterns, and mini-skirts and beehives. For the men, stick-on beards seemed to be the most popular choice, with lots of them now sticking to arms, foreheads and chests.

Brad pushed through the crowd to the kitchen, finding an empty glass and getting some water. It was freezing outside, but inside the flat he almost felt as if he were back in Perth. He'd turned the cast-iron radiators off, but the place was still steaming, even with the windows prised open to let the cold air circulate.

He felt someone press at his back. 'Sorry, it's a bit of a squash in here.' He recognised the voice instantly.

'Where have you been? Wow!' Cassidy had helped him carry all the food and drink for the party up to the flat. Then she'd disappeared to get changed. His eyes took in her short red *Star Trek* dress, complete with black knee-high boots and gold communicator pinned to her chest. She pressed the button. *'How many to beam aboard?'*

'You didn't tell me we were doing TV. Not fair. How come you get to look smart and sexy and I get to look like some flea-bitten wino?'

She laughed and moved forward. 'I'm still in the

sixties. The first episode of *Star Trek* was screened in 1966. I'm in perfect time.'

Someone pressed past her and she struggled to keep her glass of wine straight, moving so close to Brad that their entire bodies were touching. Her eyes tilted upwards towards him. 'I kind of like your too-tight shirt and shaggy wig. It suits you in a funny way.'

'Well, that outfit definitely suits you. But I feel as if you've fitted me up. I bet you had that sexy fancy-dress outfit stashed somewhere and were just looking for an excuse to give it an outing.' His broad chest could feel her warm curves pushing against him.

'You think I look sexy?' Her voice was low again and husky. Her words only heard by him. Someone else pushed past and she moved even closer in the tiny kitchen. *'How many to beam aboard?'*

They jumped. Startled by the noise. Brad grabbed her hand and pulled her through the door, past the people in the sitting room dancing to Tom Jones and the Beatles, and into the pink bedroom, pushing the door closed behind them.

Cassidy let out a little gasp. The pink shiny bedspread was gone, replaced by a plain cotton cream cover and pillowcases. But the dark pink lampshades hadn't been replaced, leaving a pink glow around the room. 'Too many people falling off your bed?'

He pulled the wig from his head, revealing his hair sticking up in all directions. 'Now, why would you think that?' There was a smile on his face as he stepped closer, pushing her against the door. His eyes were fixed on hers. His hand ran up her body, from the top of her boot, touching the bare skin on her legs, past the edge of her dress to her waist.

'Why would something like that even occur to you, Cass? Why would it even enter your mind? Because you keep telling me that we're friends. Just friends. You don't want anything more—not with someone like me, someone from Australia.' *Or someone with a missing child.*

Cassidy's heart was thudding against the inside of her chest. From the second he'd closed the door behind them she'd been picturing this in her head. No. Not true. From the first day that she'd met him she'd been picturing this in her head. It had taken her two glasses of wine to have the courage to come back to his flat tonight.

The tension had built in the last few weeks. Every lingering glance. Every fleeting touch sending sparks fluttering between them. It didn't matter how much her brain kept telling her he was the wrong fit. Her body didn't know that. And it craved his touch.

This wasn't meant to be serious. Serious had been the last thing on her mind—particularly with a man from overseas. But even though she tried to push the thoughts aside, Brad was rapidly becoming more than just a friend. She loved the sexual undercurrent between them, and the truth was she wanted to act on it. Now.

She leaned forward, just a little. Just enough to push her breasts even closer to him. If he looked down, all he would be able to see now was cleavage. *'How many to beam aboard?'* The noise startled both of them, but Brad only pulled her closer. She reached up and pulled the communicator badge from her dress, tossing it onto the bed behind them. 'I hate it when the costume takes away from the main event.'

She could see the surprise in his eyes. He'd expected

a fight. He'd expected her to give him a reason why he shouldn't be having the same thoughts she was.

She smiled, her hand reaching out and resting on his waist. 'Sometimes my body sends me different messages from my brain.'

Brad lifted a finger, running it down the side of her cheek. The lightest touch. Her response was immediate. Her face turned towards his hand, and his fingers caught the back of her head, intertwining with her hair. She leaned back into his touch, letting out a little sigh. Her eyes were closed, and she could feel his stubble scraping her chin, his warm breath near her ear. 'And which message are you listening to?' he whispered as his other hand slid under her dress.

'Which one do you think?'

She caught his head in her hands and pulled his lips towards hers. This was what she'd been waiting for.

His lips touched hers hungrily, parting quickly, his tongue pushing against hers. She wrapped her arms around his neck.

This was it. Stars were going off in her head. If he didn't keep doing this she would explode. Because everything about this felt right. And it was just a kiss—right? Where was the harm in that?

'I've waited a whole month to kiss you,' he whispered in her ear.

'Then I've only got one thing to say—don't stop.'

CHAPTER FOUR

2 November

'WHAT are you doing here?'

It was three o'clock in the morning, and the voice should have startled her, but it didn't; it washed over her like warm treacle.

She turned her head in the darkened room where she was checking a patient's obs, an automatic smile appearing on her face. 'I got called in at eleven o'clock. Two of the night-shift staff had to go home sick, and it was too late to call in any agency staff.' She wrinkled her nose. 'Sickness bug again. What are you doing here? I thought Franco was on call.'

Brad rolled his tired eyes. 'Snap. Sickness bug, Franco phoned me half an hour ago with his head stuck down a toilet.'

Cassidy nodded. 'Figures. This bug seems to hit people really quickly. Loads of the staff are down with it. Let's just hope we manage to avoid it.' She finished recording the obs in the patients chart and started walking towards the door. Brad's arm rested lightly on her waist, and although she wanted to welcome the feel of his touch, it just didn't seem right.

'No touching at work,' she whispered.

His eyes swept up and down the dimly lit corridor. 'Even when there's no one about? Where's the fun in that?' His eyes were twinkling again, and it was doing untold damage to her flip-flopping stomach. She stopped walking and leaned against the wall.

'It's like this, Dr Donovan.' She moved her arm in a circular motion. 'I'm the master of all you can survey right now, and it wouldn't do to be caught in a compromising position with one of the doctors. That would give the hospital gossips enough ammunition for the rest of the year.' She looked down the corridor again, straightening herself up, her breasts brushing against his chest.

'I may well be the only nurse on duty in this ward right now, but I've got a reputation to maintain.' She tapped her finger on his chest. 'No matter how much men of a dubious nature try to waylay me.'

Brad kept his hands lightly resting on her waist. 'Hmm, I'm liking three o'clock in the morning, Cassidy Rae. It sounds as if there might be a bit of a bad girl in there.' He had that look in his eye again—the one he'd had when he'd finally stopped kissing her a few nights ago. The one that suggested a thousand other things they could be doing if they weren't in the wrong place at the wrong time. 'We really need to improve our timing.'

He was grinning at her now. The tiny hairs on her arms were starting to stand on end. This man was infectious. Much more dangerous than any sickness bug currently sweeping the ward.

She could feel the pressure rising in her chest. How easy would it be right now for them to kiss? And how much did she want to? But it went against all her principles for conduct and professional behaviour. So why did they currently feel as if they were flying out the window?

No matter how she tried to prevent it, this man had got totally under her skin. She was falling for him hook, line and sinker. No matter how much her brain told her not to.

She tried to break the tension between them. 'What do you want, anyway? I didn't page you. Shouldn't you be in bed?' The irony of the words hit her as soon as they left her mouth, her cheeks automatically flushing. Brad and bed. Two words that should never be together in a sentence. The images had haunted her dreams for the last few nights. And she had a very *active* imagination.

His fingers tugged her just a little closer so he could whisper in her ear. 'Bed is exactly where I'm planning on being. But not here. And not alone.'

Cassidy felt her blush intensify. Was she going to deny what had been on her mind? She wasn't normally shy around men. But something about Brad was different. Something was making her cautious.

And she wasn't sure what it was. She couldn't quite put her finger on it yet. But as long as she had the slightest inclination what it was, she didn't want to lose her heart to this guy. No matter how irresistible he was.

'I've got two patients coming up. Two young guys who've—what is it you call it here?—been out on the lash?'

Cassidy laughed and nodded at his phrasing. He really was trying to embrace the Scottish words and phrases around him. She raised her eyebrows, 'Or you could call them *blootered*.'

Brad shook his head. 'I think you all deliberately

wait until I'm around and start using all these words to confuse me.' He looked out the window into the night at the pouring rain. 'One of the other nurses down in A and E called the two young guys *drookit* and *mauchit*. I have no idea what she was talking about.'

Cassidy laughed even harder. 'Look outside, that will give you a clue. *Drookit* is absolutely soaking. *Mauchit* means really dirty. I take it the guys were found lying on the street?'

Brad nodded. 'I'm getting the hang of this, though. It's...' he lifted his fingers in the air '...going like a fair down there.'

She laughed. 'See—you're learning. Bet you hadn't heard that expression before you came to Scotland.' Her brow wrinkled. 'Hang on, where is it going like a fair? In A and E?'

'The short-stay ward is full already. That's why you're getting these two. They'll need Glasgow coma scale obs done. Are you okay with that?'

Cassidy smiled. 'Of course I am. We're used to getting some minor head injuries on the ward on a Saturday night.' She walked over to the filing cabinet and pulled out the printed sheets, attaching them to two clipboards for the bottom of the beds. She turned to face him. 'You know a group of doctors at one of the local hospitals invented this over thirty years ago.' She waved the chart at him. 'Now it's used the whole world over. One of the doctors is still there. He's a professor now.'

Brad raised his eyebrows. 'Aren't you just the little fund of information at three in the morning?' He looked around again. 'Haven't you got some help? I'm not happy about you being here alone with two drunks.

There's no telling how they'll react when they finally come round.'

Cassidy pointed to a figure coming down the corridor. 'Claire, the nursing auxiliary, is on duty with me. She was just away for a break. And if I need help from another staff nurse, I can call through to next door.'

She turned her head as she heard the lift doors opening and the first of the trolleys being pulled towards the ward. 'Here they come.' She scooted into the nearby six-bedded ward and pulled the curtains around one of the beds.

Five minutes later a very young, very drunk man was positioned in the bed, wearing a pair of hospital-issue granddad pyjamas. Cassidy wrinkled her nose at the vapours emanating from him. 'Phew! He smells like a brewery. I could get anaesthetised by these fumes.' She spent a few moments checking his blood pressure and pulse, checking his limb movements and trying to elicit a verbal and motor response from him. Finally she drew her pen torch from her pocket and checked his pupil reactions.

She shook her head as she marked the observations on the chart. 'At least his pupils are equal and reactive. He's reacting to pain, but apart from that he's completely out of it.' She checked the notes from A and E. 'Any idea of a next of kin?'

Brad shook his head. 'Neither of the guys had wallets on them. This one had a student card in his pocket but that was it.'

He raised his head as the rattle of the second trolley sounded simultaneously to his pager going off. He glanced downwards at the number. 'It's A and E again. Are you sure you're okay?'

Claire had joined her at the side of the bed. 'We'll be fine, but just remember, there are no beds left up here.'

Brad nodded. 'I'll try to come back up later,' he said as he walked down the corridor towards the lift.

Cassidy spent the next hour doing neurological observations on the two patients every fifteen minutes. Both of them started to respond a little better, even if it was belligerently. It was four o'clock in the morning now—that horrible time of night for the night shift where the need to sleep seemed to smack them straight in the head. Her eyes were beginning to droop even as she walked the length of the corridor to check on her patients. Sitting down right now would be lethal—she had to keep on the move to stay awake.

A monitor started pinging in one of the nearby rooms. 'I'll get it,' she shouted to Claire. 'The leads have probably detached again.'

She walked into the room of Mr Fletcher, a man in his sixties admitted with angina. Every time he'd turned over in his sleep tonight, one of the leads attached to his chest had moved out of place.

Cassidy flicked on the light, ready to silence the alarms on the monitor. But Mr Fletcher's leads were intact. His skin was white and drawn, his lips blue and his body rigid on the bed. The monitor showed a rapid, flickering electrical line. Ventricular fibrillation. His heart wasn't beating properly at all. Even though the monitor told her what she needed to know, she took a few seconds to check for a pulse and listen for breathing.

'Claire!' She pulled the red alarm on the wall, setting off the cardiac-arrest procedure as she released the brake on the bottom of the bed and pulled the bed out from the wall. She removed the headrest from the top of the bed and pulled out the pillows. Claire appeared at her side, pulling the cardiac-arrest trolley behind her. 'I've put out the call.' She was breathing heavily.

Cassidy took a deep breath. Brad was the senior doctor carrying the arrest page tonight. If he was still down in A and E, it would take him at least five minutes to get up here. Glasgow City Hospital was an old, sprawling building, with bits added on over time. It hadn't been designed with emergencies in mind, like some of the modern, newly built hospitals were. The anaesthetist would probably take five minutes to get here, too.

It didn't matter what the monitor said. Cassidy took a few seconds to do the old-fashioned assessment of the patient. Airway. Breathing. Circulation. No pulse. No breathing.

'Start bagging,' she instructed Claire, pointing her to the head of the bed and handing her an airway as she connected up the oxygen supply to the ambu-bag. She turned the dial on the defibrillator, slapping the pads on Mr Fletcher's chest and giving it a few seconds to pick up and confirm his rhythm.

'Stand clear,' she shouted to Claire, waiting a few seconds to check she'd stood back then looking downwards to make sure she wasn't touching the collapsed metal side rails. She pressed the button and Mr Fletcher's back arched upwards as the jolt went through his body.

Her adrenaline had kicked in now. She didn't feel sleepy or tired any more. She was wide awake and on alert, watching the monitor closely for a few seconds to see if the shock had made any impact on his heart rhythm. Nothing. Still VF.

The sound of feet thudded down the corridor as Brad appeared, closely followed by one of the anaesthetists. Brad's eyes widened as he realised who the patient was. 'VF,' she said as they entered the room. 'I've shocked him once at one hundred and twenty joules.' Even though she had only been back on the ward for a month, she was on autopilot.

'What happened?' asked Brad. 'He was pain free earlier and we had him scheduled for an angiogram tomorrow.'

'Alarm sounded and I found him like this,' she said. 'He hadn't complained of chest pain at all.' She raised her knee on the bed and positioned her hands, starting the chest compressions. The anaesthetist took over from Claire and within a few seconds inserted an endotracheal tube. Cassidy continued the cycles of compressions as Brad pulled the pre-loaded syringes from the crash cart. After five cycles she stopped and their heads turned to the monitor again to check the rhythm.

'I'm giving him some epinephrine,' Brad said as he squirted it into the cannula in the back of Mr Fletcher's hand. 'Let's shock him again.' He lifted the defibrillator paddles. 'Stand clear, everyone. Shocking at two hundred joules.'

Everyone stood back as Mr Fletcher's body arched again. Cassidy went to resume the compressions. They continued for the next ten minutes with cycles of compressions, drugs and shocking. Cassidy's arms were starting to ache. It was amazing how quickly the strain of doing cardiac massage told on shoulders and arms.

'Stop!' shouted Brad. 'We've got a rhythm.' He

waited a few seconds as he watched the green line on the monitor. 'Sinus bradycardia.'

He raised his eyes from the bed. 'Cassidy, go and tell Coronary Care we're transferring a patient to them.'

She ran next door to the coronary care unit, and one of their staff members came back through with her, propping the doors open for easy transfer. They wheeled the bed through to the unit and hooked Mr Fletcher up to the monitors in the specially designed rooms. In a matter of a few moments, he was safely installed next door.

Cassidy nodded at Brad as she left him there to continue Mr Fletcher's care. Claire gathered up his belongings and took them next door while Cassidy quickly transferred him on the computer system.

She took a deep breath and heaved a sigh of relief. The adrenaline was still flooding through her system, her arms ached and her back was sore.

Claire appeared with a cup of steaming tea, which she put on the desk in front of her. 'Okay, Cassidy? I nearly jumped out of my skin when that alarm sounded. He'd been fine all night.'

Cassidy nodded. 'I hate it when that happens. Thank goodness he was attached to a cardiac monitor. I dread to think what would have happened if he hadn't been.'

A loud groan sounded from the room opposite the nurses' station. Cassidy stood back up. 'No rest for the wicked. That will be one of our head-injury patients.'

Sure enough, one of the young men was starting to come round. Cassidy started checking his obs again, pulling her pen torch from her pocket to make sure his pupils were equal and reactive. His score had gradually started to improve as he could obey simple instructions and respond—albeit grudgingly. Hangovers didn't seem to agree with him.

She moved on to the patient next door, who still appeared to be sleeping it off. As she leaned over to check his pupils, his hand reached up and grabbed her tunic. 'Get me some water,' he growled, his breath reeking of alcohol and his eyes bloodshot.

Cassidy reacted instantly, pushing him backwards with her hands to get out of his grasp. 'Don't you dare put a hand on me,' she snarled.

'Cass.' The voice was instant, sounding behind her as Brad sidestepped around her, filling the gap between her and the patient.

The sunny surfer boy with cheerful demeanour was lost. 'Don't you dare touch my staff.' He was furious, leaning over the patient.

The drunken young man slumped back against the pillows, all energy expended. 'I need some water,' he mumbled.

Brad grabbed hold of Cassidy's hand and pulled her beyond the curtains. He ran his fingers through his hair. 'He still requires neuro obs, doesn't he?'

Cassidy nodded. 'That's the first time he's woken up. His neuro obs are scheduled to continue for the next few hours.'

Brad marched over to the phone and spoke for a few moments before putting it back down. 'I don't want you or Claire going in there on your own. Not while there's a chance he's still under the influence of alcohol and might behave inappropriately. Somebody from Security will be up in a few minutes and will stay for the rest of the shift.'

He walked into the kitchen and picked up a plastic

jug and cup, running the tap to fill them with water. 'I'll take him these. You sit down.'

Cassidy didn't like anyone telling her what to do, especially in her ward. But for some reason she was quite glad that Brad had been around. It wasn't the first time a patient had manhandled her—and she was quite sure it wouldn't be the last. But there was something about it happening in the dead of night, when there weren't many other people around, that unsettled her.

And as much as she wanted to fly the flag for independence and being able to handle everything on her own, she was quite glad one of the security staff was coming up to the ward.

Brad appeared a moment later, walking behind her and putting his hands on her taut neck and shoulders. He automatically started kneading them with his warm hands. 'You okay, Cass?'

For a second she was still tense, wondering what Claire might think if she saw him touching her, but then relaxing at his touch. Her insides felt as tight as a coiled spring. What with the cardiac massage and the reaction of her patient, this was exactly what she needed. She leaned backwards a little into his touch.

'Right there,' she murmured as he hit a nerve. 'How's Mr Fletcher doing?'

Brad's voice was calm and soothing. 'He's in the right place. The staff in Coronary Care can monitor him more easily, his bradycardia stabilised with a little atropine and his blood pressure is good. We've contacted his family, and he'll be first on the list in the morning. He'll probably need a stent put in place to clear his blocked artery.'

'That's good. Mmm…keep going.'

'Your muscles are like coiled springs. Is this because of what just happened?'

She could hear the agitation in his voice.

'I hate people who react like that. How dare they when all we're trying to do is help them? He could have died out there, lying on the street with a head injury, getting battered by the elements. It makes my blood boil. If I hadn't come in when I did…' His voice tailed off then he leaned forward and wrapped his arms around her neck—just for a second—brushing a light kiss on her cheek.

It was the briefest of contacts before he straightened up, reaching for the cup of tea Claire had made a few minutes earlier and setting it down on the desk in front of her. 'Drink this.' He folded his arms and sat down in the chair next to her, perching on the edge. 'I need to go back to Coronary Care. What are you doing on Sunday? Want to grab some lunch?'

Cassidy hesitated, her stomach plunging. She had plans on Sunday. Ones she wasn't sure about including Brad in. After all, he was just a fleeting moment in her life, a 'passing fancy', her gran would have said. She wasn't ready to introduce him to her family yet. Especially in her current circumstances.

But the hesitation wasn't lost on Brad. 'What's up? Meeting your other boyfriend?' he quipped.

Her head shook automatically. 'No, no.' Then a smile appeared. 'What do you mean, my *other boyfriend*? I wasn't aware I had a boyfriend right now.' Why did those words set her heart aflutter? This wasn't what she wanted. Not with a man from thousands of miles away. Not with someone who would leave in less than a year. So why couldn't she wipe the smile off her face?

He could see the smile. *Distraction.* Was that all that Cass was? What about how'd he had felt a few minutes ago when that drunk had touched her? The guy was lucky there hadn't been a baseball bat around. Cass was getting under his skin. In more ways than one. And it was time. Time to tell her about Melody.

It would be fine. He'd tell her on Sunday. She would understand. She would get it. He had other priorities. He wanted to find his daughter, and that could take him anywhere in the world. Cassidy would be fine about it. She didn't want a serious relationship with an Australian. She obviously didn't mind the flirtation and distraction. Maybe she wouldn't even mind a little more. Something more inevitable between them.

This wasn't anything serious—she would know that. But he just didn't want anyone else near her right now.

Brad stood back up. 'Well, you do. So there.' He planted another kiss firmly on her cheek. 'And whatever you're doing on Sunday, plan on me doing it with you.' And with those words he strode down the corridor, whistling.

7 November

'We seem to be making a habit of this.' Brad smiled at Cassidy, his mouth half-hidden by the scarf wrapped around his neck, as she turned the key in the lock of the little terraced house in the East End of Glasgow.

His leather-gloved hand was at her waist and his body huddled against hers. It was freezing cold and the pavements already glistening with frost. Cassidy pushed the door open and stepped inside. 'I'm afraid it's not much warmer inside. Gran hasn't lived here for over a year, and I have the heating on a timer at mini-mum to stop the pipes from freezing.'

Brad pushed the door shut behind him, closing out the biting wind. 'I can't believe how quickly the tem-perature's dropped in the last few days. I've had to buy a coat, a hat and a scarf.'

Cassidy stepped right in front of him, her chestnut curls tickling his nose. 'And very nice you look, too.'

He leaned forward and kissed the tip of her nose, be-fore rubbing his gloved hands together. 'So what hap-pens now?'

She led him into the main room of the house and pointed at some dark teak furniture. 'The van should be here any time. It's taking the chest of drawers and sideboard in here, the wardrobe in Gran's bedroom and the refrigerator from the kitchen. The furniture goes to someone from the local homeless unit who's just been rehoused.'

'I take it there's no chance your gran will ever come home.'

Cassidy shook her head fiercely, and he could see a sheen cross her eyes. 'No. She fell and broke her arm last year. It was quite a bad break—she needed a pin inserted. She's already suffered from Alzheimer's for the past few years. I'd helped with some adaptations to her home and memory aids, but I guess I didn't really understand how bad she was.'

Cassidy lifted her hands. 'Here, in her own environ-ment, she seemed to be coping, but once she broke her arm and ended up in hospital...' Her voice trailed off and Brad wrapped his arm around her shoulders.

'So where is she now? Was there no one else to help her? Where are your mum and dad?'

'She's in a nursing home just a few miles away. And it's the second one. The first?' She shuddered, 'Don't even ask. That's why I agreed to the secondment. It meant I could spend a bit more time helping her get settled this time. Her mobility is good, but her memory is a different story—some days she doesn't even know who I am. Other days she thinks I'm my mother. I can't remember the last time she knew I was Cassidy. And now she's started to get aggressive sometimes. It's just not her at all. The only thing that helps is hearing my voice.'

The tears started to spill down her cheeks. 'I know I'm a nurse and everything but I just hate it.' Brad pulled his hand from his glove and wiped away her tears with his fingers.

He nodded slowly. So that's what the telephone calls had been about. No wonder she'd wanted some privacy to take them. 'So where's your mum and dad? Can't they help with your gran?'

Cassidy rolled her eyes. 'My mum and dad are the total opposite of me. Sometimes I feel as if I'm the parent and they're the children in this relationship. Last I heard, they were in Malaysia. They're engineers, dealing with water-pumping stations and pipelines. They basically work all over the world and hardly spend any time back here.'

His brow furrowed. He was starting to understand Cassidy a little better. Her firm stance about staying in Scotland was obviously tied into feeling responsible for her gran. 'So you don't get much support?'

She shook her head.

'Is there anything I can do to help?'

Cassidy looked around her. The pain was written all

over her face. 'Everything in this house reminds me of Gran. I packed up her clothes last month and took them to the Age Concern shop.' She walked over to a cardboard box in the corner of the room, filled with ornaments wrapped in paper, crinkling the tissue paper between her fingers. 'This all seems so final.'

The knock at the door was sharp, startling them both. Ten minutes later almost all the heavy furniture had been loaded onto the van by two burly volunteers. 'The last thing is in here.' Cassidy led them into the bedroom and pointed at the wardrobe. She stood back as the two men tilted the wardrobe on its side to get it through the narrow door. There was a clunk and a strange sliding noise.

Brad jumped forward. 'What was that? You emptied the wardrobe, didn't you, Cassidy?'

She nodded. 'I thought I had.'

He pulled open the uptilted wardrobe door and lifted up a black plastic-wrapped package that had fallen to the floor. 'You must have missed this.'

Cassidy stepped towards him and peered inside the wardrobe. 'I can't imagine how. I emptied out all the clothes last month. I was sure I got everything.' She turned the bulky package over in her hands. 'I don't know how I managed to miss this.' She gave the men a nod, and they continued out the door towards the van.

Brad thanked the men and walked back through to the bedroom. Cassidy was sitting on the bed, pulling at the plastic wrapper. There was a tiny flash of red and she gave a little gasp.

'Wow! I would never have expected this.' She shook out the tightly wrapped red wool coat and another little bundle fell to the floor. Cassidy swung the coat in front of the mirror. The coat was 1940s-style, the colour much brighter than she would have expected, with black buttons and a nipped-in waist.

'This coat is gorgeous. But I can't *ever* remember Gran wearing it. I don't even think I've seen a picture of her in it. Why on earth would she have it wrapped up at the back of her wardrobe? It looks brand new.'

Brad knelt on the floor and picked up the other package wrapped in brown paper. 'This was in there, too. Maybe you should have a look at them?'

Cassidy nodded and then gave a little shiver.

'Let's go to the coffee shop at the bottom of the road. It's too cold in here. We'll take the coat with us,' he said.

She headed through to the kitchen and pulled a plastic bag from under the sink, carefully folding the red coat and putting it inside. 'This coat feels gorgeous.' She held the edge of it up again, looking in the mirror at the door. 'And I love the colour.'

'Why don't you wear it?' Brad could see her pupils dilate, just for a second, as if she was considering the idea.

She shook her head. 'No. No, I can't. I don't know anything about it. I don't even know if it belonged to Gran.'

'Well, I think it would look perfect on you, with your dark hair and brown eyes. Red's a good colour for you. Did you inherit your colouring from your gran?'

Cassidy still had her fingers on the coat, touching it with a look of wistfulness in her eyes. 'I think so. I've only ever seen a few photos of her when she was a young girl. She was much more glamorous than me.'

Brad opened the front door as the biting wind whirled around them. He grabbed her hand. 'I've got a better idea. Why don't we get a coffee to go and just head back to my flat? It's freezing.'

Cassidy nodded as she pulled the door closed behind them and checked it was secure. They hurried over to the car and reached his flat ten minutes later, with coffee and cakes from the shop round the corner from him.

Although it was only four o'clock, the light had faded quickly and the street was already dark. 'Look!' screamed Cass. 'It's the first one!'

Brad dived to rescue the toppling coffee cups from her grasp. 'What is it?' His head flicked from side to side. 'What on earth are you talking about?'

'There!' Her eyes were lit up and her smile reached from ear to ear. He followed Cassidy's outstretched finger pointing to a flat positioned across the street above one of the shops. There, proudly displayed in the window, was a slightly bent, brightly lit-up Christmas tree.

'You have got to be joking. It's only the seventh of November. Why on earth would someone have their Christmas tree up?'

He couldn't believe the expression of absolute glee on her face. She looked like a child that had spotted Santa. 'Isn't it gorgeous?'

And there it was. That horrible twisting feeling inside his stomach. The one he was absolutely determined to avoid this year. That same empty feeling that he felt every year when he spent the whole of the Christmas season thinking about what he'd lost, what had slipped through his fingers.

He felt the wind biting at his cheek. Almost like a cold slap. Just what he needed. This year was going to be different. He'd done everything he possibly could. It was time to try and get rid of this horrible empty feeling. He'd spent last Christmas in Australia, the one before that in the US, following up some useless leads as to Alison and Melody's whereabouts.

This year would be different. That was part of the reason he'd come to Scotland. A country that had no bad memories for him. A chance to think of something new.

Cassidy's big brown eyes blinked at him in the orange lamplight. She'd pulled a hat over her curls and it suited her perfectly. 'I really want to put my tree up,' she murmured. 'But it's just too early.' She looked down at the bustling street. 'Only some of the shops have their decorations up. I wish they all had.'

This was it. This was where it started. 'Christmas means different things to different people, Cass. Not everyone loves Christmas, you know?'

He saw her flinch and pull back, confusion in her eyes. There was hesitation in her voice. 'What do you mean? Is something wrong? Did something happen to you at Christmas?'

He hesitated. How could he tell her what was currently circulating in his mind? He wasn't even sure he could put it into coherent words. Melody hadn't disappeared at Christmas, but everything about the season and the time of year just seemed to amplify the feelings, make them stronger. Most importantly, it made the yearning to see his daughter almost consume him. He blinked. She was standing in the dimmed light, her big brown eyes staring up at him with a whole host of questions.

He should tell her about Melody, he really should. But now wasn't the time or the place. A shiver crept down his spine as the cold Scottish winter crept through his clothes. A busy street filled with early festive shoppers wasn't the place to talk about his missing daughter.

And no matter how this woman was currently sending electric pulses along his skin, he wasn't entirely sure what he wanted to share. He wasn't sure he was ready.

'Brad?' Her voice cut through his thoughts, jerking him back to the passing traffic and darkened night.

He bent forward and kissed the tip of her nose, sliding his arm around her shoulders. 'Don't be silly, Cass. Nothing happened to me at Christmas.' He shrugged his shoulders as he pulled her towards him, guiding her down the street towards his flat. 'I'm just mindful that lots of the people we see in the hospital over Christmas don't have the happy stories to share that you do.'

She bit her lip, cradling the coffee cups and cakes in her arms as she matched his steps along the busy street. 'I know that. I didn't just materialise onto the medical unit from a planet far away. I've worked there a long time.'

But her words seemed lost as his steps lengthened and he pushed open the door to the close ahead of them.

Cassidy took off her bright blue parka and put it on the sofa. She'd seen something in his eyes. Almost as if a shadow had passed over them, and it had made her stomach coil. Was there something he wasn't telling her?

She pulled the coffee cups from their holder and opened the bag with the carrot cake inside. This was exactly what she needed right now. The sofa sagged next to her as Brad sat down. He was still rubbing his hands together.

'I can't believe how cold it is out there.'

She smiled at him. 'Get used to it—this is only the

start. Last year it was minus twelve on Christmas Day. My next-door neighbour is a gas engineer and his phone was ringing constantly with people's boilers breaking down.' She picked up the cup and inhaled deeply. 'Mmm. Skinny caramel latte. My favourite in the world. I haven't had one of these in ages.' She took a tiny sip then reached for the moist carrot cake.

'So I take it the fact you have a *skinny* caramel latte counteracts the effects of the carrot cake?'

She winked at him. 'Exactly.' She raised her eyes skywards. 'Finally, a man on my wavelength. They cancel each other out. And it's a skinny caramel latte with sugar-free syrup. Which means I can enjoy this all the more.' She licked the frosting from the carrot cake off the tips of her fingers.

'With this…' she nibbled a bit from the corner. '…a girl could think she was in heaven.'

'I can think of lots of other ways to put a girl in heaven,' the voice next to her mumbled.

Cassidy froze. Her second sip of coffee was currently stuck in her throat. You couldn't get much more innuendo than that. Should she respond? Or pretend she hadn't heard?

There was no denying the attraction between them. But did she really want to act on it? After a month in his company, what did she really know about Brad Donovan? She could give testimony to his medical skills and his patient care. He was amenable, well mannered and supportive to the staff.

But what did she really know about him? Only little snippets of information that he'd told her in passing. Stories about home in Australia, living in Perth and his training as a doctor. Passing remarks about childhood friends. He'd told her he had no wife or girlfriend.

So what else was it? What had made that dark shadow pass in front of his eyes? Why had he hesitated before answering the question? Or had she just imagined it all? Maybe there was nothing wrong, maybe something had caught his eye at the other side of the road, momentarily distracting him and stopping him from answering the question.

In the meantime, she could still feel that underlying buzz between them. Whenever he was near, she had visions of that night in his flat, pressed up against the wall in her sci-fi costume, wishing things could go further than they had.

Every time he touched her at work, even the merest brush of a hand was enough to set off the currents between them. It didn't matter that her head told her this wasn't sensible—he came from the other side of the world and would likely return there; her body was telling her something entirely different. Her imagination was telling her a whole host of other things...

He gave her a nudge, passing her the package he'd wedged under his jacket.

She stared down at the still-wrapped parcel in her hands, turning the brown paper package over and over.

'Are you going to open it?'

She picked at the tape in one corner. It was old, the stickiness long vanished, and it literally fell apart in her hands, revealing some white envelopes underneath. She pulled them out. Only they weren't white, they had yellowed with age, all with US postal stamps.

Her eyes lifted to meet his. Brad leaned forward, touching the pile of envelopes and spreading them out across the table. 'There must be at least twenty of them,' he said quietly. His fingers stopped at something. There, among the envelopes, was something else. A photograph. Brad slid the envelope that was covering it away and Cassidy let out a little gasp.

She leaned forward and picked up the black-and-white print. 'It's my gran!' she gasped. His head met hers as they stared at the photograph of a beautiful young woman with a smile that spread from ear to ear, wearing a beautiful coat with a nipped-in waist. Her head was turned to the side and her eyes were sparkling as she looked at the man standing next to her in a US army uniform.

Cassidy was stunned. There were a million thoughts that crowded into her mind. A million conclusions that she could jump to. But one thing stood out above all the rest. 'I've never seen her look so happy,' she whispered. 'Gran never looked like that.'

She turned to face Brad. 'I don't mean she was miserable—she was fine.' She pointed at the photograph. 'But I can't ever remember her looking like *that*.'

She didn't want to say anything else. She didn't know what to think. She'd just glimpsed a moment from the past, and it almost seemed sacred. The coat and letters had been hidden a long time ago by a woman who obviously hadn't wanted to throw them away but hadn't wanted them to be found. In a way, it almost felt like a betrayal.

She ran her finger over the photograph. 'I don't think I can even ask Gran about this. She's too far gone. I can't even remember the last time that she recognised me.'

Brad's arm wrapped around her shoulder. She could feel his breath at her neck. What would he be thinking?

The same kind of thing that she was? That her gran had lost her heart to some US soldier?

She didn't want to think like that. It seemed almost judgemental. And it seemed wrong that Brad's first glimpse into her family was revealing something she hadn't known herself.

And she couldn't pretend that it didn't hurt a little. It had been just her and Gran for the last ten years but she'd never told Cassidy anything about this. She'd been a modern woman, liberal-minded and easy to talk to. Why had she kept this to herself?

His voice was quiet and steady as he whispered in her ear. 'Don't even think about asking her about it, Cass.' He lifted the photograph from her hand and sat it back down on the table. 'Take it as it is. A happy memory from your gran's life. She's beautiful in that picture. You can see the happiness in her eyes. Why shouldn't she have had a time like that?' His finger ran down the side of her cheek. 'She looks a lot like you.'

Cassidy turned to face him. His mouth was only inches from hers and she subconsciously licked her lips. This was it. The moment she'd been waiting for.

It had taken him so long to kiss her again after the party. She didn't want to wait any longer. She didn't want to imagine any longer. She wanted to feel.

Her hands slid up around his neck as she pulled him closer. His mouth was on hers instantly, just the way she'd imagined. He pushed her backwards on the sofa, his hands on either side of her head as he kissed her, gently at first, before working his way down her neck, pushing her shirt open.

His body was warm, heating hers instantly. She could feel his whole length above her, and her hands moved from around his neck, down his back and towards his hips, pulling him closer to her.

This time there was no one else in the flat. This time they wouldn't need to stop. This time they could do what they wanted.

She pushed aside the rational side of her brain that was clamouring to be heard. She could worry about all that later. Her body was responding to him with an intensity she'd never experienced before. She'd already had a glimpse of the washboard abs when he'd changed in the doctors' office. Now she didn't just want to look—she wanted to touch, to feel, to taste.

He lifted his head, pushing himself back a little. His voice was little above a groan. 'Cass?'

The question only hung in the air for a fraction of a second. She didn't want to think about this. Right now she didn't care that he was from Australia and would probably go back there. Right now all she cared about was that he was here, *now*, with *her*.

A slow smile appeared on his face. 'Wanna stay over?'

He had no idea how sexy he was right now. His clear blue eyes were hooded with desire. She could feel his heart thudding against his chest. All for her.

She pressed herself against him again. 'I thought you'd never ask.'

He pulled her to her feet and led her towards his bedroom door, undoing the buttons on her shirt as they went. Her legs were on autopilot and she couldn't wipe the smile from her face.

He pressed her against the wall. 'I seem to remember being in this position with you before, Cassidy Rae.' His voice was deep, throaty, turning her on even more.

'I was playing hard to get,' she whispered in his ear. 'Did it work?'

He turned her around and pushed her onto the bed. 'Oh, yes.' He crawled towards her, poising himself above her. Her shirt was open now, leaving her breasts exposed in their black satin push-up bra. He bit at the edge with his teeth. 'Now, this doesn't look like ordinary underwear.' His fingers dug around her hips, sliding down the back of her jeans and finding the edge of her matching black g-string. 'Did you have something in mind when you got dressed this morning, Cass?' His low, sexy laugh sent shivers of delight down her spine.

It wasn't her normal underwear. But she could hardly even remember getting dressed this morning. Had she done this subconsciously, hoping she would end up in this position?

'Let's just say I'm a girl of many secrets.' She pulled his T-shirt over his head, revealing his pecs and tanned abdomen. If she hadn't been so turned on, she might have pulled in her stomach and worried about him seeing her curves. But from the look on his face, he liked what he was seeing. 'I have lots of gorgeous sets of underwear. If you're lucky, I'll let you see the red set,' she moaned as he started to kiss her neck, 'or the blue set...' Her hands were dipping lower on his body, to the front of his jeans where she could feel him throbbing against her. 'Or, if you're really lucky, I'll let you see the green set.'

He let out a groan. 'I can guarantee I'll love the underwear—no matter what colour. But what I love most is what's underneath. He traced his fingers down her throat as she arched her back in response. Then slid his hand underneath her, unfastening her bra strap and leaving her breasts exposed. 'Now, what can I do with these?' he murmured.

Cass pushed herself upwards, her breasts towards his mouth. 'You can start by getting rid of the rest of these clothes,' she commanded as she undid the buttons on his jeans, before wriggling out of her own. She waited as he discarded his jeans and underwear, before pushing him down on the bed and setting her legs astride him.

'I like this,' he murmured. 'A woman who likes to be in charge.'

'Oh, I'm always in charge,' she breathed in his ear as she ran her hands down his chest. 'And anyway, I'm examining your skin. You're way too tanned.' Her hands stopped at his nipples, brushing around them onto the fine hair on his chest. 'I feel it's my duty to check you for any areas of concern.' She lifted her hips and rubbed against him again.

He groaned. 'Anywhere in particular you'd like to start?'

She smiled and leaned over him again, her hardened nipples brushing against the skin on his chest. She swayed against him. 'I'll need to think about that.'

Brad let out a primal roar. He grabbed her and flipped her around on the bed so he was poised above her. 'Enough teasing. You're going to be the death of me.'

His fingers reached down and dispensed with her g-string. She could feel the heat rise inside her. She was aching for him. He touched her and she gasped, tilting her hips upwards to him. 'Oh...this is going to be so good.'

'You bet it is,' he whispered in her ear, the stubble on his jaw scraping her shoulder.

'Mmm… Where else am I going to feel that?'

'Wherever you like.'

He moved for a second, reaching into the nearby drawer, and she heard the rustle of a condom wrapper being opened. Ten seconds later he was above her again. 'Are you ready?' he whispered.

'Oh, yes…' She opened her legs further and gasped as he plunged inside her.

He stopped, just for a second. 'Okay?'

She took a deep breath, while the full sensation surrounded her. Then she pulled his hips even closer, taking him deeper inside. 'Don't you dare stop,' she groaned. 'I've got you just where I want you.'

'Ditto.' He smiled again as he moved slowly, building momentum between them as he trailed a line of kisses down the side of her face and throat.

And there it was   the fever that had been building between them for weeks. All the looks and lingering glances. All the brief touches. All the electricity buzzing around them like fireflies. The first kiss, with its strained finish. All building to this crescendo, where nothing and no one could get between them.

Cassidy could feel her skin start to tingle. Nothing else was more important than this. Nothing else had ever felt as good as this. Nothing else had ever felt this *right*. This was perfect.

She let herself go, throwing her head back and crying out his name, as she felt him stiffen at the same time.

She felt her body turn to jelly, the air whooshing out from her lungs. Brad was still above her, his whole body weight now resting on her, his heart thudding against her chest.

She let out a laugh. Sweat slicked them together as

she gave him a playful push. 'Move, mister, I can hardly breathe.'

He pushed himself up and sagged down beside her. 'Wow.'

Cassidy was breathing heavily, her eyes staring up at the ceiling and fixing on the still-pink light shade above her. She turned to the sandy-blond head on the pillow beside her, a smile creeping across her face. 'Yeah, wow,' she murmured.

CHAPTER FIVE

8 November

THE early-morning Scottish light crept across the room. Even on the greyest days the sun's rays sneaked through the clouds and scattered this room with light. Brad's brain was fuzzy. Something was different. Something had changed.

Then he felt a movement beside him, and the memories of the night before crowded into his brain. Cassidy. Wow.

Then something else hit him, charging from the dark recesses of his brain, and he stifled the groan in his throat. Melody. He hadn't told her about Melody.

He turned around in the bed, resting his hand on his arm, staring at the sleeping figure beside him. Her chestnut curls spilled across the pillow that she had wedged half under her arm as she slept on her side, facing him.

She looked beautiful. Her fair skin was smooth and unlined. Cassidy. His distraction. The woman he'd lusted after for the last month.

But his stomach clenched. He was cringing. Things in his brain just didn't add up. If Cassidy was only a distraction, why should he tell her about Melody? There should be no need.

But he knew better than that. No matter how many times he tried to use the word 'distraction' for Cassidy, she was much more than that.

In the last few weeks she had crept under his skin. Hearing her voice brought a smile to his face. Knowing she was working the same shift made his whole day seem brighter. And spending time with her outside work made the days speed past. He knew her habits—she liked to take her shoes off at the door, she sat on the left-hand side of the sofa, she only watched the news on one TV channel. His mood had lifted just by being around her.

His thoughts were always with his daughter but they didn't consume every spare second of every day.

She made him happy. Cassidy made him happy. And he was about to jeopardise all that. He knew he should have told her about Melody. He'd meant to but just hadn't found the appropriate time.

And now, after he'd slept with her, it seemed like a dirty secret. He almost wished he'd put a photo in the doctors' office in the ward as soon as he'd started there. But the truth was that office was used by lots of doctors and it wasn't appropriate to put a family picture in there. And he just hadn't been ready to answer any difficult questions about his daughter.

But now? He sagged back against the pillows. It looked as though he was hiding something. It looked as though he deliberately hadn't trusted Cassidy enough to tell her about Melody. How awkward was this conversation going to be?

He turned his head sideways to look at her again, to look at that perfect face before he ruined everything. A tiny part of him hoped that she wouldn't be annoyed at all. Maybe she would shrug her shoulders and tell him that it was fine?

Who was he kidding? How would he feel if the shoe was on the other foot? If Cassidy had a child she hadn't told him about? The thought was unimaginable. He could feel himself automatically shaking his head at the idea.

Things would be perfect if he could just freeze this moment in time. Keep everything just the way it was right now. Or, even better, just the way they'd been last night. That thought sent a smile across his face. If only…

A frown appeared on Cassidy's brow then her eyelids flickered open. Those big brown eyes that pulled him in every time. A smile appeared on her face instantly. 'Morning,' she whispered.

Relief flooded through him. She hadn't woken up and panicked. She seemed happy and comfortable around him. She obviously had no regrets about the night before. Not yet, anyway.

'Morning,' he whispered back. He couldn't help it. He was immediately drawn to her. He wanted to touch her, taste her skin again. He dropped a kiss on the tip of her nose.

A glint appeared in her eyes. Memories of last night? 'Wow,' she whispered again, her soft breath on his face.

Brad couldn't hide the smile. Her memories were obviously as good as his. If only every morning could be like this.

Her hand crept around his neck, and as much as he wanted to pull her closer and forget about everything else, he just couldn't. He had to get this over and done with.

He shifted backwards in the bed. 'How about I make you some breakfast?' His legs hit the floor before she had a chance to answer, and he pulled his underwear and jeans on rapidly. 'What would you like? Toast? Eggs? Bacon?'

Cassidy looked confused. She pushed herself upwards in the bed and adjusted the pillows behind her. 'I'll have whatever you're making,' she said quietly.

'Great. Give me five minutes and I'll give you a shout. Feel free to take a shower and freshen up.' He leaned forwards and planted another kiss on her forehead before disappearing out of the door.

Cassidy sat for a few minutes, taking deep breaths. What just happened? They'd had a fabulous night, and he'd asked her to stay over. And for a few seconds this morning when she'd woken up, everything had seemed fine. So what had made him jump out of bed like a scalded cat?

She flung back the duvet and swung her legs out of bed, wincing at the cold air in the room. There was a navy-blue dressing gown hanging up behind the bedroom door, and she wrapped it around herself, then headed to the bathroom.

She flicked the switch for the shower, grabbing an elastic band that was sitting on top of the bathroom cabinet and twisting her hair back from her face as she sat at the edge of the bath for a few moments, trying to fathom what was going on.

Was Brad regretting their night together? The thought almost made her belly ache. She couldn't imagine anything worse. Maybe he was only interested in the thrill of the chase and once that was over…

No. No, it couldn't be that. She'd got to know him over the last few weeks, and he didn't seem to be like that at all. Maybe he just felt awkward because it was the first time they'd woken up together?

Yes, that could be it. Her eyes fell to the sink. Brad had obviously been in here first as he'd left her a new toothbrush and toothpaste and a huge white soft towel. She stuck her hand under the shower. It had heated up perfectly, so she stepped into the steaming water.

There was almost a tremor on her skin. Her insides were coiling, to the point of almost feeling pain. She couldn't bear the thought of Brad wanting to walk away after their night together. And it wasn't about the humiliation or about being used. Although those things would be bad enough.

It would be the fact he didn't feel the same connection that she did. The fact that his thoughts didn't wander to her about a million times a day—the way hers did to him. It would be the fact he didn't feel the constant zing between them. Those were the things she couldn't bear.

She could still smell him on her skin and almost regretted having to wash it away, but the blue shower gel with its ocean scent reminded her of him again. She rubbed it into her body even harder, then a few minutes later stepped out of the shower and dried herself rapidly. It only took a few moments to realise she'd nothing to wear, so she padded back through to the bedroom and rummaged in a few of his drawers.

'Cassidy! Breakfast!'

The smell was drifting through the house. Eggs, bacon and tea. Perfect.

'Hey.'

She was standing in the doorway dressed in a pair of his grey jogging trousers and an oversized pale blue T-shirt. His clothes had never looked so sexy. Her hair was ruffled, some little strands around her neck still wet from the shower.

He pulled out a chair for her. 'Have a seat.' All Brad could think about right now was getting this over and done with. He had to come clean. Easier said than done.

He put the plates on the table and poured the tea while Cassidy watched him carefully. She wasn't stupid. She knew something was going on.

She took a sip of her tea, chasing her eggs around the plate with her fork. Watching. Waiting.

Brad pressed his lips together. He reached across the table and took her hand. 'Cass, there's something I need to tell you.'

He could see the tiny flare of panic in her eyes that she was trying to control. She set her tea back down on the table. Her voice was steady. 'So, what is it you want to tell me "the morning after the night before", Brad?'

He winced. There was no getting around this. Cassidy didn't even know what 'it' was—but the implication was there. If this was something important, he should have told her before he'd taken this relationship to the next level.

'I have a daughter.' The words were blurted out before he had a chance to think about it any longer.

'What?' The shocked expression on her face was very real. This was the last thing she'd expected to hear.

Brad took a deep breath. 'I have a daughter, Melody. She's nearly four.' His heart was beating against his chest, the words clambering to his mouth—he just couldn't speak quickly enough right now. 'I haven't seen in her over two years. Her mother, Alison, disappeared with her. We had a...' he flung his hands in the air '...sort of informal custody arrangement. Alison was a doctor as well, and we looked after Melody between us.'

Cassidy's face looked set in stone. 'She was your wife? Your girlfriend? The one you told me you didn't have?' Her tone said it all.

Brad spoke firmly. 'She wasn't my wife and she wasn't my girlfriend, well, not after a few months. We had a very short-lived fling that resulted in Melody. We'd broken up by the time Alison discovered she was pregnant, and neither of us were interested in getting back together.'

He leaned back in the chair, wishing he could tell the whole story in the blink of an eye. Everything about this was painful to him. Every time he spoke about things, he thought about the mistakes he had made and what he could have done differently.

Anything that could have affected the eventual outcome.

Cassidy hadn't moved. Her face was expressionless and her breakfast lay untouched in front of her.

'I don't really know what happened, Cass. I went to pick up Melody as arranged one day, and they were gone.' He flicked his hand in the air. 'Just like that.

Vanished. I was frantic. I went to Alison's work and found out she'd resigned and no one knew where she'd gone. Some of her colleagues said she'd met a doctor from the US and been head over heels in love. They thought she might have gone to the US with him.' He shook his head as a wave of desperation swept over him. It was the same every time he spoke about this.

'I hired a lawyer and two private investigators and tried to track her down. I've been trying to track her down for the last two years—with no success. I haven't seen or heard from her in two years. Right now, I have no idea how my little girl is, where she is or if she even remembers me.' His eyes were fixed on the window, staring out into space.

Cassidy felt numb. 'You have a daughter,' she said.

He nodded, it appeared, almost unconsciously.

'You have a daughter you "forgot" to tell me about?' She couldn't help it—she raised her hands in the air and made the sign of quotation marks.

She could feel rage and anger bubbling beneath the surface, ready to erupt at any moment. She hadn't imagined anything the other night. It hadn't been all in her head. It had been right before her eyes—or it should have been.

Brad looked in pain. He may have been gazing outside, but the look in his eyes was haunted. A father who had lost his child. She couldn't begin to imagine the pain that would cause. But right now she couldn't contain her anger.

'Why didn't you mention this before?'

He sighed. A huge sigh, as if the weight of the world was on his shoulders. His gaze went to his hands that were clenched in his lap. 'I know, I know, I should have. But it just never felt like the right time.'

'How about as soon as you met me?'

His brow wrinkled. 'Oh, yeah. Right. Pleased to meet you, I'm Brad Donovan. I've got a missing daughter, Melody, that I've been searching for the last two years. And before you ask—no—I've no idea why her mother disappeared with her. No—I didn't do anything wrong or mistreat my child. Yes—I've spent an absolute fortune trying to find her and I've been on two wild-goose chases to the US.' He waved his hand in frustration. 'Is that how you wanted me to tell you?'

Cassidy took a deep breath. She wanted to yell. She wanted to scream. She could see how damaged he was by all this. But she couldn't see past how hurt she felt. Hadn't he trusted her enough to tell her? He trusted her enough to sleep with her—but not to tell her about his daughter? It seemed unreal.

She looked around, her eyes scanning the walls. 'So where are they?'

His brow furrowed. 'Where are what?'

She threw her hands up in frustration. 'The photos of your daughter. I've never seen a single one. Where do you keep them?'

He grimaced and stood up. She could hear him walking through to the living room and opening a drawer. He walked through and sat a wooden framed photograph down on the table.

Cassidy felt her heart jump into her mouth as she stared at the image in front of her. The gorgeous toddler with blonde ringlets and Brad's eyes was as pretty as a picture. She felt her lip tremble and she lifted her eyes to meet his. 'You put these away when you knew I would be here?'

He nodded. 'I planned to tell you.' He hesitated, having the good grace to look shamefaced. 'I just hadn't got around to it.'

'Why didn't you tell me when I first asked you about your family? When I asked you if you had a wife or a girlfriend? When I told you about my ex-fiancé and his new Miss Spain wife? How about telling me then? Correct me if I'm wrong, but wasn't that your ideal opportunity?'

She folded her arms across her chest. It didn't matter that she'd tried to play down how hurt she'd been over her breakup with her fiancé. The fact was she'd *told* him about it—albeit in sparing detail. There was no way he was getting away with this. She didn't care about the wonderful night before. She didn't care how many times he'd taken her to heaven and back.

This was about trust. This was about honesty. This was about the things you *should* tell someone before you slept with them.

Brad shook his head. 'You make it all sound so simple, Cass.'

She cringed. The exact thought she'd had when he'd asked her about Bobby. 'It is.'

'No. It's not.' His voice was determined. 'Okay, so you may have asked me about a wife or girlfriend—and I didn't have either, so I didn't tell you any lies. And I'd only just met you then, Cass. I don't want everyone to know my business, and this isn't the easiest thing to talk about. People talk. People make judgements.' He pressed his fingers against his temples.

'When Alison and Melody vanished at first, people were suspicious about me in Australia. People, colleagues even, wondered if I'd done something to them. It was only after the Australian police confirmed they'd left on an international flight that people stopped assuming I'd done something awful.'

Cassidy felt her heart constrict. It was something she hadn't even considered. It hadn't even entered her mind that someone would think like that about Brad. How could friends or colleagues have done that?

Her head was instantly filled with stories in the media, and after only a few seconds she realised it was true. As soon as anyone went missing, suspicion was generally directed at those around them. What on earth would that feel like?

She could only imagine the worst. The frustration of not knowing where your child was. Continually shouting but not being heard. It must have been excruciating.

He leaned his elbows on the table. His fingers moved in small circles at the side of his head. 'It didn't stop there either.' He lifted his head and stared at Cassidy. 'Once people realised I hadn't done something unmentionable to them, they started to say that Alison must have done a runner with Melody to get away from me. As if I'd done something to my child.'

The words hung in the air. Too hideous for thoughts even to form.

'Oh, Brad,' she breathed. Now she understood. Now she understood the pain in his eyes. 'That's awful.'

'You bet it is.'

A lump stuck in her throat. She was angry. She was hurt. And she had no idea what this could mean for them. But right now she had to show some compassion. She stood up, the chair scraping along the kitchen floor, and walked around to the other side of the table.

Brad looked as if he was in shock. As if he was wondering what she might do next.

She might never have had a child stolen from her, but she knew what it was like to be left.

Her parents had done it. Bobby had done it.

But she was calm and lifted his hands from the table, sitting down on his knee and wrapping her hands around his neck, hugging him closely. She could feel his tense muscles beneath her fingers, and she rubbed her hand across his back, waiting for a few moments until he relaxed and the pent-up strain had started to abate.

After a few minutes she leaned back, watching him carefully.

'I'm not happy, Brad. I can't believe you didn't tell me something as important as this.'

She felt him take a deep breath. Right now his blue eyes were almost a window into his soul. She could see his regret. She could see his pain. And although hers could only pale in comparison, she wondered if he could see hers.

'I didn't mean things to turn out like this. This wasn't in my plans.'

In an instant she could almost feel his withdrawal. The hackles rose at the back of her neck. 'What do you mean?'

His hands touched her waist. 'This. Us. I didn't realise things would get so serious.'

'What did you expect? You've practically spent the last five weeks by my side. Every time I turn around, you're right there next to me. If you didn't want us to be more than friends, you should have stayed away.'

She hated how she sounded. She hated the tone of her voice, but she just couldn't help it.

The muscles on his shoulders tensed again and he blew some hair from his forehead, obviously in exasperation. What on earth was he thinking? She had a hollow feeling in her stomach. After the wonderful night before, did he want to walk away?

Everything about this was confusing. She didn't even know how she felt about the fact he had a daughter—she hadn't had time to process those thoughts. Why was she even considering any of this? Her head had always told her this relationship was a bad idea. She wanted someone who would stay in Scotland with her, and the sinking feeling in her stomach told her Brad could obviously never do that.

But her body and soul told her something else entirely. Brad was the first man in a long time that she'd been attracted to—that she'd even been interested in. She loved spending time in his company. She loved his normally easygoing manner. She loved the fact she could depend on him at work—his clinical skills and judgement were excellent.

But most of all she loved the way she felt around him. Even yesterday, in her grandmother's house, doing a task that should have made her feel sad and depressed, there had been so much comfort from having Brad around.

And as for how her body reacted to him…that was something else entirely.

Brad reached up and touched her hair, winding his fingers through one of her curls. Her head tilted instantly—an automatic response—towards the palm of his hand. His eyes were closed. 'How could I stay away from this, Cass?'

He pulled her head down and touched a gentle kiss to her lips. 'You're like a drug to me, Cassidy Rae. Apart from Melody, you're the first thing I think about when I get up in the morning and the last thing I think about when I fall asleep at night.' His eyes opened and she could tell instantly he meant every word.

This was no gentle let-down. This was no attempt to look for an excuse to end their relationship. He was every bit as confused as she was.

She pulled back. This was too much. She was getting in too deep. She pushed herself upwards, her legs trembling as she walked around to the other side of the table and pushed her untouched plate of food away.

'I can't think when you do that. I can't think straight when you touch me. It's too distracting.'

Brad let out a short laugh, shaking his head.

'What? What is it?'

'That word, Cass—distraction. That's what I thought about you at first.'

Cassidy frowned. A distraction. Hardly a flattering description. But he reached across the table and touched her hand again.

'You have no idea how I was feeling when I got here. I'd just had the year from hell in Australia. I'd been to the US twice, chasing false leads trying to find Melody. None of them worked. I'd spent a fortune and still had no idea about my daughter. Last Christmas…' He raised his eyes to the ceiling.

'Let's just say it was the worst ever. Then a few of my friends sat me down and had a conversation with me that was hard for all us. They told me I should never give up looking for Melody, but I had to accept I had a life of my own to live. And they came prepared—they had an armful of job ads for all over the world. I'd let my career slide. I'd been consumed by doing everything I could to find my daughter. The job I'd always loved had become a noose around my neck. I didn't make any mistakes but I'd lost the enthusiasm and passion for the job.

'My friends knew the career paths I'd been interested in before, and they convinced me it was the right time for a break—a change of scenery and a time for new horizons.'

He gave her a rueful smile. 'I didn't come to Scotland with the intention of meeting anyone. I came to Scotland to experience the infamous Scottish winter and the ream of medical admissions that always follow. I planned to just immerse myself in work. To try and give myself a break from constantly checking my emails and phoning the private investigator in the US.'

Cassidy didn't know what to think. A distraction. That's what he'd just called her. She couldn't stop herself from fixating on it. And it gave her the strangest sensation—a feeling of panic.

Maybe this was it. Maybe she should grab her clothes—wherever they were—and get out of here. She needed time to think. She needed a chance to get her head around what he'd just told her. Right now she was suffering from information overload.

Her gaze drifted out the kitchen and onto the coffee table in the living room. She hated that word. It made her feel worthless. As if he didn't value her. The way Bobby had made her feel when he'd left. He'd never used that word, but that's the way she'd felt—as if he'd used her as a distraction, as if he hadn't valued her enough to stay. The same way her parents had made her feel. As if she wasn't worth coming home for.

The only person who hadn't made her feel like that had been Gran. Solid. Dependable. Warm and loving. But even that had changed now. Her gran was a mere shadow of her former self. And what about those letters? She really needed to sit down and decide what she wanted to do with them.

'Cass?'

She was startled. Brad's forehead was wrinkled. He'd still been talking to her, and she'd been lost in her own thoughts. 'What?' she answered quickly.

'You didn't hear me, did you?'

She shook her head. 'You've given me a lot to think about. Maybe I should leave? Maybe you don't need any more distractions.' Her mind could only focus on one thing and she stood up again, ready to leave.

But he was quicker than her, and it took him less than a second to have her in his arms. His face was just above hers. His stubbled jaw, tanned skin and blue eyes definitely distracted *her*.

'I said it was nice to meet someone who enjoyed Christmas so much. Last year is something I don't want to repeat. I was hoping you would help try to get me into the spirit.'

She blinked. He was using her weak spot. Her Christmas rush. And he was doing it with that lazy smile on his face and his fingers winding under her T-shirt.

She sighed. 'This isn't all just going to be okay. I'm going to need some time—to see how I feel.' Then the sticking point came to the forefront of her brain. 'And are you still just using me as a distraction?'

His head moved slowly from side to side. 'I'm not using you as anything. I just want to be around you, Cass. I have no idea where this is going to go. I have no idea what's going to happen between us. But I'd like to find out. What do you say?'

There it was. That feeling. For five weeks he'd made her feel special. Made her feel wanted and important— as if she were the centre of his life. She wanted to say a hundred things. She wanted to sit him down and ask more questions. But his fingers were trailing up her side...

'I need some time to think about all this, Brad. You certainly know how to spring something on a girl.'

He pulled back a little. 'I know, and I'm sorry. I should have told you about Melody.'

Right now she didn't know what to do. She'd learned more about Brad in the last fifteen minutes than she had in the last five weeks. He was hurt, he was damaged. She had seen that in his eyes. And for the last five weeks he'd come to work every day and been a conscientious and proficient doctor. Could she have done the same?

Who did he really have here as a friend? Who was there for him to talk to, to share with, apart from her?

More importantly, did she really want to walk away right now?

It would be the sensible thing to do. She was already feeling hurt, and walking away now could save her from any more heartache in the future. But she'd still need to work with him, she'd still see him at work every single day. How would she cope then? And how would she feel if she saw him with anyone else?

The thought sent a chill down her spine. She didn't want to see him with anyone else. In her head he was already *hers*. And even if this didn't go anywhere, why shouldn't she enjoy what they had right now? She certainly wouldn't mind a repeat of last night. The sooner, the better.

Her hands wound around his neck. 'How about we try to create some new Christmas memories—some nice ones—ones that you could only experience here with me in Scotland?'

He nodded his head slowly. 'That sounds like a plan. What do I have to do in return?'

A thousand suggestions sprang to mind—most of them X-rated. She couldn't stand the pain she'd seen in his eyes earlier. But this definitely wasn't what she'd signed up for. She had to think about herself. She didn't want to end up hurt and alone. She didn't want to end up without Brad.

'I'm sure I'll think of something,' she murmured as she took him by the hand and led him back to the bedroom.

CHAPTER SIX

15 November

CASSIDY hurried up the stairs. Her cardigan was useless this morning, and her new-style uniform wasn't keeping out the freezing temperatures. She touched one of the old-fashioned radiators positioned nearby the hallway. Barely lukewarm. That was the trouble in old stone buildings with antiquated heating systems; the temperature barely rose to anything resembling normal.

The true Scottish winter had hit with a blast over the last few days. This morning, on the way to work Cassidy had slipped and skidded twice on the glistening pavements. She dreaded to think what A and E had been like last night.

Brad had been on call, so she hadn't seen him. He'd phoned her once, around midnight, to say he was expecting a few admissions and to chat for a few minutes. But things had felt a little strained—just as they had for the last week. She still couldn't get her head around all this. Not least the part he hadn't told her he had a daughter.

But the thing she was struggling with most was how much she actually liked him. It didn't matter her head had told her he was ultimately unsuitable. For the last few weeks she'd spent every minute with him. And no matter how confused she was, one emotion topped the rest. She was happy.

Brad made her happy. Spending time with him made her happy. Talking to him every day made her happy. Working with him made her happy. Cuddling up on the sofa with him made her happy. Kissing made her *very* happy, and anything else…

Her heart sank as she saw the bright lights and bustling figures at the end of the corridor. It wasn't even seven o'clock in the morning and her normally darkened ward was going like a fair.

She strode into the ward, glancing at the board. Jackie, one of her nurses, came out of the treatment room, holding a medicine cup with pills and clutching an electronic chart.

'What's going on, Jackie?' She could see instantly that the normally cool and reliable member of staff looked frazzled. Jackie had worked nights here for over twenty years—it took a lot to frazzle her.

Jackie looked pale and tired, and she had two cardigans wrapped around her. 'What do you think?' She pointed at the board. 'I'll give you a full report in a few minutes, but we've had six admissions in the last few hours and we need to clear some beds—there are another four in A and E waiting to come up.'

Cassidy nodded quickly. 'What kind of admissions?'

Jackie pointed at the window to the still-dark view outside. 'All elderly, all undernourished, two with hypothermia and the other four all with ailments affected by the cold. Just what we always see this time of year.'

The stream of elderly, vulnerable patients reminded Cassidy of her gran.

'You rang?' Lucy appeared at Cassidy's side.

'I heard you needed to transfer four patients to my ward. Thought it would be easier if I just came along, got the report and then transferred them along myself.'

Cassidy nodded. 'Perfect.' She walked over to Jackie and took the medicine cup and electronic chart from her hands. 'Introduce me to this patient and I'll take over from you, then you can hand over to Lucy before we do the report this morning.'

Jackie nodded happily. 'That's great. If we get these patients transferred, I'll give you a proper handover before the beds get filled again.' She shrugged her shoulders. 'Brad's around here somewhere. I saw him a few moments ago. He hasn't stopped all night and...' she smiled '...our normally tanned doctor is looking distinctly pale this morning.' She winked at Cass. 'I hope he hasn't been having too many late nights.'

Cassidy froze. The words sank in quickly. She didn't think that anyone knew about Brad and herself. But she should have known better. Word always spread quickly in a hospital like this.

She tried to regain her composure and pretend she hadn't heard the comment—best not to make a big deal of these things and hope the gossip would disperse quickly.

Half an hour later, with the report given and Jackie quickly leaving to go home, Cassidy gave a sigh and went to make a cup of tea. The breakfast trolley had just rolled onto the ward. The auxiliary nurses and domestics were helping the patients, and her two staff nurses had started the morning drug round.

Lucy appeared at her side. 'Make one for me, too, please. I've just taken the last patient round to my ward.'

Cassidy nodded and put two tea bags into mugs. She could kill for a skinny caramel latte right now.

Lucy nudged her. 'So, spill. What's happening with you and Dr Wonderful? I haven't seen you for over a week.'

Cassidy bit the inside of her lip. There was no point beating around the bush. Lucy would only pester her until she told anyway. She poured the boiling water into the cups.

Lucy nudged her again. 'Come on. Is the prediction going to come true? Are you going to be a Christmas bride?'

Cassidy dropped her teaspoon into the sink. 'What? Are you mad?' She'd forgotten all about smelly-cat woman and her mad predictions.

'What's wrong? I thought things were going swimmingly between you and surf boy. Come on, you must have done the dirty deed by now—surely?'

Cassidy felt the instant flush as the heat spilled into her cheeks. It was just a pity her body didn't know how to tell lies.

'I knew it! Well—tell all. Is he wonderful?'

She took a deep breath. 'Do you want me to answer everything at once?'

'I just want you to say something. Anything. What's wrong, Cass?'

'Well, in that case…' She counted off on her fingers. 'No, I definitely won't be a Christmas bride—and I'd forgotten all about that rubbish. Yes, I've done the dirty deed. Yes, it was wonderful—or it was until the next day when he told me he had a daughter.'

'A daughter? Brad has a daughter?'

Cassidy nodded slowly.

'Why hasn't he ever mentioned her? What's the big secret?'

Cassidy picked up her tea and leaned back against the sink. 'The big secret is he doesn't know where she is. Her mother vanished with her two years ago. Apparently she fell in love with some doctor from the US and didn't tell Brad anything about it. He thinks she didn't want to get into a custody battle with him, so basically she did a moonlight flit.'

Lucy looked stunned and shook her head slowly. 'Wow, he's a dark horse, isn't he? I would never have guessed.'

Cassidy sighed again. 'Neither would I.'

There was silence for a few seconds. Lucy touched her arm. 'Whoa, you've got it bad, girl, haven't you?'

Cassidy closed her eyes. 'You could say that.'

Lucy stepped in front of her, clutching her steaming cup of tea with one hand and wagging her finger with the other. 'What happened to Cassidy Rae and *"I'm never going to fall in love with another foreign doctor"*? Where did she go? And what's the big deal about Brad having a daughter? She's lost. The US is a big place, and chances are she might never be found.'

'Cassidy Rae met Brad Donovan. That's what happened. And as for his daughter, I've no idea what will happen. But one thing is for sure—ultimately he won't stay in Scotland with me.'

Lucy leaned forward and gave her a hug. 'Cassidy, you might be making a whole lot of something out of nothing.'

Cassidy stopped for a few moments. Maybe Lucy

was right. He hadn't managed to find Melody so far—
and that was with a private investigator working for
him. Maybe he would never find her? Maybe she could
just forget about Melody and start to focus on them
again?

But she still had an uneasy feeling in her stomach.
Brad wouldn't stay in Scotland—whether he found his
daughter or not. Why on earth was she pursuing a relationship with a man who wasn't right for her?

She shook her head. 'A daughter isn't nothing, Lucy.
It's a whole big something. What happens if we get serious, and then he gets a call to say his daughter has
been found? I'll be left high and dry while he jets off
somewhere to find his lost child. It's hardly the ideal
setup for a lasting relationship.'

Lucy took a sip of her tea, watching Cassidy carefully. 'That's the first time I've ever heard you say anything like that.'

'Like what?'

'The whole words—"lasting relationship". I never
even heard you say that about Mr Spain. You must really like our Dr Donovan.'

'I guess I do.' There. She'd said the words out loud.
And to someone other than herself. It almost felt like
a confession.

A little smile appeared at the corner of Lucy's mouth.
'That's what Lynn and I were talking about at Belinda
the fortune-teller's house. We'd already pegged Brad
for you and thought you'd make a nice couple.'

Cassidy stared at her as memories of that night and
their knowing nods sprang up in her brain. 'You've got
to be joking.'

Lucy shook her head, looking quite pleased with

herself. 'No. We thought you'd be a good fit together. And we were right.'

Cassidy put down her mug and started to fiddle with her hair clip. 'Well, you can't exactly say that now, can you?'

'Yes, I can. I still think you're a good fit.' She folded her arms across her chest. 'So what's been the outcome of Brad's big disclosure? Did you run screaming from the room? Have a tantrum? Go off in a huff?'

Cassidy lowered her head. 'That's just it. There's not really been an outcome. I'm still seeing him and we've talked about it a few times—but we've really only skirted around the edges.' She shrugged her shoulders. 'I've no idea what the big outcome will be.' She shook her head, 'I don't think he knows either.'

Lucy's brow puckered. She nipped Cassidy's arm. 'Who are you, and what have you done with the real Cassidy Rae? The one that always knows precisely what she, and everyone around about her, is doing?'

'Don't, Lucy. Don't remind me how much of an idiot I'm being.'

Lucy's face broke into a smile as she tipped the rest of her tea down the sink and rinsed her cup. 'I don't think you're being an idiot, Cass. For the first time in your life I think you are head over heels in love.' And with that comment she walked out the ward, leaving a shocked Cass still standing at the sink.

The rest of Cassidy's shift was bedlam. Every patient that was admitted was elderly and suffering from effects of the cold. It broke her heart.

'Is this the last one?' she asked as Brad appeared next to another patient being wheeled onto the ward.

He shook his head and ran his hand through his rumpled hair. 'Nope. I've just been paged by the doctor on-call service. They're sending another one in. Ten patients in the last twenty-four hours, all suffering from some effects of cold.' He shook his head in disbelief. 'You don't see this often in Australia. I think I've only ever looked after one case of hypothermia before. Today has been a huge learning curve.'

'Why so many?'

'The temperature apparently dropped to minus twenty last night. Some of these patients only get so-cial-care services during the week—so some of them weren't discovered until this morning. The sad thing is, only two had heating systems that weren't working. The rest were just too scared to put them on because of the huge rise in their heating bills.'

Cassidy waited as they moved their patient over into the hospital bed. He was very frail, hardly any muscle tone at all, his skin hanging in folds around his thin frame. She bundled the covers around him. 'Go and see if you can find any spare duvets or blankets,' she asked one of the nursing auxiliaries.

Brad handed over his chart. 'Frank Johnson is eighty, lives alone and has a past history of COPD and heart disease. You can see he's underweight. He hasn't been eating, and when he was admitted his temperature was thirty-four degrees centigrade. He'd got so confused he'd actually started taking his clothes off, as he thought he was overheating. He was barely conscious when the social-care staff found him this morning.'

Cassidy nodded. It wasn't the first time she'd heard this. She looked at the IV fluids currently connected—often the patients admitted with hypothermia were also dehydrated. 'What's the plan for him?'

Brad pointed to the chart. 'He's been in A and E for a few hours, and his temperature is gradually climbing. It's thirty-six now, still below normal, but he's certainly less confused. Try and get some more fluids and some food into him. I want four-hourly obs and refer him to Social Services and Dietetics. We've got to try and get him some better assistance.' He waved his hand around the ward.

'In fact, those rules apply to just about everyone that's been admitted in the last twenty-four hours.' He looked down at his own bare arms, where his hairs were practically standing on end. 'It doesn't help that this place is freezing, too. What's going on?'

Cassidy gave him a weary smile. 'Old hospital, old heating system. This place is always like this in winter.'

'Tomorrow I'm going to bring in a sleeping bag and walk about in it. Do you think they'll get the hint and try to sort this place out?'

She laughed. 'That would be a sight to see. But good luck. Look at all the staff on the ward—all wearing two cardigans over their uniforms. I hate long sleeves—it's an infection-control hazard. But the temperature in this place is ridiculous. I can hardly tell them to take them off.'

'If you come into my office, I can think of an alternative way to heat you up.'

Cassidy's cheeks instantly flushed and she looked around to check no one had heard his comment. 'Brad!'

He gave her a wicked smile. 'We both know cold temperatures can cause confusion, and it wouldn't do for the doctors and nurses to be confused. I'm just trying to keep us at the top of our game.'

She titled her head to one side. 'Dr Donovan, if the

cold is getting to you, I'll even go so far as to make you a cup of coffee. That should heat you up.'

'And if I'd prefer something else?'

'Then you'll just have to wait.' She folded her arms across her chest. It was almost time for the shift change—time to go home. And Brad must be due to finish as he'd been on call the night before. He looked knackered. As if he could keel over at any moment. But he could still manage to give her that sexy smile and those come-to-bed eyes. And no matter how much she told herself she should walk away, she just couldn't.

'I have something for you.'

'What?'

He pulled something from the pocket of his pale blue scrubs. A pair of rumpled tickets. Cassidy recognised the insignia on them instantly. Her mouth fell open. 'The skating rink! You remembered.'

'Of course I remembered. You said you wanted to go skating the night the ice rink opened in George Square so I bought us some tickets.'

She stared at the tickets. There it was again. Just when everything in her head was giving her lots of reasons to end this relationship. Just when she hadn't been alone with him for a few days and felt as though she was starting to shake him out her system—he did something like this.

Something thoughtful. Something kind. Something that would matter only to her. He'd even managed to plan ahead—a trait distinctly lacking in most men she knew.

'So are we going to capture the spirit of Christmas?' he whispered in her ear.

One look from those big blue eyes and he was instantly back in her system. Like a double-shot espresso. 'You bet ya!' She smiled at him.

20 November

'I don't think we need an ice rink. These pavements are bad enough,' Brad grumbled as he grabbed hold of Cassidy's waist to stop her skidding one more time.

She slid her hand, encased in a red leather glove, into his. 'Don't be such a grump. And look at this place, it's buzzing! Isn't it great?'

Brad looked around. He had to admit Glasgow did the whole Christmas-decoration thing well. There were gold and red Christmas lights strung along the length of Buchanan Street, twinkling against the dark night sky, trying to keep the late-night shoppers in the mood for Christmas. The street was thronged with hundreds of people, all wrapped against the bitter-cold weather, their warm breath visible in the cold night air.

But even though the lights were impressive, he couldn't take his eyes off Cassidy. She seemed to have a coat for every colour of the rainbow. And in the last few days he had seen them all.

But it was her grandmother's red wool coat that suited her most, even though it probably wouldn't withstand the freezing temperatures of tonight.

This evening Cassidy had layered up with two cardigans beneath the slim-fitting coat. She had accessorised with a black hat and scarf and red leather gloves, with a pair of thick black boots on her feet. But even in all those clothes it was her eyes that sparkled most.

As they turned the corner into George Square, the lights were even brighter.

An international Christmas market filled the edges of the square, immediately swamping them in a delicious array of smells. The ice rink took up the middle of the square, with a huge Christmas tree—still to be lit—at one end and an observation wheel at the other. Around the edges were an old-fashioned helter-skelter, a café/bar and a merry-go-round. Families were everywhere, children chattering with excitement about the lights being switched on.

For a second Brad felt something twisting around his heart. He wished more than anything that Melody could be here with him now. He'd never experienced Christmas in a cold climate, and he'd love it if his daughter could see this with him. He'd even seen an ad posted on the hospital notice-board the other day about a Santa's grotto with real, live reindeer down on the Ayrshire coast. If only he could take Melody to see something like that. The thought instantly clouded his head with difficult memories and yearnings.

He watched as a father lifted his daughter up onto one of the huge white horses with red reins on the merry-go-round. As the music started and the ride slowly began to move, he could see the father standing next to the horse, holding his daughter safely in place as her face glowed with excitement.

'Brad?'

He turned abruptly. Cassidy was watching him with her all-seeing, all-knowing brown eyes. She gave his arm a little tug. 'Are you okay?'

She followed his eyes to the merry-go-round, the question hesitating on her lips.

This wasn't the time to be melancholy. This was the time to be positive and thankful that he could create new memories with someone who tugged at his heart-strings. He reached out and grabbed her leather-gloved hand. 'Have I told you how beautiful you look tonight in your grandmother's coat? That red suits you perfectly.'

He pulled her forward for a kiss, ducking underneath the black furred hat that was currently containing her wayward curls. 'Do you remember those little girls who used to be on top of the chocolate boxes at Christmas? That's just what you look like.'

'Welcome, everyone.' The compère's voice echoed around the square and they turned to face him.

'Who is he?' Brad whispered.

'Some reality TV star,' she whispered back, 'but I've no idea which one.'

The guy was swamped in the biggest coat Brad had even seen. He obviously wasn't from around these parts. 'We're here in Glasgow tonight to light up our Christmas tree.'

There was a cheer around about them.

'Can anyone guess what colour the tree lights will be this year?'

He waited as the crowd shouted out around him. 'Let's count down and see. Altogether now, ten, nine, eight…'

Cassidy started to join in, shouting down the numbers with rest of the crowd. 'Come on, you.' She nudged him.

Brad smiled and started chanting with people around them. 'Five, four, three, two, *one*!'

There was a gasp as the tree lit up instantly with a whole host of red lights, like winter berries on the tree. A few seconds later they were joined by some tiny silver twinkling stars. A round of applause went up then, and only a few seconds later, Brad noticed Cassidy blink as a cheer erupted all around them. People were holding their hands out and laughing as the first smattering of snow appeared in tiny flakes around them. It only took a few seconds for some to land in the curls of her hair and on her cheeks. She gave a big smile, looking upwards to the dark sky. 'Nothing like a little dusting of snow for the occasion.'

Brad pulled his hand out of his thermal glove and held it out like the people around them. 'First time I've been snowed on,' he said, watching as the tiny flakes melted instantly as they touched his hand. 'This is fabulous.'

Cassidy sighed. 'Wait until the morning. If the snow lies on the roads and streets, it will be even more treacherous than before. In my experience snow generally means we'll be more busy at work.'

Brad grabbed her waist again. 'Work? Let's not talk about work. Let's go and have some fun.'

They walked around some of the nearby market stalls. Cassidy sampled some sautéed potatoes with onions and bacon then moved on to the next stall to try their vast array of chocolates. 'What's your favourite?' Brad asked. 'I'll buy you some.'

Cassidy's nose wrinkled and she glanced over her shoulder. 'Actually, I'm a tat collector. I'd prefer another ornament for my Christmas tree.'

He gave her a surprised look. 'A tree ornament instead of chocolate? I would never have guessed. Well, let's see what they've got.'

She was like a child in the proverbial sweetie shop as she oohed and aahed over tiny green sequin trees, little white angels and traditional wooden crafted Santa Claus ornaments. A few moments later Cassidy had selected a Russian doll for her tree with red and gold zigzags adorning its tiny wooden frame. 'This is perfect,' she said. 'I've never seen anything like this before.'

Brad smiled and handed over some money, but not before picking up a second one for Melody. She would have loved this stall, too.

They walked over to the nearby booth to collect their skates and spent a few minutes sitting at the side, lacing them up. Cassidy stood up, wobbling around as she tried to gain her balance. Brad appeared at her side, equally unsteady. 'Are we ready for this?' He held out his hand towards her.

They stepped onto the ice together. It was busy, families skating and wobbling with interlinked hands as they tried to find their way around the ice. Brad took a few moments to get his balance—he'd only ever skated a few times in his life but had always managed to stay upright. Cassidy, however, took him completely by surprise.

She let go of his hand and within seconds was gliding over the ice as if it was something she did every day. Her paces were long and even as she bobbed and weaved through the crowd of people on the ice. She spun round, her red coat swinging out around her. Brad held on to the side rail for a few more seconds.

'Come on, Dr Donovan, show us what you're made of!' she shouted from the middle of the rink.

She looked gorgeous. Her cheeks were flushed with colour, and the red coat with its nipped-in waist highlighted her figure perfectly. The perfect Christmas picture.

Her words were like a challenge. And no matter how unsteady he was on the ice, Brad wasn't one to ignore a challenge. He pushed himself off as best he could towards her, nearly taking out a few children in the process. He reached her in a few seconds with only a few unsteady steps and wrapped his arms around her in the middle of the rink. 'You're a scammer, Cassidy Rae. You didn't say you knew how to ice skate.'

'You didn't ask.' Her eyes were twinkling as she pushed off and spun around him again, skating backwards for a few seconds before ending in an Olympic-style twirl.

'Show-off,' he growled. 'Where on earth did you learn how to do that?'

She started skating backwards around him. 'In Australia you surf—in Scotland you skate!' She reversed into him, allowing him to collapse his arms around her waist. 'That's not strictly true,' she said. 'I skated for around five years but, to be honest, as a young girl I was a bit flighty. I tried ballet, majorettes, country dancing and horse riding before I started skating.'

His head rested on her shoulder, his nose touching her pink flushed cheek. 'I like the sound of a flighty Cassidy Rae. She sounds like fun.'

Cassidy pushed off and turned to face him again, tilting her head to one side. 'Are you trying to say I'm not fun now, Dr Donovan?'

'Oh, you're lots of fun, Ms Rae.' He tried to take a grab at her, but his unsteady gait sent him wobbling across the ice. 'Help!'

She skated alongside him and slotted her hand into his. 'Let's just take things easy. We'll just skate around in a simple circle like the rest of the people are doing.' She pointed at some kids teetering past them. 'See? Anyone can do it.'

Brad groaned and tried to push more firmly on the ice. It was easier while Cassidy was gripping his hand, and he gained confidence as they circled round and round the rink. By the time the old-fashioned klaxon sounded, signalling the end of their session, Brad felt as though he could finally stand upright with some confidence.

'Is that an hour already? I can't believe it. I was finally starting to get the hang of this.'

'We can come back again,' said Cassidy with a smile as she skated around him again. The rink was starting to empty as people crowded toward the small exit. He watched for a few seconds as Cassidy took advantage of the now-empty ice and did a few twirls. A squeal stopped her in her tracks.

Brad pushed through the throng, reaching a little girl who was being pulled up by her father and clutching her hand to her chest. Her face was pale and Brad could see a few drips of crimson blood on the ice at her feet.

'Let me have a look at her,' he said, lifting her up in his strong arms. 'I'm a doctor.' He turned his head towards Cassidy, who had appeared at his back. 'Can you ask the booth if they have a first-aid kit?'

The crowd parted easily, concerned by the cries of a child, and he walked unsteadily to the adjacent wooden bench at the side of the rink. He positioned the child underneath the nearest light and held her hand tightly for a few seconds.

'What's your name?' he asked the pale-faced, trembling little girl.

'Victoria,' she whispered. Brad smiled. It was clear she was trying very hard not to cry. Her father had his arms wrapped around her shoulders.

'She just fell over as we were waiting to get off the ice. Someone must have caught her hand with their skate.'

Cassidy appeared with the first-aid kit and opened it quickly, pulling out some gloves, antiseptic wipes, sterile dressings and elastic bandages.

Brad got off the bench and lowered himself near the ground, his face parallel with Victoria's. 'I'm just going to have a little look at your hand—just for a second. Is that okay?'

She nodded but clutched her hand even closer to her chest.

He pulled off his gloves and held his hand at the side of her face. 'Can you feel how cold my fingers are?' He touched her cheek and she flinched a little, before smiling and nodding.

He picked up the gloves. 'I'm going to put these really funky blue gloves on before I have a little look. I might want to put a special bandage on your hand—is that okay?'

Victoria nodded, still looking tearful, but held her hand out tremulously to Brad.

Brad worked swiftly. He cleared her hand from her anorak sleeve and had a quick glance at the cut before stemming the flow of blood with a sterile pad. 'I'm going to give this a quick clean and bandage it up for you.' He nodded at Cassidy as she ripped open the antiseptic wipes for him.

'Ouch!' squealed Victoria, as the wipe lightly touched her skin.

'All done,' said Brad almost simultaneously. He took one more look now that the blood was clear, then applied another sterile non-adherent pad and elastic bandage to put a little pressure on the wound. He looked at Cassidy. 'Which hospital is nearest to here?'

'The Royal Infirmary,' she answered. 'Less than five minutes in a taxi.'

Brad gave the anxious father a smile. 'I'm afraid she's going to need some stitches and the wound cleaned properly. The pad shouldn't stick to her skin and the elastic bandage gives a little pressure to stem the flow of blood before you get to the hospital. But it's not a long-term solution. Are you able to take her up to the A and E unit?'

The father nodded. He pulled a phone from his pocket and started pressing buttons. 'I have a friend who's a taxi driver in the city centre. He'll come and get us.'

Brad leaned forward and whispered in Victoria's ear. 'You're a very brave girl. And do you know what brave girls get?' He reached into his pocket and pulled out his little Russian doll. It was almost identical to the one he'd just bought for Cassidy, but this one had silver and pink zigzags and a long silver string to hang it from the tree.

'This is a special Christmas-tree decoration—just for you.'

Victoria's eyes lit up, his distraction technique working like a charm. Cassidy's felt a lump at the back of her throat that she tried to swallow. He must have bought an extra ornament when he'd paid for hers earlier. And it didn't take much imagination to know who he'd bought it for.

There it was.

Right in front of her, glowing like a beacon. All the reasons why Brad shouldn't be without his daughter. She gathered up the remnants of the first-aid kit, stuffing them back inside, and disappeared back to the booth.

She couldn't watch that. She couldn't watch him interact with a child in such an easy and relaxed manner. It showed what she already knew deep down but hadn't wanted to admit.

Brad was good with kids. No, Brad was *great* with kids. He knew just when to act and what to say. He deserved to have kids. He deserved to be with his daughter. He deserved to know where she was and play a part in her life.

And even though he hadn't said much around her over the last few days, it was clear that Melody was in the forefront of his mind.

She felt ashamed. Ashamed of the words she'd uttered and the thoughts she'd had while she'd been talking to Lucy. Thoughts that he might be willing to forget about his daughter and just have a life with her. What kind of person was she?

She'd seen the haunted look in his eyes earlier when he'd been watching the father and daughter on the merry-go-round. But she hadn't been able to say the words—to ask him if he was hurting and what she could do to help.

She looked over at him now, and he gave her a wave as he walked with Victoria and her father to a black cab parked at the side of the square. Her hand lifted automatically in response, but it was the expression on his face that was killing her.

She'd never seen Brad look so comfortable and so at ease.

She knew what he needed more than anything. He needed to find his daughter.

CHAPTER SEVEN

29 November

'Hi, Cassidy, nice to see you.'

'Hi, Grace, how's Gran today?'

The nurse walked around the desk and joined Cassidy. 'She's in here today,' she said as she walked into a large sitting room looking out over well-tended gardens. 'She's been really confused these last few days, but unusually quiet, too.'

'Is she eating okay?'

Grace nodded. 'She's eating well. She seems quite focused when she gets her meals. But as soon as she's finished, she's off wandering.' She walked over and touched Cassidy's gran on her shoulder. 'Tillie, your granddaughter is here to see you again.'

Cassidy's heart fell as her gran barely even looked up, her eyes still fixed on the garden. She gave Grace a half-hearted smile. 'Thank you, Grace.'

'No problem. Give me a shout if you need anything.'

Cassidy sat down in the chair opposite her gran. Her heart was fluttering in her chest. She was wearing her gran's red wool coat and she wondered if she would notice. She pulled off her leather gloves and reached over and took her gran's hand.

'Hi, Gran.' She brushed a kiss on her cheek.

Tillie looked at her only for a second, her confusion immediately evident. She didn't recognise Cassidy.

Cassidy took a deep breath. It had been like this for the last few months. The little spells of recognition and memory were becoming fewer and fewer. She'd had some episodes where she'd mistaken Cassidy for her mother, but it had been over a year since she'd recognised Cassidy for herself.

This was the part that broke her heart. Her gran had always been her confidante, her go-to person. The person who gave her the best advice in the world—something she badly needed right now.

She opened her bag and stared at the pile of envelopes inside. They'd revealed more than she wanted to know. But it was the photograph that haunted her most. Her gran had always been warm and caring towards her. But she couldn't remember ever seeing her gran like she was in that photograph—her eyes filled with adoration for the man standing by her side. Her whole face glowing with happiness. Had she really known her gran at all?

'I've been at the house, Gran. Everything's fine.' Her fingers caught the edge of the collar of her coat and she bit her lip nervously. 'I found this beautiful coat in the one of the cupboards. It was wrapped up with some letters.' She pulled the bundle from her bag, But Tillie's eyes were still fixed on the garden. Cassidy swallowed, trying to get rid of the lump in her throat.

The garden was covered in frost and a light dusting of snow, but the beds in front of the window brimmed with life. They were filled with evergreen bushes with red berries, coloured heather plants and deep pink pernettya plants. The planters around the edges had an eruption of coloured cyclamen and white heathers. It was beautiful.

Cassidy looked out over the horizon. Everything about this spelled Christmas to her. She wondered what plants they had in Australia at this time of year. Would there be anything as nice as this? How could anyone feel festive in a baking-hot climate?

She'd thought about that often over the last few days, the thoughts just drifting into her mind when she least expected them. She'd had numerous friends who'd emigrated and they all raved about it, saying it had been the best move of their lives. They sent her pictures of spending Christmas Day on the beach, cooking on the barbeque or having dinner in the sunshine next to the pool.

But Christmas always meant cold weather, frost and snow to Cassidy. She just couldn't imagine it any other way. Could she really feel festive in a bikini?

'Hello, dear. Who are you?'

Cassidy flinched and pushed the thoughts from her mind as her gran spoke to her, her eyes suddenly bright with life.

'I'm Cassidy, your granddaughter. I've come for a visit, Gran.'

'How lovely. Do you have any tea?'

Cassidy smiled. Her gran was a true tea genie and could drink twenty cups a day. She slid her hand into her gran's. 'I've come to tell you that I've met a nice man, Gran. One who's making me think about a lot of things.'

Tillie nodded but didn't say anything. Cassidy took

a deep breath. 'When I found your coat, I also found a parcel of letters.' She hesitated for a second. 'I hope you don't mind, but I read them, Gran. The ones from Peter Johnson, your US Air Force friend.'

She paused, waiting to see if would get any reaction. She knew some people would think she was strange, trying to have a normal conversation with a confused old lady, but to Cassidy she couldn't communicate any other way. She loved and respected her gran, and she hoped beyond hope that some of what she said might get through. 'He looked lovely, Gran.'

She pulled out the black-and-white photograph. 'I found a picture of you—you look so happy.' She couldn't help the forlorn sound to her voice as she handed the photo to her gran.

Tillie took it in her frail fingers and touched the surface of the photograph. 'So pretty,' she murmured, before handing it back.

Cassidy sat backwards in her chair. 'He wrote you some lovely letters. You never told me about him—I wish you had.' She stared out the windows, lost in thought.

She'd read the letters the night before, tears rolling down her face. Peter Johnson had met her gran while he'd been stationed in Prestwick with the US Army Air Force. His letters were full of young love and hope for the future. Filled with promises of a life in the US. Most had come from Prestwick, with a few from Indiana at a later date.

Had he been her gran's first love? What had happened to him? Had he gone back to the US and forgotten about her? Her gran could have had the chance of another life, on another continent. Had she wanted to go to the US? What had stopped her? Had she suffered from any of the doubts and confusion that she herself was feeling right now?

She looked back at her gran, who was running her fingers over the sleeve of her coat. 'I wish you could tell me, Gran.' Tears were threatening to spill down her cheeks. 'I really need some advice. I need you to tell me what I should do.'

'What a lovely colour,' her gran said suddenly, before sitting back in her chair. 'Did you bring tea?' she asked.

Cassidy gave Tillie's hand a squeeze. 'I'll go and get you some tea, Gran,' she said, standing up and heading over to the kitchen. She'd been here often enough to know where everything was kept.

The girl in the kitchen gave her a nod and handed over a teapot and two cups. She glanced at her watch. 'I thought it was about that time for your gran. I was just about to bring this over.' She smiled as Cassidy lifted up the tray, before reaching over and touching the shoulder of her coat. 'What a beautiful coat, Cassidy. It's a really nice style. It suits you.'

Cassidy blushed. 'Thank you. I found it the other day.' She nodded over her shoulder. 'It was Gran's.'

'Really? I'm surprised. It looks brand new.' She raised her eyebrows. 'I bet she cut up a storm in that coat a few years ago.'

Cassidy's felt her shoulders sag. 'I don't know, Karen. Truth is, I never saw my gran wear this coat. But I found a picture of her in it and she looked amazing.'

'I bet she did.' Karen gave her a smile. 'You know, Cassidy, I know it's hard seeing your gran like this, but you've got to remember that she's happy here. Although she's frail, her physical health is good for someone her age and most days she seems really content.'

Cassidy nodded gratefully. 'I know, Karen.' She looked over to where her gran was sitting, staring out the window again. 'I just wish I could have the old her back sometimes—even for just a few minutes.'

Karen gave her arm a squeeze. 'I know, honey.'

Cassidy carried the tea tray over and waited a few minutes before pouring a cup for her gran. She was fussy about her tea—not too weak, not too strong, with just the right amount of milk.

Cassidy kept chatting as she sat next to her. It didn't matter to her that her gran didn't understand or acknowledge what she was saying. It felt better just telling her things. In the last year she'd found that just knowing she'd told her gran something could make her feel a million times better—sometimes even help her work things out in her head.

'I've met a nice Australian man. He's a doctor who's working with me right now.' Her gran nodded and smiled. Often it seemed as if she liked to hear the music and tone of Cassidy's voice. 'The only thing is, he has a little girl who is missing right now. He really wants to find her. And when he does...' she took a deep breath '...he'll go.'

The words sounded so painful when she said them out loud.

And for a second they stopped her in her tracks.

What would she do if Brad just upped and disappeared? How would she feel if she could never see him again?

It didn't take long for the little part of her she didn't like to creep into her brain again. Chances were Melody might never be found. Brad might decide to stay in Scotland for a while longer.

She felt a wave of heat wash over her like a comfort blanket. That would be perfect. Maybe she could consider a trip to Australia? That wouldn't be so hard. It was a beautiful country and it might even be interesting to see the differences in nursing in another country.

She looked outside at the frosty weather. Her gran had started singing under her breath. A sweet lullaby that she used to sing to Cassidy as a child. Memories came flooding back, of dark nights in front of the fire cuddled up on Gran's couch.

Part of the issue for Cassidy was that she loved the Scottish winters and cold weather. As a pale-skinned Scot, she'd never been a fan of the blazing-hot sunshine. And even when she'd gone on holiday, she hadn't lain beside the pool for a fortnight; she'd needed to be up and about doing things.

Most people she knew would love the opportunity to live in a warmer climate but Cassidy had never even considered it. Not for a second.

Could she really start to consider something like that now?

Everything was making her head spin. Her relationship with Brad was becoming serious. She really needed to sit down and talk to him again.

She looked at her gran, who was sipping her tea delicately, trying to hear the words she thought her gran might say in her head.

She could imagine the elderly lady telling her not to be so pathetic. To make up her mind about what she wanted and to go get it. She could also sense the old-fashioned disapproval her gran might have about the fact Brad had a child with someone else. A child he wasn't being allowed to fulfil his parental duties towards. Her gran would certainly have had something to say about that.

But would she have been suspicious like some of Brad's colleagues in Australia? Or would she have been sympathetic towards him?

Cassidy just wasn't sure. And finding the letters and photographs made her even less sure. She'd thought she'd known everything about her gran. Turned out she hadn't. And now she'd no way of picking up those lost strands of her life.

She heaved a sigh and looked out over the garden again. She was going to have to sort this out for herself.

30 November

Brad came rushing into the restaurant ten minutes late, with his tie skewed to one side and his top button still undone. 'I'm so sorry,' he gasped as he sat down opposite her. 'There was a last-minute admission just before I left, and Luca was at a cardiac arrest so I couldn't leave.'

Cassidy gave him a smile and lifted her glass of wine towards him. 'No worries, Brad, I started without you.'

He reached over and pulled the bottle of wine from the cooler at the side of the table and filled his glass. She leaned across the table. 'Here, let me,' she said as her deft fingers did up his top button and straightened his tie.

She didn't care that he'd been late. His conscientiousness at work was one of the reasons she liked him so much.

He raised his glass to her. 'Cheers.' The glasses clinked together and Cassidy relaxed back into her chair.

Brad ducked under the table. 'Here, I bought you something.' He handed a plastic bag over to Cassidy.

She raised her eyebrows. 'Did you wrap it yourself?' she quipped.

'Ha, ha. Just look and see what it is.'

Cassidy peeked inside the plastic bag and gingerly put her hand inside—all she could see was a mixture of red and green felt. She pulled out her present and felt a mixture of surprise and a tiny bit of disappointment. It was an advent calendar, the fabric kind with pockets for each of the twenty-four days. The kind she'd told Brad she didn't like.

She looked over at him and he gave her a beaming smile. 'I thought in the spirit of making some nice Christmas memories I would try and convert you.'

She wrinkled her nose. 'Convert me? Why?'

He shrugged. 'You like the paper-type advent calendar. I always had one of these in Australia that my mum made for me. She used to put something in the pockets for only a few days at a time because she knew I would have looked ahead otherwise.' He touched the first few pockets and she heard a rustling sound. 'And they're *not* all chocolates.'

She nodded and gave him a smile. 'So, you're trying to convert me, are you? Well, I'm willing to give it a go. But how do you plan on filling up the other pockets?'

There it was. That little twinkle in his eye as he took a sip of his wine. 'That's the thing. If you want your calendar filled, you'll have to keep letting me into your flat. In fact, I'll need unlimited access.'

She loved the way his smile stretched from ear to

ear. The restaurant was dim, with subdued lighting and flickering candlelight. His eyes seemed even bluer than normal, their colour amplified as they reflected off his pale blue shirt.

'Did you plan this just so you could get into my flat?'

He shook his head, his face becoming a little more serious. 'I just think you've been a little quiet these past few days. As if something was on your mind.' His fingers reached across the table and intertwined with hers. 'I'm just trying to find a way to stay in your life.'

She felt shocked by the openness and honesty of his words. She kept her gaze stuck on the advent calendar as she tried to think of what to say. Things had been a little unsettled between them.

'I'm just a little unsure of what's happening between us,' she started slowly. She lifted her eyes. 'I like you, Brad.'

'And I like you, too, Cassidy. You know that.'

He wasn't making this any easier. It was hard enough, trying to get the words out. His fingers were tracing little circles on the palm of her hand. Just like he did after they'd made love together.

'I'm just worried that I'm getting in too deep and before we know it you'll be gone.'

His brow creased. 'Why would you think that?'

She pulled her hand away from his. It was too distracting. 'I don't know. I just think that I'm from Scotland, you're from Australia…' She threw her hands up in frustration, then levelled her gaze at him. 'I know you don't want to stay here and I don't want to move away. So where does that leave us?'

She could feel tears nestling behind her eyes. That

was the last thing she wanted to happen. She didn't want to cry.

Her mind was flooded with thoughts of her gran. Truth was, she would never find out what happened between her gran and Peter Johnson. Maybe it had only been a wartime fling, with no substance behind it. Or maybe her gran had given up the chance of a lifetime to go and live abroad with the man who'd made her face sparkle.

What Cassidy would never know was whether her gran regretted her decisions. If she could go back, would she do something different?

Was *she* about to make the same mistake?

Brad reached back over and took her hand again. 'Cassidy, I have no idea what's going to happen. All I know is I love spending time with you and I don't want it to end. I've no idea what will happen in the next few years—I've been offered an extension to my job here for another six months, and I've decided to take it. You know I'm not going to stop looking for my daughter. Is that what this is all about? Melody?'

Cassidy shook her head. 'No, it's not about Melody.' Then she hesitated. 'But I don't know what to think about all that. At the end of the day, Brad, we could continue to have a relationship for the next few months and then you could get a call one day about Melody and just disappear. I don't think I could handle that.'

And there it was, staring him in the face. All the while he was practically telling her she was bullheaded and stubborn, her biggest vulnerability lay on the table between them. Abandonment.

He'd sensed it in her for a while. When she'd mentioned her ex-fiancé, her parents or her ill grandmother. That fear of being alone.

He shook his head, the expression on his face pained. 'Remember, Cassidy, I've been on the other side of this fence. I've had someone disappear out of my life with no warning. And I know how much it hurts. I would never do that to another human being.'

She could tell her words had stung, and she hadn't meant them to. It was just so difficult to describe the mishmash of emotions in her head. Even she couldn't understand them, so how could she expect Brad to?

The waiter appeared at their side with some menus, and Cassidy pulled her hand from Brad's to take one. Her eyes ran up and down the menu quickly before Brad lifted it from her hands.

'Don't tell me, you'll have the mushrooms and the chicken.'

Cassidy groaned. 'Don't tell me I'm that predictable.' She grabbed the menu back and ran her eyes along the text again with a sinking realisation that Brad was right. She *did* always have the mushrooms and the chicken. The only time she ever deviated was if neither was on the menu.

He leaned forward, giving her that smile again. 'Why don't you surprise us both and pick something totally different? In fact, close your eyes and just point at something and order that.'

Cassidy shivered. 'Yuck.' Even the thought of doing that was too much for her. Imagine if she ended up with something she didn't like—or never ate? That would be hideous. 'I can't do that, Brad, I might get seaweed or fillet steak.'

His eyes gleamed as he did a pretend shudder.

'Mmm, and that would be awful, wouldn't it? Take this as a test, Cassidy.'

'A test for what?'

He folded his napkin in his lap, as if he was choosing his words carefully. 'For a thoroughly modern woman, you can be pretty closed-minded about some things.'

An uncomfortable feeling crept down her spine. 'What do you mean?'

'You can have some pretty fixed ideas.'

Cassidy shook her head. 'I just know my own mind. There's nothing wrong with that.'

He paused. 'I didn't say there was. But sometimes you make your mind up about things without looking at the whole picture.'

Cassidy was feeling rattled now and a little irritated. So much for a romantic dinner. 'What do you mean exactly?'

He licked his lips and she saw him take a deep breath. There was something different in his eyes. The normal laid-back look was gone. 'What I mean, Cassidy, is that you've written me—and others—off with no thought or regard for our feelings, just because we live in a different country. Now, if you'd been abroad and stayed there for a while and didn't enjoy it, it might seem a reasonable conclusion to have come to. But you haven't. You've never done it. You've never even tried. And what's more—you won't even consider it.'

He looked frustrated by her, angry even, and she felt a tight feeling spread across her chest. Not even Bobby, her Spanish fiancé, had called her like this. She'd just refused to go with him and that had been that. He hadn't questioned her reasoning behind her decision. He hadn't made *her* question her reasoning behind the decision.

But Brad hadn't finished. He was on a roll. 'It's the same with your menu choices and your Christmas traditions.' He leaned over and picked up the advent calendar. 'You say you only like the picture calendars but you've never even tried one of these, have you?' She saw his shoulders sag, tension easing out of them, and the tone of his voice altered.

'All I'm trying to do is get you to look outside your box. To look at the world that surrounds you and open your mind to other ideas, other experiences, other...' he paused before ending '...possibilities.'

He was holding his breath, waiting to see what she would say. She should stop, she should think and ponder what he was saying to her and why. But Cassidy went with her first instinct. She was mad.

She flung her napkin on the table. 'So why are you bothering with me, Brad? You don't date someone with the idea of changing them. You date someone because you like them the way they are, not the way *you* want them to be.' She spat the words at him.

'I'm not trying to change you. I like you, everything about you. But if we have any hope of a future together, you're going to have to learn to bend a little.'

'Meaning what?'

'Meaning that I would love to promise to stay with you in Scotland for the next thirty years, but what if I do get that call about my daughter? What if I do need to go to the States? That's it for us? Just like that—because you won't even consider any other possibility?'

He made it all sound so unreasonable. So closed-minded. But inside she didn't feel like that.

'Or what if I get a great opportunity to work in another country? You won't even consider coming with me? Because you can't leave Scotland?'

'But my gran, I can't leave my gran.' It was the first thing that sprang to mind. The first brick in her feeble wall of defence.

Brad shook his head. 'I'm not asking you to leave your gran, Cassidy. Even though you know she's somewhere she's been taken care of. I'm just trying to see if you'll at least *consider* the possibility.'

Silence hung in the air between them. Her temper had dissipated as quickly as it had arisen.

He was making sense. Inside she knew he was making sense. But to admit it made her seem so petty.

The waiter appeared at their side again. 'Are you ready to order?'

Cassidy didn't even glance at the menu, she just thrust it back at the waiter. 'I'll have the chilli prawns and the Cajun salmon,' she said as she looked Brad square in the eye.

She could see the pulse at the side of his neck flickering furiously. How long had he been holding all this in? Chances were he'd been waiting to say this to her for the last few weeks. And he was right.

Although there was no way she was going to admit it right now.

Tiny little thoughts of Australia had started to penetrate her brain. Little sparks, curiosity and wonder had been creeping in over the last few weeks. Would she like it there? What would it be like to be in a different country for more than a two-week holiday?

It wasn't as if she'd never left the sunny shores of Scotland. She'd been all over the world—Spain, Italy, the US, even the Bahamas. But only for two weeks at a time. And by the time the plane had hit the tarmac back at Glasgow Airport, she'd always been glad to get back home.

But she had lots of friends who'd gone to other countries to work. The most popular place lately had been Dubai. Five of the nurses she'd worked with in Glasgow City Hospital had all upped sticks and gone to work there. All of them loved it and most had no intention of coming back to Glasgow. Two other members of staff had gone to work for aid organisations—one to Africa and one to Médecins Sans Frontières.

Why was she so different? Why had she never wanted to go and work somewhere else? Why did she feel as if her roots were firmly planted in Scottish soil?

Brad lifted the wine bottle and topped up her glass. She hadn't even heard what he'd ordered. She only hoped it was chicken so she could swap her salmon for it.

He lifted his glass to her. 'So, what do you say, Cassidy? Can we raise a toast to trying new things?'

She swallowed hard, her fingers brushing the tiny pockets of the advent calendar on the table in front of her. This couldn't be too hard. She could try this, couldn't she?

He was staring across the table at her, with those big blue eyes, tanned skin and perfect smile. Everything about him made her stomach still lurch. She'd never felt like this before. Could she honestly just walk away?

This had to be worth fighting for.

CHAPTER EIGHT

4 December

CASSIDY woke up with a smile on her face. She glanced at the calendar hanging on her wall. Maybe embracing new change wasn't such a bad thing.

Brad's gifts had proved personal and thoughtful. She'd found an orange Belgian chocolate in the first pocket—one that she'd remarked on that night at the George Square market. For once she hadn't been instantly offended by the thought of a chocolate-filled calendar.

Next had been a tiny green sequin Christmas tree complete with red string, and in the third pocket she'd found a sprig of mistletoe.

It only took her seconds to push her feet into her red slippers and wrap her dressing gown around her shoulders. Brad had been on call again last night, so she hadn't seen him.

Her brow wrinkled. Pocket number four looked distinctly flat—maybe he hadn't had time to put something in there yet? She flicked the switch on the kettle and pulled a cup from the cupboard, before finally touching the pocket. There was a faint rustling noise. She pulled a piece of paper from the pocket and unfolded it.

It said, *'Look under the tree—not everything can fit in these tiny pockets!'*

She left the kettle boiling and walked through to her living room. There, under the tree he'd helped her decorate a few days before, was a red, glistening parcel. She couldn't wipe the smile from her face as she unwrapped the paper. It was a book. But not just any book. It was the latest thriller from her favourite Glasgow author— one she'd been meaning to buy herself.

Cassidy sagged back against the cushions on her sofa. Yet another thoughtful gift. One that meant something to her. Picked up from a chance conversation they'd had in the middle of the night on one shift.

She looked out at the overcast sky. It was going to be another miserable day. Time to wrap up warmly and head up the frosty hill to the hospital. She heard a noise at her door—a key turning in the lock and a whoosh of cold air blasting across the room.

'Brad, what are you doing here?'

Brad was barely recognisable among the layers of clothing he was wearing. All she could really see clearly were his blue eyes peering out from the balaclava-type headwear he'd started wearing to protect himself from the cold. He was brandishing some cups. 'A skinny caramel latte for my favourite woman.'

She smiled. 'I'd hug you, but you're too cold.'

He sat down next to her, hands clenched around his cup. 'I'd take off my jacket but let me heat up first. It's Baltic out there.'

She laughed. 'So, you're finally connecting with our

language. That's something I would normally say—
not you.'

He nudged her. 'You must be rubbing off on me.' He
bent over, his cold nose brushing against her, and she
let out a squeal.

'Get away, ice man!' He wrapped his arms around
her, trapping her on the sofa.

'This is an emergency. I need some body heat. I can't
take these cold winters!'

She pretended to squirm as he held her tight. 'Drink
your coffee. That will heat you up.'

'I can think of a better way to heat up,' he whispered
as he grabbed her hand and led her back through to her
warm bed.

10 December

Today she had a magic wand. Pocket ten had held another little note that had led her to find it wrapped in
silver paper, balanced on the branches of the tree.

He'd asked her favourite film character the other
night and she'd declared she'd always wanted to be
Glinda, the good witch of the north, from *The Wizard
of Oz*. So he'd bought her a magic wand. And right
now she really wanted to wave it above her medical
receiving unit.

In the last twenty-four hours every single one of the
thirty beds in the unit had been emptied and refilled.
Patients were never supposed to stay in the medical
receiving unit. Patients were supposed to be assessed
and transferred to one of the other wards, but the current rate of transfer was ridiculous, for both the staff
and the patients.

She replaced the phone receiver. Her staff was run ragged. The bed manager was getting snarky—she had patients in A and E waiting to be admitted. The normally pristine ward looked chaotic. There were a few random patient belonging bags sitting at the nurses' station, obviously misplaced or forgotten in the preceding few hours. And as for the ward clerk—she'd disappeared in tears five minutes ago.

Cassidy took a deep breath. This was the story of Scottish hospitals in the middle of an icy winter. It was only eight o'clock in the morning. She had to take control of this situation. Something was going to give. And she didn't want it to be her—or her staff.

She lifted her hands above her head. 'Everyone, stop!'

For a second there was silence. Cassidy never raised her voice on the ward and her staff looked startled. A few heads stuck out from doors down the corridor.

'Everyone...' she gestured her hands towards the desk '...come here. This will take five minutes.'

Her bewildered staff walked towards the nursing station. Some were carrying electronic nursing notes, some bed linen and towels.

Cassidy waited until they'd all assembled. One of the phlebotomists and ECG technicians appeared, too. She took another deep breath.

'Everyone, let's calm down. I want you all to take a deep breath and tell me calmly what help you need.' She laid one hand on the desk. 'I can tell you that right now, no matter what the bed manager says, we will not move another patient until after lunchtime today. We need time to assess these patients properly.'

She gestured to the bags on the floor. 'We need to

make sure that patients' belongings don't go astray.' She lowered her voice. 'More importantly, I need my team to know that they do a good job.'

She could see the visible calm descending on the ward as the rumble of the meal trolley could be heard approaching. 'What about the patients in A and E?' asked one of the younger staff nurses.

Cassidy shook her head. 'A and E is full of competent nursing staff. They are more than capable of starting the assessments for their patients. I'm going to phone them now and tell them to arrange breakfast and lunch for those patients. They won't be moving any more up here until after lunchtime.'

A number of shoulders relaxed around her.

'What about the bed manager?'

Cassidy smiled. 'Let me deal with her. Now...' she looked over at the staff surrounding her '...Fiona and Claire, go for your tea break. Michael...' she nodded to the tall, dark-haired nurse beside her '...you start the drug round. Linda and Ann, you help Joanne, the domestic, with the breakfasts.' The two auxiliaries scurried off, glad to have a simple task to perform.

Cassidy noticed Janice, the ward clerk, sniffing at her side. 'What's wrong, Janice?'

'It's the off-duty. It was supposed to be in for yesterday. But there's still a few shifts that need to be covered.'

Cassidy's eyes swept over the blank spaces in the book. Her brain shifted into gear. One of her senior staff nurses had asked if she could start taking over the off-duty rota. And she'd made an absolute mess of it, something Cassidy would have to deal with at a later date.

Just what she would have expected. One short for

the night shift on Christmas Eve. The same thing happened every year without fail.

Her mind drifted back to the night at smelly-cat-woman's house. She almost cringed as she remembered she'd offered to do the night shift if she was a Christmas bride.

She could almost laugh out loud. Although the thought didn't seem anything like as ridiculous as it had before.

Things between her and Brad were good—better than good. Her brain had started to rationalise things for her. Australia was one day away. All twenty-four hours of one day, but still only one day away from Scotland.

The more stories he told her about his life there, the more curious she became. But something else was becoming clearer to her. Just like it had when Brad had naturally came home to her flat the other day after his shift had finished.

She wanted to see him all the time. She wanted to be with him all the time. If he was on call and she didn't see him one day, she missed him. Something that had hit her like a bolt out of the blue.

Cassidy had spent the last two years living life on her own. Her gran's memory had deteriorated to the point she didn't recognise Cassidy, and it had left her feeling even more alone than before. She rarely heard from her parents. But all of sudden it felt as if she had family again.

And having Brad around just felt so *right*.

She didn't expect to be a Christmas bride, but she did expect to have Brad in her future.

She pointed. 'Swap these two around. Lorna prefers

her night shifts together. And I'll cover the night shift on Christmas Eve. Okay?'

'Are you sure?' The clerk was looking at her through red-rimmed eyes.

She gave her shoulder a squeeze. 'Yes, I'm sure. Now, just send it in and go make yourself a cup of tea.'

She went through to her office and made an uncomfortable call to the bed manager then walked quickly through the ward, helping the auxiliaries sit some patients up in bed for breakfast and helping another few patients into chairs. Luca appeared at her side and started reviewing some of the patients who had been admitted overnight. He gave her a smile. 'I hear you're leading a revolt up here this morning.'

She nodded. 'Happy to join in?'

'Absolutely. I feel as if I hardly got to see some of these patients in A and E.'

'It was the same for my staff. We weren't getting the chance to assess the patients properly before we sent them on.' She looked up and down the length of the ward, which seemed much calmer. 'I'm not allowing that to happen. We have a duty of care to these patients and I won't compromise.'

'Tell that to the bed manager.'

'I just did.' She shrugged her shoulders. 'Although she hates me right now, first and foremost she is a nurse, so she does understand the issues.'

The phone started ringing again, and since she'd sent the ward clerk off for tea, Cassidy leaned forward and picked it up. 'Medical receiving unit, Sister Rae speaking. Can I help you?'

The words she heard chilled her to the bone, and she

gestured frantically to Luca for a piece of paper and then started scribbling furiously.

'What's wrong?' he asked as she replaced the phone.

'It's my grandmother. She's had a fall at the nursing home—they think she might have broken her hip.' She started to look around about her, searching for her bag. 'I need to go. They've taken her to another hospital at the other side of the city.'

Luca stood up. 'What can I do?'

Cassidy started pulling on the cardigan that was draped over her chair. She couldn't think straight. She couldn't think at all. The rational parts of her brain had stopped working. Gran was in her eighties and had chest problems. How often did an elderly person have problems with the anaesthetic? What if this was the last time she'd ever see her gran again?

She started to pace up the corridor. 'Michael, are you there?'

His head ducked out from behind a set of curtains.

'I'm really sorry but I need to go. It's an emergency—my gran. They think she might have broken her hip.'

'Of course, Cassidy. No problem.'

'You've got the keys to the drug trolley, haven't you? Here's the controlled-drug key.' She unpinned it from inside her uniform pocket. 'Can you let Lucy, Sister Burns from next door, know that I've had to leave?' She was babbling and she knew it.

'Cassidy, we'll be fine. I'll get some help from next door if we need it. And I won't start transferring any patients until after lunch.' He gave her a quick hug, then placed a hand firmly at her back. 'Now, go.'

* * *

His pager sounded again, and Brad growled and rolled over. 'I'm sleeping. I'm not on call any more. Leave me alone,' he groaned.

But the pager wasn't listening. It sounded again. And again. And again.

Brad was mad. Last night had been ridiculous. He hadn't stopped—not even for a minute. And on the way to work last night his Mini had made the strangest sound then phutted to a stop at the side of the road. And all he wanted to do this morning was lie in his bed and vegetate.

He flung back the covers, squinting at the light coming through the blinds, and lifted the pager to his scrunched-up eyes.

'Call Joe immediately.'

All of a sudden he was wide awake, his heart thumping in his chest. Joe Scott was his very expensive, US private investigator. He emailed Brad every few weeks, telling him any leads he was following and how he was getting on.

They had an understanding. Joe knew that Brad was a doctor, frequently on call, and had agreed that Joe would only contact Brad via his pager if something significant turned up. It had seemed the easiest solution as messages to a busy hospital could be lost, and depending on his rota sometimes Brad could be away from his house and normal emails for a few days at a time.

He reached for his phone, pushing in the number that was ingrained there.

'Joe, it's Brad Donovan. What have you found?'

'Haven't you read the email I sent you? I sent you some photographs.'

It took a few seconds for Brad's ears to adjust to the

American accent. Email. He hadn't looked at his emails for two days.

He moved automatically to his laptop, his bare feet padding across the floor. It took for ever to boot up.

'I'm just opening the email now, Joe,' he said. 'Give me a few minutes.' He wasn't sure what was waking him up more quickly—the shock phone call or the cold air.

The email took for ever to open. He could sense Joe waiting impatiently at the other end of the phone. He didn't even read the content, just clicked on one of the attached photographs.

There she was. Blonde ringlets framing her face, dressed in a green puffy coat, throwing back her head and laughing. It was a beautiful sight.

'Is it her?' The US voice cut into his thoughts.

For a moment he couldn't speak. She'd grown so much. She looked like a proper little girl now—a little lady even, rather than a toddler. His eyes swept the surrounding area. Alison was standing in the background, holding a baby. She was laughing, too. Melody was positioned on the pebbled shoreline of a lake and was clutching stones in her hands.

He tried not to let the rage overwhelm him. He couldn't let that get in the way right now. This was the first time he'd laid eyes on his little girl in nearly two years.

'Brad? Are you there?' The voice was strained now, obviously worried by his lack of response.

'Yes,' he croaked. 'It's Melody.' There was an unfamiliar sensation overwhelming him right now. It was a mixture of relief, joy, bitterness and excitement.

'Great. I was sure I'd found them, but needed you to confirm it.'

Brad's mind started to race. His eyes couldn't move from the photograph. They looked to be out in the middle of nowhere.

'Where are they?'

'North Woods, Wisconsin. Lots of hills and dense woods, terrible phone and internet reception. Took the photo two days ago. You were right about Alison, she got married. Her name is now Alison Johnson. Married to Blane Johnson—a paediatrician in Wisconsin—and they have a baby daughter, Temperance.'

Brad could tell he was reading from the notes in front of him. But he didn't care. He still couldn't believe it. And the picture was crystal clear. Not some blurry snap, which he might have expected. He could almost reach out and touch her. Did she remember him? Did she remember she had a dad who loved her very much?

His fingers brushed the screen. She looked happy. She looked healthy. Part of him gave a little sigh of relief. His daughter was alive, happy and healthy. For any parent, that should be the most important thing.

He was trying so hard to keep a lid on his feelings. He'd spent the last two years thinking about what he'd do when he found her. Thoughts of taking his time and trying to contact Alison separately, engaging a lawyer, getting advice on his legal rights in another country, finding out about extradition from that particular state in the US. And now all those rational, sensible thoughts were flying out the window.

Something registered in his brain—geography had never been his strong point. 'Where is it? Where's North Woods, Wisconsin?'

He heard Joe let out a guffaw. 'I thought you might ask that. Not the most straightforward place to get to. For you, the nearest international airports are Minnesota or Chicago. I don't think you can get a flight from Glasgow to either of them direct. Probably best to fly from Glasgow via Amsterdam and then Chicago. I'll make arrangements for you from there. Just let me know if you're coming into O'Hare or Midway International.'

Brad nodded. Chicago—some place that he'd heard of. He'd be able to find a flight there. 'I'll get online now. I'll get the quickest flight out that I can. Give me a couple of hours and I'll email you back the details.'

'No problem, son. See you soon.'

Brad put down the phone. His hands were shaking. He clicked into the rest of the email. There were four photographs. Two pictures of Alison with her baby and two of Melody. She was still his little girl. She had his blond hair and blue eyes. She even had his smile. And if he played his cards right, he would get to see her again.

He quickly dialled another number he had in his phone. A US attorney he'd been put in touch with who specialised in family law. Best to get some advice before he set foot on US soil. The last thing he wanted to do was cause a scene and get deported.

His brain whirring, he opened a travel website to search for flights. Only one from Glasgow. Leaving in six hours. He didn't hesitate. A few clicks and he was booked. He'd already been to the US in the last two years and knew his machine-readable passport meant he didn't need a visa.

This was it—he was finally going to see his daughter again.

Then something else hit him. Cassidy. He had to tell Cassidy.

He looked at the clock. It wouldn't take him long to pack. He groaned as he remembered his Mini still abandoned at the side of the road. He could get a taxi to the airport. But he couldn't leave without speaking to Cassidy first. It took a few minutes to wrap up his call to the lawyer then he pulled on his jogging trousers and trainers. He could run up the hill to the hospital. Cassidy would be on the ward. He could speak to her there.

He remembered that look on her face in the restaurant. She'd worried about this moment. And to be honest, he'd reached the stage that he'd wondered if this would ever happen.

And now it had.

And he had to go.

But he wouldn't go without speaking to Cassidy. Without reassuring her that he would come back for her. He loved his daughter with his whole heart. But he loved Cassidy, too, and he wanted her to be a part of his life. He looked over to the table where he had an array of little gifts organised for her—all to be placed in the pockets of the calendar. He would do that once he got back from the hospital.

First he had to reassure her. First, he had to tell her that he loved her.

'Where is she?'

'Where's who?' Michael was in the middle of drawing up some heparin. 'Who are you looking for?'

'Cassidy, of course!' Who did that big oaf think he would be looking for? He was out of breath, panting.

He wasn't really dressed for the cold, with just a T-shirt and tracksuit top in place, and the run up the hill in the biting cold hadn't helped.

Michael's face paled a little. 'Oh, I take it you haven't heard?'

'Haven't heard what?' Brad's frustration was growing by the second.

'Cassidy had to leave. Her gran had a fall in the nursing home and they thought she might have broken her hip. They are taking her to the Wallace Hospital—on the other side of the city. Cassidy left about an hour ago.'

Brad felt the air whoosh out from him. He pulled out his phone and started dialling her number. But it connected directly to her voice mail.

'Not supposed to use that in here,' muttered Michael.

Brad grabbed his arm. 'How far away is the Wallace? How would I get there at this time of day?' This was the worst possible time for his car to die.

Michael frowned. 'You in a hurry?'

Brad nodded. 'I need to see Cassidy, speak to the boss and arrange a few days off, then get to the airport.'

'You are joking, aren't you?' Michael's eyebrows were raised.

'No. No, I'm not. Give me some directions.'

Michael shook his head. 'At this time of day it will be a bit of a nightmare. You'd need to take the clockwork orange...'

'The what?'

'The underground. That's what we call it around here. You'd need to take the clockwork orange to Cessnock and then get the bus to the hospital. It'll take you about an hour.' He looked at the clock on the wall opposite. 'What time do you need to get to the airport?

Because you'll need to get a train to Paisley for that. Then a bus to the airport.'

Brad's head was currently mush. There was no way he was going to get across the city—find Cassidy in a strange hospital, get back, pack and get to the airport in time.

He threw up his hands in frustration and left the hospital, walking back down the hill towards his flat.

He tried her phone again three times and sent her two text messages—but it was obvious she had her phone switched off. What could he do?

He got back home and pulled the biggest suitcase he had from the wardrobe and started throwing things inside. Jeans, jumpers, boots, T-shirts—anything he could think of.

He sat down and tried her phone again. Straight to voice mail. 'Cassidy—it's Brad. I heard about your gran. I'm really sorry and I hope she's okay. I really, really need to speak to you and I don't want to do it over the phone. Please phone me back as soon as you get this message. Please...' He hesitated for a second. 'I love you, Cass.'

He put the phone down. A wave of regret was washing over him. The first time he told her he loved her should have been when he was staring into her big brown eyes—not leaving a message on a phone. But he needed to let her know how he felt. She had to know how much she meant to him.

He looked at the rest of the items on the table. Her flat was only five minutes away—he could go around now and put them in the calendar for her. He could also take some time to write her a letter and explain what had happened. That way, if he didn't get to speak to her, she'd know he'd never meant to leave like this.

He looked at the clock again. Did he really not have the time to get to the other side of the city and back? His heart fell. He knew he didn't. Latest check-in time at the airport was two hours before his flight left. He would never make it. This was the only flight to Chicago that left in the next three days. He had to be on it. The chance to see his daughter again was just too important. He'd waited too long for this moment. He couldn't put this off, no matter how much he wanted to see Cassidy.

He picked up the items from the table and grabbed his keys. He had to try and make this right.

Cassidy leaned back against the wall. The cool hospital concrete was freezing, cutting straight through her thin top, but she welcomed it as she felt completely frazzled. Six hours after she'd got here, her gran was finally being wheeled to Theatre. Her hip was definitely fractured and she was in pain. The orthopaedic surgeon had tried to put her off until the next day, but he hadn't met Cassidy Rae before.

She'd waited until she was sure her gran had disappeared along the corridor to Theatre before she started rummaging around her bag. She badly needed a coffee. Her mobile clattered to the floor as she tried to find her purse.

She picked it up and switched it back on. It had sounded earlier in the A and E department and one of the staff had told her to switch it off. The phone buzzed back into life and started to beep constantly.

Text message from Brad. *'Phone me.'*

Another text message from Brad. *'Phone me as soon as you get this.'*

Text message. *Two voice-mail messages.*

Cassidy felt her heart start to flutter in her chest. She hadn't managed to phone Brad since her gran's accident. Was he worried about her? Or was it something else?

She walked along the corridor and out of the main door, standing to one side and pressing the phone to her ear. She listened to the first message. What on earth was wrong? What didn't he want to say on the phone? Her brain started to panic so much she almost missed the end of the message. *'I love you.'*

Brad had just told her he loved her. On the phone. And while she wanted the warm feeling to spread throughout her body, she couldn't help feeling something was wrong. His voice—the tone of it.

Had something happened to him? She pressed for the next message.

'Cassidy, honey, I'm so sorry. I really wanted to speak to you. I've left you a letter at home—it explains everything. I will be back, I promise. And I'll phone you as soon as I get there. And I'll email you as soon as I get near a computer. I love you, Cassidy.'

Get back from where? Her fingers scrolled for his name and pressed 'dial'. It rang and then diverted to voice mail. His phone must be switched off.

Where was he?

Her agitation was rising. She didn't need this right now. Her gran was in Theatre. She should be concentrating on that. And he should be here with her, helping her through this. Where was he?

She sent him a quick text. *'Still at hospital with Gran. What's going on? Won't be home for a few hours.'*

Maybe he'd been called into work again? Maybe that was it. But something inside her didn't agree.

She walked back inside. There was nothing she could do right now. She had to stay here and be with her gran. There was no telling how she'd be when she woke from her anaesthetic. Cassidy wanted to be close.

And no matter how much she wanted to know what was going on with Brad, he'd just have to wait.

CHAPTER NINE

20 December

THE alarm sounded and Cassidy groaned and thumped the reset button with her hand. Even stretching out from under the warm duvet for a second was too cold. She heard a little muffled sound and seconds later felt a little draught at the bottom of the duvet.

Bert. The alarm had woken him and he was cold, too, so he'd sneaked into the bottom of her bed just as he'd done for the last ten days.

Ten days. Two hundred and forty hours—no, it had actually been forty-seven hours since she'd last spoken to Brad.

Sometimes when she woke in the morning—just for a millisecond—she thought everything was all right again. But then she remembered he was gone, searching for his daughter in North-blooming-Woods, Wisconsin. She'd had to look the place up on the internet—she didn't even know where it was.

By the time she'd got back from the hospital that night, Brad's flight had been in the air for four hours. He was long gone.

And although it helped just a little that he'd tried to

contact her and that he'd left her a letter, it didn't take away from the fact that he'd gone. Just like that. At the drop of a hat.

She knew she was being unreasonable. He'd waited nearly two years to find his daughter—of course he should go. But her heart wasn't as rational as her head tried to be.

Her heart was broken in two.

What if he never came back? What if the only way he could have contact with his daughter was to stay in Wisconsin? What if he fell back in love with Melody's mother?

Every irrational thought in the world had circulated in her mind constantly for the last ten days and nights. Even Bert wasn't helping.

He kept looking at the door and sniffing around Brad's shoes in the hope he would reappear again.

She had to be the unluckiest woman in the world. Twice Brad had phoned her mobile—and both times she had missed his call. Both times she'd been working and both times she'd been with a patient.

He'd phoned the ward one day but she hadn't been on duty. And when he'd phoned the flat she'd been visiting her gran, who was still in hospital.

Every time she tried to call him back she'd received an 'unobtainable' signal.

He'd warned her. He'd warned her that North Woods was aptly named, surrounded by thick woods and hills with poor reception for mobiles and internet connections.

He'd sent two emails letting her know that he'd contacted a family lawyer and made contact with Alison. After some fraught negotiations he'd been allowed su-

pervised access to see Melody twice. They were currently stuck in the land of legal mumbo-jumbo, trying to
figure out the parental rights of two Australians in the
US. Alison was covered—she'd married an American.
But Brad's position was more difficult, particularly
when he was officially only on 'holiday'.

It didn't help that his lawyer was advising him to
look at extradition since Melody had been removed
from Australia without permission.

She really, really wanted to talk to him.

She wanted to hear his voice, feel his arms around
her, feel his body pressed next to hers. Particularly now.
A warm dog around her feet might be nice, but it just
didn't cut it.

She didn't even feel festive any more. Her favourite
time of year had been blighted by the fact the man she
loved was on the other side of the Atlantic. The flight
had taken fourteen hours to reach Chicago, and then another few for the air transfer to North Woods. It wasn't
exactly the easiest place to get to. And it wouldn't be
the easiest place to get home from either.

But as soon as he did, she knew what she was going
to do. She knew what she was going to say. This forced
separation had clarified everything for her. She'd made
up her mind.

Now all she could do was wait.

Brad's heart was in his mouth. His little girl seemed
completely unfazed by him. Alison was another matter entirely.

Ten days of trying to keep his temper in check. Ten
days of biting back all the things he really, really wanted
to say.

Once she'd got over the initial shock, Alison had been shamed into a visit at his lawyer's office. She'd brought her husband along, who seemed equally outraged that Brad had dared to appear into their lives in North Woods, Wisconsin.

It hadn't taken long for his lawyer to go through the legal aspects of removing a child from another country without parental consent. Alison's lawyer had been surprisingly quiet and encouraged his client to agree in principle to some short supervised access spells.

He'd been here ten days and had spent three hours with his daughter.

He'd also spent innumerable hours trying to contact Cassidy back home.

Home? Scotland?

In Brad's mind right now, home was wherever Cassidy was. Wherever they could be together. He wanted to spend hours on the phone to her, talking through things with her and telling her how he felt.

But North Woods didn't seem to be a place with normal communication methods in mind—and to be fair, Joe, his private detective, had warned him about this. In theory, he would have managed to co-ordinate time differences, shift patterns and visiting schedules. But reality was much harder. Right now it seemed as if an old-fashioned carrier pigeon would be more effective than modern-day technology.

He glanced at his watch. Time for another visit. Time to see his gorgeous blonde, curly-headed daughter, who could skim stones across the lake like a professional. Time to get the wheels in motion to learn about more permanent types of access. Time to set up an agreed method of communication between them all. One that meant he could talk to his beautiful daughter without having to face the minefield that was her mother.

Time to get his life in order.

22 December

A Christmas bride. That's what smelly-cat woman had told her. Was there any chance she could go and demand her twenty quid back?

Right now it felt as if she'd been conned. False pretences. That's what they called it. But she'd never heard of a fortune-teller being sued. Just as well she'd never believed any of it.

Cassidy tugged her thick black boots on, trying to ignore the trickle of water inside that instantly soaked through her sock. There was about three feet of snow outside. It had been the same last night when she'd come home from work.

If she'd been organised—or cared enough—she would have stuffed her already soaked boots with newspaper and stuck them under the radiator. Instead, she'd flung them across the room and fallen into bed instantly.

She couldn't even be bothered to prepare something to eat. Her cupboards were a disgrace. Oh, if she wanted chocolate or crisps or bakery items like chocolate éclairs or cupcakes, she was fine. If she wanted anything substantial to eat, she was well and truly snookered.

Cassidy pulled on a cardigan, her gran's red wool coat and a black furry hat. It shouldn't take too long to get up the hill to the hospital. Her only problem would be if the pavement hadn't been gritted. Yesterday she'd picked up three people who'd slipped, trying to climb the hill, and caught another as he'd almost slid past her.

Maybe a coffee would help? A skinny caramel latte would be perfect.

She gave Bert a pat on the way out—even he was too intelligent to want to go out in this weather.

The cold air instantly stung her cheeks. Snow was starting to fall again already. Within a few hours there could easily be another few feet on the ground. Getting home again would be a nightmare.

The aroma caught her. The smell of a freshly prepared caramel latte. She closed her eyes. Heaven on earth.

'Cassidy?'

The voice stopped her in her tracks. It was quiet. Like a question. Unsure, uncertain.

'Brad!'

She didn't hesitate. She didn't care who was in the street around them. She didn't worry about the slippery pavement covered in snow beneath her feet. She launched herself at him.

'Oof…'

He fell backwards and the latte he'd been carrying toppled, leaving a trail of pale brown on the white snow.

'Why didn't you tell me you were coming home? When did you arrive? Do you know how many times I tried to phone you? What on earth is wrong with that place? Why can't you get a decent signal there? And how dare you tell me you love me in a message?' She finished by slapping her gloved hand on his chest. Her knees pinned him to the ground beneath her.

All he could see was her face. Her curls were escaping from the sides of the black furry hat and her cheeks were tinged with red. A face that he'd longed to see for the last twelve days. It looked perfect.

He lifted his head from the snow. 'Is this a happy-to-see-me greeting or a mad-as-hell greeting?'

She furrowed her brow for a second then she broke into a smile and bent towards him, kissing the tip of his nose. 'What do you think?'

His head sagged back against the snow. 'Thank goodness.' He moved underneath her. 'Can I get up now?'

Her grin spread from ear to ear as she turned her head sideways and noticed people staring at them lying on the pavement. 'I suppose so.'

He stood up and brushed the snow from his back. 'I've missed you,' he said as he wrapped his arm around her shoulders.

'Me, too.'

'Can we go inside?'

'Yes, I mean no. I want to do something first. I promised myself I would do something the next time I saw you. Come with me.' She grabbed his hand, waiting until he'd grabbed the handle of his wheeled suitcase and pulled him across the road.

'Sounds ominous. Where are we going?'

'You'll see.'

She walked quickly along the road, in her excitement almost forgetting he was pulling a heavy suitcase through snow. But in a few moments she stopped and smiled. 'In here,' she said.

He looked around him, puzzled by the surroundings. They'd moved away from the busy street to a small church with an even smaller cemetery, virtually hidden from the road. Its tiny spire was the only thing that made it noticeable among the surrounding buildings.

'I didn't even know this was here.'

'Lots of people don't. But two hundred years ago this was one of the main roads into Glasgow.'

He waited while she pushed open an iron gate and walked behind the railings. He followed her in, totally bemused.

'What on earth are we doing here? Is this the church you normally go to? You've never mentioned it.' He looked around at the old worn gravestones. Some of the writing was barely visible now, washed away through time, wind, rain and grime. 'Looks like no one's been buried here in a very long time.'

Cassidy nodded and pulled him under one of the trees. All of a sudden her rose-tinged cheeks looked pale. He could feel the tremors in her skin under her coat. The snow was starting to coat the fur on her hat in a white haze.

Her voice was shaking as she started to speak. 'You told me you loved me.'

He clasped his hands around her. 'And I do, Cassidy. I didn't want to tell you like that, but things happened so quickly and I didn't want you to think I'd just walked away. I wanted you to know how I felt about you. I wanted you to know that I was definitely coming back.' His voice tailed off.

'I didn't want you to think I was abandoning you.' It was so important to him. To tell her that he wasn't like Bobby or her parents. To tell her that he would never abandon her. That he wanted to be with her for ever.

Her eyes were glazed with hidden tears, but she didn't look unhappy. Just very determined.

'What is it, Cassidy? What's wrong?'

'I was wrong. When I spoke to you about Christmas

and its traditions and not leaving Scotland—I was wrong.'

The cold air was making her breath come out in a steam. Short blasts.

'You were right when you said it was about the people—or person—you spend it with.' Her eyes swept around them, taking in the ancient church and graveyard. 'I love Scotland. You know I love Scotland. But I love you more and I want to be wherever you are.'

Brad blinked, snowflakes getting in his eyes. A two-hour flight, followed by another fourteen-hour flight, all worrying about Cassidy. How she would be, whether she would forgive him for leaving without saying goodbye, whether she would be angry with him. 'You love me,' he said slowly, his sense of relief sending a flood of warm blood through his chilled skin.

She nodded, the smile on her face reaching right up into her brown eyes.

'You love me,' he said again.

'Yes, yes, I love you. Do you want me to shout it out loud?' Her voice rose, sending some birds fluttering from the tree above.

He bent his head and kissed her. Taking her sweet lips against his own, pulling her close to him, keeping out all the cold that surrounded them. He'd wanted to do nothing else for the last twelve days. Twelve days and twelve long nights without Cassidy in his arms had driven him crazy.

'How do you feel about fourteen-hour flights?' he whispered.

She pulled backwards a little, nodding slowly. 'To North Woods, Wisconsin?' She reached up, pulling her hand from her red leather glove and running her finger down the side of his cheek. 'I think that's something we can do together.'

He sucked in a breath. She was prepared to go with him to see his daughter. She was prepared to meet the challenge of their life together. She'd come full circle. Just like he had. Eighteen months ago he couldn't have been lower. Cassidy had lit up his world in every way possible. He couldn't imagine life without her.

A shiver stole down his spine. He nuzzled into her neck. 'You've still not told me, what are we doing here, Cass?'

He watched her take a deep breath. She looked at him steadily. 'I've decided I'm a modern woman and want to embrace life—in every way possible. I've always loved this place—especially in the winter.' She swept her arm across the scene. 'How do you feel about this as a wedding setting?'

Brad froze. She hadn't. She hadn't just said that, had she?

She looked terrified. Now that the words were out, she looked as if she could faint on the spot.

'Did you just propose?' He lifted his eyebrow at her in disbelief.

'I think so.' She trembled.

He picked her up and spun her around. 'Isn't this supposed to be my job? Aren't I supposed to go down on one knee and propose to you with a single red rose and a diamond ring?' He pressed his face next to hers, his lips connecting with hers again.

'You were taking too long,' she mumbled. 'It took you a full month to kiss me. What chance did I have?' She hesitated. 'So what do you think?' There was fear in her voice, still that little piece of uncertainty.

'I think you should look in pocket twenty-four of your calendar.'

'What?' She looked momentarily stunned. Not the answer she was expecting.

Cassidy's brain was desperately trying to click into gear. She'd just asked the biggest question in her life. What kind of an answer was that? She hadn't looked at the calendar since the night Brad had left—she'd just assumed he wouldn't have had a chance to fill it before he'd gone.

He set her feet down on the ground. The grin on his face spread from ear to ear, his head, shoulders and eyelashes covered in snowflakes. 'Well, I'm not entirely a modern man. This is my job.' He dropped to one knee on the snow-covered grass. 'So much for taking too long—let's just cut right to the chase. Cassidy Rae, will you do me the honour of being my wife? Will you promise to love, honour and keep me, in sickness and in health, for as long as we both shall live?'

She dropped to her knees beside him. 'That's not a proposal.' She looked stunned. 'That's a wedding vow.'

'That's okay,' he whispered, pulling her even closer. 'I've already got the wedding ring.'

Her eyes widened. 'Pocket twenty-four?'

He nodded. 'Pocket twenty-four. I didn't know there was a church around here. I was hoping that we could say our own vows.'

She giggled. 'Looks like I'm going to be a Christmas bride after all.'

He looked completely confused. 'What on earth are you talking about?'

She smiled. 'Well, one day I might tell you a little story...'

EPILOGUE

One year later

'YOU'VE got to pick the best stones, Cassidy. They need to be flat on both sides.' The blue eyes regarded her seriously before the little face broke into a broad smile. 'That's why I always win,' she whispered, giving a conspiratorial glance over her shoulder towards Brad, who was standing at the lakeside waiting for them both.

'What's going on with my girls?' he shouted.

Melody held her gloved hand out towards Cassidy as they walked back over to Brad.

Cassidy looked down at the blonde curls spilling out from the green woolly hat. She gave Brad a smile. This was their third visit to North Woods, Wisconsin, and Brad had finally been allowed some unsupervised access to his child. Melody was a loving, easy child who, luckily enough, seemed totally oblivious to the tensions between her natural parents.

She spoke to Brad online every week and had been happy to meet Cassidy, loving the fact that her dad had a Scottish wife. She'd even painted Cassidy a picture of them all living in a Scottish castle.

Cassidy winked at Brad. 'Melody and I needed some time to make our plan. We think we've found a sixer.'

'A sixer? What on earth is that?' He shook his head in amusement at them both.

Melody's voice piped up. 'You should know what a sixer is, Daddy.' The stone-skimming champion looked at him seriously, holding up the flat grey stone in her hand like an winning prize. 'This stone will skim across the water *six* times before it goes under.'

'Aha.' He knelt down beside her, touching the stone with his finger, 'A sixer? Really?' He shook his head and folded him arm across his chest. 'No way. Not that stone.'

'It really is, Daddy.'

Brad's face broke into a big smile as he straightened up and slung his arm around Cassidy's shoulder. 'Prove it.'

They watched as Melody took her position at the lakeside edge, narrowing her gaze and pulling her hand back to her shoulder. She let out a yell as she released the stone, sending it skimming over the flat water, bouncing across the lake.

Cassidy leaned against Brad's shoulder. 'One, two, three, four, five, six. Your daughter was absolutely right. It was a sixer. Now, where does she get that skill from, I wonder?'

He laughed. 'Her dad, definitely her dad. I could throw a mean ball as a kid.'

He picked up Melody, who was shrieking over her success. 'What a star!' he shouted as he threw her into the air, catching her in his arms and spinning her round.

Cassidy pulled her red wool coat further around her,

trying to ward off the biting cold. North Woods was nearly as cold as Glasgow at this time of year.

Brad came over and whispered in her ear. 'Happy anniversary, Mrs Donovan.' His cold nose was pressed against her cheek as he wrapped his arms around her waist.

Cassidy felt herself relax against him. After all her worries, all her stresses, things had worked out just fine. They'd married two weeks after his proposal in the churchyard—as quickly as they legally could.

Her gran had recovered quickly from her broken hip and recuperated back in the nursing home with some expert care. She was on a new drug trial, and although her Alzheimer's hadn't improved, it certainly hadn't got any worse. The relief for Cassidy was that the episodes of aggression seemed to have abated. She still visited her gran as often as possible but she was confident in the care the nursing home provided.

That had given her the freedom she'd needed to join Brad on a two-month visit to Australia and on three trips to the States to see Melody.

After a few tense months, Alison's lawyer had finally talked some sense into his client and visiting rights had been sorted out. It meant that every few months they could have Melody for a week at a time to stay with them.

Brad had looked at a few jobs nearby and been interviewed for a position at the local hospital. Cassidy had just seen an ad for a specialist nurse to help set up an anticoagulant clinic and knew it was just what she was looking for. There was only one more thing that could make this perfect.

She turned round and put her arms around his neck.

'Happy anniversary, Dr Donovan.' She kissed him on his cold lips.

'So how do you feel about North Woods, Wisconsin?' he asked, his smile reaching from one ear to the other.

Cassidy looked over her shoulder at the lake with ice around the edges and thick trees surrounding it. 'I think it has potential.' She smiled.

He raised his eyebrows. 'Potential? Potential for what?'

He was waiting. Waiting to see what she would say. He didn't know she'd just found an ad for her dream job. He didn't know that there had been a message from the hospital after he'd left to collect Melody, offering him the job he'd just been interviewed for. But all of that could wait. Right now she wanted the chance to still surprise her new husband.

She rose up on the tips of her toes and whispered in his ear, 'I think North Woods, Wisconsin might be a nice place to make a baby.'

His jaw dropped and his eyes twinkled as he picked her up and spun her round. 'You know, Mrs Donovan, I think you could be right.'

* * * * *

SINGLE DAD'S HOLIDAY WEDDING

BY
PATRICIA THAYER

Originally born and raised in Muncie, Indiana, **Patricia Thayer** is the second of eight children. She attended Ball State University, and soon afterwards headed West. Over the years she's made frequent visits back to the Midwest, trying to keep up with her growing family.

Patricia has called Orange County, California, home for many years. She not only enjoys the warm climate, but also the company and support of other published authors in the local writers' organisation. For the past eighteen years she has had the unwavering support and encouragement of her critique group. It's a sisterhood like no other.

When she's not working on a story, you might find her travelling the United States and Europe, taking in the scenery and doing story research while thoroughly enjoying herself, accompanied by Steve, her husband for over thirty-five years. Together, they have three grown sons and four grandsons. As she calls them: her own true-life heroes. On rare days off from writing you might catch her at Disneyland, spoiling those grandkids rotten! She also volunteers for the Grandparent Autism Network.

Patricia has written for over twenty years, and has authored more than forty-six books. She has been nominated for both a National Readers' Choice Award and the prestigious RITA® Award. Her book NOTHING SHORT OF A MIRACLE won an *RT Book Reviews* Reviewers' Choice award.

A longtime member of Romance Writers of America, she has served as President and held many other board positions for her local chapter in Orange County. She's a firm believer in giving back.

Check her website, www.patriciathayer.com, for upcoming books.

To my Vine Street Sisters.
I've enjoyed our time together. Bless you all.

CHAPTER ONE

SHE still wasn't sure if coming here was a good idea.

Lorelei Hutchinson drove along First Street to the downtown area of the small community of Destiny, Colorado. She reached the historic square and parked her rental car in an angled spot by a huge three-tiered fountain. The centerpiece of the brick-lined plaza was trimmed with a hedge and benches for visitors. A pathway led to a park where children were playing.

She got out, wrapped her coat sweater tighter against the cold autumn temperature and walked closer to watch the water cascade over the marble structure. After nearly twenty years many of her memories had faded, but some were just as vivid as if they'd happened yesterday.

One Christmas she remembered the fountain water was red, the giant tree decorated with multicolored lights and ornaments and everyone singing carols. She had a family then.

A rush of emotions hit her when she recalled being in this exact spot, holding her father's hand as he took her to the park swings. One of the rare occasions she'd spent time with the man. He'd always been too busy building his empire. Too busy for his wife and daughter. So many times she had wanted just a little of his attention, his love. She never got it.

Now it was too late. Lyle Hutchinson was gone.

With a cleansing breath, she turned toward the rows of storefront buildings. She smiled. Not many towns had this step-back-into-the-nineteen-thirties look, but it seemed that Destiny was thriving.

The wind blew dried leaves as she crossed the two-lane street and strolled past Clark's Hardware Store and Save More Pharmacy, where her mother took her for candy and ice cream cones as a child. A good memory. She sure could use some of those right now.

There was a new addition to the block, a bridal shop called Rocky Mountain Bridal Shop. She kept walking, past an antiques store toward a law office with the name Paige Keenan Larkin, Attorney at Law, stenciled on the glass.

She paused at the door to the office. This was her father's town, not hers. Lyle Hutchinson had made sure of that. That was why she needed someone on her side. She pushed the door open and a bell tinkled as she walked into the reception area.

The light coming through the windows of the store-front office illuminated the high ceilings and hardwood floors that smelled of polish and age, but also gave off a homey feeling.

She heard the sound of high heels against the bare floors as a petite woman came down the long hall. She had dark brown hair worn in a blunt cut that brushed her shoulders. A white tailored blouse tucked into a black shirt gave her a professional look.

A bright smile appeared. "Lorelei Hutchinson? I'm Paige Larkin. Welcome home."

* * *

After exchanging pleasantries, Lori was ushered into a small conference room to find a middle-aged man seated at the head of the table, going through a folder. No doubt, her father's attorney.

He saw her and stood. "Lorelei Hutchinson, I'm Dennis Bradley."

She shook his offered hand. "Mr. Bradley."

When the lawyer phoned her last week, and told her of her father's sudden death and that she'd been mentioned in his will, she was shocked about both. She hadn't seen or talked with her father since she'd been seven years old.

All Lori was hoping for now was that she could come into town today, sign any papers for Lyle's will and leave tomorrow.

The middle-aged attorney began, "First of all, Lorelei, I want to express my condolences for your loss. Lyle wasn't only my business associate, but my friend, too." He glanced at Paige and back at her. "I agreed to see you today knowing your reluctance. Your father wanted the formal reading of his will at Hutchinson House tomorrow."

Great. Not the plans she had. "Mr. Bradley, as you know, I haven't seen my father in years. I'm not sure why you insisted I come here." He'd sent her the airline ticket and reserved a rental car. "If Lyle Hutchinson left me anything, couldn't you have sent it to me?"

The man frowned. "As I explained on the phone, Ms. Hutchinson, you're Lyle's sole heir." He shook his head. "And that's all I'm at liberty to say until tomorrow at the reading of the will. Please just stay until then. Believe me, it will benefit not only you, but this town."

Before she could comprehend or react to the news,

the door opened and another man walked into the room. He looked her over and said, "So the prodigal daughter finally made it to town."

The big man had a rough edge to him, his dark hair a little on the shaggy side. He was dressed in charcoal trousers and a collared shirt, minus the tie. His hooded blue-eyed gaze fringed by spiky black lashes didn't waver from her.

Paige stood. "Jace, you shouldn't be here. This is a private meeting between me and my client."

He didn't retreat. "I just wanted to make sure she doesn't take the money and run. Lyle had obligations he needed to fulfill before that happens."

Lori wasn't sure how to handle this—Jace's attack. But having heard of her father's shrewd business deals, she wasn't surprised by the man's anger.

"I'm Lorelei Hutchinson, Mr...."

He stepped closer. "Yeager. Jace Yeager. Your father and I were partners on a construction project until I realized Lyle pulled one over on me."

"Jace," Bradley warned. "Work stopped because of Lyle's death."

The man made a snorting sound. "It wouldn't have if Lyle had put his share of money into the business account in the first place." He glared at Lori. "Sorry if my impatience bothers you, but I've been waiting nearly three weeks and so have my men."

"Be patient a little while longer," Bradley told him. "Everything should be resolved tomorrow."

That didn't appease Mr. Yeager. "You don't understand. I can't keep the project site shut down indefinitely, or I go broke." He turned that heated look on her and she oddly felt a stirring. "It seems tomorrow you're coming into all the money. I want you to know that a chunk of that belongs to me."

Lori fought a gasp. "Look, Mr. Yeager, I don't know anything about your partnership with Lyle, but I'll have Paige look into it."

Jace Yeager had to work hard to keep himself under control. Okay, so he wasn't doing a very good job. When he'd heard that Lorelei Hutchinson was coming today, he only saw red. Was she going to stroll in here, grab her daddy's money and take off? He wasn't going to be on the losing end with a woman again.

Not when his business was on the chopping block, along with his and Cassie's future. Just about every dime he had was wrapped up in this project. And it was already coming to the end of October as it was, with only bad weather on the horizon. It needed to be completed without any more delays.

Jace looked over Lyle's daughter. The pretty blonde with big brown eyes stared back at him. She had a clean-scrubbed look with a dusting of freckles across her nose, and very little makeup.

Okay, she wasn't what he expected, but he'd been wrong about women before. And the last thing he wanted to do was work for her. After his ex-wife, he wasn't going to let another woman have all the control.

He looked at Bradley. "What does Lyle's will say?"

"It won't be read until tomorrow."

Lori saw Jace Yeager's frustration, and felt obligated to say, "Maybe then we'll have some news about the project."

He glared. "There's no doubt I will. I might not have your father's money, Ms. Hutchinson, but I'll fight to keep what's mine."

Yeager turned and stormed out right past a tall redheaded woman who was rushing in. "Oh, dear," she said, "I was hoping I could get here in time." Her green eyes lit up when she saw Lori. "Hi, I'm Morgan Keenan Hilliard."

"Lori Hutchinson," Lori said as she went to shake Morgan's hand.

"It's nice to meet you. As mayor, I wanted to be here to welcome you back to town, and to try and slow down Jace. Not an easy job."

Since Paige and Bradley had their heads together going over papers, they walked out into the hall. "I'm not sure if you remember me."

"I remember a lot about Destiny. Like you and your sisters. You were a little older than I was in school, but everyone knew about the Keenan girls."

Morgan smiled. "And of course being Lyle's daughter, everyone knew of you, too. I hope you have good memories of our town."

Except for her parents' marriage falling apart, along with her childhood. "Mostly, especially the decorated Christmas tree in the square. Do you still do that?"

Morgan smiled. "Oh, yes and it's grown bigger and better every year." She paused. "Our mom said you have a reservation at the inn for tonight."

She nodded. "I don't feel right about staying at the house."

The redhead gripped her hand. "You don't have to explain. I only want your visit here to be as pleasant as possible. If there is anything else, any details about your father's funeral."

Lori quickly shook her head. "Not now."

Morgan quickly changed the subject. "Look, I know

Jace isn't giving you a very good impression at the moment, but he's having some trouble with the Mountain Heritage complex."

"I take it my father was involved in it, too."

Morgan waved her hand. "We can save that discussion for another time. You need to rest after your trip. Be warned, Mom will ask you to dinner…with the family."

Lori wasn't really up to it. She wanted a room and a bed, and to make a quick call back home to her sister.

Morgan must have sensed it. "It's only the family and no business, or probing questions. We'll probably bore you to death talking about kids."

Lori relaxed. She truly didn't want to think about what would happen tomorrow.

"You're right. That's what I need tonight."

That evening as Jace was driving to the Keenan Inn, he came to the conclusion that he'd blown his chance earlier today. He tapped his fist against the steering wheel, angry about the entire mess.

"Daaad, you're not listening."

Jace looked in the rearview mirror to the backseat. "What, sweetie?"

"Do I look all right?"

He glanced over his shoulder. His daughter, Cassandra Marie Yeager, was a pretty girl. She had on stretchy jean pants that covered coltish long legs and a pink sweater that had ruffles around the hem. Her long blond hair had curled around her face with a few tiny braids. Something she'd talked him into helping with.

"You look nice. But you always do."

"We're going to Ellie's grandmother's house. Ellie Larkin is my best friend."

"I think she'll like your outfit."

"What about my hair?"

"Honey, I've always loved your blond curls. The braids are a nice touch."

That brought a big smile to her face and a tightening in his throat. All he ever wanted was for her to be happy.

When they'd moved here six months ago, it hadn't been easy for her. He still only had temporary custody of his daughter. It was supposed to be only during the time when her mother remarried a guy from England. Jace had different plans. He wanted to make Cassie's life here with him permanent. Optimistic that could happen, he went out and bought a run-down house with horse property. Although it needed a lot of work, it felt like the perfect home for them. A couple horses helped coax his seven-year-old daughter into adjusting a little faster to their new life.

A life away from a mother who'd planned to take his Cassie off to Europe. He was so afraid that his little girl would end up in boarding school and he'd only get to see her on holidays.

No, he wouldn't let that happen. A product of the foster care system himself, he'd always longed for a home and family. It hadn't worked out with ex-wife Shelly, and that mistake cost him dearly—a big divorce settlement that had nearly wiped him out. Jace hadn't cared about the money, not if he got his daughter. He only hoped they weren't going to be homeless anytime soon.

His thoughts turned to Lorelei Hutchinson. He didn't like how he reacted to her. Why had she angered him so much? He knew why. She had nothing to do with Lyle's business dealings. But she was due to inherit a lot of money tomorrow, and he could be handed the shaft at the same time. It could cost him everything that mattered. His daughter. No, he wouldn't let that happen.

He pulled up in front of the beautiful three-story Victorian home painted dove-gray with white shutters and trim. The Keenan Inn was a historical landmark, a bed-and-breakfast that was also the home of Tim and Claire Keenan. Jace had heard the story about how three tiny girls had been left with them to raise as their own. That would be Morgan, Paige and Leah. After college all three returned to Destiny to marry and raise their own families.

Right now there was someone else staying in the inn—Lorelei Hutchinson. Somehow he had to convince her that this downtown project needed to move forward. Not only for him, but also for Destiny.

Just then Tim Keenan came out the front door, followed closely by some of their grandkids, Corey, Ellie and Kate.

His daughter grabbed her overnight bag and was out of the car before he could say anything. He climbed out, too.

Tim Keenan waved from the porch. "Hello, Jace."

"Hi, Tim." He walked toward him. "Thank you for inviting Cassie to the sleepover. I think she's getting tired of her father's bad company."

"You have a lot on your mind."

Tim was in his early sixties, but he looked a lot younger. His wife was also attractive, and one of the best cooks in town. He knew that because the Keenans had been the first to stop by when he and Cassie moved into their house. They'd brought enough food for a week.

"Hey, why don't you stay for supper, too?"

He wasn't surprised by the invitation. "Probably not a good idea. I don't think I made much of an impression on Ms. Hutchinson."

The big Irishman grinned. "Have faith, son, and use a little charm. Give Paige a chance to help resolve this." They started toward the door, as Tim continued, "I'm concerned about Lorelei. She wasn't very old, maybe seven, when her parents divorced. Lyle wrote them off, both his ex-wife and his daughter. As far as I know, he never visited her. Now, she has to deal with her estranged father's mess."

Jace felt his chest tighten because this woman's scenario hit too close to home. "That's the trouble with divorce, it's the kids who lose."

They stepped through a wide front door with an etched glass oval that read Keenan Inn and into the lobby. The walls were an ecru color that highlighted the heavy oak wainscoting. A staircase with a hand-carved banister was open all the way to the second floor. All the wood, including the hardwood floors, were polished to a high gloss. He suspected he wasn't the only one who was an expert at restoration.

"This house still amazes me," he said.

"Thanks," Tim acknowledged. "It's been a lot of work over the years, but so worth it. The bed-and-breakfast has allowed me to spend more time with Claire and my girls."

Jace shook his head. "I can't imagine having three daughters."

Keenan's smile brightened. "You have one who gives you joy. I'm a lucky man, I tripled that joy." Tim sobered. "Too bad Lyle didn't feel the same about his child. Maybe we wouldn't be having this conversation tonight."

The sound of laughter drifted in from the back of the house. "That sounds encouraging," Tim said. "Come on, son. Let's go enjoy the evening."

They walked through a large dining room with several small tables covered in white tablecloths for the inn's guests. They continued through a pantry and into a huge kitchen.

Okay, Jace was impressed. There was a large working area with an eight-burner cooktop and industrial-sized oven and refrigerator, and all stainless steel counters, including the prep station. On one side a bank of windows showed the vast lawn and wooded area out back and, of course, a view of the San Juan Mountains. A group of women were gathered at the large round table. He recognized all of them. Morgan because she was married to his good friend Justin Hilliard, another business owner in town. Paige he'd met briefly before today. The petite blonde was Leah Keenan Rawlins. She lived outside of town with her rancher husband, Holt.

And Lorelei.

Tonight, she seemed different, more approachable. She was dressed in nice-fitting jeans, a light blue sweater and a pair of sneakers on her feet. Her hair was pulled back into a ponytail and it brushed her shoulders when she turned her head. She looked about eighteen, which meant whatever he was feeling about her was totally inappropriate.

Those rich, chocolate-brown eyes turned toward him and her smile faded. "Mr. Yeager?"

He went to the group. "It's Jace."

"And I go by Lori," she told him.

He didn't want to like her. He couldn't afford to, not with his future in the balance. "Okay."

"Oh, Jace." Claire Keenan came up to them. "Good, you're able to stay for dinner. We don't get to see enough of you." She smiled. "I get to see your daughter when I volunteer at school."

He nodded. "And I'm happy Ellie and Cassie are friends. Thank you for including her in the kids' sleepovers." He glanced out the window to see his daughter running around with the other children. Happy. "Your granddaughter Ellie helped Cassie adjust to the move here."

Claire's smile was warm. "We all want to make sure you both got settled in and are happy."

That all depended on so many things, he thought. "You've certainly done that."

The older woman turned to Lori. "I wish I could talk you into staying longer. One day isn't much time." Claire looked back at Jace. "Lori is a second grade teacher in Colorado Springs."

Lori didn't want to correct Claire Keenan. She *had* been a second grade teacher before she'd been laid off last month. So she didn't mind that her dear father had decided to leave her a little something. It would be greatly appreciated.

But, no, she couldn't stay. Only long enough to finish up Lyle's unfinished business. She hoped that would be concluded by tomorrow.

Claire excused herself. Tim arrived, handed them both glasses of wine and wandered off, too, leaving them alone.

Lori took a sip of wine, trying not to be too obvious

as she glanced at the large-built man with the broad shoulders and narrow waist. No flab there. He definitely did physical work for a living.

"How long have you lived in Destiny, Mr.... Jace?"

"About six months, and I'm hoping to make it permanent."

She didn't look away. "I'm sure things will be straightened out tomorrow."

"I'm glad someone is optimistic."

She sighed. "Look, can't we put this away for the evening? I've had a long day."

He studied her with those deep blue eyes. "If you'd rather I leave, I will. I was only planning to drop my daughter off."

In the past few hours Lori had learned more about Jace Yeager. She knew that Lyle probably had the upper hand with the partnership. "As long as you don't try to pin me down on something I know nothing about. It isn't going to get us anywhere except frustrated."

He raised his glass in salute. "And I'm way beyond that."

CHAPTER TWO

Two hours later, after a delicious pot roast dinner, Lori stood on the back deck at the Keenan Inn. She'd said her goodbyes to everyone at the front door, but wasn't ready to go upstairs to bed yet.

She looked up at the full moon over the mountain peak and wondered what she was doing here. Couldn't she have had a lawyer back in Colorado Springs handle this? First of all, she didn't have the extra money to spend on an attorney when she didn't have a job and very little savings. She needed every penny.

So this was the last place she needed to be, especially with someone like Jace Yeager. She didn't want to deal with him. She only planned to come here, sign any papers to her father's estate and leave.

Now there was another complication, the Mountain Heritage complex. She had to make sure the project moved forward before she left town. She didn't need to be told again that the project would mean employment for several dozen people in Destiny.

"Why, Dad? Why are you doing this?" He hadn't wanted her all those years, now suddenly his daughter needed to return to his town. How many years had she ached for him to come and visit her, or to send for her.

Even a phone call would have been nice. The scars he'd caused made it hard for his daughter to trust. Anyone.

She felt a warm tear on her cold cheek and brushed it away. No. She refused to cry over a man who couldn't give her his time.

"Are you sad?"

Hearing the child's voice, Lori turned around to find Jace Yeager's daughter, Cassie.

Lori put on a smile. "A little. It's been a long time since I've been here. A lot of memories."

The young girl stood under the porch light. "I cried, too, when my daddy made me come here."

"It's hard to move to a new place."

"At first I didn't like it 'cause our house was ugly. When it rained, the ceiling had holes in it." She giggled. "Daddy had to put pans out to catch all the water. My bedroom needed the walls fixed, too. So I had to sleep downstairs by the fireplace while some men put on a new roof."

"So your dad fixed everything?"

She nodded. "He painted my room pink and made me a princess bed like he promised. And I have a horse named Dixie, and Ellie is my best friend."

Her opinion of Jace Yeager just went up several notches. "Sounds like you're a very lucky girl."

The smile disappeared. "But my mommy might come and make me go away."

Jace Yeager didn't have custody of his daughter? "Does your mom live close?"

The child shook her head. "No, she's gonna live in England, but I don't want to live there. I miss her, but I like it here with Daddy, too."

It sounded familiar. "I'm sure they'll work it out."

The girl studied her with the same piercing blue eyes as her father. "Are you going to live here and teach second grade? My school already has Mrs. Miller."

"And I bet you like her, too. No, I'm not going to teach in town, I'm only here for a visit. My dad died not too long ago, and I have to take care of some things."

"Is that why you were crying, because you're sad?"

"Cassie…"

They both turned around and saw Jace.

"Oh, Daddy," Cassie said.

Jace Yeager didn't look happy as he came up the steps. "Ellie's been looking for you." He studied Lori. "The rest of the girls took the party upstairs."

"Oh, I gotta go." She reached up as her father leaned over and kissed her. "'Bye, Daddy, 'bye, Miss Lori." The child took off.

Jace looked at Lori Hutchinson as his gaze locked on her dark eyes.

Finally Lori broke the connection. "I thought you'd left."

"I'd planned to, but I got caught up at the front porch with the Keenans."

He had wanted to speak to Paige, hoping she could give him some encouragement. She'd said she'd work to find a solution to help everyone. Then she rounded up her husband, Sheriff Reed Larkin, leaving her daughters Ellie and Rachel for Grandma Claire's sleepover.

The other sisters, Morgan and Leah, kissed their parents and thanked them for keeping the kids. He caught the look exchanged between the couples, knowing they had a rare night alone. The shared intimacy had him envious, and he turned away. He, too, planned to leave when he spotted his daughter on the back deck with Lori.

"And I was finishing my coffee." He'd had two glasses of wine at dinner. He had to be extra careful, not wanting to give his ex-wife any ammunition. "Well, I should head home."

She nodded. "Your daughter is adorable."

"Thank you. I think so." Jace had to cool it with Lori Hutchinson. "I just wanted to say something before tomorrow...."

She raised a hand. "I told you, I'll do everything I can to get your project operational again."

He just looked at her.

"Whether you believe it or not, I don't plan to cause any more delays than necessary."

"I wish I could believe that."

"After the meeting, how about I come by the building site and tell you what happened?"

He shook his head. "The site's been shut down. Until this matter is settled, I can't afford to pay the subcontractors. So you see there's a lot at stake for me."

"And I understand that. But I still have no idea what's going to happen tomorrow, or what Lyle Hutchinson's plans are. It's not a secret that I haven't seen the man in years." She blinked several times, fighting tears. "He's dead now." Her voice was hoarse. "And I feel nothing."

Jace was learning quickly that Lyle Hutchinson was a piece of work. "Okay, we can both agree your father was a bastard."

She turned toward the railing. "The worst thing is, you probably knew the man better than I did." She glanced over her shoulder. "So you tell me, Jace Yeager, what is my father planning for me? For his town."

* * *

Tim Keenan stood at the big picture window at the inn as he waved at the last of dinner guests left.

He was a lucky man. He loved his wife and his family. He'd been blessed with a great life running the inn for the past thirty-plus years. Mostly he enjoyed people and prided himself on being able to read body language.

For example, Jace and Lori had been dancing around each other all night. Not too close, but never out of eye sight. And the looks shared between them…oh, my.

Claire came down the steps and toward him, slipping into his arms. "I got the girls settled down for now, but I have a feeling they're plotting against me."

He kissed her cheek. "Not those little angels."

She smiled. "Seems you thought the same about your daughters, too."

"They are angels." He thought about the years raising his girls. And the grandchildren. "And we're truly blessed." He glanced out to see the lonely-looking woman on the porch. Not everyone was as lucky.

Lori watched from the inn's porch as Jace walked to his truck. He was strong and a little cocky. She had to like that about him. She also liked the way he interacted with his daughter. Clearly they loved each other. What about his ex-wife? She seemed to have moved on, in Europe. Who broke it off? She couldn't help but wonder what woman in her right mind would leave a man like Jace Yeager. She straightened. There could be a lot of reasons. Reasons she didn't need to think about. Even though she'd seen his intensity over the project, she'd also seen the gentleness in those work-roughened hands when he touched his daughter.

She shivered. One thing was, he wasn't going to be

put off about the project. And she couldn't wait for this mess to be settled. Then she could put her past behind her and move on.

She walked inside and up to the second floor. Overhead she heard the muffled voices of the kids. Her room was at the front of the house. A large canopy bed had an overstuffed print comforter opposite a brick fireplace. She took out her cell phone and checked her messages. Two missed calls.

Fear hit her as she listened to the message from Gina. She could hear the panic in her half sister's voice, but it had been like that since childhood.

Lori's mother had remarried shortly after moving to Colorado Springs. Not her best idea, losing Lyle's alimony, but Jocelyn was the type of woman who needed a man. She just hadn't been good at picking the right ones. Her short union with Dave Williams had produced a daughter, Regina. Lori had been the one who raised her, until big sister had gone off to college.

Without Lori around, and given the neglect of their mother, Gina had run wild and ended up pregnant and married to her boyfriend, Eric Lowell, at barely eighteen. Except for Gina's son, Zack, her life had been a mess ever since. It became worse when her husband became abusive, though the marriage ended with the man going to jail. Now Lori was tangled up in this mess, too.

She punched in the number. "Gina, what happened?"

"Oh, Lori, I think Eric found us."

Over a year ago, Lori had moved her sister into her apartment while Eric served a jail sentence for drug possession and spousal abuse. This hadn't been the first time he'd smacked Gina around, but the first conviction. That was the reason they'd planned to move out of state when Lori had been notified about Lyle's death.

"No, Gina, he doesn't get out until the first of the month."

"Maybe he got an early release."

"Detective Rogers would have called you. You still have a few weeks."

"What about you? Are you flying home soon?"

She knew this delay would worry Gina more. "I can't yet. I still need to meet with the lawyer tomorrow."

She heard a sigh. "I'm sorry, Lori. You've done so much for us. You have a life of your own."

"No, Gina. You're my sister. Zack is my nephew. I told you, I won't let Eric hurt you again. But I still need a day or so to get things straightened out. Then hopefully we'll have some money to start over and get away from Eric." She prayed that her father had left her something. Since their mother had died a few years ago, there wasn't anything holding them in Colorado Springs. They could go anywhere. "Think about where you and Zack want to move to." Preferably somewhere they needed a second grade teacher.

"No, you decide, Lori. We'll go anywhere you want. We just can't stay here. I won't survive it."

Lori could hear the fear in her voice. "I promise I'll do whatever it takes to keep you safe. Now go get some sleep and give my special guy a kiss from me."

Lori hung up the phone and hoped everything she said was true. Unlike Lyle Hutchinson, she didn't walk away from family.

The next morning, Lori was up early. She was used to being at school ahead of her students to plan the day.

Not anymore. Not since she'd gotten her pink slip at the start of the school year. She'd been told it was because of cutbacks and low enrollment, but she wondered if it was due to the trouble Eric had caused her at the up-scale private school where she taught.

No, she couldn't think about that now. She needed to have a clear head for the meeting. Was Lyle Hutchinson as wealthy as people said? Normally she wouldn't care, but it could help both her and Gina relocate to another part of the country. Somewhere Gina could raise Zack without the fear of her ex-husband coming after her again. Enough money so Lori had time to find a job.

She drove her car to the end of First Street. A six-foot, wrought-iron fence circled the property that had belonged to the Hutchinsons for over the past hundred years. Her heart raced as she raised her eyes and saw the majestic, three-story white house perched on the hilltop surrounded by trees. Memories bombarded her as she eased past the stone pillars at the gate entrance. The gold plaque read Hutchinson House.

She drove along the hedge-lined circular drive toward the house. She looked over the vast manicured lawn and remembered running through the thick grass, and a swing hanging from a tree out back. She parked in front of the house behind a familiar truck of Jace Yeager. Oh, no. Was the man following her?

Then she saw him standing on the porch leaning against the ornate wrought-iron railing. He was dressed in jeans and a denim shirt and heavy work boots. Without any effort, this man managed to conjure up all sorts of fantasies that had nothing to do with business.

She pulled herself out of her daydream. What was he doing here?

He came down the steps to meet her.

She got out of her car. "Jace, is there a problem?"

He raised a hand in defense. "Mr. Bradley called me this morning. Said he needed me here for after the reading."

Lori was confused. "Why?"

"I hope it's to tell me it's a go-ahead on the Mountain Heritage project."

They started up the steps when she saw a man in a khaki work uniform come around the side porch. He looked to be in his late sixties, maybe seventies. When he got closer she saw something familiar.

"Uncle Charlie?"

The man's weathered face brightened as he smiled. "You remember me, Miss Lorelei?"

"Of course I do. You built me my tree swing." She felt tears sting her eyes. "You let me help plant flowers, too."

He nodded and gripped her hands in his. "That was a lot of years ago, missy. You were a tiny bit of a thing." His tired eyes locked on hers. "You've turned into a beautiful young lady." His grip tightened. "I'm so sorry about your father."

Before Lori could say anything more, another car pulled up. Paige Larkin stepped out of her SUV. Briefcase in hand, she walked up the steps toward them.

They shook hands and Paige spoke briefly to Charlie before the man walked off. Paige turned to Jace. "So you've been summoned, too."

"I got a call from Bradley first thing this morning."

Paige frowned. "Dennis must have a reason for wanting you here." She turned back to her client. "Let's not speculate until we hear what's in Lyle's will."

Lori nodded and together they walked up to the large porch, where greenery filled the pots on either side of the wide door with the leaded glass panels.

She knew that her great-great-grandfather had built this house during the height of the mining era. It was said that Raymond Hutchinson never trusted banks. That was why he didn't lose much during the Great Depression.

They went inside the huge entry with high-gloss hardwood floors. A crystal chandelier hung from the high ceiling and underneath was a round table adorned with a large vase of fresh-cut flowers. The winding staircase circled up to the second story, the banister of hand-carved oak. Cream and deep maroon brocade wallpaper added a formality to the space.

Lori released a breath. "Oh, my."

She was reminded of Jace's presence when he let out a low whistle. "Nice."

"Do you remember this house?" Paige asked.

"Not much. I spent most of my time in the sunroom off the kitchen."

Paige shook her head. "Well, I wouldn't be surprised if this becomes yours. And then you can go anywhere in it you want."

Lori started to tell her she didn't want any part of this house when a thin woman came rushing into the room. Her gray hair was pulled back into a bun. She looked familiar as she smiled and her hazel eyes sparkled. Lori suddenly recognized her.

"Maggie?" she managed to say.

The woman nodded with watery eyes. "Miss Lorelei."

"I can't believe it." Lori didn't hesitate, and went

and hugged the woman. It felt good to be wrapped in the housekeeper's arms again. Years ago, Maggie had been her nanny.

"It's good to have you home." The older woman stepped back and her gaze searched Lori's face. "How pretty you are."

Lori felt herself blush. She wasn't used to all this attention. "Thank you, Maggie."

The housekeeper turned sad. "I'm so sorry about your father." Then squeezed her hands tighter. "I want you to know he went in his sleep. They said a heart attack. Maybe if we would have been there…"

Lori could only nod. "No. He couldn't be helped." She had no idea this would be so hard.

Dennis Bradley walked down the hall. "Good. You made it." He turned and nodded toward Jace. "Mr. Yeager, would you mind waiting a few minutes until I've gone over the will with Ms. Hutchinson?"

"Not a problem." He looked at Maggie and smiled. "I wonder if you could find a cup of coffee for me."

"I'll bring some out."

Once she left, the lawyer said, "We should get started."

He motioned them down the hall and into an office. Lori paused at the doorway. The walls were a deep green with dark stained wainscoting. The plush carpet was slate-gray. Bradley sat down behind the huge desk that already had a folder open.

After they were seated, the lawyer began, "I'll read through Lyle's requests. His first was that the will be read here at the family home." He handed Paige and her copies. "We can go over any details later."

The lawyer slipped on his glasses. "I don't know if

you knew that Lyle had remarried for a short time about ten years ago."

Nothing about her father surprised her. She shook her head.

"There was a prenuptial agreement, then two years later a divorce." He glanced down at the paper. "Lyle did have one other relative, a distant cousin who lives back in Ohio." He read off the generous sum left to Adam Johnson. Also he read the amount given to the household staff, which included Maggie and Charlie.

"I'm glad my father remembered them," Lori said.

Bradley smiled. "They were loyal to him for a lot of years." He sighed. "Now, let's move on to the main part of the will.

"Lyle Hutchinson has bequeathed to his only living child, Lorelei Marie Hutchinson, all his holdings in Hutchinson Corp." He read off the businesses, including Destiny Community Bank, two silver mines, Sunny Hill and Lucky Day. There were six buildings on First Street, and this house at 100 North Street along with all its contents, the furnishings and artwork.

Lori was stunned. "Are you sure this is right?" She looked down at Paige's copy to see the monetary amount stated. "My father was worth this much?"

Bradley nodded. "Lyle was a shrewd businessman. Maybe it was because your grandfather Billy lost nearly everything with his bad investments and eccentric living. Lyle spent years rebuilding the family name and recouping the money. And he also invested a lot into this town."

Bradley looked at her, then at Paige. "Are there any questions?"

Lori gave a sideways glance to her lawyer.

"I probably will once we go over everything."

Bradley nodded. "Call me whenever you need to. Now, for the rest I think Mr. Yeager should hear this. Do you have any objections, Lorelei?" With her agreement, he went to the door and had Jace come in.

He sat down in the chair next to Lori.

Bradley looked at Jace. "Whatever you thought, Mr. Yeager, Lyle went into the Heritage project honestly. The business complex was to promote more jobs and revenue for the town. He wasn't trying to swindle you. As we all know, his death was sudden and unexpected."

Jace nodded. "Of course I understand, but you have to see my side, too. I need to finish this job, get tenants in and paying rent."

Bradley nodded and looked at Lori. "And that will happen if Lorelei will agree to the terms."

"Of course I'll agree to finish this project."

"There is a stipulation in the will." Bradley paused. "You are the last living heir in the Hutchinson line, Lorelei. And this town was founded by your great-great-grandfather, Raymond William Hutchinson, after he struck it rich mining gold and silver. But other business has been coming to Destiny and your father invested wisely. He wants you to continue the tradition."

"And I will," she promised. "I plan to release money right away so the work on Mountain Heritage complex can resume."

Bradley exchanged a look with Paige, then continued on to say, "Everything your father left you is only yours if you take over as CEO of Hutchinson Corporation... and stay in Destiny for the next year."

CHAPTER THREE

LORI had trouble catching her breath. Why? Why would her father want her to stay here to run his company?

"Are you all right?" Jace asked.

She nodded, but it was a lie. "Excuse me." She got up and hurried from the room. Instead of going out the front door, she headed in the other direction.

She ended up in the large kitchen with rows of white cabinets and marble countertops. Of course it was different than she remembered. The old stove was gone, replaced with a huge stainless steel one with black grates.

Suddenly the smell of coffee assaulted her nose and she nearly gagged.

"Miss Lorelei, are you all right?"

She turned around to see a concerned Maggie. She managed a nod. "I just need some air." She fought to walk slowly to the back door and stepped out onto the porch. She drew in a long breath of the brisk air and released it, trying to slow her rapidly beating heart.

Two weeks ago, she couldn't say she even remembered her life here, or the father who hadn't had any time for her. Then the call came about Lyle's death, and she'd been swept up into a whirlwind of emotions and confusion. She couldn't even get herself to visit his grave site.

"Are you sure you're okay?"

She turned around and found Jace standing in the doorway. A shiver ran through her and she pulled her sweater coat tighter around her. "You were there. Would you be okay?"

He came to the railing. "Hell, with that kind of money, I could solve a lot of problems."

She caught a hint of his familiar scent, soap and just his own clean manly smell. She shifted away. She didn't need him distracting her, or his opinion.

"Easy for you to say, your life is here, and you wouldn't have to pull up and move." Lori stole a glance at him. "Or have Lyle Hutchinson running that life."

Jace didn't know the exact amount of money Lyle had left his daughter, but knew it had to be sizable from the investigation Jace had done before he'd entered into the Mountain Heritage project. And he needed that project to move ahead, no matter what he had to do. "It's only a year out of your life."

She glared at him. "That I have no control of."

He studied her face. She was pretty with her small straight nose and big brown eyes. His attention went to her mouth and her perfectly formed lips. He glanced away from the distraction.

Yet, how could he not worry about Lorelei Hutchinson when her decision could put his own livelihood in jeopardy? His other concern was having any more delays, especially when the weather could be a problem. This was business. Only.

"Look, I get it that you and your father had problems,

but you can't change that now. He put you in charge of his company. Surely you can't walk away."

She sent him another piercing look. "My father didn't have a problem walking away from his daughter."

He tried to tell himself she wasn't his problem. Then he remembered if she didn't take over the company, then that was exactly what he'd have to do. Walk away from Cassie. "Then don't walk away like he did. This town needs Hutchinson Corporation to exist."

"Don't you think I know that?"

He sat on the porch railing facing her. "I know it's a three-hundred-mile move from Colorado Springs, but you'll have a great income and a place to live." He nodded toward the house. Then he remembered. "I know you'll have to give up your teaching job."

She glanced out at the lawn. "That I don't have to worry about. I was laid off when the school year started. I have my résumé out in several places."

Jace felt bad for her, but at the same time was hopeful. "It's a bad time for teachers. So maybe it's time for a change. Why can't you take over your father's company?"

"There's so many reasons I can't even count them. First of all, I'm not qualified. I have limited business experience. I could lose everything by managing things badly."

He felt a twinge of hope. "You can learn. Besides, Lyle has lawyers and accountants for a lot of it. I'll be the person at the construction site. You can check out my credentials. I'm damn good at what I do."

This time she studied him.

"I can give you references in Denver," he offered.

Lori couldn't help but be curious. Her life had been

exposed, yet she knew nothing about him. "Why did you leave there? Denver."

"Divorce. I had to sell the business to divide the joint assets. Moving here was my best chance to make a good home for my daughter. Best chance at getting full custody."

She might not like the man's bad attitude toward her, but wanting to be a good father gave him a lot of points.

"Once I finish Mountain Heritage and the spaces are leased, I'll have some revenue coming in. It'll allow me to control my work hours. I can pick and choose construction jobs so I can spend more time with Cassie." His gaze met hers. "Best of all, Destiny is a great place to raise children."

She smiled. "That I remember about this town, and how they decorated at Christmas."

She watched conflict play across his face. "That's what I want Cassie to experience, too. I don't want her in some boarding school in Europe because her mother doesn't have time for her." He stood, and quickly changed the subject. "I also have several men that are depending on this job."

"I need to talk to my lawyer before I can make any decision." And she needed to speak to Gina. Her sister weighed heavily in this decision. She turned toward Jace. "I know you were hoping for more."

He nodded. "Of course I was, but I can't wait much longer. Just so you know, I'll be contacting my own lawyer. I have to protect my investment."

Lori tried not to act surprised as she nodded. Jace Yeager finally said his goodbye as he stepped off the porch and walked around the house to the driveway.

She heard his truck start up. Just one more problem to deal with.

"Thanks, Dad." She glanced skyward. "You couldn't give me the time of day when you were alive, but now that you're gone, you turn my life upside down."

She walked back inside the house and back into her father's office. Paige and Mr. Bradley had their heads together. They spent the next twenty minutes going over all the details. She could contest the will, but if she lost, she'd lose everything and so would this town.

Mr. Bradley checked his watch, gathered up his papers and put them in his briefcase. "Lorelei, if you need anything else from me, just call." He handed her a business card. "There's one other thing I didn't get a chance to tell you. You only have seventy-two hours to make your decision," he said then walked out the door.

Lori looked at Paige. "How can I make a life-changing decision in three days?"

"I know it's difficult, Lori, but there isn't a choice. What can I say? Lyle liked being in control." The brunette smiled. "Sorry, I hate to speak ill of the dead."

"No need to apologize. Over the years, my mother never had anything nice to say about the man. It doesn't seem as if he ever changed."

She thought about what Lyle had done to Jace Yeager. The man would lose everything he'd invested in this project if he couldn't complete it. She closed her eyes. "What should I do?"

"Are you asking me as your lawyer or as a citizen of Destiny?"

"Both."

"As your lawyer, if you turn down Lyle's bequest, the corporation and the partnerships would be dissolved and all moneys would be given to charity. You'd get nothing, Lori." Paige went on to add, "As a citizen of a town I love, I hope you accept. Hutchinson Corporation employs many of the people in this community."

She groaned. "Lyle really did own this town."

Paige shrugged. "A fair share of it. But remember, the Hutchinsons built this town with the money they got from mining." She smiled. "Times are changing, though. My brother-in-law Justin is moving at a pretty good pace to take that status. He has an extreme skiing business. And don't count out Jace Yeager. He's got some other projects in the works."

"And now he's tied up in this mess," Lori said. "Dear Lord, you all must have hated my father."

"Like I said there's always been a Hutchinson here to deal with. Your grandfather Billy was a piece of work, too. He'd done a few shady deals in his time. The family has done a lot of good for Destiny." She tried not to smile. "Maybe Lyle was a little arrogant about it."

"And now it looks like you all have me to continue the tradition."

Paige raised an eyebrow. "Does that mean you're staying?"

"Do I have a choice?" She knew it was all about Lyle protecting the Hutchinsons' legacy. Not about his daughter's needs or wants. He had never cared about that.

Well, she had to think about what was best for her family. She and Gina had planned to move away from Colorado, and her sister's ex-husband. Most important they had to be safe. Could Eric find them here in Destiny? Would he try? Of course he would if he had any idea where to look.

If Lori decided to stay, at least she could afford to hire a bodyguard. "I need to talk to my sister. She would have to move here, too."

Paige nodded. "I understand. So when you make your decision give me a call anytime. I need to get back to the office." Her lawyer walked out, leaving her alone.

Lori went to the desk, sat down and opened the file. She stared once again at the exorbitant amount of money her father was worth. Although she was far from comfortable taking anything from Lyle, how could she walk away from this? The money would help her sister and nephew so much. Not to mention the other people in Destiny.

But she'd have to be able to work with Jace Yeager, too. The man had his own anger issues when it came to a Hutchinson. Could she handle that, or him? No, she doubted any woman could, but if she stayed out of his way, they might be able to be partners.

She took her cell phone from her purse and punched in the familiar number. When Gina answered, she said, "How would you feel about moving into a big house in Destiny?"

The next morning, Jace took his daughter to school then drove to the site. He needed to do everything he could to save this project. That meant convince Lori Hutchinson to stay. And that was what he planned to do.

He unlocked the chain-link fence that surrounded the deserted construction site. After opening the gate, he climbed back into his truck, pulled inside and parked in front of the two-story structure. The outside was nearly completed, except for some facade work.

Yet, inside was a different story. The loft apartments

upstairs were still only framed in and the same with the retail stores/office spaces on the bottom floor. He got out as the cool wind caused him to shove his cowboy hat down on his head. Checking the sky overhead, he could feel the moisture in the air. They were predicting rain for later today. How soon before it turned to snow? He'd seen it snow in October, in Colorado.

He heard a car and looked toward the dirt road to see Lori pull in next to his truck and get out. Though tall and slender, she still didn't reach his chin. He glanced down at her booted feet, then did a slow gaze over those long legs encased in a pair of worn jeans. Even in the cold air, his body took notice.

Calm down, boy. She was off-limits.

His gaze shot to her face. "Good morning. Welcome to Mountain Heritage."

"Morning," Lori returned as she burrowed deeper in her coat. "I hope this tour is going to be on the inside," she said. "It's really cold."

He nodded. "Come on."

He led her along the makeshift path through the maze of building materials to the entry. He'd been surprised when he'd gotten the call last night from her, saying she wanted to see Mountain Heritage.

"As you can see, the outside is nearly completed, just a little work left on the trim." He unlocked the door, and let her inside.

"We're ready to blow in insulation and hang Sheetrock. The electricians have completed the rough wiring." He glanced at her, but couldn't read anything from her expression. "This is going to be a green building, totally energy efficient, from the solar panels on the roof, to the tankless water heaters. Best of all, the outside of the structure blends in with the surrounding buildings. But this complex will offer so much more."

He pushed open the double doors and allowed her to go in first. He followed as she walked into the main lobby. This was where it all looked so different. The open concept was what he loved the most about the business complex. He'd done most of the design himself and was proud of how well it was turning out.

The framework of a winding staircase to the second-story balcony still needed the wooden banister. He motioned for her to follow him across the subfloor to the back hall, finding the elevators. He explained about the hardwood floors and the large stone fireplace.

"It's so large."

"We need the space to entice our clients. These back elevators lead to the ten loft apartments upstairs. Both Lyle and I figured they'd rent pretty well to the winter skiers. Of course our ideal renter would be long-term. We were hoping to make it a great place to live, shop and dine all without leaving the premises.

"We have a tentative agreement to lease office spaces for a ski rental company from Justin Hilliard. He's planning on doing a line of custom skis and snowboards."

"How soon were you supposed to have this all completed?"

Was she going to stay? "We'd been on schedule for the end of November." Now he was hoping he still had a full crew. Some of the subcontractors he'd been working with had come up from Durango.

Lori felt ignorant. She'd never been to a construction site. Doubts filled her again as she wondered for the hundredth time if she'd be any good taking over for

Lyle. So many people were depending on her. "How are you at teaching, Jace?"

He looked confused, then said, "I guess that depends on the student and how willing they are to learn."

"She's very serious." She released a sigh. "It looks like we're going to be partners."

Damn. Jace had a woman for his partner, a woman who didn't know squat about construction. And he was even taking her to lunch. He'd do whatever it took to provide for his daughter.

He escorted Lori into a booth at the local coffee shop, the Silver Spoon. He hadn't expected her to accept his lunch invitation, but they'd spent the past two hours at the site, going over everything that would need to happen in the next seven weeks to meet completion. She took notes, a lot of notes.

He'd made a call to his project manager, Toby Edwards, and had asked him to get together a crew. Within an hour, his foreman had called back to tell him they got most of the people on board to start first thing in the morning.

So it seemed natural that he would take her to lunch to celebrate. He glanced across the table. She still looked a little shell-shocked from all the information she'd consumed this morning, but she hadn't complained once.

"This place is nice, homey," she said. "Reminds me of the café I worked in during college."

Okay, that surprised him. "It's your typical family-run restaurant that serves good home cooking, a hearty breakfast in the morning and steak for supper. Outside of a steak house, there isn't any fine dining in Destiny, and Durango is forty-eight miles away. We're hoping a restaurant will be added to our complex. Not only more revenue for us, but more choice when you want to go out."

He smiled and Lori felt a sudden rush go through her. No. No. No. She didn't want to think about Jace Yeager being a man. Well, he was a man, just not the man she needed to be interested in. He was far too handsome, too distracting, and they would be working together. Correction, he was doing the work, she would be watching…and learning.

"I hear from your daughter that you've been remodeling your house."

"Restoration," he corrected. "And yes, it's a lot of work, but I enjoy it. So many people just want to tear out and put in new. There is so much you can save. I'm refinishing the hardwood floors, and stripping the crown moldings and the built-in cabinet in the dining room. What I've replaced is an outdated furnace and water heater."

She smiled. "And the roof?"

He raised an eyebrow.

She went on to say, "Cassie told me that you had to put out pans when it rained."

She caught a hint of his smile, making him even more handsome. "Yeah, we had a few adventurous nights. We stayed dry, though."

She couldn't help but be curious about him, but no more personal questions. Focus on his profession. "I bet my father's house could use some updating, too."

"I wouldn't know. Yesterday was the first time I'd been there. I conducted all my business with Lyle in his office at the bank."

She didn't get the chance to comment as the middle-aged waitress came to the table carrying two mugs and a coffeepot. With their nods, she filled the cups.

"Hi, Jace. How's that little one of yours?"

"She keeps me on my toes." He smiled. "Helen, this is Lorelei Hutchinson. Lori, this is Helen Turner. She and her husband, Alan, are the owners of the Silver Spoon."

The woman smiled. "It's nice to meet you, Ms. Hutchinson. I'm sorry about your father."

"Thank you. And please, call me Lori."

"Will you be staying in town long?" the woman asked.

Lori glanced at Jace. "It looks that way."

She couldn't tell if Helen was happy about that or not. They placed their order and the woman walked away.

"I guess she hasn't decided if she's happy about me staying."

Jace leaned forward. "Everyone is curious about what you're going to do. Whether you'll change things at Hutchinson Corp." He shrugged. "These days everyone worries about their jobs."

"I don't want that to happen. That's one of the main reasons I'm staying in town."

Jace leaned back in the booth. "Of course it has nothing to do with the millions your father left you."

Lori felt the shock. "Money doesn't solve every problem."

"My ex-wife thought it did."

Before she could react to Jace's bitter words, Helen brought their food to the table. Their focus turned to their meal until a middle-aged man approached their booth.

"Excuse me, ma'am, sir," he began hesitantly. "Helen told me that you're Mr. Hutchinson's daughter."

Lori smiled. "I am Lori Hutchinson and you are…?"

"Mac Burleson."

She had a feeling that he wasn't just here to be neighborly. Had her father done something to him? "It's nice to meet you, Mr. Burleson."

Mr. Burleson looked to be in his early thirties. Dressed in faded jeans, a denim shirt and warm winter jacket, he held his battered cowboy hat in his hands. "I hope you'll pardon the intrusion, ma'am, but your father and I had business before his death. First, I'm sorry for your loss."

She nodded. "Thank you."

"I was also wondering if you'll be taking over his position at the bank."

She was startled by the question. "To be honest with you, Mr. Burleson, I haven't had much chance to decide what my involvement would be. Is there a problem?"

The man was nervous. "It's just that, Mr. Neal, in the loan department, is going to foreclose on my house next week." The man glanced at Jace, then back at her.

"I know I've been late on my payments, but I haven't been able to find work in a while. No one is hiring…." He stopped and gathered his emotions. "I have three kids, Miss Hutchinson. If I can have a little more time, I swear I'll catch up. Just don't make my family leave their home."

Lori was caught off guard. Her father planned to evict a family?

"Mac," Jace said, drawing the man's attention, "do you have any experience working construction?"

Hope lit up the man's tired eyes. "I've worked on a

few crews. I can hang drywall and do rough framing. Heck, I'll even clean up trash." He swallowed hard. "I'm not too proud to do anything to feed my family."

Lori felt an ache building in her stomach as Jace talked. "If you can report to the Mountain Heritage site tomorrow morning at seven, I'll give you a chance to prove yourself."

"I'll be there," Mac promised. "Thank you."

Jace nodded. "Report to the foreman, Toby."

Mac shook Jace's hand. "I won't let you down, Mr. Yeager." He turned back to Lori. "Could you tell Mr. Neal that I have a job now? And maybe give me a few months to catch up on my payments."

Lori's heart ached. She didn't even know her loan officer, but it seemed she needed to meet him right away. "Mac, I can't make any promises, but give me a few days and I'll get back to you."

He shook her hand. "That's all I can ask. Thank you, Ms. Hutchinson." He walked away.

Lori released a sigh. "I guess I have a lot more to do now than worry about one building."

"Your job as Hutchinson CEO covers a lot of areas."

Helen came over to the table, this time wearing a grin.

"I hoped you've enjoyed your lunch."

"Great as usual," Jace said.

The waitress started to turn away, then stopped and said, "By the way, it's on the house." She picked up the bill from the table. "Thank you both for what you did for Mac."

"I haven't done anything yet," Lori clarified, now afraid she'd spoken too soon.

"You both gave him hope. He's had a rough time of

late." Helen blinked. "A few years ago, he left the army and came back home a decorated war hero. At the very least, he deserves our respect, and a chance. So thank you for taking the time to listen to him." The woman turned and walked back toward the kitchen.

She looked at Jace, remembering what he said about her inheritance. She also wasn't sure she liked being compared to his ex. "I better go and stop by the bank." She pushed her plate away. "Who knows, maybe all those 'millions' just might do some good."

CHAPTER FOUR

LORI couldn't decide if she was hurt or angry over Jace's assumption about the inheritance. She'd lost her appetite and excused herself immediately after lunch.

She was glad when he didn't try to stop her, because she had a lot of thinking to do without the opinion of a man she'd be working with. And who seemed to have a lot of issues about women.

Was he like her father? What she'd learned from her mother about Lyle over the years had been his need to control, whether in business or his personal life. When Jocelyn Hutchinson couldn't take any more she'd gotten out of the marriage, but their child had still been trapped in the middle of her parents' feud. The scars they'd caused made it hard for Lori to trust.

But was coming back to Destiny worth putting her smack-dab into dealing with the past? All the childhood hurt and pain? It also put her in charge of Lyle's domain, and his business dealings, including the Mountain Heritage complex. And a lot more time with the handsome but irritating Jace Yeager.

The man had been right about something. She had a lot of money and it could do a lot of good. She recalled the look of hope on Mac Burleson's face and knew she needed to find an answer for the man.

She crossed the street to Destiny Community Bank. The two-story brick structure was probably from her grandfather's era. With renewed confidence she walked inside to a large open space with four teller windows. Along the wall were portraits of generations of the Hutchinson men—Raymond, William, Billy and Lyle. They were all strangers to her. She studied her handsome father's picture. This man especially.

She turned around and found several of the bank customers watching her. She put on a smile and they greeted her the same way as if they knew who she was.

She went to the reception desk and spoke to the young brunette woman seated there. "Is it possible to see Mr. Neal? Tell him Lorelei Hutchinson is here."

"Yes, Miss Hutchinson." The woman picked up the phone, and when she hung up said, "Mr. Neal said to have a seat and he'll be out…shortly."

Lori wasn't in the mood to wait. "Is he in a meeting?"

The girl shook her head.

"Then I'll just head to his office. Where is it?"

The receptionist stood and together they went toward a row of offices. "Actually, he's in Mr. Hutchinson's office."

Lori smiled. "Oh, is he? Excuse me, I didn't get your name."

"It's Erin Peters."

"Well, Erin, it's very nice to meet you. I'm Lori." She stuck out her hand. "Have you worked at the bank for long?"

"Three years. I've been taking college classes for my business degree."

"That's nice to know. I'm sure my father appreciated his employees continuing their education."

Erin only nodded as they walked toward the office at the end of the hall. Lori knocked right under the name-plate on the last door that read Lyle W. Hutchinson. She paused as she gathered courage, then turned the knob and walked in.

There was a balding man of about fifty seated behind her father's desk. He seemed busy trying to stack folders. When he saw her he froze, then quickly put on a smile.

"Well, you must be Lorelei Hutchinson." He rounded the desk. "I'm Gary Neal. It's a pleasure to finally meet you. Lyle talked about you often."

She shook his hand, seriously doubting Lyle said much about her. Her father hadn't taken the time to know her. Now, did she have to prove herself worthy of being his daughter?

"Hello, Mr. Neal."

"First off, I want to express my deepest sympathies for your loss. Lyle and I were not only colleagues, but friends. So if there is anything you need..."

"Thank you, I'm fine." She nodded. "I've only been in town a few days, but I wanted to stop by the bank. I'm sure you've already heard that I'm going to be staying in Destiny."

He nodded. "Dennis Bradley explained as much."

She hesitated. "Good. Do you have a few minutes to talk with me?"

"Of course."

Still feeling brave, she walked behind the desk and took the seat in her father's chair as if she belonged.

She didn't miss the surprise on the loan officer's face. "Where's your office, Mr. Neal?"

He blinked, then finally said, "It's two doors down the hall. Since your father's death, I've had to access some files from here. Lyle was hands-on when it came to bank business. I'm his assistant manager."

"Good. Then you're who I need to speak with." She motioned for him to sit down, but she was feeling a little shaky trying to pull this off. This man could be perfectly wonderful at his job, but she needed to trust him. "I take it you handle the mortgage loans." With his nod, she asked, "What do you know about the Mac Burleson mortgage?"

The man frowned. "Funny you should ask, I was just working on the Burleson file."

"Could I have a look?"

He hesitated, then relented. "It's a shame we're going to have to start foreclosure proceedings in a few days."

Neal dug through the stack, located the file and handed it to her. She looked over pages of delinquent notices, the huge late fees. And an interest rate that was nearly three points higher than the norm. No wonder the man was six months behind. "Has Mr. Burleson paid anything during all this time?"

"Yes, but it could barely cover the interest."

"Why didn't you help him by dropping the interest rate and lowering the payments?"

"It's not the bank's policy. Your father—"

"Well, my father is gone now, and he wanted me to take over in his place."

"I'm *sure* he did, but with your limited experience…"

"That may be, but I feel that given the state of the economy we need to help people, too. It's a rough time."

She knew firsthand. "I want to stop the foreclosure, or at least delay it."

"But Mr. Burleson isn't even employed."

"As of an hour ago, he's gotten a job offer." She looked at the remaining eight files. "Are these other homes to be foreclosed on, too?"

The loan officer looked reluctant to answer, but nodded. "Would you please halt all proceedings until I have a look at each case? I want to try everything to keep these families in their homes." She stood. "Maybe if we can set up a meeting next week and see what we can come up with."

Mr. Neal stood. "This isn't bank policy. If people aren't held accountable for their debts, we'd be out of business. I'm sure your father wouldn't agree with this, either."

For the first time in days, Lori felt as if she were doing the right thing. "As I said before, my father left me in charge. Do you have a problem with that, Mr. Neal?"

With the shaking of his head, she tossed out one more request. "Good. I also need money transferred into the escrow account for the Mountain Heritage project as soon as possible. Mr. Yeager will have his crew back to work first thing in the morning. And if you have any questions about my position here, talk to Mr. Bradley."

She walked out to the reception desk and found Jace standing there, talking with Erin. He was smiling at the pretty brunette woman. Why not? He was handsome and single. And why did she even care?

He finally saw her and walked over. "Hi, Lori."

"What are you doing here? I told you that I'd get the money for the project."

"I know you did, but that's not why I'm here—"

"I'm really busy now, Jace. Could we do this later?" She cut him off and turned to the receptionist. "Erin, would you schedule a meeting for all employees for nine o'clock tomorrow in the conference room?"

With Erin's agreement, Lori walked out of the bank, feeling Jace's gaze on her. She couldn't deal with him. She had more pressing things to do, like moving out of the inn and into her father's house, where she had to face more ghosts.

Jace was angry that he let Lori get to him. He'd wasted his afternoon chasing after a woman who didn't want to be found. At least not by him.

He hadn't blamed Lori for walking out on him at lunch. Okay, maybe he had no right to say what he did to her. Damn. He'd let his past dictate his feelings about women. Like it or not, Lori Hutchinson was his partner. More importantly, she had the money to keep the project going. If he wanted any chance of keeping Cassie he had to complete his job.

An apology was due to Lori. And he needed to deliver it in person. If only she'd give him a minute to listen to him. He also needed her to sign some papers that needed her authorization.

Jace left the bank to meet up with his foreman to finalize the crew for tomorrow. Then the search for Lori continued as he'd gone around town and ended up at the inn, where he finally got an answer as to her whereabouts.

He had to pick up Cassie from school, but went straight to the Hutchinson house after. He drove through the gates, hoping he could come up with something to say to her. The last thing he wanted was to start off on the wrong foot.

"Wow! Daddy, this is pretty. Does Ms. Lori really live here?"

He parked in the driveway and saw the rental car there. "Yes, she does. It was her father's, now it's hers."

He climbed out and helped Cassie from the backseat. They went up the steps as the front door opened and Maggie appeared. "This is a wonderful day. First, Ms. Lorelei comes home and now, Mr. Yeager and this beautiful child come to visit."

"Hi, Maggie," Jace said. "This is my daughter, Cassie. Cassie, this is Maggie."

They exchanged greetings then the housekeeper opened the door wider.

"I'd like to see Lori if she isn't too busy."

"Of course." Maggie motioned them inside the entry. "She's in her father's upstairs office." The housekeeper looked at Cassie. "Why don't I take you into the kitchen and see if there are some fresh baked cookies on my cooling rack? They're so good along with some milk." The housekeeper looked concerned. "Coming back here is hard for her."

"I expect it is. Are you sure it's okay?"

Maggie smiled. "I think that would be good. The office is the first door on the left."

Still he hesitated.

"You should go up," the woman said. "She could use a friend right about now."

Jace glanced up the curved staircase and murmured, "I'm not sure she'd call me 'friend' right now."

* * *

Lori had trouble deciding where to put her things. There were six bedrooms and a master suite. One had been turned into an office, and the one next to it was non-descript, with only a queen-size bed covered by a soft floral comforter. It had a connecting bath, so that was where she put her one bag.

She unpacked the few items she had, but went into her father's office. She couldn't get into his computer because she didn't have access.

"Okay, need to make a call to Dennis Bradley first thing tomorrow."

What she knew for sure was she needed to have someone to work with. Someone she trusted. As far as she knew her father had worked out of his office at the bank and from home. Did Lyle handle everything himself? Had he not trusted anyone? She rubbed her hands over her face. She didn't know the man. She stood up and walked out.

In the hall curiosity got the best of her and she began to look around. She peeked into the next room, then the next until she came to the master suite. She opened the door but didn't go inside.

The dark room had a big four-poster bed that dominated the space. The windows were covered with heavy brocade drapes and the bedspread was the same fabric. The furniture was also stained dark. Bits and pieces of childhood memories hit her. She pushed them aside and journeyed on to the next room. She paused at the door, feeling a little shaky, then she turned the knob and pushed it open.

She gasped, seeing the familiar pale pink walls. The double bed with the sheer white canopy and matching sheer curtains. There was a miniature table with stuffed animals seated in the matching chairs as if waiting for a tea party.

Oh, my God.

Nothing had been changed since she'd lived here. Lori crossed the room to the bed where a brown teddy bear was propped against the pillow.

"Buddy?" She picked up the furry toy, feeling a rush of emotions, along with the memory of her father bringing the stuffed animal home one night.

She hugged the bear close and fought tears. No, she didn't want to feel like this. She didn't want to care about the man who didn't want her. Yet, she couldn't stop the flood of tears. A sob tore from her throat as she sank down onto the mattress and cried.

"Lori?"

She heard Jace's voice and stiffened. She quickly walked to the window, wiping her eyes. She fought to compose herself before she had to face him.

He followed her, refusing to be ignored.

"It's okay to be sad," he said, his voice husky and soft.

She finally swung around. "Don't talk about what you know nothing about."

Jace was taken aback by her anger. "It seems that everything I've said to you today has been wrong. I won't bother you again."

She stopped him. "No, please, don't go."

She wiped the last of the tears off her face. "It's me who should apologize for my rudeness. You caught me at a bad moment. Why are you here?"

"Maggie sent me up to Lyle's office. I have some papers for you to sign, but they can wait. Believe it or not, Lori, I came to apologize for what I said to you at lunch. I had no right to judge your motivation."

Jace glanced around the bedroom and hated what he was feeling. What Lyle must have felt when his daughter left. Would this happen to him if his ex got Cassie back? "I take it you were about six or seven when you left here?"

She nodded. "It was so long ago, I feel silly for letting it upset me now."

"You were old enough to have memories. Your childhood affects you all your life. It was your father who chose not to spend time with you." It seemed odd, he thought, because Lyle had kept her room like a shrine.

Lori suddenly brightened as if all the pain went away. "Well, as you can see, I'll need to do some painting. My sister, Gina, is coming soon along with my nephew, Zack." She put on a smile. "I don't think he'd like a pink bedroom."

Before Jace could say anything, he heard his daughter calling for him. "I'm in here, Cassie. I picked her up from school, and I wanted to see you before work tomorrow. To make sure everything is okay…between us."

The expression on his seven-year-old's face was priceless as she stopped at the door. "Oh, it's so pretty." She looked at Lori. "Do you have a little girl, too?"

An hour later, with Cassie busy doing homework at the kitchen table, Jace and Lori went to do their work in Lyle's office.

"I hate that you have to keep going over everything again and again," Lori told him.

"It's not a problem. Better now, when I'm around to answer your questions. There aren't too many decisions to make right now. If you'd like to put in some input on finishes, like tile and countertops, you're more than welcome. A woman's touch." He held up a hand. "I didn't mean anything about that. A second opinion would be nice."

"I'd like that."

She smiled and he felt a tightening in his gut. Damn. He looked back at the work sheet.

"Well, the crew is showing up tomorrow to start the finish work on the outside. If we're lucky the weather will hold and we can complete everything before the snow comes."

"Will it affect the work inside?"

"Only if we can't get the materials to the site because the roads aren't passable."

She nodded, chewing her bottom lip. He found it hard to look away.

"What about Mac Burleson? Do you really have a job for him?"

Jace nodded. "If he can do the work."

"I wonder if Mac can paint," Lori said.

Jace looked at her to see a mischievous grin on her pretty face. She wasn't beautiful as much as striking. Those sparkling brown eyes and full mouth… "That was probably going to be one of his jobs—priming the walls once they're up. What were you thinking?"

"I doubt my father has done much work on this house in years." She shrugged. "I don't mind so much for myself, but Gina and Zack. I want this place…" She glanced around the dark room. "A little more homey. I want to talk to Charlie and see what he has to say about repairs."

"How soon are you expecting your family?"

"Next week. Gina is packing and putting most of the furniture in storage." She sighed. "I should go back to help her, but I want to make sure there won't be any holdup on the project."

Jace needed to remember that her entire life had been turned upside down by Lyle's death. "It's a shame you have to leave everything behind, like your friends. A boyfriend...?"

She looked surprised at his question. Not as much as he was. He stood and went to the window. "I only meant, Lyle had you make a tough choice."

"No, I don't have a boyfriend at the moment, and my sister is my best friend. So sometimes a fresh start is good." She turned the tables on him. "Isn't that why you came to Destiny?"

He didn't look at her, but that didn't mean he couldn't catch her scent, or wasn't aware of her closeness. He took a step back. "I came here to make a life for my daughter. She's everything to me."

Lori smiled at him and again his body took notice. "From what I've seen, Cassie feels the same way about you. You're a good father."

"Thank you. I'm not perfect. But I do try and want to make the job permanent."

His gaze went back to her. Darn. What was it about her that drew him? Suddenly he thought about his ex-wife, and the caution flag came out. He needed to stay focused on two things—business and his daughter.

A happy Cassie skipped into the room and rushed to him. "Maggie said to tell you that dinner is ready."

"Oh, honey. We should head home." He glanced at his watch. "Maybe another time."

"No, Daddy. We can't go. I helped Maggie make the biscuits, so we have to stay and eat them."

He was caught as he looked down at his daughter, then at Lori.

"I can't believe you're passing up a home-cooked meal, Jace Yeager," Lori said. "Maggie's biscuits are the best around, and probably even better with Cassie helping."

"Please, Daddy. I'll go to bed right on time. I won't argue or anything."

Jace looked back at Lori. It was her first night here, and would probably be a rough one.

Lori smiled. "Now that's a hard offer to turn down."

"You're no help," he told Lori.

"Sorry, us girls have to stick together."

That was what he was afraid of. He was losing more than just this round. He hated that he didn't mind one bit.

"Okay, but we can't stay long. We have a bedtime schedule."

"I promise, I'll go to bed right on time," Cassie said, then took off toward the kitchen.

He looked at a smiling Lori. "Okay, I'm a pushover."

"Buck up, Dad. It's only going to get worse before it gets better."

Suddenly their eyes locked and the amused look disappeared. Lori was the first to speak. "Please, I want you to stay for dinner. I think we both agree that eating alone isn't fun."

"Yes, we can agree on that."

He followed Lori into the kitchen, knowing this

woman could easily fill those lonely times. He just couldn't let that happen. No more women for a while, at least not over the age of seven.

CHAPTER FIVE

AT EIGHT-THIRTY the next morning, Lori was up and dressed, and grabbed a travel mug of coffee from Maggie, then she was out the door to the construction site. Not that she didn't think Jace could do his job, but she wanted to meet the crew and assure them that there wouldn't be any more delays with the project.

When she pulled through the gate and saw the buzz of activity, she was suddenly concerned about disturbing everyone.

She had every right to be here, she thought as she climbed out of her car and watched the men working on the trim work of the two-story structure. Jace hadn't wasted any time.

She walked carefully on the soggy ground. Okay, she needed more protection than her loafers. A good pair of sturdy boots was on her list. She headed up the plywood-covered path when a young man dressed in jeans, a denim work shirt and lace-up steel-toed boots came toward her.

He gave her a big smile and tipped back his hard hat. "Can I help you, ma'am?"

"I'm looking for Jace Yeager."

The man's smile grew bigger. "Aren't they all? I'm Mike Parker, maybe I can help you."

All? Lori couldn't help but wonder what that meant. She started to speak when she heard a familiar voice call out. They both turned to see Jace. He was dressed pretty much like the others, but he had on a leather vest over a black Henley shirt even though the temperature was in the low fifties.

Lori froze as he gave her a once-over. He didn't look happy to see her as he made his way toward them.

Jace ignored her as he looked at Mike. "Don't you have anything to do?"

"I was headed to my truck for some tools." He nodded to her. "And I ran across this nice lady. Sorry, I didn't catch your name."

"Lori Hutchinson."

Mike let out a low whistle. "So you're the big boss? I can't tell you how good it is to meet you, Ms. Hutchinson."

She tried not to cringe at the description. "It's Lori. I'm not anyone's boss. Jace is in charge of this project."

That was when Jace spoke up. "Mike, they've finished spraying the insulation up in the lofts, so I need you to get started hanging drywall."

"Right, I'll get on it." He tipped his hat to Lori. "Nice to meet you, ma'am."

"Nice to meet you, too, Mike."

She watched him hurry off, then turned back to Jace. "Good morning. Seems you've been busy. What time did you start?"

"I had a partial crew in at five."

"What about Cassie?"

He seemed surprised at her question. "I wasn't here,

but my foreman was. My daughter comes first, Lori. She always will."

"I didn't mean... I apologize."

That didn't ease the scowl on his face. "Were we supposed to meet this morning?"

She shook her head. "No."

"Did you come to work?" He looked over her attire. "You're not exactly dressed for a construction site."

She glanced down at her dark trousers and soft blue sweater under her coat. "I have an appointment at the bank later this morning. I wanted to stop here first to see if everything got off okay. Do you need anything?"

"No, it's fine. I know it looks a little chaotic, but things are running pretty smoothly for the first day back to work. It's most of the same crew so they know what I expect from them."

Lori had no doubt that Jace Yeager was good at his job. "So everything is on schedule?"

"If the weather holds." The wind picked up and brushed her hair back. "Come inside where it's a little warmer," he said. "I'll introduce you to the foreman."

"I don't want to disturb him."

"As you can see, it's a little late for that." He nodded toward the men who were watching.

She could feel a blush rising over her face as she followed Jace inside the building to a worktable that had blueprints spread out on top. A middle-aged man was talking with another workman.

"Hey, Toby," Jace called as he reached into a bin and pulled out a hard hat. He came to her and placed it on her head. "You need to wear this if you come here. Safety rules."

Their eyes met. "Thank you."

Toby walked up to them. "What, Jace?"

"This is Lori Hutchinson. Lori, this is my foreman, Toby Edwards."

The man smiled at her and tiny lines crinkled around his eyes. "So you're the one who saved this guy's as... sets."

Lori felt Jace tense. "I'd say I was just lucky to inherit some money," she told Toby. "Speaking of money..." She turned to Jace. "Were the funds transferred into the Mountain Heritage account?"

He nodded. "Yes. We're expecting materials to be delivered later today."

"Good." She glanced around, feeling a little excited about being a part of this. "It's nice to see all the work going on." It was a little noisy with the saws and nail guns.

Jace watched Lori. He wasn't expecting her here. Not that she didn't have a right, but she was a big distraction. He caught the guys watching her, too. Okay, they were curious about their attractive new boss. He hoped that was all it was. There could be a problem if she stopped by every day. And not only for his men, either. He eyed her pretty face and those big brown eyes that a man could get lost in.

No way. One woman had already cost him his career and future, and maybe his daughter. He wasn't going to get involved with another, especially in his workplace. Or any other place. He thought about the cozy dinner last night in the Hutchinson kitchen.

It was a little too cozy.

Enough reminiscing, he thought, and stuck his fingers in his mouth, letting go with a piercing whistle. "Let's get this over with so we can all get on with our day." All work stopped and the men came to the center of the main room.

"Everyone, this is Lorelei Hutchinson. Since Lyle Hutchinson's death, Lori will be taking over in her father's place. It's thanks to her we're all back to work on this project." The men let go with cheers and whistles. Jace forced a smile, knowing this was a means to get this project completed. But damn, being beholden to a woman stuck in his craw. "Okay, now back to work."

"Thank you," Lori said. "So many people in town have been looking at me like I have two heads."

"Has someone said anything to you?" he asked.

"No, but they're wondering what I'm going to do." She shrugged. "Maybe I should just make a big announcement in the town square. 'Hey, everyone, I'm not here to cause trouble.'"

A strange protective feeling came over him. "Now that the project has started up again, maybe they'll stop worrying."

"I hope so. I'm bringing my sister and nephew here to live. I want to be part of this community."

"What you did for Mac Burleson yesterday was a pretty good start."

"Oh, Mac. Is he here?"

Jace nodded. "Yeah, he was here waiting when Toby opened the gates."

She glanced around the area. "How is he doing?"

"Good so far."

She looked up at Jace. "There he is. Would you mind if I talked to him for a moment?"

"No, not a problem."

She walked across the large entry to the wall. Jace watched her acknowledge a lot of the workers before she got to Mac. She smiled and the man returned it. In fact he was smiling the whole time Lori was talking. Then he shook her hand and Lori walked back. "I just hired Mac to paint a couple of bedrooms at the house."

"Hey, are you stealing my help?"

"No. He's agreed to come over this weekend with his brother and paint the upstairs. I don't think my nephew wants to sleep in a pink room."

Jace nodded, knowing she would be erasing the last of her own memories of her childhood. "There are other bedrooms for him to sleep in."

"I know, but it should have been changed years ago."

"Maybe there was a reason why it hadn't been."

She looked at him. He saw pain, but also hope. "Lyle Hutchinson knew where I was since I left here twenty-two years ago. My father could have invited me back anytime. He chose not to."

Lori turned to walk out and he hurried to catch up with her. "Look, Lori. I don't know the situation."

She stopped abruptly. "That's right, you don't." She closed her eyes. "Look, it was a long time ago. My father is gone, and I'll never know why he never came to see me. And now, why in heaven's name does he want me to run his company?"

"I can't answer that, either."

"I've dealt with it. So now I move on and start my new life with Gina and Zack. I want them to have a fresh start here, in a new place, a new house and especially a new bedroom for my seven-year-old nephew."

Jace frowned. "I take it Zack is without his father."

Lori straightened. "His parents are divorced." She glanced around. "I should be going."

"I need to get back, too."

They started walking toward the door. "If there's anything you need," she offered, "just give me a call. You have my cell phone number. I'll be at the bank most of today."

He walked her out. "I can handle things here." Then he felt bad. "Maybe in a few days if you're available we could go over some samples of tiles and flooring."

She looked surprised at his request. "I'd like that. I want to be a part of this project."

Her steps slowed as she made her way over the uneven boards. He took Lori's arm, helping her along the path.

"What about the bank?"

"I doubt Mr. Neal will enjoy having me around." She stopped suddenly and nearly lost her balance. "Oh," she gasped.

"I got you." He caught her in his arms. Suddenly her trim body was plastered up against him. Even with her coat he wasn't immune to her soft curves. And he liked it. Too much. He finally got her back on her feet. "You need practical boots if you come to a construction site. Go to Travers's Outfitters and get some that are waterproof. You don't want to be caught in bad weather without protection."

She stopped next to her compact car. "I need a lot of things since I'll be living here awhile."

"Like a car that will get through the snow. This thing will put you in a ditch on the first bad day. Get something with bulk to it. You'll be driving your family around."

She nodded. "I guess I need to head down to Durango and visit a dealership next week when my sister flies in."

Before he could stop himself, he offered, "If you need any help, let me know."

She gave him a surprised look, mirroring his own feelings.

Two hours later, Lori glanced across the conference table at the Destiny Community Bank's loan officers, Gary Neal, Harold Brownlee and Larry McClain. The gentlemen's club. "I disagree. In this day and age, we need to work with people and help adjust their loans."

"In my experience," Neal said, "if we start giving handouts, people will take advantage. And no one will pay us."

She tried to remain calm, but she was so far out of her element it wasn't funny.

"I never said this is a handout, more like a hand up. All I suggested is we lower the interest rates on these loans." She pointed to the eight mortgages. "Two points. Waive the late fees and penalties. Just give these families a fighting chance to keep their homes. We'll get the money we loaned back." She paused to see their stunned looks and wondered if she were crazy, too.

She hurried on to say, "Mac Burleson has a job now, but he can't catch up on his mortgage if we don't help him."

"We've always done things this way," Larry McClain said. "Your father would never—"

Lori stiffened. "Well, I'm not my father, but he did put me in charge. In fact, I'm going to become more involved in day-to-day working here at the bank. I can see that there aren't any women in management positions. That needs to change, too."

The threesome gave each other panicked looks. "That's not true. Mary O'Brien manages the tellers."

Were these men from the Dark Ages? "I mean women in decision-making positions. It's a changing world out there and we need to keep up. I've seen the profit sheet for this bank. Over the years, it's done very well."

Neal spoke up again. "You can't come in here and just change everything. You're a schoolteacher."

Lori held her temper. "I became an expert when my father put me in charge of his company. Just so you know, not only am I a good teacher, but I also minored in business. So, gentlemen, whether you like it or not, I'm here."

She was feeling a little shaky. What if she was making a mistake? She glanced at her watch. "I think we've said about everything that needs to be said for now. Good morning." She took her purse and walked out.

She needed someone here on her side. She walked to Erin's desk.

The girl smiled when she approached. "Hello, Ms. Hutchinson. How was your meeting?"

"Not as productive as I would have liked." She sat down in the chair next to the desk. "Erin, could you help me?"

The girl nodded. "If I can."

"I'm looking for someone, a woman who is qualified for a managerial position. Could you give me some candidates?"

The pretty brunette looked surprised, but then answered. "That would be Mary O'Brien and Lisa Kramer. They've both worked for the bank for over five years.

I know Lisa has a college degree. I'm not sure Mary does, but she practically runs this bank."

"That's good to know, because I need someone to help me." She was going to need a lot of help. Since her father had never promoted a woman that was one of the things she needed to change. Immediately.

"Could you call a meeting with all the employees?" She looked at her watch. "And call the Silver Spoon and have them send over sandwiches and drinks."

Erin smiled. "This is going to be fun."

"We're going to need our strength to get this bank into the twenty-first century."

Two mornings later, Lori had been awakened by a call from a sick Claire Keenan, asking her for a favor. Would Lori like to take her place as a volunteer in the second grade classroom this afternoon?

There might have been several other things to do, but Lori found she wanted to check out the school. After her trip to the paint store and picking her colors for the bedroom, she had her purchase sent to the house.

She grabbed a quick lunch at the Silver Spoon, and after a friendly chat with Helen, she arrived at Destiny Elementary with time to spare. She went through the office then was taken down the hall to the second grade classroom.

Outside, she was greeted by the teacher. "It's good to meet you, I'm Julie Miller."

"Lori Hutchinson. I'm substituting for Claire Keenan. She's sick."

The young strawberry blonde smiled eagerly. "I'm glad you could make it. I've heard a lot about you."

"Well, I guess Lyle's long-lost daughter would be news in a small town."

Julie smiled. "No, I heard it all from Cassie Yeager. Seems you live in a castle and have a princess bedroom like hers."

That brought a smile to Lori's lips, too. "If only."

"I also heard you teach second grade."

"I did. I was laid off this year."

"I'm sorry to hear that, but you're welcome to come and help out in my class anytime. But it sounds like you've been pretty busy with other projects around town."

Lori blinked. "You must have a good source."

"My sister, Erin, works at the bank. You've really impressed her."

"Oh, Erin. She's been a big help showing me around. There do need to be some changes."

Julie smiled brightly. "I can't tell you how happy I am that you came to Destiny and I hope you stay."

"I'll be here for this year anyway. In fact, my sister and her son will be coming in next week. Zack will be in second grade."

"That's wonderful. Then you'll want to see how I run my class."

Julie Miller opened the door to a room that was buzzing with about twenty-five seven-year-olds. The room was divided in sections, half with desks, the other half with tables and a circle of chairs for reading time.

Suddenly two little blonde girls came up to her— Ellie Larkin and Cassie Yeager.

"Miss Lori, what are you doing here?" Cassie asked.

"Hi, girls. Ellie, your grandmother isn't feeling well today."

Both girls looked worried. "Really?" Ellie said.

"It's nothing serious, don't worry. But she asked if I'd come in her place."

They got excited again. "We're going to try out for our Christmas program today."

"That's wonderful," Lori said. This was what she missed about teaching, the children's enthusiasm.

"It's called Destiny's First Christmas," Cassie said as she clasped her hands together. "And everyone gets to be in it."

"But we want to be the angels," Ellie added.

Just then Mrs. Miller got their attention. "Okay, class, you need to return to your desks. We have a special guest today and we need to show her how well-behaved we are so she'll want to come back." A bright smile. "Maybe Miss Hutchinson will help us with our Christmas play."

CHAPTER SIX

LATER that evening, Jace finally headed home. He was beat to say the least. A twelve-hour day was usually nothing for him, but he'd been off for three weeks. He needed to oversee everything today to make sure that the schedule for tomorrow went off without a hitch. The one thing he knew, he didn't like to be away from Cassie that long. Luckily, he had good childcare.

He came up the road and the welcoming two-story clapboard house came into view. Although the sun had set an hour ago, he had installed plenty of lighting to illuminate the grounds, including the small barn. He had a lot of work yet to do on the place, but a new roof and paint job made the house livable for now.

The barn had been redone, plus he'd added stalls for his two horses, Rocky and Dixie. Maybe it was a luxury he couldn't afford right now, but it was something that had helped Cassie adjust to her move. Luckily he'd been able to hire the neighbor's teenage son to do the feeding and cleaning.

Jace frowned at the sight of a new SUV parked by the back door. Had Heather, the babysitter, gotten a new car? Then dread washed over him. Was it his ex-wife?

Panic surged through him as he got out of his truck

and hurried up the back steps into the mudroom. After shucking his boots, he walked into the kitchen. He froze, then almost with relief, he sagged against the counter when he saw his daughter at the kitchen table with Lori Hutchinson.

He took a moment and watched the interaction of the two. Their blond heads together, working on the math paper. Then Lori reached out and stroked Cassie's hair and it looked as natural as if they were mother and daughter. His throat suddenly went dry. His business partner had a whole new side to her, a very appealing side.

Too appealing. Lorelei Hutchinson was beginning to be more than a business partner and a pretty face. She had him thinking about the things he'd always wanted in his life. In his daughter's life.

Cassie finally turned to him. "Daddy." She got up and rushed over to him. "You're home."

He hugged her, but his gaze was on Lori. "Yes, sorry I'm so late."

"It's okay," she said. "Miss Lori drove me home." His daughter gave him a bright smile. "She's helping me with my homework."

"I thought Mrs. Keenan was going to do that." He'd made the arrangements with her yesterday.

Lori stood. "Claire would have, but she got sick. I took over for her this afternoon in Cassie's classroom, and I offered to bring her home. I knew you would be busy at the site."

Jace tensed. "My daughter is a priority. I'm never too busy to be here for her. At the very least I should have been called." He glanced around for the teenager who he depended on. "Where's Heather?"

"She had a 'mergency at her house," Cassie told him.

He turned to the jean-clad Lori. She didn't look much older than the high school babysitter.

"We tried to call you but I got your voice mail," Lori said. "It wasn't a problem for me to stay with Cassie until you got home."

Jace felt the air go out of him, remembering he hadn't had his phone on him. He wasn't sure where it was at the site. He looked at Lori. "Thank you. I guess I got wrapped up in getting things back on target at the job site."

"It's okay, Daddy." His daughter looked up at him. "'Cause we made supper."

Great. All he needed was for this woman to get involved in his personal life. "You didn't need to do that."

Lori caught on pretty quickly that Jace didn't want her here. She'd gotten rejection before, so why had his bothered her so much?

"Look, it's just some potato soup and corn bread." She checked her watch. "Oh, my, it's late, I should go."

"No!" Cassie said. "You have to stay. You said you'd help me practice my part in the play." She turned back to her father. "Daddy, Miss Lori has to stay."

Lori hated to put Jace on the spot. Whatever the issues he had about women, she didn't want to know. She had enough to deal with. "It's okay, Cassie, we'll work on it another time."

"But Miss Lori, you wanted to show Daddy your new car, too."

Lori picked up her coat and was slipping it on when Jace came after her.

"Cassie's right, Lori. Please stay."

His husky voice stopped her, but those blue eyes convinced her to change her mind about leaving.

His voice lowered when he continued. "I was rude. I should thank you for spending time with my daughter." He smiled. "Please, stay for supper and let me make it up to you."

Lori glanced away, knowing this man was trouble. She wasn't his type. Men like Jace Yeager didn't give her much notice. *Keep it light.* "We're getting an early start on the Christmas pageant. How are you at playing the part of an angel?"

Cassie giggled.

He smiled, too. "Maybe I'd do better playing a devil."

She had no doubt. "I guess I could write in that part."

She knew coming here would be crossing the line. They worked together, but it needed to stay business. Instead she was in Jace Yeager's home. And even with all the unfinished projects he had going on, it already felt like a real home. It set off a different kind of yearning inside her. That elusive traditional family she'd always wanted. Something all the money from her inheritance couldn't buy her.

Two hours later, Jace finished up the supper dishes, recalling the laughter he heard from his daughter and their guest.

It let him know how much Cassie missed having another female around. A mother. He tensed. Shelly Yeager—soon-to-be Layfield—had never been the typical mother. She'd only cared about money and her social status and her daughter ranked a poor second. More than anything he wanted to give Cassie a home and a life where she'd grow up happy and well-adjusted. He could only do that if she was with him. He'd do whatever it took to keep it that way.

In the past, money, mostly his, had pacified Shelly. Now, she'd landed another prospective husband, a rich one. So she had even more power to keep turning the screws on him, threatening to take Cassie back.

He climbed the steps to his daughter's bedroom and found her already dressed in pajamas. Lori was sitting with her on the canopy bed reading her a story.

His chest tightened at the domestic scene. They looked so much alike they could be mother and daughter. He quickly shook away the thought and walked in.

"The end," Lori said as she closed the book and Cassie yawned.

"I see a very sleepy little girl."

"No, Daddy." She yawned again. "I want another story."

He shook his head and looked at Lori. "The rule is only one bedtime story on a school night." He checked his watch. "Besides, we've taken up enough of Lori's time tonight."

Cassie looked at her. "I'm sorry."

"No, don't be sorry, Cassie." She hugged the girl. "I enjoyed every minute. I told you I read to my nephew."

Cassie's eyes brightened. "Daddy, Lori's nephew, Zack, is coming here to live. He's going to be in my class."

"That'll be nice. How about we talk about it tomorrow? Now, you go to sleep."

Jace watched Lori and his daughter exchange another hug, then she got up and left the room. After he kissed his daughter, he turned off the light and headed downstairs. He found Lori putting on her coat and heading for the back door.

"Trying to make your escape?"

She turned around. "I'm sure you're tired, too."

He walked to her. "I think you might win that contest. Spending four hours with my daughter, not counting the time at school, had to be exhausting."

She smiled. "Remember, I'm a trained professional."

His gut tightened at the teasing glint in her incredible eyes. "And I know my daughter. She can try anyone's patience, but she's the love of my life."

He saw Lori's expression turn a little sad. "She's a lucky little girl." She turned away. "I should get home."

Something made him go after her. Before she could make it to the back door, he reached for her and turned her around. "I wish things could have been different for you, Lori. I'm sorry that you had to suffer as a child."

She shook her head. "It was a long time ago and I've dealt with it."

"Hey, you can't fool a foster kid. I was in the system most of my life. We're experts on rejection."

Her gaze went to his, those brown eyes compelling. "What happened to your family?"

"My parents were in a car accident when I was eight. What relatives I had didn't want me, so I went into foster care."

"Oh, Jace," she whispered.

Her little breathless gasp caused a different kind of reaction from him. Then he saw the tears in her eyes.

His chest tightened. "Hey, don't. I survived. Look at me. A success story."

Jace reached out and touched her cheek. The next thing he knew he pulled her toward him, then wrapped her in his arms. He silenced a groan as he felt her sweet body tucked against his. It had been so long since he'd held a woman. So long since he'd felt the warmth, the glorious softness.

He pulled back trying to put some space between them, but couldn't seem to let her go. His gaze went to her face; her dark eyes mirrored the same desire. He was in big trouble.

He lowered his head and whispered, "This is probably a really bad idea." His mouth brushed over hers, once, then again. Each time she made a little breathy sound that ripped at his gut until he couldn't resist any longer and he captured her tempting mouth.

She wrapped her arms around his neck and leaned into him as her fingers played with the hair at his nape. He pushed his tongue into her mouth and found heaven. She was the sweetest woman he'd ever tasted, and the last thing he ever wanted to do was stop. He wanted so much more, but also knew he couldn't have it.

He tore his mouth away and took a step back. "Damn, woman. You pack a punch. I just can't…"

"It's okay." She pulled her coat tighter. "It would be crazy to start something."

He couldn't believe how badly he wanted to. "Right. Bad idea. We're business partners. Besides, I have room for only one female in my life. Cassie."

Her gaze wouldn't meet his. "I should go."

"Let me walk you out."

"No, you don't need to do that. It's too cold."

He tried to make light of the situation. "Right now, I could use a blast of cold air." He followed her out. Grabbing his coat off the hook, he slipped it on as they went through the mudroom. The frigid air hit him hard as they hurried out to the well-lit driveway and around to her side of the car.

"Nice ride." He glanced over the four-wheel-drive SUV. "You're ready for the snow." He held on to the door so she couldn't rush off. "Are you coming by the site tomorrow?"

"No." She paused. "Unless you need me for something."

He found he wanted to see her again. "I guess not."

"Okay then, good night, Jace."

"Thank you, Lori. Thank you for being there for Cassie."

"You're welcome. Goodbye." She shut her door and started the engine and was backing out of the drive before Jace could stop her. That was the last thing he needed to do. He didn't need to be involved with this woman.

Any woman.

It would be a long time before he could trust again. But if he let her, Lori Hutchinson could come close to melting his cold, cold heart.

Lori had spent the past two days at the bank where she'd been trying to familiarize herself with her father's business dealings. How many people expected her to fail at this?

She'd stayed far away from Jace Yeager, although that didn't change the fact that she'd been thinking about him.

Had he been thinking about her? No. If he had been, wouldn't he have called? Or maybe he'd resisted, knowing getting involved could create more problems.

Lori looked up from the desk as Erin walked into

the office. The receptionist had been such a big help to her, going through files and being the liaison between Lori and Dennis Bradley's office.

Erin sat down in the chair across from the desk. "I found this in an old personnel file, and it's kind of interesting. Kaley Sims did used to work for Mr. Hutchinson. It states that she managed his properties up until two years ago."

Lori had found this woman's notes on several contracts. "Why isn't she working for him now?"

Erin gave her a funny look and glanced away.

"You know something?"

"It's just some bank gossip, but there might have been something between Kaley and Mr. Hutchinson, beyond professional."

So her father had someone after his divorce. "I take it they were discreet."

"They went to business and social functions together, but no one saw any signs of affection between them."

Lori shrugged. "Maybe that's the reason Kaley left here. She wanted more from Lyle."

"If you want to talk to her, I could call her mother and see if she's available to come back to work here."

Lori needed the help. "I guess it wouldn't hurt to call. I sure could use the help, especially someone who already knows the business. I don't want to put in twelve-hour days."

Had Lyle Hutchinson become that much of a recluse that all he did was work? She was curious. Had her father driven off Kaley?

"Okay, I'll make the call tomorrow," Erin said as she stood. "Is there anything more you need today?"

Lori checked her watch. It was after five o'clock. "I'm sorry. You need to get home."

"Normally I'd stay, but I have a date tonight."

Lori smiled, feeling a little twinge of envy, and immediately thought about Jace. Since the kiss she hadn't heard a word from him in two days. *Stop.* She couldn't let one kiss affect her. She wasn't a teenager. "Well, you're great, Erin. I'm grateful to have all your help." She paused. "How would you like to be my assistant?"

"Really?"

"Really. But you have to promise to stay in college. We can schedule hours around your classes, and you'll get a pay raise."

"Oh, wow. Thank you. I'd love to be your assistant." Erin reached out and shook her hand. "And everyone thought you coming to town would be a bad thing."

"Oh, they did, huh?"

This time, Erin hesitated. "I think they thought that a lot of jobs might be lost." The pretty brunette beamed. "Instead, you've come here and come up with ideas so people can save their homes, and you're helping women advance, too."

Lori was happy she could do something. "So it's a good thing?"

"Very good." The girl turned and left the office.

Lori sank back into her father's overstuffed leather chair. "Lyle Hutchinson, you must have really been some kind of tyrant. What made you so unhappy?"

She thought about the sizable amount of money Lyle had acquired over the years. When the waiting period was over next year, she'd never be able to spend it all. She could give the money away. Right now, she received a large income just from his properties.

Sadness hit her hard. Seeing how her father lived, she realized he'd died a lonely man. Outside his few male friends, he didn't go out with anyone. "I was always there, Dad. Just a call away. Your daughter. I would have loved to spend time with you."

It might be too late for a family with her father, but there was a second chance, because she had a sister and nephew. Gina and Zack would always be her family.

A few days had passed and Jace hadn't been able to get Lori, or the kiss, out of his head. Even working nonstop at the site couldn't keep his mind from wandering back to Lori Hutchinson. Until work came to a sudden halt when problems with the staircase came up and didn't meet code. They had to make some changes in the design.

He needed Lori's okay to move ahead with the architect's revisions. He went by the bank, but discovered she was at home. So that was where he was headed when he realized he was looking forward to seeing her. Glad for the excuse.

He pulled up out front, sat there a moment to pull it together. Then he jerked open the door and got out of his truck. The early November day was cold. He looked up at the gray sky, glad that they'd finished the outside of the building. At the very least they would get some rain.

He walked up to the porch, but slowed his steps at the door, feeling his heart rate accelerate.

He hadn't seen Lori since the night at his house. When she had been in his arms. He released a breath. Even time away didn't change the fact that he was eager to see her.

Maggie opened the door with her usual smile. "Mr. Yeager. It's nice to see you again."

He stepped inside. "Hi, Maggie. Is Lori here?" He held up his folder. "I have more papers for her to sign," he said, suddenly hearing the noises coming from upstairs.

"Oh, she's here." Maggie grinned. "Been working all day trying to get things finished before her sister and nephew's arrival tomorrow. Charlie's helping." There was a big thud and Maggie looked concerned. "But maybe you should have a look."

Jace nodded. He headed for the stairs and took them two at a time to shorten the trip. He walked down the hall and was surprised when he found the source of the noise. It was coming from the room across from Lori's childhood bedroom.

He looked in the slightly open door and found Charlie and Lori kneeling on the floor with sections of wood spread out. The two were engrossed in reading a sheet of directions.

Lori brushed back a strand of hair, revealing her pretty face. Then his heart went soaring and his body heated up as she reached for something and her jeans pulled taut over her cute, rounded bottom.

"It says right here that *A* goes into *B*. Okay we got that, but I can't find the next piece." She held up the sheet of paper. "Do you see this one?"

Hiding his amusement, Jace stepped into the room. "Could you two use some help?"

They both swung around. "Mr. Yeager," Charlie said and got to his feet. "Oh, yes, we could use your expertise. And since you're here to help, I'll go do my work." The older man left, looking relieved.

Jace turned back at Lori. "What are you building?"

"Bunk beds," she offered.

Jace pulled off his jacket as he glanced over the stacks of boxes. "Why not buy it assembled?"

Lori stood. "I didn't have time to go to Durango, so I got them online. I didn't realize it would come in boxes."

"You should have called me. I would have sent Mac over." He took the paper from her. Their hands brushed, and he quickly busied himself by looking over the directions. "Okay, let's lay out the rails and the end pieces."

Lori took one end and he took the other. He set the bolts, then went to her end. He was close and could breathe in her scent, which distracted the hell out of him. He finally got the bolt tightened. He got up and went to the other side, away from temptation, but she followed him.

Over the next hour, they'd become engrossed in building the elaborate bunk-bed set. They stood back and looked over their accomplishment.

"Not bad work." He glanced at the woman beside him and saw her blink. "What's wrong?"

She shook her head. "Zack is going to love it. He's had to share a room with his mother the past few months. Thank you for this."

"Not a problem," he told her. "You helped me out with Cassie. I know how much you want to make a home for your sister and your nephew."

"They've had a rough time of it lately." She put on a smile. "It's going to be great for them to be here."

Jace looked around the freshly painted blue room. "I thought you were going to put Zack in your old bedroom."

She shrugged. "I tried, but I couldn't bring myself

to touch it." She looked at him and he saw the pain in her eyes. "I guess I'm still trying to figure out why my father kept it the same all these years. Crazy, huh?"

Unable to help himself, he draped his arm across her shoulders. "It's okay, Lori. You have a lot to work through. You've pulled up your roots and come back here. There's a lot to deal with."

She looked up. "But I have the funds now to take care of my family."

That was the one thing that kind of bothered him. He'd been pretty well-off financially before his divorce, but to have a woman with so much money when he was trying to scrape by hit him in his pride. But he truly thought it bothered her more.

"So how does it feel to have that kind of money?"

She scrunched up her nose. "Oddly strange," she admitted. "It's far too much. I'm the kind of girl who's had to work all my life, and when I lost my job a few months ago, I was really worried about what was going to happen, especially for Gina and Zack."

"They have you now."

She looked up at him, her eyes bright and rich in color. "And I have them. I wouldn't stay here in Destiny, money or no money, if they couldn't be with me. Their safety and well-being is the most important thing to me."

He frowned. "Why wouldn't they be safe here?"

She glanced away. "It's just a worry I have."

He touched her chin to get her to look at him. "Lori, what aren't you telling me? Is someone threatening you or your family?"

She finally looked at him. "It's Gina's ex-husband. He'll be getting out of jail soon."

"Why did he go to jail?"

"Look, Jace, I'm not sure Gina wants anyone to know her private business."

"I'm not a gossip. If your family needs protection then I want to help."

Lori was surprised at his offer. She wasn't used to anyone helping them. "Eric is in for drug possession and spousal abuse. He swore when he got out he'd make Gina pay for having him arrested."

She felt Jace tense. "So that's why you were headed out of state?"

She nodded.

"Does this Eric guy know where Gina is moving to?"

"No one knows. We haven't even told Zack. I want so badly for Gina to make a life here. She has full custody of her son, but we're still afraid of what the man might do."

"This house has a security system. I hope you're using it."

She nodded.

"And I think you should have protection for yourself, also. You're worth a lot of money and you could be a target for threats from this guy. Maybe a security guard isn't out of the question."

"I can't let my life be dictated by a coward."

Jace clenched his fists. "I don't care for a creep who gets his jollies by beating women, either, but you still need to take precautions. Not an armed guard, but maybe a security man disguised as a gardener or handyman."

She hesitated. "If Gina will agree."

"What about you? I'm sure you've had some run-ins with your brother-in-law."

Lori shivered, recalling Eric's threats.

Jace's eyes narrowed. "Did he hurt you, too?"

"Just a few shoves here and there, but I couldn't let him hurt Gina."

He cursed and walked away, then came back to her. He reached out and cupped her face. "He put his hands on you, Lori. No man ever has the right to do that unless the woman wants it."

She stared into his eyes. That was the problem. She wanted Jace's hands on her. Badly.

CHAPTER SEVEN

Jace had trouble letting go of Lori. He knew the minute he touched her again this would happen.

He cursed under his breath. "This isn't a good idea." His gaze searched her pretty face, those bedroom eyes, then he stopped at her perfect rosy mouth. He suddenly felt like a man dying of thirst. Especially when her tongue darted out over her lips. With a groan, he leaned down and brushed his mouth across hers, hearing her quick intake of breath.

"I swore I'd stay away from you. We shouldn't start something...." His mouth brushed over hers again and then again. "My life doesn't need to get any more complicated."

"Mine, either," she whispered.

He fought the smile, but it didn't stop the hunger, or the anticipation of the kiss he so desperately wanted more than his next breath.

Then Lori took the decision out of his hands as she rose up on her toes and pressed her mouth against his. That was all it took. His arms circled her waist and he pulled her against him, unable to tolerate the space between them any longer. Their bodies meshed so easily it was as if they were meant to be together. All he knew was he didn't want to let her go anytime soon.

His mouth slanted over hers, wanting to taste her, but all too quickly they were getting carried away.

He tore his mouth from hers, and trailed kisses along her jaw to her ear. "I could get drunk on you." Then he let his tongue trace her earlobe, feeling her shiver. He found her mouth again for another hungry kiss.

Then suddenly the sound of his cell phone brought him back to reality. He stepped back, and his gaze was drawn to Lori's thoroughly kissed mouth. Desire shot through him and he had to turn away.

"Yeager," he growled into the phone.

"Hey, Jace," Toby said. "What happened? I thought you were coming right back."

He glanced over his shoulder at Lori. "Sorry, something came up. I'm heading back now." He shut his phone. "I'm needed at the site."

"Of course," Lori said, wrapping honey-blond strands behind her ear. "I can't thank you enough for your help. I couldn't have done this on my own."

Unable to resist, he went back to her and stole another kiss. They were both breathless by the time he released her. "Your sister and nephew arrive tomorrow, right?"

She nodded.

"Okay, I'll have a security guy in place here before you get back from the airport." When Lori started to disagree, he put his finger over those very inviting lips. "He'll work with Charlie so Gina doesn't have to know. I want you and your family safe."

Lori smiled. "I wasn't going to disagree. I think it's a good idea."

He blinked. "You're agreeing with me? That's a first."

"Don't get used to it, Yeager."

The next afternoon, Lori had agreed to let Charlie drive her father's town car the 47 miles to the Durango airport to pick up Gina and Zack.

She couldn't hide her excitement as she watched her sister and nephew come out of the terminal. She gave them a big hug, then herded them into the backseat of the car while Charlie stowed the few belongings in the trunk.

They talked all the way to Destiny. It was as if they'd been apart for months instead of only two weeks.

Lori kept hugging her seven-year-old nephew beside her in the backseat. She'd missed him. "Zack. I was able to work in the second grade classroom last week and met your teacher, Mrs. Miller. I think you're going to like her."

The little dark-haired child didn't look happy. "But I don't know any kids."

"The class knows you're coming. And there's Ellie and Cassie, who will help you learn your way around the school."

"Girls?"

That brought a smile as Lori looked at her sister. Although beautiful, with her rich, dark brown hair and wide green eyes, Regina Williams Lowell looked a little pale and far too thin. Lori hoped she could erase her sister's fear once she knew she was safe living in Destiny. And her son would blossom here, too.

"It might take a little time, Zack, but I know you'll make lots of friends."

They drove through town, past the square and fountain, then down the row of storefronts. "Just wait. Soon they'll be putting up a big Christmas tree with colorful lights. The whole town will be decorated."

"Can we have a Christmas tree at your house?"

Suddenly Lori got excited. This was going to be a special holiday. And a new year that meant a fresh beginning for all of them. "You bet we can. And you can pick out a really big one."

Zack grinned as they pulled through the gate. "Wow!" The boy's eyes lit up. "Mom, are we really going to live here?"

"We sure are." Gina looked like a kid herself. "Although, I can hardly believe it myself."

Lori glanced at her sister's face. "That was my first reaction, too. Welcome to Hutchinson House."

Charlie drove up the long drive and stopped in front of the house. He opened the back door and helped them out, then sent them up the porch steps.

Maggie swung open the front door and opened her arms. "Welcome, welcome," the older woman said as she swept them inside the warm house. First, the older woman embraced Zack, then Gina.

"We're so happy you're here. Oh, my, and to have a child in this big house again is wonderful."

"It's so big," Zack said. "What if I get lost?"

"Don't worry. Charlie will show you around. The important thing to remember is there are two sets of stairs. One leads down here." Maggie pointed to the circular staircase. "Most important, the other one leads to the kitchen and I'm usually there."

Zack looked a little more comfortable after the quick explanation.

Maggie turned to Gina and smiled. "Goodness, my, you look so much like Lorelei and your mother. Your coloring might be different, but there's no doubt you're sisters. And both beautiful."

Her sister seemed embarrassed. "Thank you."

"How was your flight?"

"Not too bad, especially sitting in first class." Gina glanced at Lori. "It was a big treat for Zack and me."

"Well, we're planning on a lot of treats for Master Zack." The older woman placed her hands on the boy's shoulders. "After you go and see your new bedroom, come down to the kitchen so you can tell me all your favorite foods. And if it's okay with your mother you can sample some of my cookies." Maggie raised a hand and glanced at Gina. "I promise not to spoil his appetite for our special dinner tonight."

"The way my son eats, I doubt anything can." Gina smiled, which made Lori hopeful that her sister would start relaxing.

"We're also having a couple of guests for dinner," Maggie announced. "Mr. Yeager and his daughter, Cassie. And before you frown, Zack, the girl has a horse. That's a good friend to have."

Lori was surprised by the news, and a little too happy, feeling a stir of excitement. Maybe he was bringing the security guard they'd talked about.

Maggie gave her the answer. "Jace has something to discuss with you. So I invited them both to dinner."

Her nephew called to her. "Can I go see my new bedroom, Aunt Lori?"

"Sure. How about we all head up and see it?"

The child ran ahead of them, following Charlie up the steps with the bags.

Lori hung back with Gina. "Lori, you never said the place was a—" she looked around the huge entry, her eyes wide "—mansion."

"Okay, so the Hutchinson family liked things on the large size. Now that you and Zack are here, it's already starting to feel more like a home." She hugged her sister again. "I want you and Zack to think of this place as home. More important, I want you to feel safe here."

Gina looked a little panicked. "Just so long as Eric never finds us."

Another precaution had been for Gina to take back her maiden name, Williams.

"If he shows up in Destiny, you can believe he'll be arrested." Jace had convinced her to let Sheriff Reed Larkin in on the situation.

"Does everyone in town know?"

Lori shook her head. "No, only the people who work here at the house. And Jace Yeager, my business partner. He suggested that I hire some security." Lori raised a hand. "Only just as a precaution."

"That has to cost a lot of money."

Lori smiled. "Look at this place, Gina. Lyle Hutchinson might have been a lousy father, but he knew how to make money. And taking care of you and Zack is worth whatever it costs."

Tears filled her sister's eyes. "Thank you."

Before Lori started crying, too, she said, "Come on, I hope you like your bedroom. It's got a connecting bath with Zack's room."

They started up the steps arm in arm. "I can't imagine I wouldn't love it."

"If you don't like it, you can redo it. You're the one

with experience. In fact, I'd be happy if you would redo the entire place."

Gina turned to Lori. "Decorating a boutique window doesn't make me a professional." She looked around. "It's so grand as it is."

Lori knew what her sister had been thinking. There had been a lot of times when their living quarters hadn't been that great, especially when Gina was married. Being a school dropout, Eric hadn't been able to do much, and he spent his paycheck on alcohol instead of diapers.

"This is our fresh start, Gina. You don't have to worry about Eric anymore. I'm not going to let anything happen to either you or Zack."

Lori prayed that was a promise she could keep.

Three hours later, Jace walked up the steps to the Hutchinson home, carrying a bottle of wine and flowers. He normally didn't take Cassie out on a school night, but this was a special occasion and he knew how it was to be the new kid in town.

Okay, the truth was he wanted to see Lori. He'd tried to keep focused on work, but she was messing with his head. Last night he couldn't sleep, recalling their kisses, but he knew from now on that he had to keep his hands to himself. If Shelly got wind of any of this, she would make his life miserable just for the hell of it.

He had to focus on Cassie and getting the project completed on time. That was all. Once he had custody settled, he could think about a life for himself.

The front door opened and a little boy stuck his head out. "Hi," he said shyly.

His daughter answered back. "Hi. You're Zack. I'm Cassie Yeager. You're going to be in my class at school."

The boy looked up at Jace as if asking for help. His daughter never had a problem with being shy.

"I'm Jace. I think your aunt is expecting us."

Zack nodded. "You want to come in?"

"Sounds good. It's a little cold out here."

The door opened wider as another woman appeared. She smiled, showing off the resemblance to Lori.

"Hello, you must be Gina. I'm Jace Yeager. I'm Lori's business partner."

She took his hand. "It's nice to meet you."

"This is my daughter, Cassie."

His daughter beamed as she came up to Gina. "Hi, Miss Gina. My dad brought you flowers and for Miss Lori, wine. And I bought Zack a school sweatshirt." She held up the burgundy-colored shirt with Destiny Elementary School printed on it.

"Hello, Cassie. That's very nice."

Cassie turned to Zack. "My dad said you have a new bedroom."

"Yeah, it's cool."

"Can I see it?"

Zack looked at his mother for permission. With Gina's nod the two seven-year-olds took off upstairs.

"My son's a little shy," Gina admitted.

"Well, that won't last long if Cassie has anything to say about it."

He finally got a smile out of the pretty dark-haired woman with green eyes. There was definitely a strong resemblance between the two sisters, except for their coloring. Both women were lovely.

"Here, these are for you. Welcome to Destiny."

He watched her blush as she took the bouquet. "Thank you."

"It's rough having to pick up and move everything. I had to do it about six months ago, but it was worth it. Destiny is a wonderful place to raise kids. Cassie loves it here."

"I'm glad." Gina hesitated. "Lori said she told you about my...situation."

He watched her hesitation, maybe more embarrassment. "I assure you, Gina, no one else will know about your past. It's no one's business. Your sister only wants you safe. I agreed to help her take some precautions."

"I appreciate it, really. I'm sure Eric wouldn't think to look for us here. He knows nothing about Lori's father." She sighed. "But I wouldn't put anything past him. So I thank you for the extra security."

Jace was about to speak when Lori came down the steps. She was wearing a black turtleneck sweater and gray slacks. He was caught up in her grace as she descended the winding stairs. She smiled at him, and his insides went all haywire.

Lori felt Jace's gaze on her and it made her nervous, also a little warm. She'd missed seeing him. The last time had only been a little over twenty-four hours ago when he'd helped her with the bed, and they almost fell into it. A warm shiver moved up her spine. How did he feel about it?

She walked across the tiled floor, seeing her sister holding flowers. That was so nice of him. "Hi, Jace."

"Lori."

She went to him. "Sorry, I wasn't here when you arrived. I just saw Cassie upstairs."

"Has she reorganized Zack's bedroom yet?"

Lori couldn't help but laugh. "I think he's safe for the moment."

Gina spoke up. "Excuse me. I'll go put these in water, then go up and have the kids wash up for dinner." She turned and walked to the kitchen.

Jace looked at Lori. "I don't want to barge in on your family dinner."

"You're not at all. You're always welcome here," she told him, knowing that was probably admitting too much. "Maggie loves to have company. She hasn't been able to cook this much in a long time."

"Anytime she wants company tell her I'll be here." He held up the bottle. "I brought wine."

Lori smiled. "Why don't we open it?"

"Lead the way," he said and they started toward the dining room. Lori watched as he stared at the dark burgundy wallpaper, dark-stained wainscoting and long, long table with the upholstered chairs, also dark.

"It's pretty bad. This room is like a mausoleum. It's going to be my first redecorating project. In fact, I'll put Gina in charge. I hope you don't mind eating in the kitchen."

"I prefer the kitchen." He glanced down at his jeans and sweater pulled over a collared shirt. He followed Lori to the sideboard. In actuality, he preferred her over it all, but he tried to stay focused on the conversation. "As you can see, I'm not dressed for anything fancy."

Lori thought he was dressed perfectly. The man would look good in…nothing. Oh, no. *Don't think about that.* She busied herself by opening a drawer and searching for a corkscrew. Once she found it, she handed it to him, then crossed to the glass-front hutch and took out two crystal wineglasses.

"Gina won't drink, so we'll have to toast my sister and nephew's arrival on our own."

"I think I can handle that." He managed to uncork the bottle and when she brought over the glasses, he filled them with the rosy liquid.

He held out the stemmed glass to her. She brushed his hand and tried to remain calm. It was only a drink, she told herself.

Jace picked up his. "To yours, Gina's and Zack's new home," he said.

Lori took a slow sip, allowing herself to enjoy the sweet taste. She took another, and soon the alcohol went to her head, making her feel a little more relaxed. Then her eyes connected with Jace, and suddenly her heart was racing once again.

"This tastes nice," she said, unable to get her mouth to work. "I mean, I'm not much of a drinker, but I like this."

His deep sapphire gaze never left hers as he set his glass down on the sideboard. "Let me see." Then he leaned forward and touched his mouth to hers.

She froze, unable to do anything but feel as his firm mouth caressed her lips, coaxing her to open for him with a stroke of his tongue.

She whimpered as her hand rested against his chest, feeling his pounding heart. She only ached for more.

He pulled back a little. "You're right. Sweet." He took her glass from her and set it down beside his. "But I need another taste to be sure."

He bent down and took her mouth again. She went willingly as her arms circled his neck, and she wanted to close out the rest of the world. Just the two of them. She refused to think about how stupid it was to let this happen with Jace. When his tongue stroked against hers, and he drew her against his body, she lost all common sense.

Then it quickly returned when the sound of footsteps overhead alerted them to the fact that the kids were coming.

He broke off, and pressed his head against hers. "Damn, Lorelei Hutchinson, if you don't make me forget my own name."

She could only manage a nod. Then he leaned forward again. "Not that you don't look beautiful thoroughly kissed, but you might have to answer too many questions."

She smoothed her hair. "Tell everyone I'll be in shortly." She took off, knowing she was a fool when it came to this man. It had to stop before someone got hurt.

Jace had trouble concentrating on his pot roast dinner. Why couldn't he keep his hands off Lori? She wasn't even his type. Not that he had a type. He'd sworn off women for the time being. So why had he been trying to play tonsil hockey with her just thirty minutes ago?

"Daddy?"

He turned to his daughter. "What, Cassie?"

"Can Zack go riding with me tomorrow?"

Jace glanced at Gina and saw her concerned look. "Maybe it's a little cold right now, sweetheart. Let Zack and his mother get settled in first. Besides, you both have school all day."

Those pretty blue eyes blinked up at him. "I know, Daddy," she said. "I'm gonna help Zack get used to the class."

Jace fought a smile and stole a glance at Lori, then at the poor boy who'd become his daughter's newest project. "I'm sure Zack appreciates all your help, sweetheart, but remember, Miss Lori is a teacher. She can help, too."

The child looked deflated. "Oh."

"I can sure use your help," Lori said. "And we're all going to be working on the Christmas play together. I'm sure Zack would like to do that."

"I guess," he said. "Are there other boys in the play?"

Cassie nodded. "Everyone is in the play. Cody Peters and Owen Hansen and Willie Burns." She smiled. "And now, you."

Jace wasn't sure he liked how his daughter was smiling at Zack. *Oh, no, not her first crush.*

Maggie came in with dessert and after everyone enjoyed the chocolate cake, the kids were excused and went up to Zack's bedroom.

"Seems like they've become fast friends," Gina said. "I thank you, Jace. Your daughter is helping my son a lot." She glanced at her sister. "I hated that Zack had to go through all the pain of the last few years."

"You need to put that in the past. This is a new start."

Lori reached over and covered her sister's hand. "It's a new beginning, Gina. We're going to keep you safe."

"Lori's right," Jace told her. "The security guard is on duty as we speak. Wyatt McCray will be touring the grounds during the night. He's moved into the room behind the garage. His cover will be he's working with Charlie. No one is going to hurt you or your son again."

Tears formed in Gina's eyes. "Thank you."

Lori spoke up. "Has Eric been released yet?"

"Detective Rogers said he is scheduled to get out this Friday."

"Good." Jace nodded. "You and Zack were gone before he had a chance to know what your plans were. The fewer people who know the better. So we three, Maggie, Charlie, Wyatt and Sheriff Larkin are the only people who know about your situation. You're divorced, and your past life is private."

"I'm grateful, Jace. Thank you." Gina stood. "I think I'll go check on the kids."

Lori watched her sister leave. "She's still scared to death."

"I know," Jace said, hating that he couldn't do more. "And I almost wish the creep would show up here so I could get my hands on him."

"No, I don't want that man anywhere near them ever again. Zack still has nightmares." She put on a smile. "Thank you for all your help."

His gaze held hers for longer than necessary. "Hey, we're partners."

Problem was, he wanted to be so much more.

CHAPTER EIGHT

BY THE end of the week Gina and Zack had settled in and were getting into a routine. Her nephew had started school and was making new friends. Of course, Cassie was still taking charge of Zack's social schedule.

Life was great, Lori thought, as she arrived at the bank that cold, gray November morning. Thank goodness her car had seat warmers to ward off the near-freezing temperatures. She thought about the upcoming holidays and couldn't help but smile. Her family would all be together.

She also thought of Jace. She wanted to invite him and Cassie to Thanksgiving at the house. Would he come? The memory of the kisses they'd shared caused a shiver down her spine. She was crazy to think about a future with the man, especially when he'd been telling her all along he didn't want to get involved.

As she entered her office, she decided not to go to the construction site unless absolutely necessary. Besides, she had plenty to do at the bank to keep her busy for a long time. She looked down at the several stacks of files and paperwork covering the desktop. The last thing she wanted to do was spend all her time managing the number of properties, and the rest of the time at the bank. If only she could hire someone to oversee it all. And she didn't trust the "three amigos" loan officers to handle things on their own. They'd already thought she was in over her head. Maybe she was, but she wasn't going to let them see it.

She'd been working nearly two hours when there was a knock on the door. "Come in," Lori called.

Erin walked in. She wore a simple black A-line skirt and a pin-striped red-and-white blouse. She was carrying a coffee mug and a white paper sack. "Break time?"

"Thank you, I could use it. Everything is getting a little blurry."

"You should have more than coffee. Helen sent over some scones from the Silver Spoon. A thank-you for putting a six-month moratorium on foreclosures."

Lori thought of her own childhood after her mother remarried. They'd had some rough times over the years. "I refuse to let this bank play Scrooge especially with Christmas coming soon. The first thing on the agenda for the first of next year is reworking these loans."

Erin smiled. "You know, the other bank officers aren't happy with your decision."

Lori took a sip of her drink. "Yes. Mr. Neal has already decided to retire." She thought about the generous retirement package her father had given him. He wouldn't be giving up his lifestyle.

"Oh, I almost forgot," Erin said. "I located Kaley Sims. She's working for a management company in Durango. I have the phone number."

"Good. Would you put in a call to her and see if she's willing to talk with me?"

"Of course. Anything else?"

Erin was so efficient at her job, Lori wasn't sure what she would have done without her.

"There is one thing. In looking over my father's properties, I found a place called—" she searched through the list "—Hidden Hills Lodge. I'm not sure if it's a rental property, or what. It doesn't show any reported income."

"Maybe it was a place Mr. Hutchinson had for his personal use. Do you want me to find out more about it?"

Lori shook her head. "No, you have more than enough to do now." Maybe she would look into this herself. She had a great GPS in her new car. Surely she could find her way. She stood. "I'm going to be gone the rest of the afternoon. If you need me, call me on my cell phone."

Maybe it was time she delved a little further into her father's past and the opportunity was right in front of her.

Later that afternoon, Jace got out of his truck as snow flurries floated in the air, clinging to his coat and hat. He took a breath as he walked to the bank. Okay, he'd been avoiding going anywhere he might see Lori Hutchinson. He couldn't seem to keep his hands off the woman, but since he needed her signature on some changes in the project, he didn't have a choice.

He walked through the doors and Erin greeted him. "Is Miss Hutchinson in?"

"No, she's not. She left about noon."

"She go home?"

"No, I've tried to reach her there. I also tried her cell

phone, but it goes to voice mail." Erin frowned. "I'm worried about her, especially with this weather."

Suddenly Jace was concerned, too. "And she didn't say where she was going? A property? Out to the site?"

"That's what I'm worried about. I think she might have gone to the Hidden Hills Lodge."

"Where is this place?"

Erin sat down at her desk and printed out directions from the computer. Jace looked them over. He wasn't sure about this area, only that it was pretty rural.

He wrote down his number and handed it to Erin. "Give me a call if Lori gets in touch with you."

He left as he pulled out his cell phone and gave Claire Keenan a call, asking if she'd watch Cassie a little later, then he hung up and glanced up at the sky. An odd feeling came over him, and not a good one. "Where are you, Lori?"

An hour later, Lori had turned off the highway to a private road, just as her GPS had instructed her to do. She shifted her car into four-wheel drive and began to move slowly along the narrowing path.

It wasn't long before she realized coming today wasn't a good idea. Deciding to go back, she shifted her SUV into Reverse and pushed on the gas pedal, and all that happened was the tires began to spin.

"Great. Please, I don't need this." She glanced out her windshield as her wipers pushed away the blowing snow, which didn't look like it was going to stop anytime soon.

She took out her cell phone. No signal. The one thing that was working was her GPS and it showed her destination was a quarter mile up the road. What should she do? Stay in the car, or walk to Hidden Hills Lodge?

She buttoned her coat, wrapped her scarf around her neck and grabbed a flashlight. She turned on her emergency blinkers and climbed out as the blowing snow hit her. She started her trek up the dirt road and her fear rose. What if she got lost and froze to death? Her thoughts turned to Gina and Zack. And Jace. She cared more about the man than she even wanted to admit. And she wanted to see him again. She quickened her pace, keeping to the center of the dirt road.

Ten minutes later, cold and tired, she finally saw the structure through the blowing snow. It was almost like a mirage in the middle of the trees. She hurried up the steps to the porch and tried the door. Locked.

"Key, where are you?" she murmured, hating to break a window. It took a few minutes, but she found a metal box behind the log bench. After unlocking the dead bolt with nearly frozen fingers, she hurried into the dark structure and closed the door. She reached for the switch on the wall and light illuminated the huge main room. With a gasp, she glanced around. The walls were made out of rough logs and the open-beam ceiling showed off the loft area overhead. Below the upstairs were two doorways leading to bedrooms. The floors were high-gloss pine with large area rugs and overstuffed furniture was arranged in front of a massive fireplace. She found a thermostat on the wall and flipped it, immediately hearing the heater come on.

Shivering, Lori walked to the fireplace and added some logs. With the aid of the gas starter, flames shot over the wood. She sat on the hearth, feeling warmth begin to seep through her chilled body.

Once warmed, she got up and looked around. The kitchen was tucked in the back side of the structure, revealing granite counters and dark cabinets.

She checked out the two bedrooms and a bath on the main floor. Then she climbed up to the loft and found another bedroom. One of the walls was all windows with a view of the forest. She walked into the connecting bathroom. This one had a soaker tub and a huge walk-in shower.

"I guess if you have to be stranded in a snowstorm, a mountain retreat isn't a bad place to be." At least she'd stay warm until someone found her. When? Next spring?

She came back downstairs trying to think of a plan to get her back to town, when a sudden noise drew her attention. She froze as the door opened and Jace Yeager walked in.

"Jace!" she cried and leaped into his arms.

He held her close and whispered, "I take it you're happy to see me."

Jace didn't want to let Lori go. Thank God, she was safe. When he found her deserted car, he wasn't sure if she would find cover.

He pulled back. "Are you crazy, woman? Why did you go out in this weather?"

She blinked back the obvious tears in her eyes. "It wasn't this bad when I started out. Besides, I didn't think it was that far. I tried to go back when the weather turned, but my car got stuck. How did you know where I went?"

"I stopped by the bank. Erin was worried because she couldn't get ahold of you."

"No cell service."

Jace pulled out his phone and examined it. "I have a few bars." He walked toward the front door, where the signal seemed to be a little stronger. "I'll call the Keenans." He punched in the number and prayed he could get a message out. Tim answered.

"Tim. It's Jace." He went on to explain what had happened and that Lori was with him. Most importantly they were safe. He asked Tim to keep Cassie, then to call Lori's sister and let her know they wouldn't be back tonight. "Tell Cassie I love her and not to worry."

He flipped the phone closed and looked around the large room, then he turned back to Lori. "Tim will call Gina and let her know you're okay."

Lori's eyes widened. "We're not going back now?"

He shook his head. "Can't risk it. The storm is too bad so we're safer staying put." That was only partly true. He glanced around, knowing being alone with Lori wasn't safe anywhere. "I'd say this isn't a bad place to be stranded in." He looked at her. "This is one of your properties?"

She nodded. "I think my father came here...to get away."

Jace grinned. "So this was Lyle's secret hideaway?"

Lori frowned. "Please, I don't want that picture in my mind."

Jace looked around at the structure. "Well, whatever he used it for, it's well built. And it seems to have all the modern conveniences."

He went on a search, and found two bedrooms, then a utility room off the kitchen. There was a large generator and tankless water system. "Bingo," he called to Lori. "All the conveniences of home. In fact, it's better than back home." He nodded to the fire. "Propane gas for the kitchen stove and most importantly there's heat."

Lori looked at him. "You really think my father used this place for his own personal use?"

Jace shrugged. "Or he let clients use it. Come on, Lori, did you think your father lived like a monk?"

She shrugged. "Truthfully, I hadn't thought much about my father's personal business in a long time. So what if he came here." She walked to the kitchen. "Maybe we should look for something to eat." Opening the cabinets, she found some canned goods, soup, beans and tuna.

Jace opened the refrigerator. Empty, but the freezer was filled with different cuts of meat, steaks, chicken. "I'll say one thing about Lyle. He believed in being prepared." He pulled out two steaks. "Hungry?"

She arched an eyebrow. "Are you cooking?"

"Hey, I can cook." He took the meat from the package, put it on a plate and into the microwave to defrost. "I've been on my own for a long time."

Lori had wondered about his childhood since he'd mentioned that he'd been in foster care. "How old were you?"

"At eighteen they release you. So you're on your own," he told her as he found a can of green beans in another cabinet. "I got a job working construction and signed up for college classes."

Jace didn't have it much better than she did, Lori thought. "That had to be hard for you."

"Not too bad," Jace said. "I found out later, I had a small inheritance from my parents. It was in trust until I turned twenty-five." He turned on the broiler in the oven then washed his hands. "I used it to start my company. Yeager Construction."

Lori found she liked listening to Jace talk. He was a confident man, in his words and movements. Okay, so she more than liked him.

The microwave dinged and he took out the meat. "How about a little seasoning for your steak?" He held up a small jar.

"Sure."

He added the rub to the meat. She watched as he worked efficiently to prepare the meal. She couldn't help but wonder about how those broad hands and tapered fingers would feel against her skin.

She suddenly heard her name and looked at him. "What?"

He gave her an odd look. "How do you like your steak?"

"Any way you fix it is fine," she said, not really caring at all. Then he smiled and she couldn't find enough air to draw into her lungs.

He winked. "Medium rare it is," he said and slid the tray into the broiler.

Pull it together, girl, she told herself then went to the cupboard. She got out two plates and some flatware from the drawer, then set the table by the fire. No need for candles. She glanced around the room. It looked so intimate.

She went and found a can of pineapple and opened it, then heated the green beans just as the steaks came off the broiler.

Jace added another log to the fire, then they sat down to dinner. "Man, this looks good. Too bad we can't do a salad and some garlic bread."

"I find it amazing that there's so much food here."

"Your father struck me as well prepared. Hold on a minute." He got up, went into the utility room and came out with a bottle of wine. "In every way."

He opened the bottle and poured two glasses. He took them to the table, sat in his chair and began to cut his steak. "If he used this place, he wanted all the comforts money could buy," Jace said, nodding to the wine.

"I'm wondering who he shared all this with."

Jace took a drink. "You might never know. One thing for sure, Lyle had good taste."

She took a sip from her glass, too, and had to agree. Then she began to eat, discovering she was hungry. "I guess I'm still the daughter who wonders why he was such a loner, not even finding time for his only child."

"We can spend hours on that subject." Jace continued to eat. "Some people aren't cut out for the job of parenting."

She hated that her father's rejection still bothered her after all these years. She wanted to think she'd moved on. Maybe not.

She turned her attention back to the conversation. "Shelly hated anything to do with being a mother," Jace said. "That's why I can't let her have Cassie."

"Does Cassie want to live with her mother?"

"Cassie wants to be *loved* by her mother, but my ex is too selfish. She's been jealous of her daughter since her birth. And I'll do anything to prevent Cassie from taking a backseat to that. I know how it feels."

"Cassie's lucky she has you."

He smiled. "It's easy to love that little girl. I know I spoil her, but she's been so happy since she moved here. I have to make it permanent."

Lori put on a smile. "You're a good father, Jace Yeager." She placed her hand on his arm. "I'll help you in any way I can."

He stopped eating. "What do you mean? Help. I can afford to handle this custody battle on my own."

She shook her head. "I know that. I only meant that I know what it's like to not have a father in my life. I was offering moral support, nothing else. But don't be too bullheaded to take any and everything you can to keep your daughter. She needs you in her life, more than you know." Lori stood and carried her plate to the sink. Her appetite was gone.

He came to her. "I'm sorry, Lori."

She could feel his heat behind her. Good Lord, the man made his presence known. She wanted desperately to lean back into him. "For years Lyle Hutchinson never even acknowledged that I existed. I can't tell you how much that hurt."

She hated feeling needy. When Jace turned her around and touched her cheek, she couldn't deny she wanted his comfort.

"I can't imagine doing that to my child. I don't want to think about Cassie not being in my life. I know from experience that adults do dumb things, and in the end it's the kids that get hurt the most."

Lori felt a tear drop and he wiped it away. "It's not fair."

Jace leaned forward. "I wish I could change it." He brushed his mouth across hers. "I wish I could make you feel better."

She released a shaky breath. "What you're doing is nice."

His blue-eyed gaze searched her face. "Damn, Lori.

What I'm thinking about doing with you isn't nice."
Then he pulled her close and captured her mouth. Desire
burst within her, if possible more intense than ever before, pooling deep in her center. She could feel his heat
even through their clothes as she arched into his body.
She whimpered her need as his tongue danced against
hers.

"You make me want so many things," he breathed
as his tongue tormented her skin. He found his way to
her collarbone. "I want you, Lorelei Hutchinson." His
mouth closed over hers once again, giving her a hint of
the pleasure this man offered her.

She arched against him, her fingers threading
through his hair, holding him close. Mouths slanted,
their tongues mated as his hands moved over her back
and down to her bottom, pulling her closer to feel his
desire.

Jace was on the edge. On hearing her soft moan, he
drew back with his last ounce of sanity. Then he made
the mistake of looking into her eyes and all good intentions flew out the window. "Tell me to stop now, Lori."

She swallowed. "I can't, Jace. I don't want you to
stop."

His heart skipped a beat as he swung her up into his
arms. With a quick glance around, he headed to one of
the rooms under the loft, only caring there was a bed
past the door.

The daylight was fading, but there was enough light
from the main room. He set her down next to a four-
poster bed. He captured her mouth in a long kiss, then
reached behind her and threw back the thick comforter.

He returned to her. "I've dreamed of being with you

like this." He drew her into his arms. "So be sure you want the same."

She nodded.

He let out a frustrated breath. "You have to do better than that, Lori."

"I'm very sure, Jace."

Those big brown eyes looked up at him. He inhaled her soft scent and was lost, so lost that he couldn't think about anything except sharing this intimacy with this special woman.

His mouth descended to hers and the rest of the snowstorm and the world disappeared. There was only the two of them caught up in their own storm.

CHAPTER NINE

SOMETIME around dawn, Jace woke suddenly, aware he wasn't alone in bed. And it wasn't his bed. He blinked and raised his head from the pillow to find Lori beside him. He bit back a groan as images of last night came flooding into his mind.

He'd come looking for her, afraid she'd been stranded in the freak storm. He found her all right, and had given in to temptation. They'd made love last night. Right now her sweet body pressed against his had him aching again.

He lay his head back on the pillow. Why did she have to come into his life now? He didn't have anything to offer her. Not a future anyway. He couldn't let anyone distract him from getting custody of Cassie.

Lori stirred, then rolled over and peered at him through the dim light. Her soft yellow hair was mussed, but definitely added to her sex appeal.

"Hi," she said in a husky voice that had him thinking about forgetting everything and getting lost in her once again.

"Hi, yourself."

She pulled the sheet up to cover her breasts. "I guess

this is what they call the awkward morning-after moment."

He knew Lori well enough to know that she wasn't the type to jump into bed with just any man. That wasn't the type he needed right now. "The last thing I want to do is make you feel uncomfortable," he said, and leaned toward her. "It's just us, Lori."

She glanced away shyly. "I haven't had a relationship since college."

He found that made him happy. "That's hard to believe." He touched her face. "You're a very beautiful woman, Lorelei Hutchinson."

"Thank you." She glanced away. "I didn't have time for a personal life. Gina and Zack needed me."

"I take it Gina's ex has caused her and you a lot of trouble."

She nodded. "Sober Eric had a mean streak, but when drunk he was really scary. Even with his obvious abuse, it took a lot to convince Gina that the man would never change. Then one day he went after Zack and she finally realized how dangerous he was. That's what it took for her to go to court and testify against him. After that Eric threatened to come after her." Lori's large eyes met his. "That's why it was so hard for me to come to Destiny. When my father made the stipulation in the will about staying a year, I wasn't sure if I could."

"I'm glad you did," he told her, unable to stop touching her. His hand moved over her bare arm, her skin so soft.

She looked surprised. "Is that because I rescued your project?"

"No, it's because you're beautiful and generous." He decided not to fight whatever was going on between them any longer. He leaned down and brushed his mouth over hers, enjoying that she eagerly opened for him. He drew back and added, "You've also taken time with Cassie. Before we moved here she didn't have much female attention."

Lori wasn't sure what she'd expected this morning, but not this. "It's easy to be nice to her. Cassie's a sweet girl."

"Hey, what about me?"

She wrinkled her nose. "I wouldn't call you sweet. Not your disposition anyway."

"Maybe I can change your mind." He caressed her mouth again. "Is that any better?"

"Fishing for a compliment?"

He shifted against her. "How about we continue this without conversation?"

Though Lori wanted the same thing, they needed to get home. "Shouldn't we think about heading back?"

"It's barely dawn." He started working his magic as his mouth moved upward along her jawline. "What's your hurry?" His tongue circled her ear. "Are you trying to get rid of me?"

She gasped, unable to fight the sensation. "No, it's just that it's…" She forgot what she wanted to say as his lips continued along her neck. "Don't we need to leave?"

He raised his head and she could see the desire in his eyes. "I want to do one thing right and it only involves the two of us." He arched an eyebrow. "But if you'd rather go out in that cold weather and start digging out, I'll do it. Your choice."

Lori knew what she wanted, all right. This man. But the fear was that she could never really have him. Last night and these few early hours might be all she would ever have. She wrapped her arms around his neck and pulled his mouth down to hers. "I choose you."

Two hours later, Jace stood at the railing on the cabin porch, drinking coffee. The sun was bright, reflecting off the ten inches of snow covering the ground. The highways would be plowed by now, but not the private road that led to the cabin. He had four-wheel drive on his truck, so they could probably get out and make it to the main road. It better be sooner than later before he got in any deeper.

He had no regrets being with Lori. Making love with her had been incredible. He'd never felt anything like it in his life. Even the best times during his marriage hadn't come close to what he'd shared with Lori.

In just the past three weeks, he'd come to care about this woman more than he had any business doing. But he had strong feelings for Lori and that scared the hell out of him.

Worse, there was no guarantee and he couldn't even offer her a future. He had no extra money. Hell, he needed to rebuild his business. He had to get things settled with the custody issue before he could have a personal life. The question was, would he be able to walk away from Lori? Did he want to?

The front door opened and she stepped out. "I wondered where you went."

"Sorry." He pulled up the collar on her coat and kissed her. "I was just figuring out if we can make it back to town."

"I wouldn't mind getting stuck here a few more days," she admitted. "It's beautiful."

He wouldn't mind pushing reality away for a little

time with this woman. "That would be nice, but we both have jobs to do. Family to take care of."

"Oh, gosh. Gina. I bet she's going crazy with worry."

"Tim called her last night."

"She'll still worry, and be afraid."

Jace wondered who worried about Lori. Seemed she took care of everyone else. "Gina and Zack have Wyatt McCray, Lori. He'll protect them."

"I know," she said with a smile.

His heart began pounding in his chest. The effect she had on him could be a big distraction.

"Thank you for giving us that peace of mind. You've been so kind."

He wondered if she'd always think that. "I didn't do that much."

Those dark eyes locked with his. "You seem to be there whenever I need you."

He found he might not mind being that man. He leaned down to kiss her when he heard something and looked toward the road. "Looks like we're getting rescued."

Jace pointed to a large truck with a plow attached to the front. It stopped a few yards from the door and Toby and Joe climbed out.

Smiling brightly, his foreman called, "I hear someone here might need a ride back to town."

"Toby," Lori cried and hurried down the steps Jace had cleared earlier.

He watched as she ran through the snow to get to Toby. She hugged the big foreman. Jace felt a stab of jealousy stir inside him, but he didn't have any right to claim her. Not yet, maybe never.

* * *

After stopping to get Jace's truck, the ride back to town took about thirty minutes. He followed behind the plow truck until they reached the highway. After Lori gave Toby her car keys, she got into Jace's truck and drove to the Keenan Inn.

She knew she should probably go straight to the house but asked Toby to tow her car to the inn. Besides, she wasn't ready to leave Jace yet.

When they got to the porch, the door opened and they were immediately greeted by Claire and Tim.

"Well, you had yourself quite an adventure," Tim said.

Lori felt a blush rising up her neck as they crossed the threshold. "I guess I should pay better attention to the weather forecast before heading out into the countryside. I did discover my father has a lovely cabin. Thank goodness there was heat."

"Where's Cassie?" Jace asked, looking around.

Claire looked worried. "She's in the kitchen. She's with one of our new guests."

Lori caught Jace's frown. Then he took off and Lori followed him through the dining area and into the large kitchen.

She found Cassie at the counter with a tall, statuesque woman. Her hair was a glossy black in a blunt shoulder-length cut. Her face was flawless, her eyes an azure-blue. She was a beautiful woman until she flashed a hard look at Jace.

The child ran to him. "Daddy. Daddy, you're back."

"Yes, baby." He hugged his daughter. "I told you we got stuck in the snow."

Cassie looked at Lori. "Miss Lori, did you get stuck, too?"

"Yes, your daddy found me."

The child turned back to her father and whispered, "Daddy, don't let Mommy take me away."

Shelly Yeager stood and walked toward them. "Hello, Jace." She gave Lori a once-over. "It's nice to see that you could make it back to take care of our daughter."

"Shelly. What are you doing here?"

"I came to take my little girl home, of course."

An hour later, Lori's car had arrived and she got in and drove home to find a relieved Gina. She'd taken a long shower and gotten dressed in clean clothes, but couldn't push aside the memories from last night. The incredible night she'd shared with Jace, then reality hit them in the face with Shelly Yeager.

She couldn't stop thinking about Cassie and what her mother had said. Was she going to take the child back to Denver? No, Jace couldn't lose his daughter. She wished she could help him, like he'd helped her.

Lori came downstairs to find her sister in the dining room working with Wyatt. The security guard was a retired army man in his forties with buzz-cut hair. She smiled. He didn't look out of place pulling down twenty-year-old brocade drapes. No doubt this wasn't in the man's job description.

Standing back, Maggie was smiling at what was going on. "It's about time someone got rid of those awful things, don't you think?"

"The room does look brighter." Lori had put her sister in charge of making changes to the house. Gina had told her a few days ago about the plans for the dining room. This was good since it had taken her sister's mind off her ex-husband and any trouble he could cause.

Gina finally turned around. "Oh, yes, you look better now. Still a little tired, but better." She walked over as Maggie left the room. "You okay?"

Lori wasn't sure what she was. "I'm fine. We'll talk later." She sighed, not ready to share what had happened with Jace. "So what are you doing in here?"

Her sister smiled. "I hope you don't mind. I decided to take you up on your suggestion and redo the room. I'm going to order some sheer curtains and light-colored linen drapes. Then I'll plan to strip the wallpaper and paint." She went to the sideboard to find the paint chips. "I've narrowed it down to either shaker beige, or winter sunshine."

Lori tried to focus on her sister's selection and push Jace out of her head. It wasn't working. "You're the decorator, you decide."

"Well, since I'm going to keep the woodwork dark, I'm thinking shaker beige." She glanced at Wyatt. "What do you like?"

Lori found herself smiling. At least something was going well today.

"I can do anything I damn well please," Shelly told Jace as she paced her suite upstairs at the inn. Cassie stayed downstairs with the Keenans while her parents talked.

Jace knew better than to get into a fight with this woman. "I thought you wanted me to have Cassie until the first of next year. You were going to be on an extended honeymoon."

Shelly glanced away. "Plans change."

She was hiding something. "So you're going to just rip Cassie out of school and drag her back to Denver? Well, that's as far as you're going, Shelly. You can't take her out of state, and forget about out of the country." He glanced around the large room and into the connecting bedroom. "Where is your so-called duke?"

Shelly glared at him. "His name is Edmund. And he's not a duke." She raised her head as if she was better than everyone. That was always what Shelly wanted to be, but she had come from the same background he had. "He might not be a duke, but he's got money and a bloodline linked to the royal family. And he can take care of me."

That always got to him. He could never make enough money to satisfy her. "I'm happy for you, Shelly. So why are you here and not with…Edmund?"

"There's been a delay in our wedding plans. I might be having second thoughts. So I decided I'd come to see Cassie. And you. You were always good at calming me down."

Something was up with her, and Jace was going to find out what it was. First stop was to visit his lawyer, Paige Keenan Larkin. No one was taking Cassie away from him.

That afternoon, Lori went into her office at the bank. She had to do something to keep her mind off what had happened at the cabin. She also had to think realistically. She couldn't hold out hope about having a future with Jace. His ex-wife showing up in Destiny proved that.

The most important thing she had to remember was that a child was in the middle of this mess. That meant Cassie's welfare had to come first. She had to stay away from Jace Yeager.

A sudden knock brought her back to the present. "Come in."

Jace walked into her office and her breath caught in her throat. Would she ever stop reacting to this man? Her gaze roamed over Jace's six-foot-two frame, recalling how she'd clung to those broad shoulders.

"Lori."

"Jace. What are you doing here?"

"I needed to see you."

Once again she got caught up in his clean-shaven face. Suddenly the memory of his beard stubble moving against her skin caused her to shiver. The sensation had nearly driven her out of her mind.

He closed the door and went to her desk. "I thought we should talk."

She managed a smile, hoping she was covering her insecurities. "There's no need to. Cassie's mother is in town and you need to take care of them. I understand."

"There's nothing to understand except I don't want you caught up in this mess. I have no idea what Shelly is even doing in Destiny. She was supposed to be in England, married and heading off on her honeymoon."

Lori stood. "Did she give you any explanation?"

"Only that plans change," he told her as he crossed the room toward her.

Lori wanted to back away, to tell Jace to leave, that being together now could be dangerous. Instead, she rounded the desk and met him in the middle of the room.

It wasn't planned, but she didn't turn away when his head descended and his mouth captured hers. She surrendered to his eager assault and returned the kiss, hungry for this man. Finally she came to her senses and broke away. "We shouldn't be doing this."

"Are we breaking any laws?"

"But I don't think Shelly was happy when I walked into the inn with you today."

"It's none of her business."

"Jace, you need to get along with her. At least for Cassie's sake."

He pressed his head against hers. "It's funny. Shelly thinks I'm not worthy of her, but she has this need to interfere in my life."

Lori sighed. "I'm so sorry, Jace."

He drew back. "That's the reason I don't want you involved in this fight, Lori. Maybe it would be best if we cool it for a while. I have to think about Cassie."

Lori knew in her head this was the way it had to be, but her heart still ached. She was losing someone she truly cared about. She managed to nod. "Of course. Besides, we both have too much going on to think that far in the future, or at least to make any promises."

This time he looked surprised.

She moved away from him, or he might see how she truly felt. "Come on, Jace. We work together. Last night we gave in to an attraction. It might not have been the wisest thing to do, but it happened."

He studied her a moment. "Are you saying you regret it?"

"That's not the point."

Jace glared at her. The hell it wasn't. He wanted to reach for her, wanted her to admit more than she was. To tell him how incredible their night was. The worst of it was she couldn't do it any more than he could. "You're right."

She nodded. "Goodbye, Jace."

That was the last thing he wanted to hear, but he would only hurt her more if he stayed. He nodded and walked toward the door. It was a lot harder than he ever dreamed it would be, but he couldn't drag Lori into his fight.

CHAPTER TEN

OVER the next three days, Lori felt like she was walking around in a fog. After the incredible night with Jace, then his quick, easy dismissal of it, how could she not? It would be so easy to pull the covers over her head and just stay in bed. If she were living alone she might do just that. Instead she'd stayed home and gotten involved in Gina's redecorating projects. She tried to fill her time with other things, rather than thinking about a tall, dark and handsome contractor.

Then she'd gotten a call from Erin, telling her that Kaley Sims was in town and had agreed to see her. Anxious for the meeting, Lori arrived right at one o'clock and found an attractive woman with short, honey-blond hair and striking gray eyes waiting in her office.

"Ms. Sims. I'm Lori Hutchinson."

Kaley Sims stood up and they shook hands. "It's nice to meet you. And please call me Kaley." The woman studied her and smiled. "I see some resemblance. You have Lyle's eyes." The woman sobered. "I am sorry to hear of his passing."

"Thank you." Lori motioned for Kaley to sit in the chair across from the desk. "I can't tell you how happy

I am that you agreed to meet with me. I see in my files that you worked for my father a few years back."

Kaley nodded. "I was selling real estate in Destiny before he offered me a job as his property manager. I worked for Lyle about three years."

"You managed all his properties?"

"I did."

"I'm impressed," Lori said with a smile. "He has a big operation. I can't handle it all, nor do I have the experience to deal with the properties."

Kaley seemed to relax. "I was a single mother, so I needed the money. And the market was different then. Now, property values are a lot lower. You'd lose a fortune selling in this market."

"See, that's something I don't know. You've probably heard that my father left me in charge of all this."

Kaley's eyes widened, then she smiled. "Lyle would be proud. He talked about you a few times."

Lori froze. "He did?" Why did she still want Lyle's approval?

Kaley looked thoughtful. "One day I came in and found him looking at pictures of you. I think you were about eight or nine in the photo. And of course, Destiny being a small town, everyone knew about your parents' divorce. I mentioned to Lyle how cute you were and he should have you come back for a visit. He said he blew his chance."

Lori felt her chest tighten as she fought tears. This wasn't the time to relive the past. She blinked rapidly at the flooding emotions.

Kaley looked panicked. "I'm sorry, I didn't mean to make you sad."

Lori put on a smile, finding she liked this woman.

"You didn't. I never heard anything from my father since the day I left Destiny."

Kaley sighed. "That was Lyle. The only family he had was his father. Poor Billy had lived to be ninety-two and ended up in the nursing home outside of town until his death a few years ago." Kaley studied her. "Do you remember your grandfather?

Lori shook her head. "No, he wasn't around that I recall."

"You were probably lucky. Old Billy boy was what my mother called a hell-raiser. He was one of the last of the miners. Spent his gold as fast as he dug it out. Story has it that he loved gambling and women." Kaley raised an eyebrow. "His exploits were well-known around town. He was nearly broke when he suffered a stroke. It was Lyle who took over running what was left of the family fortune."

"Looks like he did a pretty good job," Lori said.

Kaley nodded in agreement. "I worked for the man, so I know how driven he was." She paused. "I also went with him to visit his father. Old Billy Hutchinson never had a good word to say to his son."

Lori didn't want to get her hopes up that there was something redeeming about Lyle Hutchinson.

Nor did she want to know about any personal relationship her father might have had with Kaley.

She quickly brought herself back to the present. "Well, I didn't ask you to come in to reminisce about my childhood. I was wondering if you'd be interested in coming back here and being my property manager." When Kaley started to speak, Lori stopped her. "I'll double whatever my father paid you."

The woman looked shocked to say the least. "You want me to work for you?"

Lori shook her head. "No, I want you to work *with* me. You have a good business sense, or my father wouldn't have trusted you. The one thing my father didn't offer, I will. There's a place in this company for advancement. Seems the women employees have been overlooked."

Kaley laughed. "I'm sure your father is somewhere cursing your words."

For the first time in two days, Lori laughed. It felt good. "So what do you say, Kaley?"

"I hear around town that you have to stay a year before you get your inheritance. Will you leave after that?"

Lori thought about her sister and nephew. How easily they had adapted to their new life. How Lori herself had, but could she be around Jace knowing she'd never have a life with the man?

She looked at Kaley. "News does travel fast, but no, I want to stay. I care about the residents of Destiny and I want to see the town prosper. Maybe it's my Hutchinson blood, but I can't let the town die away. That's why I need your help. I want to bring more businesses here and create more jobs."

The pretty woman studied her. "I'd like that, too, but there's one thing you need to know about your father and me—"

Lori raised her hand to stop her. "No, I don't need to know anything about your personal life. Makes no difference to me. I only care that you want to work for Hutchinson Corporation." Lori mentioned a yearly salary and benefits.

"Looks like you've got me on your team."

Lori smiled. "How soon can you start?"

"Give me a week to get moved back and get my daughter, Heather, settled in school."

"Let me know if there's anything I can do to help." The phone began to ring. She said goodbye to Kaley then answered.

"Lori Hutchinson."

"Hello, Lori. It's Claire Keenan. I hope I'm not interrupting you."

"Of course not, Claire. What can I do for you?"

"I need a big favor."

Tim Keenan eyed his wife of nearly forty years as she hung up the phone. He knew when she was planning something.

"Okay, what's going on, Claire?"

She turned those gorgeous green eyes toward him. She was also trying to distract him. "Whatever do you mean?"

"I thought you were looking forward to your afternoon volunteering in Ellie's class."

"I was," she admitted. "But I think Lori might need it more. She has to miss teaching. Besides, they're starting the Christmas pageant practice. She's volunteered to help."

Tim arched an eyebrow. "I'd say she has plenty to do taking over for Lyle. What's the real reason?"

"Did you happen to notice Lori and Jace when they were here the other day?"

"You mean after they'd been stranded at the cabin overnight? It was hard not to."

She nodded. "There were several looks exchanged between them." She sighed. "That only proves what

I've known from the moment I saw them together. They would be so perfect for each other, if only they got the chance."

He drew his wife into his arms. Besides her big emerald-green eyes, her loving heart was what drew him to her. The feel of her close still stirred him. "Playing matchmaker again?"

"It's just a little nudge. I'm hoping maybe they'll catch a glimpse of each other when Jace picks up Cassie."

"Sounds good in theory, but what about Shelly Yeager?" He raised his eyes toward the ceiling. The suite on the second floor was still occupied by the ex-wife. "She's been all but shadowing Jace's every move."

A mischievous smile appeared on his bride's lovely face. "I have plans for her."

About four-thirty that afternoon, Jace pulled up at the school and parked his truck. He was tired. More like exhausted ever since Shelly had arrived in town. And she showed no sign of leaving anytime soon. Something was up with her, but he couldn't figure out what it was.

He climbed out of his truck and started toward the auditorium. The last thing he wanted to do was anger his ex so much she'd walk away with Cassie. That was the only reason he'd put up with her dogging him everywhere, including several trips to the construction site. She even showed up at his house most evenings.

He hoped that Paige Larkin would get things in order, and fast, so he could finally go to the judge and stop Shelly's daily threats to take their daughter back to Denver. He liked the fact that Cassie got to spend time with her mother, but only if Shelly didn't end up hurting her.

No, he didn't trust Shelly one bit.

He opened the large door and walked into the theater-style room. Up on stage were several kids along with some teachers giving directions. That was when he caught sight of the petite blonde that haunted his dreams.

He froze as he took in Lori. She had on dark slacks and a gray sweater that revealed her curves and small waist. He closed his eyes and could see her lying naked on the big bed, her hair spread out on the pillow, her arms open wide to him.

He released a long breath. As much as he'd tried to forget Lori, she wouldn't leave his head, or his heart. All right, he'd come to care about her, but that didn't mean he could do anything about it.

The rehearsal ended and his daughter came running toward him. "Daddy! Daddy!" She ran into his arms and hugged him. "Did you see me practice?"

He loved seeing her enthusiasm. "I sure did."

Jace glanced up to see Lori coming toward them. His heart thudded in his chest as his gaze ate her up. Those dark eyes, her bright smile. His attention went to her mouth as he recalled how sweet she tasted. He quickly pulled himself back to the present, realizing the direction of his thoughts.

"Hello, Lori."

Her gaze avoided his. "Hi, Jace."

"Looks like you've got your hands full here."

"I don't mind at all. I love working with the kids. I gladly volunteered."

Why couldn't he have met this woman years ago?

Cassie drew his attention back to her. "Daddy, did you know that our play is called *Destiny's First Christmas?* It's about Lori's great-great grandfather Raymond Hutchinson. On Christmas Eve, he was working in his mine, 'The Lucky Strike,' and found gold. That night he made a promise to his wife to build a town."

Jace looked at Lori. "Not exactly the traditional Christmas story."

She shrugged. "Not my choice, but the kids voted to do this one. Probably because of my father's passing."

"No, I'd say because of you. You've made a lot of positive changes in the last month."

She shook her head. "Just trying to bring Lyle Hutchinson's business practices into the new century."

Jace found he didn't want to leave, but he couldn't keep staring at her and remembering how it was to hold her in his arms and make love to her.

Cassie tugged on his coat sleeve. "Daddy, I forgot to tell you, Miss Lori invited us to her house for Thanksgiving."

That surprised Jace.

"She's invited a whole bunch of people. It's going to be a big party. Can we go?"

The last thing he wanted to do was disappoint his daughter. "We'll talk about it. Why don't you go get your books." After he sent Cassie off, he turned back to Lori. "Please, don't feel you have to invite us."

"I don't. I wanted to invite you and Cassie, Jace. Besides, practically everyone else in town is coming. The Keenans and Erin and her family. A lot of the bank employees." She glanced away, not meeting his eyes. "And I plan to extend the invitation to Toby and the construction crew. There's going to be a lot of people at the house. I did it mainly for Gina and Zack so they could meet everyone. So you and Cassie are welcome."

Jace wanted so badly to reach out and touch her. He told himself that would be enough, but that was a lie. He wanted her like he'd never wanted a woman ever. "If you're sure."

She frowned. "Of course. We're business partners."

And that was all they could be, he thought. "Speaking of that, you need to come by the site. We're down to doing the finish trim work and adding fixtures. I'd like your opinion on how things are turning out."

She nodded. "How soon to completion?"

"Toby estimates two weeks."

"That's great. Then we can concentrate on getting the spaces rented. I can help with that since I've hired a property manager, Kaley Sims. If it's okay with you, I'd like her to come by and talk with you about listing the loft apartments."

Jace smiled. "So she's handling the rest of your properties?"

Lori nodded. "Yes, she worked for my father years ago, so she knows what she's doing. I convinced her to come back to work with me."

"Good, I'm ready to get this done."

She stiffened. "And you don't have to deal with a rookie partner."

He cursed. "Ah, Lori, I didn't mean it that way. It's just with all the delays we've had, I'm ready to be finished. You're a great partner. I'd work with you again."

She looked surprised. "You would?"

"In a heartbeat." He took a step toward her. There was so much he wanted to say, but he had no right to make promises when he wasn't sure what was in store for him and Cassie. He was in the middle of a messy custody battle. "Just come by the site tomorrow."

Lori started to speak when he heard his name called. He turned around to find Shelly coming toward him. Great. He didn't need this.

He turned back around but Lori had walked off. He wanted to go after her, but he couldn't, not until he got things settled. He'd better do it quickly, or he might lose one of the best things that ever happened to him.

The next week, Lori did what Jace asked and came by the site. She'd purposely stayed away from the project to avoid the man, so she was amazed at the difference.

The chain-link fence had been removed. They'd already started to do some stone landscape. Planters and retaining walls had been built, and a parking area.

"I'm impressed," Kaley said as she got out of the car and looked at the two-story wood-and-stone structure.

So was Lori. "Wait until you see the inside."

They headed up the path to the double-door entry. The door swung open and Toby greeted them with a big smile.

"Well, it's about time you showed up again."

Lori returned the smile. "Well, I knew you were in charge so I didn't worry about things getting done. Hello, Toby."

After a greeting, the foreman turned to Kaley and grinned. "Well, well, who's your friend, Lori?"

Lori made the introductions. "Kaley Sims, Hutchinson Corp's property manager, Toby Edwards."

"So you're not just a pretty face," Toby said.

"And you'd be wise to remember that, Mr. Edwards."

She took a step toward him, grinning. "Now, let's go see if this place looks as good as Lori says it does."

"Well, damn. You're making my day brighter and brighter."

Lori was surprised to see these two throw off sparks. "Go on ahead and don't mind me," she called as the two took off, not paying any attention to her.

She stepped through the entry and gasped as she looked around. The dark hardwood floors had been laid and the massive fireplace completed. She eyed the golden tones of the stacked stones that ran all the way from the hearth to the open-beam ceiling.

Then her attention went to the main attraction of the huge room. The arching staircase. The new design was an improvement from the old as the natural wood banister wrapped around the edge of the first floor, showing off the mezzanine. A front desk had been built for a receptionist for the tenants.

"So how do you like it so far?"

Lori swung around to see Jace. "It looks wonderful."

Then she took in the man. In his usual uniform of faded jeans and a dark Henley shirt, Jace also wore a carpenter's tool belt around his waist. Somehow that even looked sexy.

"Am I disturbing your work?"

He grinned. "Darlin', you've been disturbing a lot more than my work since the minute I met you."

Jace was in a good mood today. Although Shelly had no plans to leave town, he had talked to Paige first thing that morning. He now had a court date and also a preliminary injunction so Shelly couldn't run off with Cassie. At least not until after the custody hearing back in Denver.

"We butted heads a lot, too," she said.

He leaned forward and breathed, "And there were times when we couldn't keep our hands off each other." Before she could do more than gasp, he took her hand. "Come on, I want to show you around."

"I need to go with Toby and Kaley."

He led her up the staircase. "I think Toby can handle the job." He took her into the first loft apartment, showing off ebony-colored hardwood floors. The open kitchen had dark-colored cabinets, but the counters weren't installed yet. "Here are some granite samples for the countertops and tile for the backsplash."

He watched her study the light-colored granite, with the earth-toned contrasting tile. The other was a glossy black, with white subway tile. "I like the earth tone," she told him.

He smiled. "My choice, too. The next stop is the bathroom." He led her across the main living space, where the floor-to-ceiling windows stopped her.

"Oh, Jace. This is a wonderful view."

He stood behind her, careful not to touch her as they glanced out the window at the San Juan Mountains. He worked hard to concentrate on the snow-filled creases in the rock formations and evergreen trees dotting the landscape. "It's almost as beautiful as the view from the cabin."

She glanced up at him and he saw the longing in her dark eyes. "It was lovely there, wasn't it?"

"You were even more beautiful, Lori."

She shook her head. "Don't, Jace. We decided that we shouldn't be involved."

"What if I can't stay away from you?"

Lori closed her eyes. She didn't want to hope and be

hurt in the end. Then his mouth closed over hers and she lost all reasonable thoughts. With a whimper of need she moved her hands up his chest and around his neck and gave in to the feelings.

He broke off the kiss. "I've missed you, Lori. I missed holding you, touching you, kissing you."

"Jace…"

His mouth found hers again and again.

Finally the sound of voices broke them apart. His gaze searched her face. "Lucky for you we're not alone. I'm pretty close to losing control." He sighed. "And with you, Lorelei Hutchinson, that happens every time I get close." He pulled her against him so there was no doubt. "Please, say you'll come by the house tonight. There are so many things I want to tell you."

Lori wanted to hope that everything would work out with Jace. Yet, still Shelly Yeager lingered in town. The last thing Lori wanted was to jeopardize Jace getting custody of his daughter.

Yet, she wanted them both—Jace and Cassie—in her life. Question was, was she ready to fight for what she wanted? Yes. "What time?"

CHAPTER ELEVEN

AT THE site, Jace kept checking his watch, but it was only two o'clock. He had three more hours before he could call it a day and see Lori again.

He was crazy to add any more complications to his life, but he hadn't been able to get her out of his head. For weeks, he'd tried to deny his feelings, tried to convince himself that he didn't care about Lori, but he did care. A lot.

He hadn't been able to forget her or what happened between them. The night at the cabin, what they'd shared, made him think it was possible to have a relationship again. Tonight, when she came by the house, he planned to tell her. He only hoped she could be patient and hang in there a little while longer, until this custody mess was finally straightened out.

"Hey, are you listening?"

Jace turned toward his friend Justin Hilliard. "Sorry, what did you say?"

Justin smiled. "Seems you have something or someone else on your mind."

"Yeah, I do. But I can't do anything about it right now so I'd rather not talk about it."

"I understand. If you need a friend to talk later, I'm your guy. I'll even buy the beer."

Justin was the one who'd brought him to Destiny after Yeager Construction tanked following his divorce. He'd always be grateful. "I appreciate that."

His friend nodded. "Now, tell me when can I move in?" He motioned around the office space on the main floor at the Mountain Heritage complex.

"Is next week soon enough?"

"Great. I'll have Morgan go shopping for office furniture. And I'll need a loft apartment upstairs for out-of-town clients. Is there someone handling the loft rentals?"

Jace nodded. "Kaley Sims. I'll have her get in touch with you to negotiate the lease."

"Good. I'm available all this week." Justin studied Jace. "So what are your plans for your next project?"

"Not sure." That much was true. "I've been so wrapped up in getting this project completed, I haven't thought that far ahead." He had Lori on his mind. "I know I'd like to stay here, of course, but until I get this custody mess taken care of, I'm still in limbo."

"Like I said, let me know if I can help." Justin slapped him on the back. "Just don't let Shelly get away with anything."

"Believe me, I won't." She'd taken him to the cleaners once. No more. "Besides, Paige is handling it all for me."

Justin nodded. "Yeah, my sister-in-law is one of the best. She'll do everything she can to straighten this out."

God, he hoped so. Jace wanted nothing more than to end Shelly's threats.

They walked out of the office space and Justin said, "If you think you'd be ready to start another project by March, let me know."

Jace stopped. He was definitely interested. "What kind of project?"

"It's an idea I've had in the works awhile. I waited until I had the right partner in place, and now, it's in the designing stages."

Jace was more than intrigued. "So what is it?"

"A mountain bike racing school and trails. I bought several acres of land about five miles outside of town and plan to build a track. I'm bringing in a pro racer, Ryan Donnelly, to design it."

"I don't do landscaping."

Justin smiled. "I know. I want your company to handle the structures, cabins to house the students and instructors, including a main building to serve meals and a pro shop."

They walked through the main area of the building as Justin continued. "Eventually, I hope to work with Ryan to design bikes. I want the plant to be right here in Destiny." Justin arched an eyebrow. "I want you to handle it all, Jace."

This was a dream come true. "And I want the project, Justin. By early spring I could have the subs and crew in place to start." He worked to hold in his excitement. "But I'll need the plans by February."

Justin nodded. "Shouldn't be a problem."

Now if his personal life straightened out by then. With this new project he could move forward, make a fresh start. He thought about Lori. He couldn't wait to tell her. Tonight. This could be their new beginning.

* * *

By six o'clock, Lori had gathered her things and left the office. She went home, showered and changed into a nice pair of slacks and white angora sweater. Excited about spending the evening with Jace, she took extra time with her clothes and makeup.

Her pulse raced as she realized how badly she wanted to be with him. He was everything she'd ever dreamed the man she loved could be. Handsome, caring and a good father. What woman wouldn't dream about forever with him?

She walked back into the connecting bedroom to find Gina.

"Sorry, Lori, I didn't mean to disturb you. I know you plan to go out tonight."

"You never could disturb me," Lori assured her sister. "Is something wrong?"

Gina smiled. "No. For the first time in a very long time, everything is going right." She went to her sister. "Thanks to you. I never thought I could feel this happy again. And Zack…"

Lori hugged her, praying that continued. That Eric would leave them alone. "We're family, Gina. Besides, it's Lyle's money."

"No, you were there for us long before you inherited the Hutchinson money. You were always there for me."

"You're my sister and Zack is my nephew. Where else would I be?"

"Having a life?" Gina said. "And finding someone special."

Lori wanted to believe. "I think that has already happened."

Her sister smiled. "If Jace Yeager is as smart as I think he is, he'll snatch you up."

Of course, Lori hoped that tonight the man would make some kind of commitment, but she also knew he had to tread cautiously. They both did. "Let's just see what happens."

About eight o'clock that evening, Jace had put Cassie to bed, but she made him promise when Lori got there she would come up to say good-night. He was happy that his daughter got along with her.

He smiled, knowing he'd have Lori all to himself for the rest of the evening. There were so many things he wanted to tell Lori tonight. He wanted them to move ahead together.

He checked on the dinners he'd picked up from the Silver Spoon. Then he took the wine out of the refrigerator and got two glasses from the cupboard. He looked around his half-finished kitchen.

Okay, this place had been neglected too long. It was going to be his top priority. He could probably make some headway by Christmas. Thanksgiving at the Hutchinson house, and maybe, Christmas dinner at the Yeager house. That would be his goal.

He hoped to have the rest of his life in order by then, too. His daughter with him and Lori with them. He'd made a start with the custody hearing.

He saw the flash of headlights as a car pulled into the drive. His heart began to pound when he saw Lori climb out and walk up the steps to the back porch. He opened the door and greeted her with a smile.

"Hi, there."

She smiled. "Hi. Sorry I'm late."

Jace drew her into his arms because he couldn't go any longer without touching her, holding her. "Well, you're here now and that's all that matters. I missed you." He kissed her, a slow but intense meeting of their mouths, only making him hungry for more.

He didn't want to let go of her, but he promised himself he'd go slow. He tore his mouth away. "Maybe we should dial it down a little." He tugged at her heavy coat. "At least until I feed you."

She smiled. "I am a little hungry." She brushed her hair back and looked around. "Where's Cassie?"

"I'm losing out to the kid, huh? She's upstairs in bed." He led her into the kitchen. "I told her you'd come up and say good-night. I hope you don't mind."

"Of course not." Lori started off, but he brought her back to him for another intense kiss. "Just remember you're mine for the rest of the night."

"I'll be right back."

Jace's heart pounded as he watched the cute sway of her hips as she walked out of the kitchen and up the stairs.

He sighed and worked to get it together. "You got it bad, Yeager." He turned down the lights, and put on some music from the sound system, then lit the candles on the table. Back at the kitchen counter, he opened the chilled bottle of wine and filled the glasses at the two place settings.

It was impossible not to remember their dinner together at the cabin. He wanted nothing more than to have a repeat of that night. But that couldn't happen. Not with Cassie here. He blew out a breath. There was no doubt in his mind, they'd be together again. And soon.

Smiling, Lori walked down the steps and it turned into a grin when she saw Jace in the kitchen. "That's what I like about you, Yeager. You're just not a handsome face, you're domestic, too."

Jace turned around and tossed her a sexy smile. "I can be whatever you want."

Her heart shot off racing. *How about the man who loves me?* she asked silently as he came to her and drew her against him. She wanted nothing more than to stay wrapped in his arms, to close out the rest of the world.

She looked up at him. "Kiss me, Jace."

"My pleasure, ma'am." He lowered his head, brushing her mouth with his. She opened for him, but he was a little more playful and took nibbling bites out of her bottom lip.

With her whimper of need, he captured her mouth in a searing kiss. By the time he pulled back, her knees were weak and she had trouble catching her breath. "Wow."

He raised an eyebrow. "That was just an appetizer." He stepped back. "But before I go back to sampling you again, we better eat."

She was a little disappointed, but knew it was better to slow things down a little. She accepted the wine he offered her.

She sipped it and let the sweet taste linger in her mouth. She caught Jace watching her and smiled, then took another sip. "How was your day at the site?"

"Oh, I meant to tell you that Justin stopped by. Besides the office space, he wants to lease a loft apartment. I gave him Kaley's number."

"Good." She raised her glass. "The first of many, I hope."

"You and me both. Justin might want more than one apartment. I'm hoping Kaley can convince him of that.

Maybe give him a few incentives like a six-month re-
duction in the rent."

"That sounds good. Is that usually done in real estate?"

He nodded. "All the time." He walked her to the table
and sat her down, then began filling their plates with
roast chicken and mashed potatoes. "The Silver Spoon's
Thursday night special."

Lori took a bite. "It's very good."

"Come spring," he began, "I'll barbecue us some
steaks on the grill. That's my specialty."

She paused, her fork to her mouth. He was talking
about the future. "I'd like that."

He winked and took a bite of food as they continued
to talk about Mountain Heritage, then he told her about
Justin's offer for the racing bike school.

"Oh, Jace, you have to be excited about that."

Jace wanted to be, but there were still problems
looming overhead. Like getting permanent custody of
his daughter. He prayed that Paige could pull this off.
"There's still a lot to work out."

Lori nodded.

He didn't want to talk about it right now. This was
just for them. No troubles, no worries, just them. Yet,
he knew he couldn't make her any promises. He'd never
thought he'd find someone like Lori, someone he'd want
to dream about a future together.

The meal finished, they carried the dishes to the sink
and left them. He offered her coffee, but she refused it.

A soft ballad came on the radio. He drew her into his
arms and began slowly dancing her around the kitchen
and into the family room, where soft flames in the fireplace added to the mood. He placed his hands against

her back, pulling his swaying body against hers. "I want you, Lori," he whispered. "Never have I wanted a woman as much as you." His lips trailed along her jaw, feeling her shiver. He finally reached his destination. "Never." He closed his mouth over hers, and pushed his tongue inside tasting her, stroking her.

His hands were busy, too, reaching under her sweater, cupping her breasts.

"Jace," she moaned. "Please."

"I definitely want to please you." He kissed her again and was quickly getting to the point of no return.

"Well, well. Isn't this cozy?"

Jace jerked back and caught sight of Shelly standing in the doorway. He immediately turned Lori away from view. "What are you doing here?"

The tall brunette pushed away from the doorjamb and walked into the room as if she had every right to be there.

"Since no one was answering the phone, I came to see what the problem was." She gave Lori a once-over. "Now I know why. You're having a little party here while our daughter is asleep upstairs."

"That's my business, Shelly. And that doesn't give you the right to come into my house without an invitation. And you weren't invited."

"I don't need to be. I have custody of Cassie." She shot an angry look at Lori. "In fact I think I should remove her from here right now."

Lori gasped.

Jace got angry. "I wouldn't try it, Shelly."

"Try and stop me."

When she started to move past him, Jace stepped in

front of her. "You can't. I have an injunction that says she stays with me until the court hearing."

She glared. "I know. I got served today."

So that was why she showed up. "And this should be settled in court."

"I want my daughter. Now!"

"Stop it! Mommy, Daddy, don't fight!"

They all turned and saw Cassie standing at the bottom of the stairs.

Lori wanted to go to the child, but it wasn't her place.

Jace took over and went to his daughter's side. "Oh, baby. I'm sorry we woke you."

"You and Mommy were fighting again?"

"I'm sorry. We're trying to work something out and we got a little loud."

"Please, I don't want you to fight anymore."

Jace looked at Lori. "Will you take Cassie back to her room?" With her nod, he glanced down at his daughter. "I'll be up in a minute."

Shelly came over and kissed her daughter and sent her along.

Once they were alone, Jace took Shelly's arm and walked her out to the utility room. "I'm not going to let you come here and upset Cassie like that."

"You're just mad because I interrupted your rendezvous with little Miss Heiress."

"Leave Lori out of this. She's a respectable person in this town."

"And you're sleeping with her."

Jace had to hold his temper. "We've done nothing wrong. If you think so, then talk to the judge. I'll see you in court, Shelly."

Shelly's face reddened in anger. "Don't think you've

won, Jace Yeager. This is not going to end in your favor."

He held on to his temper. "Why, Shelly? Why are we arguing about this? You know Cassie is better off here. She's made friends and is doing great in school. I have a job that has me home every night." He stopped in front of the woman he once loved, but now he only felt sorry for. "When you get married, Shelly, I will let you see her anytime you want."

"That might not happen. So the game plan will change."

"Oh, Cassie."

Lori cradled the small form against her as they sat on the bed. She inhaled the soft powdery smell and realized how much Cassie had come to mean to her. She could easily become addicted to this nightly ritual.

She silently cursed Shelly Yeager. How could anyone drag a child into this mess? "I wish I could make it better, sweetheart."

The child's lip quivered as she looked up. "Nobody can. They always fight."

"I'm sorry. That doesn't mean they don't love you. They just have to work out what's best for you."

A tear ran down the girl's cheek. "I want to live here with Daddy, but if I do, Mommy will go away." Cassie's big blue eyes looked up at her, and Lori could feel her pain. "And she's gonna forget about me." She started to sob and Lori drew her into a tight embrace.

"Oh, sweetheart, have you told your father how you feel?"

The child pulled back, looking panicked. "No! I don't

want them to fight anymore." Her face crumpled again. "So please don't tell Daddy."

"Don't tell me what?"

They both looked toward the door to see Jace. "Nothing." Cassie wiped her eyes. "I'm just talking to Miss Lori."

Lori got up and Jace sat down to face his daughter. "Sweetheart, I'm sorry."

The little girl suddenly collapsed into her father's arms. Lori backed out of the room, not wanting to intrude. She realized right away how much this custody battle had affected the child.

And Cassie had to come first.

Lori couldn't help but wonder if they could get through this situation unscathed, or would Shelly follow through on her threats?

Lori's chest tightened. She'd never forget the heartache she'd felt when she had to leave her childhood home. Her father standing on the porch. That had been the last time she'd ever seen Lyle Hutchinson. Oh, God. She couldn't let that happen to this little girl. No matter what it cost her.

Cassie finally went to sleep and Jace walked out into the hall, but he didn't go downstairs yet. Heartsick over his daughter's distress, he needed some time to pull himself together. Cassie had been dealing with problems he and her mother had caused. No child should have to choose which parent to love, which parent to be loyal to.

He sighed, knowing he had to do something about it.

Jace made his way down the steps and found Lori standing in the kitchen. He went to her and pulled her into a tight embrace. "I guess we should talk." He released her and walked around the kitchen in a daze. "You want something to drink?"

"No," she said. "Is Cassie asleep?"

He nodded, feeling the rush of emotions as he went and poured himself a glass. "I'm so angry at Shelly for starting all this."

"Divorce isn't easy for anyone, kids especially." Lori closed her eyes momentarily. "Cassie needs constant re-assurance that her daddy's going to be around."

Jace tried to draw a breath, but it was hard. "And I have been right here for her. I've been doing everything possible to keep her with me."

He immediately realized the harshness of his words. "I'm sorry, Lori, that you had to witness this." He pulled her close, grateful that she didn't resist. "I'm so frus-trated." He held her tightly. "I've worked so hard to have a good relationship with my daughter."

Lori pulled back, knowing there wasn't any sim-ple solution. "I know, but Cassie is still caught in the middle."

"This is all a game to Shelly."

It wasn't for the rest of the people involved. "Well, she is here and you have to deal with her. For Cassie's sake."

"I've been doing that," he told her. "Paige has got-ten a court date for a custody hearing with a judge in Denver."

Lori was surprised by Jace's news. "That's good. When?"

"This coming Monday."

She told herself not to react, not to be hurt that he hadn't said anything before now. "So soon?"

He studied her with those intense blue eyes. "If we

don't do it now, the holidays are coming up. It could be delayed until January. By then Shelly might have taken Cassie to Europe." He paused. "I was going to tell you about it tonight."

That didn't take away the pain of his leaving. "How long will you be gone?"

"Probably just a few days. Don't worry, Toby has the project under control."

She shook her head. "You think I'm concerned about that when Cassie's future is in jeopardy?"

He shook his head. "Of course not, Lori. I know you care about her."

"I care about both of you. I want this to work, because she should be with you."

He looked at her, his blue eyes intense. "I'm going to see that happens no matter what the judge's decision is."

Lori felt her heart skip a beat. "Does that mean you'll move back to Denver?"

He nodded slowly. "I hope there's another way. I don't want to leave here, but if that's the end result of this hearing...there's no choice."

He might be going away, she thought, fighting tears. "Cassie's your daughter, so of course you have to go there. You have to fight for her."

"I care about you, Lori. A lot. I know you have a year commitment here, or I'd ask—"

"Then don't, Jace," she interrupted, forcing a smile. "Neither one of us is ready to jump into a relationship. Like you said, we both have other commitments."

His gaze locked on hers. "I want to say the hell with all of Shelly's games, but I can't. Bottom line is, I can't give you any promises."

And she couldn't beg him to. There was too much

at stake here. Most importantly, a little girl. Lori had once been that little girl whose father let her go. Cassie deserved better.

Lori couldn't meet his eyes. She fisted her hands so he wouldn't see her shaking. "It's too soon to make plans when we don't know the future."

"Is it? What about what happened between us at the cabin? Unless it didn't mean anything to you."

She swallowed hard. "Of course it did." She'd always have those incredible memories. "It was…special."

"Seems not as special for you as it was for me."

She had to get away from him. "I'm sorry, Jace. I need to go. I hope everything works out for you and Cassie." She headed toward the door and paused. She took one last look at the man she loved. "Goodbye, Jace."

When he didn't say anything to stop her, she hurried out the door and got into her car. Starting the engine, she headed for the highway. He hadn't even asked her to wait it out. Tears filled her eyes, blurring her vision, until she had to stop.

She cried for her loss, for letting this between her and Jace to get this far. She never should have let herself fall in love with this wonderful man. A man she couldn't have. She'd finally opened herself and let love in, only to be hurt again.

She brushed away more tears, praying that the pain would stop. That the loneliness would go away soon. This was what she got for starting to dream of that happy ending.

The only consolation was she wouldn't let another little girl go through the misery she had. She would never prevent Jace from having his daughter.

CHAPTER TWELVE

THAT night, sleep eluded Lori.

When she'd gotten home earlier she'd made up an excuse to go to her room. She hadn't been in the mood to talk about her evening with Jace. Not even with Gina. And what good would it do? Neither one of them had a choice in the matter. There was nothing to say except they couldn't be together.

But after several hours of tossing and turning, she got out of bed. Restless, she ended up wandering around the big house. She checked in on her sleeping nephew and pulled the covers around him, knowing Jace would do the same thing with Cassie. Smiling, she realized that had been one of the reasons she'd fallen in love with the man. His relationship with his daughter was part of that. She would miss them both so much if they couldn't come back here. What were Jace's chances of getting custody? Probably slim.

Lori walked down the hall, passing her childhood bedroom. She stopped, wanting nothing more than to shake the feeling of abandonment she'd had since her mother took her away from here.

She slipped inside, waiting as the moonlight coming through the window lit her path to the canopy bed.

Loneliness swept through her as more memories flooded back. Her absent father had been too busy for her. He'd been too busy making money and that meant he hadn't been home much.

Then long-forgotten images flashed though her mind. There had been some happy times. She remembered sitting at the dinner table, hearing her parents' laughter. Lyle wasn't very demonstrative, but she would always cherish the time he'd spent with her. Guess he'd been as loving as he was able to be.

She smiled, thinking of those good-night kisses she would treasure. She brushed away a tear as she turned on a bedside lamp and caught sight of the stuffed animals lined up on the windowsill.

Another memory hit her. "Oh, Daddy, you gave me all of these."

"Lorelei?"

Lori turned to find Maggie standing in the doorway. She was wearing her robe over a long gown. "Oh, Maggie, did I wake you?"

The housekeeper walked in. "No, I was up getting something to drink. This old house has a lot creaks and I know them all. When I heard someone walking around, I thought it might be the boy." The older woman eyed the stuffed animals. "Land sakes, child. You can't keep coming in here and getting all sad."

"No, Maggie. Really, I'm fine." She smiled as she wiped away the tears and held out one of her childhood animals. "Look. I remembered that Dad bought this for me." She reached for another. "He bought these, too." She gathered all them in her arms.

Maggie smiled. "I'm glad you remember those times."

And so much more. "Every time he went on a business trip, he came home with a toy for me." Another memory. "And when he was home he would come into my bedroom and kiss me good-night." Tears flooded her eyes. "He loved me, Maggie."

"Of course he loved you. You were his little girl, his pride and joy."

"Then why, Maggie? Why didn't he want me?"

The housekeeper shook her head. "It wasn't that." She hesitated, then said, "You never knew your grandfather Billy. If you had you might understand your father better."

"Kaley Sims mentioned him. She said he'd gone into a nursing home after a stroke."

Maggie made a huffing sound. "It was probably better than he deserved. That man was a terrible example as a parent. What Lyle went through as a child was... Let's just say, Billy wasn't much of a human being, so I won't go into his fathering skills."

"Wouldn't that make Lyle a better one?"

Maggie took hold of Lori's hands and they sank down to sit on the window seat. "I believe your dad did the best he could, honey. When Billy nearly lost all the family money, and that included the bank, this town almost didn't survive. Your father spent a lot of years rebuilding the family wealth, and trying to get Billy's approval."

Maggie continued, "Your mother didn't like being neglected, either. She wanted all of her husband's attention. I think she left hoping Lyle would come after both of you. Your father took it as another rejection and just shut down."

Lori had no doubt Jocelyn Hutchinson would do that to get attention. "But he had a daughter who loved him."

Maggie looked sad. "I know. I wish I had a better answer for you. I recall a few phone conversations between your mother and father. He asked Jocelyn to bring you here. She refused. When your mother remarried, he told me that you'd do better without him."

She felt a spark of hope. "He wanted me to come back here?"

Maggie nodded. "For Christmas that first year. He told me once how much you loved the tree lights in the town square."

A tear ran down Lori's cheek. She had no idea he would remember.

Maggie pulled her into a comforting embrace. "He kept this room the same, hoping to have you back here. So keep hanging on to the good memories, child. I know that was what your father did."

Lori pulled back. "How can I?"

The housekeeper brushed back Lori's hair. "Because your father knew he caused enough pain over the years." Maggie smiled through her own tears. "Think about it, Lorelei. Your father finally brought you home. No mistaking, he wanted you here."

Lori began to sob over the lost years that father and daughter would never get back. The tears were cleansing, and she had some answers.

"Lori?"

Lori looked at the open door to find her sister. "Oh, Gina. Sorry, did we wake you?"

"I was just checking on Zack."

Maggie hugged them both. "Share with your sister, Lorelei. It will get better each time." The older woman left.

"Should I be worried?" Gina asked once they were alone.

"Not any longer. I've learned a lot about my father. Lyle wasn't perfect, but he loved me in his way." Lori went on to explain about her discovery.

"I'm so glad," Gina agreed. "Every child needs those good memories." She hesitated. "That's what I hope for Zack."

"He'll have those good memories. I promise," Lori told her, thinking about Cassie, too.

Lori never wanted that child to go through what she had. So that meant she had to accept it. Accept she might not be able to have Jace Yeager.

Gina's voice broke into her thoughts.

Lori looked at her. "What?"

"Something else is bothering you. Would it have anything to do with Jace? Did you two have a fight?" Gina asked, frowning. "Oh, no, it's his ex-wife causing trouble, isn't it?"

Lori agreed. "Jace has to go back to Denver for the custody case. If he loses, he wants to live close by Cassie. That means he'll have to move back there."

"I wish I could hate the guy, but he's a great father." Gina suddenly grinned. "So move to Denver."

Lori would in a minute. "I can't until I fulfill Lyle's will. If I leave before the year is up, the town might not survive."

"That doesn't mean you can't go visit Jace for long weekends."

She could go for that. Would Jace want a long-distance relationship? "He hasn't asked me."

Gina jumped up. "Of course he hasn't. He doesn't know anything yet. Lori, I believe Jace Yeager loves you. And if he can, he'll do whatever it takes to get Cassie and come back here to you."

Lori was heartened with her sister's enthusiasm. "You sure seem to have a better outlook toward men these days."

Her sister shrugged. "Maybe they aren't all jerks like Eric. I've met a few here in town that seem really nice. Now, that doesn't mean I want to get involved with any of them. I'm happy concentrating on raising Zack."

If one good thing came out of returning to Destiny it was helping Gina and Zack have a chance at a new life. "And we have each other."

"Always." Gina nodded. "Now, we need something to do to keep you busy." She looked around what once had been a little girl's room. "This entire house, at the very least, needs a fresh coat of paint. We should redecorate the master suite, so you can move in there."

Lori knew Gina was trying to distract her, and she loved her for it. "The place is a little big for us, don't you think?"

"Of course it is. It's a mansion."

Lori turned to her sister. "What about moving into a smaller place?"

Her sister blinked. "Are you going to sell this house?"

She shook her head. "We have to live here for now. I think maybe Hutchinson House can be rented out for weddings and parties and the proceeds could go to the town." She couldn't help but wonder if Jace and Cassie would be living here in Destiny, too. "What do you think of that?"

"Lori, I think that's a wonderful idea." She hesitated.

"And you've been generous to Zack and me. But I feel I need to contribute, too. I know this mess with Eric still has me frightened, but thanks to you, I've felt safer than I have for years."

"I'm glad." Lori had already checked on her ex-brother-in-law. She'd contacted the police detective on the case. Eric had been staying with his family in Colorado Springs.

"I need a job," Gina blurted out. "It's not that I'm not grateful to you for everything, but I want to be more independent. I have to set a good example for my son. I don't want him to think he has an easy ride in life."

Lori hugged her, knowing the hell she'd gone through for years. "So you want a job. I just happen to have one."

Her sister frowned. "Lori, you can't make up a job for me."

"I hate to tell you, sis, but most of the people in Destiny work for Hutchinson Corp. And honestly, I'm not making this job up. Kaley Sims is going to advertise the Mountain Heritage spaces to rent and she needs to stage them. You're the perfect decorator to do it. So what do you say?"

Gina gave her a big smile. "I say, when do I start?"

"I'll talk to Kaley in the morning." Lori smiled, but inside she was hurting. Everyone was moving forward, but she couldn't, not knowing what her future held. "Come on, we both need to get some sleep."

They walked back to their rooms. Lori climbed in bed just as her cell phone rang. She reached for it off her nightstand.

She glanced at the familiar caller ID. "Jace," she answered. "Is something wrong?"

"No, nothing's wrong. I'm sorry I called so late. I just wanted to let you know that Cassie and I are leaving."

She already knew that. "When?"

"First thing in the morning."

So soon.

Jace went on. "Toby has everything under control at the site. There are only a few finishing touches before the last walk through. Kaley Sims is now handling the Heritage project. I'll pass on the news to her."

"I appreciate that," she told him. "Is there anything else?"

Lori begged silently that he'd ask her to wait for him. At least tell her he cared.

"I hated the way we left things last night," he finally said. "God, Lori, I wish it could be different."

She swallowed back the lump in her throat. "You're doing what's right, Jace."

"I know. I just needed to hear your voice," he told her and there was a long pause. "Goodbye, Lori." Then he hung up.

The silence was deafening. She lay back in her bed, pulling up the covers to protect her from the loneliness. It didn't help. Nothing would help but Jace.

"Why are you dead set on making my life hell?" Jace demanded as he stepped through the door into his one-time Denver home the next day. Something else that Shelly had gotten from their divorce.

He glanced around the spacious entry of the re-furbished Victorian. The hardwood floors he'd refinished himself, along with the plaster on the walls. He stopped the search when unpleasant memories of his marriage hit him. He turned back to Shelly to see her stubborn look.

"You're the one who had me served with papers."

"Because you came to Destiny and disrupted Cassie's life. I'm done with your games, Shelly. It's time we settle this."

"Well, that's too bad." She strolled across the room to the three windows that overlooked the street. "I'm Cassie's mother, and after today, the judge will see that I should have our child permanently. Where is our daughter?"

"She's in good hands." Paige had offered to watch her back at the hotel while he tried to straighten out a few things. "She's with Paige Larkin."

Shelly frowned. "So what are you willing to give up to spend time with Cassie? Your little girlfriend?"

"I'm not willing to give up anything. Besides, my personal life is none of your business." He prayed he still had one. Not only couldn't he make any promises to Lori, but he also couldn't even tell her his feelings.

"It is if you're living with her with our child. Maybe the judge should know, too."

"Stop with the threats, Shelly." He walked toward the front door. He opened the door and glanced out at the man on the porch and motioned to him to come inside.

Shelly looked at Jace suspiciously. "What are you up to?"

"You're the one who plays games, Shelly. So if I can't talk any sense into you, maybe he can." He prayed that all his hard work would pay off and not backfire in his face.

"Don't push me, Jace. You'll only lose." She gasped as Edmund Layfield stepped through the front door.

The distinguished gentleman was in his early fifties. He was dressed in a business suit and had thick gray hair. Jace had spent only an hour with the man and realized that he truly loved Shelly. Edmund also liked Cassie, but didn't particularly want to raise another child full-time, since his kids were grown.

Shelly came out of her trance. "Edmund, what are you doing here?"

"I came to see you, love. And I'm not leaving here until I convince you that we're meant to be together." He reached out and pulled her into his arms. That was when Jace made his exit.

For the first time in days, he realized that maybe they could come to a compromise. They all might get what they wanted. His thoughts turned to Lori. And that included him.

Tim parked the small SUV next to several other cars at Hutchinson House. It was Thanksgiving and half the town had been invited to have dinner here.

"Are you okay with this?" he asked Claire.

She smiled. "Normally no, but I can share this special day with Lori and Gina. It's important they feel a part of Destiny." She sighed. "Besides, all the kids and grandkids will be here." She smiled. "It's all about family being together. If only we would hear from Jace. You'd think our own daughter could give us some information."

He reached across the car and took his wife's hand. "Come on, Claire, you know Paige is Jace's lawyer."

"I know, I know, client/lawyer confidentiality." She frowned. "But I've seen how sad Lori is. If two people should be together, it's them."

"And if it's meant to be it will work out."

"I've been praying so hard for that."

It had been a week, and not a word from Jace. Lori had tried to stay positive—after all, it was Thanksgiving.

She looked around the festive dining room. The long table could seat twenty. There were two other tables set up in the entry to seat another twenty. And with the kids' table in the sunroom off the kitchen, everyone would have a place.

Maggie had cooked three turkeys and with Claire's two baked hams and many side dishes from everyone, she couldn't imagine not having enough food.

"Miss Hutchinson."

Lori turned to see Mac Burleson. "Mac, I asked you to call me Lori."

"Doesn't seem right," he told her.

"It seems very right to me. Unless you don't consider me a friend."

His eyes rounded. "You're a very good friend. I'm so grateful—"

"You did it," she interrupted. "You proved yourself at every job you've taken on. You make us all proud."

"Thank you…Lori." He smiled. "Is there anything else you want me to do?"

Some laughing kids ran by, chasing each other. She smiled at their antics. Her father would probably hate this. "Enjoy today. We have a lot to be thankful for." She knew she was so lucky, but two important people weren't here to share it with her.

"Hurry, Daddy, we're gonna be late for Thanksgiving."

Jace smiled, but it didn't relax him as he drove his

truck down First Street toward Hutchinson House. "We'll get there, sweetheart."

He glanced toward the backseat where his daughter was strapped in. They'd been gone a week, having stayed in Denver longer than planned. With the lawyers' help, they'd worked out the custody issue without a judge having to make the decision.

And in the end, it had been Cassie who'd told her mother that she wanted to live in Destiny with her daddy and all her friends and her horse. Shelly finally agreed, but wanted visitation in the summers and holidays. So Jace became the custodial parent. There was only one other thing that could make him happier. Lori.

"I just can't wait to see Ellie and Mrs. K. and Miss Lori, to tell everybody that I get to live here and be in the Christmas pageant."

"I can't wait, either," he told his daughter, praying that a certain pretty blonde felt the same about the news.

"Daddy, are you gonna ask Miss Lori today?"

On the flight home, Jace had told her how he felt about Lori and about her being a part of their lives. That was crazy, considering he hadn't even talked with Lori yet.

"Not sure. There's going to be a lot of people there today. It might have to wait, so you have to keep it a secret, okay?"

"Okay, but could I tell Ellie about Mommy's wedding? And that I'm going to go visit a real castle this summer?"

He smiled. "Yes, about the wedding, but the castle is only going to happen if I can get time off work." He was definitely going with her. He hoped Lori could go, too.

His heart began to race as he pulled up and climbed

out of the truck. He grabbed the wine and hurried after his daughter to the front door.

When they rang the bell, the door opened and Zack poked his head out. "Hi, Cassie. Hi, Mr. Jace."

"Hi, Zack. We came for Thanksgiving."

The boy grinned and opened the door wider and allowed them into the entryway filled with a long table decorated with colorful flowers and a paper turkey centerpiece. Cassie took off before he could stop her.

Jace was soon greeted by Justin and Morgan, then Tim Keenan and Paige and Reed Larkin joined them. He wanted to join in the conversation, but his eyes kept searching for a glimpse of Lori.

"She's in the kitchen."

He glanced at Justin. "Who?"

"As if you two are fooling anyone," his friend said. "You need to go to Lori before she comes out here and sees you."

Jace nodded and took off toward the kitchen. He knew his way around this house, but there were so many people here it was hard to maneuver. How was he going to be able to get her alone?

He saw Maggie at the counter. Without asking anything, she nodded toward the sunroom. He walked there as kids ran past him. Okay, so they weren't going to have any privacy.

Then he saw her and everyone else seemed to disappear from view. She was seated on the floor with some of the little kids. She was holding a toddler who'd been crying, and she managed to turn the tears into a smile before the child wandered off. Jace fell in love with her all over again.

Lori stood. Dressed in black slacks and a soft blue

sweater he ached to pull her close and just hold her. Tell her how much he'd missed her. How much he wanted her…

She finally turned in his direction. Her hair was in an array of curls that danced around her pretty face. Her chocolate eyes locked on his. "You're back."

That was a dumb thing to say, Lori thought as she looked up at Jace. So much for cool and calm.

"Hello, Lori."

"Hi, Jace." She didn't take a step toward him. "Is Cassie with you? Please tell me that she's with you."

He beamed. "Yes, she is." He glanced around. "I need to talk to you. There are so many things I have to tell you."

Just then Maggie broke in. "Sorry to interrupt but dinner is on the table. And Tim Keenan is ready to say the blessing."

Lori glanced back at Jace. "I'm sorry. Can we talk later?" Without waiting for an answer, Lori took off and headed toward the front of the house. She felt Jace following behind her as they reached the dining room. Hopeful, she added an extra place at the table for him.

She smiled at all her family and the new friends she was sharing today with. That included Jace and Cassie.

It grew quiet and someone handed her a champagne glass. "First of all, Gina, Zack and I want to thank you all for coming today. I hope this is the first of many visits to Hutchinson House. I want you all to feel welcome, so you'll come back here." She raised her glass. "To friends, and to Destiny." After everyone took a drink, she had Tim Keenan say the blessing.

The group broke up, and mothers went off to fill

their children's plates and settle them in the sunroom. Maggie stood by, watching for any emergencies. Lori ended up back at the head table, while Gina was seated at the entry table. Somehow Jace was seated at her table, but at the opposite end. Every so often, he'd smile at her.

She kept telling herself in a few hours they could be alone. After dinner, she went into the kitchen to check on dessert and finally saw Cassie.

"Miss Lori." The girl came and hugged her. "I got to come back."

"I know. Your daddy told me."

"Did he tell you about the wedding?" Cassie's tiny hand slapped over her mouth. "Oh, no, I wasn't supposed to tell you about that."

"Whose wedding? Your mommy's?" When Cassie didn't answer, she asked, "Your daddy's?"

The child giggled. "Both of 'em. But don't tell Daddy I told you. It's a surprise."

Lori could barely take her next breath. Was that why Jace said he got Cassie? He had to remarry Shelly?

She couldn't do this. She turned and found Jace behind her, holding her coat. "Okay, we need to get out of here and talk." He grinned. "I know just the place."

She gasped. "There's no need to tell me. I already heard from Cassie about the wedding. I hope you and Shelly will be happy."

He frowned. "What? You think that Shelly and I…" He cursed.

Lori held up her hand to stop him, but he took it in his.

"We're definitely going to talk about this," he began. "We need to get a few things straightened out. Now."

"I can't leave now."

"So we should just talk here. I'm sure all your guests would love to hear what I have to say," he said, and held out her coat.

"Why are you doing this?" she asked, keeping her voice low.

"I hate the fact that you even have to ask. I hope I can change that." When she hesitated, he asked, "Can't you even give me a few minutes to hear me out? To listen to what I have to say."

Lori wasn't sure what to do, only that she didn't want a scene here. She slipped on her coat and told Maggie she was leaving for a little while.

The housekeeper smiled and waved them on saying, "It's about time."

CHAPTER THIRTEEN

TWENTY minutes later, Jace was still furious as he pulled off the highway. The sun had already set, but he knew the way to the cabin.

"Why are you bringing me here?" Lori asked.

"So we can talk without anyone interrupting us." He glanced across the bench seat. "But if you want, I'll take you back home."

He watched her profile in the shadowed light. She closed her eyes then whispered, "No, it might be good if we talk. At least to clear the air."

"Oh, darlin', I plan to do more than clear the air."

Lori jerked her head around and even in the darkness he could see she was glaring. She opened her mouth but he stopped her words.

"Hold that thought. We're here." He pulled into the parking space and climbed out. No more snow had fallen since the last time he'd followed her here. It hadn't gotten any warmer, either.

He pulled his sheepskin coat together to ward off the cold as he went around to Lori's side. After helping her out, they hurried up to the lit porch. He took the key from his pocket and rushed on to explain, "I stopped by earlier." He unlocked the door, pushed it open and turned on the light inside the door.

"After you," he told her, watching surprise cross her pretty face. "Come on, let's get inside where it's warm."

Lori felt Jace's hand against her back, nudging her in. Once inside she stopped and looked around, trying not to think about the last time they'd been here. It didn't work. Memories flooded her head. How incredible it had been being in Jace's arms, making love with him.

"Just let me get a fire started." Jace went straight to the fireplace, where logs had been placed on the grate. He turned on the gas and the flames shot over the wood. He lit the candles that were lined up along the mantel, then turned to her. "You should be warm in a few minutes."

She recalled another time he hadn't waited for the fire to warm her. She pushed away the thought and walked to the table where she saw a vase of fresh flowers. Red roses. She faced him. "You bought these?"

He nodded.

"So you'd planned to bring me here?"

He pulled off his jacket and went to her. "I've been thinking about it since I left Denver. I want to be with you alone, to talk to you."

With her heart racing, she returned to the fire and held out her hands to warm them. Mostly, she wanted to gather her thoughts, but she was overwhelmed by this man. She wanted to be hopeful, but she also recalled what Jace had told her. He didn't want to get involved with another woman.

"Are you ready to listen to what I have to say?"

She stared into the fire. "So now you want to talk?

Why didn't you call me before? Let me know what was going on."

"Because I didn't know myself until recently. I was in mediation during the day with Shelly and her lawyers. At night, I was trying to ease my daughter's fears." His sapphire gaze met hers. "And I guess I've been so used to doing things on my own, I didn't know how to depend on someone else."

"You didn't have to be alone. I was here for you."

"I know that now. Yet, in the end, I had to make the decision based on my daughter's well-being. It was hard to know what was best for Cassie. Was I being selfish wanting her with me?"

Hearing his stress, she turned, but didn't go to him. "Oh, Jace. No, you weren't being selfish. You love Cassie enough to want to give her stability. I also believe that you love your daughter enough that if Shelly could give Cassie what she needed, you'd let her have custody."

He smiled. "It always amazes me how you seem to know me so well."

That wasn't true, she thought, praying he wanted the same thing she did. To be together. "Not so. I have no idea why you brought me here, especially since I haven't heard a word in the past week. And what about this wedding?"

This time he came to her. He stood so close, she could inhale his wonderful scent. The only sounds were the logs crackling in the fire as she waited for an explanation.

Then he took her hand. "I might have helped a little with a nudge to Edmund. He took it from there and went to see Shelly. They were married yesterday by the same judge who helped with the custody case. I escorted Cassie to her mother's wedding."

"Shelly got married?"

"Yes. I thought things would go smoother if I helped Shelly settle her problem with her now-husband. I contacted him the day I arrived, and got him to come with me to Shelly's place." He shrugged. "They took it from there, and now they're headed to England for their honeymoon and his family."

Jace met her dark eyes and nearly lost his concentration. "Before Shelly left we managed to sit down and decide what would be best for our daughter. In the end, Cassie told her mother she wanted to live with me in Destiny."

"That had to be hard on Shelly."

Jace nodded. "But she gets visitation, summers and holidays. She can't take Cassie out of the country until she's older." He studied Lori's pretty face and his stomach tightened. He wanted her desperately.

"It all finally got settled yesterday, and Cassie and I caught the first flight back here...and came to see you."

He reached for her hand and tugged her closer. "I want more, Lori. More than just having my daughter in my life. I also want you. No, not just want you, but need you."

Not giving her a chance to resist, his mouth came down on hers in an all-consuming kiss. He couldn't resist her, either. His hands moved over her back, going downward to her hips, drawing her against him.

With a gasp, she pulled back. "You're not playing fair," she accused.

"I want you, Lorelei Hutchinson. I'll use any means possible to have you."

"Wait." Lori pushed him away, not liking this. "What are you exactly talking about? Seduction?" She deserved more. "I won't be that secret woman in your life, Jace, that you pull out whenever it's convenient."

He frowned. "Whoa. Who said anything about that…" He stopped as if to regroup.

"First of all, I'm sorry that I ever made you feel that way. I asked a lot of you when I left here, and I know I should have called you. Believe me I wanted to, but I was so afraid that if I did, I'd confess how I felt about you. I didn't have a right yet. I needed all my concentration on Cassie. You and I both know what it's like to lose parents. I would do anything not to have that happen to my daughter." His gaze bore into hers. "No matter how much I care about you, Lori, I couldn't abandon my child and come to you." He swallowed. "No matter how much I wanted to. Not matter how much I love you."

She closed her eyes.

"No, look at me, Lori. I'm not your father. I'm never going to leave you, ever. How could I when I can't seem to be able to live without you. Even if I had to move back to Denver because of Cassie, I would have figured out a way to come and be with you, too."

"You love me?"

He drew her close and nodded. "From the top of your pretty blond hair, to your incredible brown eyes, down to your cute little ruby-red painted toes." He kissed her forehead, then brushed his lips against each eyelid. His mouth continued a journey to her cheek, then she shivered as he reached her ear. "I'll tell you about all your other delicious body parts later," he promised, then pulled back and looked down at her. "If you'll let me."

"Oh, Jace. I love you, too," she whispered.

"I was hoping you felt that way." He pulled her into his arms and kissed her deeply. By the time he released her they were both breathing hard.

"We better slow down a minute, or I'll forget what I was about to do." He went to his coat and pulled a small box out of his jacket pocket, then returned to Lori.

Her eyes grew round. "Jace?"

He felt a little shaky. "I want this to be perfect, but if I manage to mess up something, just remember how much I love you." He drew a breath. "Lorelei Hutchinson, I probably can't offer you a perfect life. I have a home that's still under construction. A business that isn't off the ground yet." His eyes met hers. "And a daughter that I'm going to ask you to be a mother to."

A tear ran down her cheek. "Oh, Jace, don't you know, those are assets. And I couldn't love Cassie any more than if she were my own."

"She loves you, too."

"So she's okay with me and you?"

He nodded. "She even approved of the ring." He opened the box and she gasped at the square-cut diamond solitaire with the platinum band.

"Oh, my. It's beautiful."

That was his cue. He got down on one knee. "Lorelei Hutchinson, you are my heart. Will you marry me?"

She touched his face with her hands and kissed him softly. "Yes, Jace, oh, yes."

With her mouth still against his, he rose and wrapped his arms around her as he deepened the kiss. He couldn't let her go. Ever.

He finally broke off the kiss, then slipped the ring on her finger. He kissed her softly, then pulled back. "Give me one second, then we'll have the rest of the night."

Lori nodded and looked down at her ring. She couldn't believe this was really happening. "Good, I'm going to need your full attention the rest of the night to convince me that this isn't a fairy tale."

He grinned, took out his cell phone and punched in a number. "You got it." He put it to his ear. "Hi, sweetheart," Jace said into the receiver. "She said yes." He looked at Lori and winked. "Yes, we'll celebrate tomorrow. I love you, too." He ended the call. "I hope you don't mind. Cassie wanted to know what your answer was."

"I don't mind at all. I think we have enough love that I can share it with your daughter." She wrapped her arms around his waist. "But maybe tonight, I'll let you show me."

"Not just tonight, Lori. Always. Forever."

EPILOGUE

It was nearly Christmas in Destiny.

This year, the town council had asked Lori to light the big tree in the town square. She was honored, to say the least. Of course, she didn't do it alone. She'd invited Zack and Cassie to help throw the switch that lit the fifty-foot ponderosa pine.

While enjoying the colorful light show and the children's choir singing carols, she recalled the first day she'd arrived in Destiny. She felt so alone, then she started meeting the people here. That included one stubborn contractor who made her heart race. Made her aware of what she'd been missing in life.

For Lori there were bittersweet memories, too. Her father was gone and she'd never had the chance to have a relationship with him. But with her new family, she wasn't going to be alone. Not only Gina and Zack, but also her future husband, Jace, and a stepdaughter, Cassie.

Suddenly she felt a pair of arms slip around her waist from behind. She smiled and leaned back against Jace's broad chest.

"So are you enjoying your big night?" he said against her ear.

"Oh, yes." She smiled, recalling the last time she'd been here with her father. She called them treasured memories now. "But I have to say, I'm glad the school play is over."

"Until next year," he reminded her.

"Very funny. I'm planning to be really busy."

"You do too much as it is," he said as they watched the children's choir singing beside the tree. He tightened his hold, his large body shielding her from the cold night. "Between the mortgage and college scholarship programs, you have no free time."

She and Jace had made the decision together about taking only a small part of the inheritance to put away for the kids; the rest would go back into the town. They both made an excellent income from Hutchinson Corp properties.

"I want to get the programs up and ready for when my father's money comes through next fall." She stole a glance over her shoulder at him. "You'd be proud of me. I've turned over my job on the mortgage committee to Erin. She'll go to all the meetings, and I'll work from her recommendations."

"However you get it done, you're a pretty special lady to be so generous to this town."

She turned in his arms. "I only want to be your special lady."

He grew serious. "You are, Lori, and will always be." He kissed her sweetly. "How about we ditch this place for something a little more private."

"Oh, I'd like that, but you know we can't. For one thing, Cassie and Zack are singing." They both looked at the children. "And we're all invited back to the Keenan Inn for a party and to finalize our wedding plans. It's going to be a big undertaking for Claire and Gina to pull this off, especially with the holidays."

"I know, the first wedding at Hutchinson House," he said.

"The first of many, I hope," she reminded him.

Jace had to smile. With the exception of Cassie's birth, he couldn't remember ever being this happy. Now he had it all, the woman he loved and his daughter permanently. "So I guess a wild night together is out of the question."

"Of course not. It's just postponed for a few weeks."

"Until New Year's Eve," he finished. The date they'd chosen for their wedding. "That's a long three weeks off." Even longer since they'd spent most of their time with Cassie trying to help her adjust to the new arrangement. He hated having to send Lori home every night.

"You sure we can't sneak off to the cabin tonight?"

She gave him a quick kiss. "Just hold that thought and I promise to make it worth your while after the wedding."

"You being here with me now has made my dreams come true."

Hutchinson House never looked so beautiful.

On New Year's Eve Lori stood at the window of the master suite. She could see over the wide yard toward the front of the property.

The ornate gates were covered with thousands of tiny silver lights and many more were strung along the hedges. It was only a prelude for what was to come as the wedding guests approached the end of the circular drive and the grand house on the hill.

The porch railings were draped in fresh garland, and

more lights were intermixed with the yards of green-ery that smelled of Christmas. White poinsettias edged the steps leading to the wide front door trimmed with a huge fresh-cut wreath.

Lori smiled. The Hutchinson/Yeager wedding was going to be the first of many parties in this house.

Gina came in dressed in a long dark green grown. "Oh, Lori. You look so beautiful."

Lori glanced down at her wedding dress. She'd fallen in love with the floor-length ivory gown the second she'd seen it at Rocky Mountain Bridal Shop, from the top of the sweetheart neckline, to the fitted jeweled bodice with a drop waist and satin skirt. Her hair was pulled back, adorned with a floral headband attached to a long tulle veil.

"I hope Jace thinks so."

Gina handed her a deep red rose bouquet. "He will."

She felt tears forming. "I'm so lucky to have found him, and Cassie."

Gina blinked, too. "They're lucky to have you." She gripped Lori's hand. "I love you, sis. Thank you for al-ways being there for us."

"Hey, you were there for me, too. And nothing will change. We're still family. I'm only going to be a few miles from your new place." Lori frowned, knowing they had arranged to live in their own house. "You feel okay about the move?"

Her sister nodded. "Zack and I are going to be fine."

Lori knew that. Her sister was working with Kaley, having hours that enabled her to be home when Zack got out of school. She still worried about Eric showing up someday, but they'd all keep an eye out.

Gina straightened. "Okay, let's get your special day started."

They walked into the hall toward the head of the stairs where Charlie was waiting. She couldn't lie, every girl dreamed of walking down the aisle escorted by her father. She wasn't any different. At least now she'd been able to make peace with it all.

She whispered, "I'll always miss you, Dad."

Smiling, Charlie had tears in his eyes when she arrived. "Oh, Miss Lorelei, you are a vision. I'm so honored to escort you today."

She gripped his hands. "Thank you, Charlie."

The older man offered her his arm. "I know there's an anxious young man waiting for his bride."

The music began and Cassie and Zack, the flower girl and ring bearer, started down the petal-covered stairs. The banister entwined with more garland that wound down to the large entry. Next Gina began her descent. Once her sister reached the bottom the music swelled.

Holding tight on to Charlie, Lori's heart raced when she made her way down. Once she touched the bottom steps, she took it all in.

The room was filled with flowers: roses, carnations and poinsettias, all white. Rows of wooden chairs, filled with family and friends, lined either side of the runner that led through the entry and into the dining room and ended at a white trellis covered in greenery. And underneath stood Jace. The man who was going to share her life.

Jace's breath caught when his gaze met Lori's. She was beautiful. His heart swelled. He never knew he could love someone so much.

She made her way to him and he had to stop himself from going to her. Finally she arrived and he took her hand. When he locked on her big brown eyes, everything else seemed to fade away. There was only her. It was just the two of them exchanging vows, making the life commitment.

The minister began the ceremony and the vows were exchanged. Jace listened to her speak and was humbled by her words.

Then came his turn. He somehow managed to get the emotional words past his tight throat. Then Justin passed him the ring, and he slipped the platinum band on her finger. He held out his hand so she could do the same.

He gripped both her hands and the minister finally pronounced them husband and wife. Jace leaned down, took her in his arms and kissed her.

There were cheers as the minister announced, "It's my pleasure to introduce to you, Mr. and Mrs. Jace Yeager."

Jace held his bride close, never wanting to let her go. She was his heart, his life, the mother of his future children.

It had been a long journey but they had found each other. He pulled back and looked at his bride. "Hello, Mrs. Yeager."

With tears in her eyes, she answered, "Hello, Mr. Yeager."

Together they walked down the aisle hand in hand past the well-wishers toward their future together. It was their Destiny.

* * * * *

MILLS & BOON®
By Request

RELIVE THE ROMANCE WITH THE BEST OF THE BEST

1215/05